Watercolours in the Rain

Jo Lambert

Editor: Elaine Denning
www.elainedenning.com

Cover Design: Jane Dixon Smith
www.jdsmith-design.com

Formatting: Rebecca Emin
www.gingersnapbooks.co.uk

Author Links:
Website: www.jolambertbooks.com
Blog: www.jolambertwriter.wordpress.com

Also by Jo Lambert

When Tomorrow Comes
Love Lies and Promises
The Ghost of You and Me
Between Today and Yesterday
The Other Side of Morning
Summer Moved On

For Josette and Marie...

AUGUST 2012

JESS

I am missing those cloudless cerulean skies and warm waters of Cala Los Rosas already. An uneventful flight has brought me back from my two weeks in the Med to the UK and the real world. Stepping out of the aircraft on this cool summer evening, I haul my tote over my shoulder and pull up the collar of my light jacket to protect me against the slight chill in the air as the sun dips below the horizon. Following the others, I cross the tarmac to where the bus waits to take us to the terminal.

Ten minutes later I'm hanging around the baggage carousel with the rest of the EasyJet passengers from Palma and waiting expectantly for my luggage. Spotting my case, I'm grateful to a helpful fellow traveller who assists me as I attempt to capture it. I emerge into the airport's entrance hall, my case following obediently behind me, and am greeted by a sea of expectant faces, all anticipating the arrival of friends or relatives. And suddenly there he is. With his hazel eyes and untidy brown hair, his six foot frame is a sight for sore eyes. Alex Cadwallader, or Roo as he's known to those close to him, is very special. We've been together since we were twelve years old and over that time he's become my closest friend and confidant.

'Welcome home,' he says as he takes my case from me and pulls me into a warm brotherly hug. I breathe in his expensive cologne, feeling his familiar warmth as he cradles me against him.

We leave the terminal and head for the car park. He slows his pace, allowing me to keep up with his long legged strides, firing questions at me non-stop as we walk. 'How was the weather in Majorca? How is Amber? Has Mads moved in with her boat builder yet? Is the bar still doing well?' I meet each one with positive responses: yes, the weather was fabulous, my aunt is fine and her cousin is now living with handsome widower Juan Ortega and his small son Santiago. And El Barco Rojo - not so much a bar but a beautiful beach restaurant - is thriving. The place has seen an increase in diners – both locals and tourists - due to the arrival of new chef Jorge, who has completely revamped the menu. I tell Roo all of this and also remind him once more that the next time I visit he should come with me. He smiles and apologises. The promise is always there but his work as a solicitor in his father's Bristol office regularly conspires to throw up something at the last minute, which sees him having to cancel.

'Did you have any more thoughts about your future while you were away?' Roo asks as he unlocks his BMW and slides my suitcase onto the back seat. He's referring to my thoughts about finding another teaching post. I've been at St Helens for nearly two years and it's time to move on. I need a new challenge. Deciding to keep him in suspense, I slip into the grey leather interior of the car and secure my seatbelt. He joins me, belts himself in and as he starts the car I smile and say, 'Yes, I have made a decision. Oxford is a beautiful city, the children are wonderful but I do miss country life. What I'd love is a teaching post in a village school. I could rent a cottage and find local stables so I could take a horse out on a regular basis. It would be my idea of bliss...and before you say anything,' I wave a warning finger at him, 'it doesn't mean I'm planning to return home.'

'Why not? Don't you miss everyone in Lynbrook?' he asks as we exit the airport car park and head towards the main road.

'How can I possibly miss them, Roo? I see them when I'm home for school holidays. And in between I'm in regular touch on the phone.'

Oh come on, stop making excuses. You know Rufus would love to have you back,' He argues, 'With Sally married and gone he could do with some female company behind the bar.'

'There's just a slight flaw in your argument,' I insist, pulling my tote onto my lap as I hear the muffled sound of my mobile. 'Even if he does, I've already checked and currently there are no teaching jobs anywhere near Lynbrook. I can't simply up sticks and expect my father to put me up while I wait for the right job to turn up. I need to work.'

I rummage around in my bag and find my phone. Opening it up a familiar ID appears on my screen. 'It's Dad,' I tell him, glad of a respite from our verbal sparring. 'He's probably calling to check I've arrived safely.'

The voice on the phone isn't the normal cheerful one I'm used to. Despite the fact he's asking similar questions to Roo about my holiday, I'm instantly aware something is very wrong.

'Jess...' he pauses, clearing his throat, 'there's no easy way to tell you this, but while you were away I had a call from Scotland. Leo passed away two days ago.'

I draw in a breath; so many questions are racing through my mind. Leo is Rufus's older brother. He is also the man I thought was my father for the first eighteen years of my life. We share a lot of history, not all of it pleasant. 'That's terrible,' I respond, finally finding my voice, 'how did it happen?'

'A heart attack at work. By the time the ambulance arrived it was too late.'

'Are you okay?' I ask, turning my head to look at Roo and catching his curious expression. He simply nods, understanding I'll explain everything once the call is over. But my first thought is how this news has affected my father. They were never close; in fact Leo could be quite obnoxious at times. Rufus was the sunshine to Leo's shadow. The light to his darkness. In the years I lived with him and Amber, I remember him as a sour individual living on a diet of disapproval and prejudice.

'Me? Yes,' Rufus says, and I can visualise him pushing his dark hair back off his face as he speaks. 'Bit of a shock, I guess. Never had him down as a cardiac case, but then I've not seen him in over six years.'

'Did he ever marry again?' I ask.

'No. That reminds me,' he gives a distracted sigh, 'I'll

need to ring Amber, let her know. Even though their relationship ended badly I'm sure she'll want to pay her last respects.'

'Yes, she probably will.'

As I agree, it occurs to me how complicated my family life has been. Throughout my childhood I rarely saw Leo. His job regularly took him away, project managing the construction of some shopping mall or luxury hotel in the Middle East. In his absence my mother, Diana, regularly abandoned the family home to mix and mingle with her party- loving friends. I became a pass the parcel child; farmed out to anyone who was available to look after me. Mostly, it was overnight stays but on occasions it ran into days when someone or other lured her up to London for dinner or the opening of a new play in the West End. I was thirteen when they divorced. When my mother left with her new husband for a life abroad, Leo was in the middle of a large contract in Riyadh. He made arrangements for Rufus to look after me until he returned. It was almost three years before I saw him again. I guess some people might find that strange, but, you see, I'd grown up fully aware neither of my parents had any real interest in me. When Leo did make it back to the UK, he brought Amber, his new wife, with him. Like Rufus, she was kind-hearted and caring. Still keeping in regular touch with my uncle, I returned to live with them. To the outside world we had a comfortable middle-class life. But behind closed doors, Amber and I existed under the regime of a strict and controlling man. Someone who had my future mapped out: education, marriage – everything.

'The funeral is next Thursday; Milton Bay Crematorium. He specifically asked for the internment to be there,' I hear Rufus's voice as it pulls me from my troubled memories. 'Can you make it?'

'Of course,' I say without hesitation. However awful Leo was, he's still family.

'He's left all the arrangements in the hands of his solicitors. They're sending a representative to attend the funeral and a room's been hired at The Driftwood Spars

Hotel for the reading of the will afterwards.'

'Well, thankfully, that's something I won't have to hang around for,' I say dismissively, not really interested in hearing what he's left or to whom.

'Sorry to be a party pooper darling girl,' Rufus replies, 'ducking out's not an option...apparently we've both had a mention.'

The new crematorium, two miles from my South Devon home town of Milton Bay, sits on a gentle curve on the road to Teignmouth, overlooking the sea. It's a peaceful place with trees, neat lawn areas and borders full of colourful flowers. There's a Garden of Remembrance, a flat grassy area where small memorial plaques sit next to each other in neat rows. The whole place has an air of tranquillity and I find myself hoping Leo, wherever he is, has found peace too. Roo is with me, quiet and serious in a dark suit and black tie. Apart from the two of us, the only other mourners are Rufus, Amber, who has flown in from Spain, and a tall thin balding man in his late forties, who must be Leo's Scottish lawyer. We emerge into the sunshine after the service, the next stop town, and the reading of Leo's will. During the journey back to Milton Bay, I exchange a few brief words with the other occupants of the car. The rest of the time I gaze in silence at the world passing outside the window, wondering not only what Leo has left me, but given our relationship, why.

The Driftwood Spars Hotel sits one end of the town's rather splendid Victorian esplanade. With white walls under a grey tiled roof and an impressive pale columned canopied entrance, the hotel's public rooms have huge windows facing the sea. Rufus leaves his vehicle in the small car park at the rear and we make our way around to the front, through the main door into the foyer. A slim redheaded receptionist greets us and we are directed towards a heavy wooden door marked *The Drake Room*. As it closes behind us, I catch a glimpse of Amber and Roo who have already settled themselves in the lounge and are in the process of ordering drinks, a waiter hovering next to them.

Inside the room, six chairs are neatly arranged around a rectangular table, a tray with coffee set at one end. The solicitor, Elliot McIntyre, introduces himself, his handshake firm, his voice a warm Scottish baritone. Sitting directly opposite Rufus and me, he busies himself, pulling documents from his briefcase. I organise three cups of coffee before re-joining them.

McIntyre clears his throat and opens the file in front of him. He begins with the usual introductory lines I've heard so many times in films and on TV. His accent, rich and heavy, blurs my concentration which, as I sip my coffee, focuses itself a few yards outside the window on a small dark haired boy in green shorts who is getting to grips with a large ice cream. He could be any one of my pupils and I love the delighted expression on his face as his small pink tongue laces itself around the smooth coldness of his treat. The sound of Rufus's name being mentioned pulls me rudely back to the room. I hear the solicitor's voice announcing Leo has left him ... a car? I turn to look at Rufus. He slides his cup and saucer onto the table and raises eyebrows in surprise.

McIntyre's hand skims over his bald head and his gaze runs between both of us as he announces this is not just any car but a Porsche classic worth nearly £80,000. I draw in a deep breath. Although he was moderately wealthy, I wonder how my uncle has come to possess such a vehicle. And if Rufus has this, what's in store for me? After draining his coffee cup the solicitor continues and I realise I'm about to find out.

'To my niece, Jessica Hayden, the bulk of my estate...' he hesitates and I see the semblance of a smile in his dark eyes as he registers my surprise before returning to consult the document in front of him '...which comprises the following property and investment portfolio.' He looks up at me and the smile is there again.

'Property? Investments?' I echo, as I sit there stunned. 'I

had no idea he had…' my voice trails away.

'Mr Hayden spent years buying property. He accumulated a substantial collection of rental homes in the south of England and in Scotland. And as for his home in the Bieldside district of Aberdeen, well that is currently valued at over £500,000. He was also very successful with his investments,' McIntyre says matter-of-factly as he extracts a document from the file and slides it across the table towards me. 'Here is a detailed list of everything he's left you.'

I pick up the sheet of paper and stare at it for a moment, trying to take in what's written there. Leo's four bedroom home, the properties he currently owns and details of his investments are all neatly recorded on the left side of the sheet with their individual values on the right. As I reach the very bottom and see the total, my hand goes to my mouth. Shocked and stunned by what is there, I shake my head. 'But why would he do this?' I ask. 'He never really cared for me.'

McIntyre clears his throat again. 'I understand your reaction, Miss Hayden…Jess, but can I just tell you something? During the time I was your uncle's solicitor I became well acquainted with him. The Leo Hayden I came to know was totally different from the one who lived here in Milton Bay. His years in Scotland gave him time to reflect on his actions, his foolishness and the damage he had caused both to himself and others. When we drew up this will he said he needed to make amends, to right the wrongs he had been responsible for. For not giving you the love you deserved, Jess, and for unfairly loading the blame onto you, Rufus, for what happened with his first wife. He also realised your lodger…'

'Lily…Lily Stevenson?' I offer.

'Yes, McIntyre nods, 'Lily. She duped him. He had something of a mid-life crisis. He believed himself in love with her and that she returned his affection. It foolishly led him to share the one thing he shouldn't have…your family's secret. That you were Rufus's child. I understand from Leo, Lily was the one who made you aware of this.'

'Yes, we had a very heated argument. That's when it all came out,' I confirm, but am reluctant to admit our row was because I'd discovered she had been seeing my boyfriend Zac Rayner: good looking, arrogant, and as it turned out, thoroughly untrustworthy.

'And as a result it led to the breakup of your family?'

I nod silently, trying to block the memories of the chaos Lily caused: Amber beginning divorce proceedings, Leo retreating back to his job in Scotland while I left everything I had ever known behind to make a new life with Rufus in Lynbrook.

'The whole episode played on his mind a great deal, you know,' McIntyre continues, 'but he didn't feel he could come back and face you both. So he decided to do the next best thing.' He opens his hands, indicating the will, which lies on the table in front of him. 'This became the way for him to find redemption, to apologise for his weaknesses and ask your forgiveness.

I nod, feeling wetness on my cheeks. I bow my head, my teeth tugging at my lower lip, totally overcome by what I've just been told. I feel Rufus's reassuring touch on my arm and I lift my head to look at him. Judging by the moisture gathering in his eyes, he too has been affected by all of this.

'Three and a half million.' The words come out in a whisper as I wipe my tears away with the back of my hand and pass him the sheet I have been holding. 'Leo has left me three and a half million pounds.'

TALÚN

Pulling my horse to a halt and surveying the landscape, I realise how much I love the month of August. It's a time when everything we've been working for here all year comes together. In the distance I can see the two massive yellow combines with their attendant tractors and grain hoppers keeping pace. This is just one small part of the work that's undertaken on Hawkeswood Estates. Alongside wheat, oats and barley, we grow every kind of fruit and vegetable – oh and there's an award winning

14

vineyard too. Then there's the livestock - cattle, sheep, pigs and poultry and of course the horses, which are my area of expertise. Norfolk is a vast, flat landscape with endless skies and my family, the Hawkeswoods, own and farm a huge swathe of it. With contracts in the UK and across Europe into Russia, my grandfather, Marcus, has built the company into a global brand. Rumours are even circulating of a possible knighthood.

It seems impossible but this coming September I will have been here for five years. I had another life before. One which seems so distant it feels as if it was lived by somebody else. When I arrived here I was poor and penniless, escaping from a broken love affair that had almost destroyed me. Now I'm heir to a multi-million pound food and livestock empire. Today I have everything I could possibly want, although... My thoughts immediately turn to Fliss and Emily, both lost to me now. Fliss healed the hurt. She made me forget that other life, where I was foolish enough to believe I had found the special someone I could commit to long term. Of course, some of the blame for what happened was mine. I behaved badly too, and it might be said I deserved my fate. But it shattered my faith in womankind and afterwards I vowed to avoid them at all costs.

Fliss joined us as Marcus's PA six months after I arrived. With a father in the diplomatic service, she'd lived all over the world. Amberleigh was her first opportunity to put down roots. She brought with her a wicked sense of humour and an infectious laugh. She wasn't conventionally pretty but she definitely had something special about her – probably the reason Marcus picked her. I liked the fact she wasn't pushy or deliberately flirty as most women seemed to be around me, the Hawkeswood heir. She didn't care who I was, she treated me the same way she treated everyone else. And she told it like it was. She had a refreshing honesty about her which I grew to love. I guess that's why I fell for her, because she was different from the others. She wrapped her love around me like a comforting blanket. We had an end of summer wedding eighteen months later and moved into our own home on the estate. The morning over breakfast when she told me we were going to have a baby, I thought everything was coming together at last. When Emily Rose arrived with a combination of my dark hair and Fliss's blue eyes, my world was perfect. And then four months later I lost everything.

It was mid-January and we'd been to a late lunch with my grandparents. Fliss always insisted on driving home on these occasions. It wasn't just the alcohol, although I had been very careful, it was concern for our beautiful daughter, Emily. Driving with even the slightest hint of alcohol in my blood was a no-no for Fliss. So, on family occasions when Emily came along, Fliss was always the one behind the wheel on the drive home.

As usual I'd argued. 'I'm fine,' I'd said, pulling the car keys from my pocket and dangling them just out of her reach. 'It will be quiet on the road, it's not a problem. I'll be careful, I promise.'

'Oh no you don't.' She'd wrestled the keys from my hand under the amused gaze of my grandfather. 'Better to be safe than sorry.' My grandmother, Anna, agreed. 'She's right,' she added, 'better safe than sorry.'

Those words were to echo in my head for a long time afterwards. I was right, the roads were empty but they were also dark and wet, and there was no moon that night. Fliss was no slouch behind the wheel. The route was flat and straight and as usual she put her foot down. I remember we'd just entered a stretch of road bordered by fir trees. I twisted around in my seat for a quick check on Emily and when I turned back...

It all happened so fast; a huge explosive thud as metal collided with flesh and bone. There was no time to avoid the collision, to do anything but react. The deer had run straight out into the road and hit the car. Fliss struggled with the wheel as the car slewed to the right. I learned afterwards that it had hit a patch of black ice, which sent it careering into the trees. I remember leaving the road, Fliss was screaming, the baby crying. Then the driver's side of the car collided with a tree, flipping it over. The car horn, alarm and airbags seemed to activate simultaneously, just before my head hit something hard and the world dissolved into blackness.

I close my eyes as I try to blot out the sudden and vivid visions playing in my head. Raising my hand, I gently massage my temple with my fingers.

'Talún?' I feel a hand on my arm and look up. I've been so focused on my memories of the accident, I wasn't aware that my grandmother had ridden up to join me. 'Are you okay?' I hear her ask. I open my eyes, see her concerned expression as she scans my face, and realise she's caught sight of the moisture gathering in my eyes. 'Memories again?' she asks.

I nod and wipe my hand across my face. I can't keep anything from someone like Anna. My grandfather's second wife is ten years younger than him, a beautiful woman with blonde hair and calm grey eyes. Those eyes miss nothing and understand everything. 'My fault,' I say, 'I shouldn't have let the genie out of the bottle.'

'Maybe you need to get away from familiar places for a while,' she suggests, 'take a holiday. You've been putting in too many late nights at the stud. All this work isn't good for you; you need something else in your life.'

'I'm fine,' I reassure her. The last thing I want is time alone, even if it's in a warmer, more exotic location than Norfolk. No, I've no desire to be anywhere but here, where at least I have company and work to keep me occupied well into the evening.

'Then maybe you need another sort of diversion,' she says, sounding as if she already has something in mind.

I shake my head. I know where this is going. It's almost two years since I lost my wife and daughter. I should be closing the door on my grief and moving forward. Marcus isn't getting any younger – seventy two next birthday – and it's no secret that he's keen to have me settled with another family to make sure there is a future generation to continue the business. But you can't simply conjure up a new and lasting relationship, it's not that simple. You have to want to find that special person first and, currently a new love is the last thing I'm looking for.

'You need a distraction.' I hear Anna's words again. 'A building project maybe.'

'A building project?' I query, managing a smile, wondering where a suggestion like that has come from. 'I'd be a fish out of water. Horses are all I know.'

'Silly,' she waves away my amusement, 'that's not what I meant. You make a purchase...land or a house needing work. You employ a first class architect to design or make the changes needed and get someone else to do the hod carrying.'

'Anna, I don't want my own house.' I balk at the thought. 'Living at Amberleigh isn't perfect but at least I'm not alone.'

'You're not building for yourself.' She rolls her eyes in mock exasperation. 'You're building to sell. For profit. Who knows? You might even find you enjoy it so much you want to do it again. And,' she pauses for a moment, 'it might be just the thing to get your life back on track.'

'Back on track? As in looking for a new wife?' I hear the irritation in my voice as I glance at her before taking my gaze back to the combines.

'Absolutely not.' I can tell by the tone in her voice that I've upset her.

'I'm sorry.' I turn in the saddle, my eyes meeting hers. 'I didn't mean to snap, it's just...' my voice trails away.

'It's okay, I understand.' She reaches out to give my arm a reassuring pat. 'Talún, Marcus and I would love to see you settled again, but you're the one who's in control of how and when that happens. No one is going to put any pressure on you. What is important is we help you find a purpose in life once more.'

She's right, of course. I've been putting in extra hours at the stud because I have no real enthusiasm for anything other than work. As soon as I was discharged from hospital after the accident I returned to recuperate at Amberleigh, my grandparents' Regency manor house. I never set foot in the home I shared with Fliss and Emily again. Anna dealt with everything. I think her aim was to minimise my grief. When I arrived home, my room was just as it had been before I left to get married. There was nothing left to anchor me to my previous life with my wife and child.

During the ten days I lay in hospital drifting in and out of consciousness, my wife and daughter were buried in the family plot at St Swithin's. I pay regular visits to lay flowers, trying to accept the fact they are gone and I have to find my own way in the world again. I'm not sure about life after death but I want to believe, if indeed it does exist, they are with my mother and are at peace. However, for me, left behind, even after all this time, I sometimes struggle. The only thing that keeps me sane is my love of horses. Bringing new foals into the world is the most satisfying part of working in a stud. My job keeps me there long into the evening. By the time I reach home and my suite in the west wing I'm exhausted and sleep comes easily, although on occasions I have to encourage it with a little alcohol. Not too much, though or I could easily drift into deeper, darker waters.

'Well, what do you think?' Anna's voice intrudes into my thoughts and I turn to look at her. The expression on her face tells me she's hoping I'll agree, potentially turning myself into another Nick Knowles, fronting a team of polo shirted DIY SOS helpers.

'Let me think about it.' I answer in an attempt to slow things down. After considering my reply she gives thoughtful nod. I relax, happy I've at least bought myself a breathing space. Because knowing her this subject is far from over. And now it's time to leave before she hits me with another plan to help me back into the world I once knew. Gently I ease my horse's head around and with a farewell wave I leave, heading back down the lane towards Amberleigh and another day of work at the equestrian centre there.

OCTOBER 2012

LILY

This child is going to be the death of me. He's always in scrapes and I can't begin to count the number of times I've been sitting in A & E waiting to be seen. The blonde, Scottish triage nurse who always seems to be here too has already taken a look at him, greeting us like old friends. 'Hello,' she says, staring at Josh's bandaged leg, 'and what's the wee laddie been up to this time?'

The problem is my "wee laddie" is always in trouble. A real chip off the old block, I tell myself, remembering how his father, Pauli, used to get into all sorts of grief with his so-called mates, Robbie and Kenny. Petty criminals all three of them, until Josh came along and Pauli promised to mend his ways. Now my son is following in his father's footsteps. Not along a path of criminality, though. He's a good kid and wouldn't dream of getting into any real trouble. No, Josh's problem is, like Pauli he's easily led...and curious. Added to that, he's the clumsiest child on the planet and is always managing to hurt himself in some way. This morning when I wasn't looking, he sneaked out into the garden only to return moments later with his leg covered in blood. So here I am calling work to say I've been delayed, then calling Sonya his childminder to tell her I'm in the Emergency Department with Josh... again.

'I'm sorry, Mummy,' he says, looking up at me with a noisy sniff, his big blue eyes peeking at me from beneath his untidy blond fringe, his face reminding me so much of his father. Rummaging in my jacket pocket, I find a crumpled tissue and hand it to him.

'Here,' I instruct softly, 'wipe your nose.' He does and hands it back. I shake my head. 'Keep it,' I tell him.

'It was an accident. I tripped,' he sniffs again, and I hear echoes of Pauli in his voice. God, he's been gone four years and sometimes I still can't believe how it happened. For most of the time we were together he was in and out of prison. Makes him sound like a real villain, doesn't it? And that is so far from the truth. He was simply not clever enough to avoid getting caught. He worked as a delivery driver for Glen Maddox, a local fat cat who hid his criminal activities behind legitimate businesses. Glen had a lot of less than honest stuff going on and used Pauli and his two ham-fisted mates, Robbie and Kenny, for the petty pilfering. Poor Pauli was convinced they'd eventually be given a job which would net them all enough to retire on. His dream was for us to run a beach bar in Spain. Sadly, that's all it ever was: a dream.

The year before Josh was born, the three of them spent several months on remand following some bungled job. In the end, Glen greased a few palms and got them off. Pauli came home with promises to change, the way he always did, but it wasn't long before he was sucked back onto the criminal merry-go-round again. When I found I was pregnant with Josh I discovered I had a weapon, something to make him stop and think about what he was doing and where it would ultimately lead. For once in his life he actually listened. To my surprise, he was really excited about becoming a father. He got his act together, managed to get us another rented house in a better part of the town and with his newly-acquired HGV licence, moved to another company. Overnight he became a different man.

He managed to get a few days off when Josh was born but it wasn't long before I was alone again. It was clear he was bored at home and couldn't wait to get back to work. When the opportunity came up to drive abroad he jumped at it. 'The money will make such a difference, babe,' he said as he hugged me, not listening to my protests about really needing him here. The two weeks he was away seemed like a month. Although Josh was not a demanding baby, it had been a complicated birth which had taken its toll on me physically. That on its own would have been bad enough, but with a sprinkling of post-natal depression on top, things became much, much worse. I had no family; I abandoned them long ago. My father was a bully and my mother the alcoholic doormat he wiped his feet on. Four older brothers disappeared from home as soon as they were old enough and had never kept in touch. Pauli had no relatives I knew of either, which meant I really was alone. And then two days after Pauli had left on his first long haul drive to Italy, my next door neighbour, Rosie, turned up on the doorstep with a present for Josh.

I don't do friends, in fact experience has shown me, for whatever reason, that other women don't really like me. Until that morning I'd only ever seen Rosie half a dozen times – hanging out washing or returning from shopping with her toddler. Then there she was on the doorstep, all big eyed and smiley, offering me not only a gift, but some company as well. I studied her for a moment as she stood there chattering on about how she realised we'd had a baby and thought it would be a nice gesture to bring it a present. Overweight, with long dark untidy hair and a round homely face punctured by a nose ring, she didn't have a lot going for her. As she handed me the small package I noticed her namesake tattoo - a small rose which sat between the thumb and index finger of her right hand. With her oversized green jumper, long patterned skirt and worn Doc Martens she reminded me of the kind of women TV cameras zoom in on at environmental protests. Although I wasn't really interested in her, I told myself at least it was another human bringing conversation to my otherwise silent world. So I invited her in for coffee, watched as she enthused over Josh and simply let her talk.

'I've just turned twenty one,' she told me as she chattered on. 'Mia's father, Jack, isn't with us any longer. We met at Glastonbury three years ago. He's a poet...writes songs, too. He's very creative, needs his own space...but he loves Mia...wants her to be part of his life. He supports us as best he can and has her at weekends.'

Her words triggered the memory of a battered camper van pulling up in the street on Friday evenings. I wasn't sure I'd be willing to hand Josh over to the scruffy dropout in faded denims behind the wheel, and then I wondered why I cared. It wasn't any of my business really.

Rosie had a part time catering job at the local hospital

where there was a crèche. She told me how good the staff were and how Mia did all sorts of stuff like finger painting and making things with play doh. She also had regular visits from her mother and sister, two equally plump, scruffy women who both lived just outside Exeter. When she asked me what Pauli did for a living she seemed really horrified to learn he'd left me for a long distance driving job so soon after Josh's birth. 'We needed the money,' I told her.

'What, no support from your family?' she asked.

'Too far away.' I shook my head. It was a lie, but what else could I say?

'Friends?' The probing went on.

'I'm a bit shy,' I said, biting my lip. 'I did meet other pregnant women at ante-natal clinics but, well, they were all a bit cliquey.'

'Oh, poor you,' she said, stroking my arm and making a sad face. 'Well I'm here and if you need me, just shout, d'you hear? And I can babysit anytime you and your man...'

'Pauli,' I said, 'his name's Pauli.'

'...anytime you and Pauli want a break. You know,' she swivelled her shoulders and laughed, 'a bit of a night out. It's no trouble.'

I smiled and thanked her, half listening as she began to tell me more about herself. I realised that although I might not want this friendship it would at least give me an opportunity to get Pauli to take me out and free me up from my domestic prison occasionally.

The Italian job paid really well and Pauli decided he wanted to volunteer for more international trips. 'The money's really good, babe,' he said. 'It'll make all the difference.' Suddenly I didn't care about the money. I had missed him and the most important thing was having my man home every night. Rosie had elected to become my friend but it wasn't the same as having a husband around. I told him I needed him here but he simply waved away my concerns and did what he wanted to do. On my own I began to feel resentful. I hated the restrictions motherhood placed on me. Not just the domestic stuff but being chained to this small individual whose needs seemed to override everything else in my life. Trips into town made me feel worse. Windows full of pretty summer clothes, pavements full of laughing, happy, fashionable young women on their lunch breaks. How I longed for that life again, remembering those days when I lived with the Haydens as their lodger. Leo Hayden was in my debt for saving him from being mugged. My plausible lie of being homeless saw me moving to middle class suburbia with a generous monthly allowance while Pauli was on remand. Life was good then; I dressed and felt like a million dollars, unlike now, where since Josh's birth, everything was old and didn't fit properly. I felt shabby and out of step with everyone else. It seemed as if I wasn't a person any longer, simply a functional part of the house like the TV or the washing machine. But, I convinced myself, if Pauli's money was going to make a difference, maybe I might get those dresses I'd seen in Wallis, and with Rosie happy to babysit, a night out somewhere. But strangely, although Pauli was on good money, there never seemed to be any spare. There were always excuses - bills to be paid, things needed for the house or repairs on the car, which was old and unreliable. I didn't think I was asking for much, just something to cheer me up and stop this feeling of being at odds with the rest of the world. Of course, every time I asked, Pauli would give me a hug and say, 'Next month hun, I promise.' But next month came and went, and then another and nothing changed. And all the time my resentment was deepening.

That was when the rows started. They were small at first, but when he began slamming out of the house and coming back late with alcohol on his breath I really flipped.

'If you can go out and drink money away, how come I can't have my dresses?' I demanded, 'or a meal. One meal, a night out together like we used to,' I complained over breakfast one morning. Seeing his irritable expression, I changed tactics. 'I think it would be great to spend more time together,' I said, looking at him from under my fringe, 'and I'd like to look nice. Wouldn't you like that, too? The dresses aren't too dear and I told you Rosie said she would babysit.'

'I'm not having a scruffy hippie in here looking after my son,' he said. 'I can't believe she works anywhere near food with that bloody hair of hers.'

'She ties it back and she tells me they wear hats... and she's not a hippie, Pauli, she's my friend.'

'Friend!' He gave a scornful snort. 'You must be scraping the bottom of the barrel. Well, I'm not letting that walking health hazard near Josh...end of,' he said, before pushing his chair back and leaving the room.

Josh was four months old when Pauli's company decided to set up a driver rota for continental trips, which reduced his absences to a fortnight every six weeks. Whatever the reason behind the decision it was good news for me. I had my man back. It meant we had less money coming in and I trimmed my demands to one dress and a pair of shoes plus the meal out. But Pauli wouldn't budge and accused me of being selfish. Selfish? Well, I wasn't going to let a comment like that go unchallenged, not when he'd come home from town with a new shirt and Levis the previous Saturday. This time my comments saw him slamming out of the front door and disappearing until late. It soon became a regular occurrence every time we clashed. But there were moments when he was different. Like the times we would take Josh for walks at the weekend, mostly to the park where we'd buy coffee in cardboard cups from the small kiosk there. These were times when we talked about our son and our future together. But now Pauli seemed to have closed off completely. He seemed remote; unapproachable. However, I brushed away my fears. He was the only one bringing in money and, according to him, because of the rota we were on a tight budget. Therefore, I reasoned, he probably had a lot on his mind, things he didn't want to worry me with. Maybe it was time to rein in my demands for a while. Something was bound to come up, I thought. I simply had to be patient.

A month later, Rosie came around to tell me about a newly advertised ten hour a week job in the hospital catering department and I thought, yes, I can do this. We'll have more money and I can get my life back again. But Pauli didn't agree. Wouldn't agree. 'You need to be home with Josh,' he argued. His tone, so different from the quiet, easy going husband I'd known for the past four years, told me he didn't expect to be argued with. This wasn't the Pauli I knew. My mild mannered husband seemed to have disappeared and I wasn't at all happy about the cold hard stranger who had taken his place.

'But Josh will be perfectly safe,' I explained to him. 'The crèche takes babies from three months and Rosie says the staff are very experienced.'

'Rosie says. Rosie says,' he mimicked. 'Why can't you get it through your head I don't want him dumped in some hospital nursery with a load of other grubby kids giving him God knows what. Those sorts of places are a breeding ground for germs.'

'That's ridiculous,' I said. 'Don't *you* realise the difference the money would make? I might be able to make myself look decent for a change.'

'Ah, it's all about you, is it? I might have known.'

'I look a mess, Pauli. My clothes don't fit and I'd really like to get my hair cut properly, not have to do it myself.'

I thought he might understand how I felt. I even managed to squeeze out a few tears to support my case. But from the tired expression on his face and the way he sucked in his breath, I knew what was coming next wasn't what I wanted to hear.

'I said no, Lily.' His voice was calm but there was a frosty edge to it. 'You do understand no, don't you?'

Sarcasm I could do without. 'Yes, and I also understand male pride and stupidity, too,' I fired back. 'You're being totally unreasonable. In fact, I actually think I'm beginning to hate you.' I hadn't meant to say that, but he was making me feel so angry and frustrated that it simply slipped out.

A huge row followed. We threw insults at each other,

neither of us really taking in what the other was saying, and when we both eventually calmed down he stood there shaking his head.

'I can't go on like this anymore. If you want the bloody job that badly then take it,' he said, 'but don't expect me to stay. I've had enough of all this rowing and you being such a miserable, demanding bitch, always wanting things I can't provide you with.' He stared at the floor for a moment before he raised his eyes to look at me again. 'All I want is a quiet life with you and Josh but it's not working, is it? Nothing's working. When I'm away it's wrong, now I'm back you're still moaning all the time. I just don't want to be here anymore.'

I was stunned that this was how he saw our situation. He was the one who'd caused it all and here he was planning to leave. As panic began to flood through me, I heard him promise to set up regular maintenance payments for Josh and to cover the rent. Alone, I thought. I'd be totally alone and I couldn't allow that to happen. I needed Pauli here. *We* needed Pauli here. I was scared because I could see I was being pushed into a worse situation than I'd been in when he was on remand. Because this time it wasn't going to be just me I had to look out for, there was the baby as well. Why couldn't he see he was part of the problem? Why was he so bloody difficult?

'You're bluffing,' I said. 'You wouldn't. You couldn't.'

'I have to,' he said. 'I really have to.'

'If you find me such a miserable cow then it's partly your fault,' I threw back at him. 'You make things worse, disappearing all the time. Three nights a week, maybe more lately, you leave after you've eaten and don't return until I'm in bed. You're not back with Maddox again, are you?'

'Of course not, you silly bitch.' He tutted under his breath. 'You're doing my head in that's all, and I can't stay.' He went all quiet and stared at the floor again, then simply turned and disappeared out into the hall. Wondering what he planned to do next, I followed him up the stairs to our room, watching in dismay as he pulled out a heavy canvas bag and began packing.

'You can't leave,' I said, desperately trying to hide the panic in my voice. 'Where will you go?'

'I've plenty of mates. I'll crash out on someone's sofa,' he said as he began pulling items from the hangers in the wardrobe.

'Robbie or Kenny's, I suppose.'

'Get it through your head, those days are over. I'm not that man anymore.' The anger in his voice woke Josh.

His cries took me away from Pauli's packing. I picked him up, realising he needed changing. When I came out of the small bedroom with him in my arms, Pauli was half way down the stairs. I called after him, following him down to the front door, wanting him to stop and turn around, hoping seeing Josh's small, tearful face would make him have a change of heart. No chance. He simply opened the door and walked out into the night.

'You'll be back,' I shouted from the doorway as he threw the bag into the back of the car. 'You won't leave us...you can't leave us.'

Pauli did return the next evening, not for me or his son but to collect the rest of his clothes in what looked like a new suitcase. He pushed past me. He didn't want to talk. He wouldn't even look at me. Rosie came around afterwards carrying a bottle of wine. Jack had picked Mia up for the weekend so she was on her own. She had heard our raised voices from the other evening and had just seen Pauli leave with his case.

'Men are stupid,' she said as she unscrewed the cap of the chilled bottle of Chardonnay and filled the two glasses I'd provided. 'Don't worry,' she added, handing me one of them, 'he'll be back after he's got over his man-fit. I've seen him with Josh. He loves him, he'd never leave.'

'Jack did,' I said, taking a sip.

'Jack never promised to stay. We never exchanged vows or stuff like that.' She took a sip of her wine. 'I told you he's a poet and a song writer. A free spirit. We enjoyed our time together and he wants Mia in his life, but he doesn't do domestic. It's not a problem,' she said with a contented smile, 'it works well for both of us. I'm happy.'

I didn't say anything but decided Jack was one of those selfish sods who wanted life on his own terms. Much like Pauli was doing at the moment. If he didn't come back, I wondered whether I could live like Rosie. The notion upset me and I brushed it away. She's right, I thought, he's just having a bit of a man crisis.

A week later Pauli returned. Taking a seat at the kitchen table, he waited for me to join him.

'I've got something to tell you,' he said, splaying his hands across the smooth Formica surface as I pulled up a chair. 'I've...uh...been offered another job.'

'I see.' The way he was sitting there looking embarrassed, the thought crossed my mind he might be planning to apologise and tell me everything was going to be all right.

'It's not here.'

'Right.' I sat still, clasping my hands together, not wanting to make any move or say anything that would interrupt. It was all up to him and once he'd told me about the new job and what it would mean for us I'd tell him I was sorry for what had happened. I'd then say I was glad we were going to be making a new start and promise...well, anything really, if it would guarantee I'd have him back and his regular money coming in.

'It's in Manchester,' he said in one quick breath, 'another company. I'll be doing permanent trips abroad.'

'Manchester?' The word almost tumbled out of my mouth, 'I see.' I nodded. 'We'll be moving, will we?'

'No Lily, *we* won't. I will.'

'Oh.' I bit my lip. 'But you'll be back between journeys?'

'Not exactly.' He gave an uncomfortable lift of his shoulders and stared at his clasped hands, a sure sign he was about to deliver bad news. 'I think,' he said quietly looking across the table at me, 'it might be a good idea for us to have some time apart.'

'No Pauli, that's not fair.' I glared at him. 'You have responsibilities. You can't just swan off to Manchester and make a new life for yourself. What about us?'

'You'll be taken care of. I'll send money, I promise.'

'So you think as long as you're sending us regular money, everything is fine? Is that it? But what about Josh growing up? He needs you here.'

'Look, I just need a few months to sort myself out then I'll send for you.' He said rubbing a tired hand across his face. 'I'm sorry, I'm just not very good with this parenting thing. I looked forward to it, I really did. I was over the moon in fact, but I didn't expect it to turn into this. You moaning all the time, wanting what we can't afford, the house a complete tip, nights when Josh won't settle...and now he's teething, well it's got worse. I rarely get a decent night's sleep. I don't want to be here Lily.' He shook his head miserably. 'Driving abroad was great, it got me away from all of this, but when they changed the rotas, to be quite honest coming through the door each night all I wanted to do was to turn around and run. Taking this job and having a complete break for a few months is the only way I feel I can solve our problems. By the time we're back together again Josh won't be a baby any more. That's something I know I can handle. I've bought another car so I'll leave you the Focus...you'll have wheels...and money.'

'You coward,' I said, feeling my temper build as I watched him leave. 'You bloody coward.' I wanted to pummel him, to make him see what he was doing to me and Josh. What did he think my life had been like? Four months of sun filled laughter? And he'd found the money for another car. How, if we were supposedly strapped for cash? Suddenly I wanted to do something to hurt him as badly as he was hurting us. Being a volatile red head, I'm prone to simply opening my mouth and letting the most destructive, hurtful things come spilling out. And that is exactly what happened on this occasion. As he turned, I uttered the words I knew would cut the deepest as my mouth ran away with me once more. 'Go then, who cares?' I taunted. 'Bugger off to Manchester, Josh won't miss you. It's not as if you're his real father anyway.'

His fingers were wrapped around the handle of the door as he swung around to look at me. 'What did you say?'

Eyes narrowing, his voice came out in a low growl.

For a moment I honestly thought I'd gone too far, that for the first time in his life Pauli might commit an act of violence against me. I could even see the headlines: *Police arrest husband as wife found strangled.* But he didn't. Instead, he was quite calm as he delivered his reply. One that meant he was severing all ties and I really was on my own.

'Right,' he said with a careless shrug, 'well I suggest you look Josh's real father up and get him to support both of you from now on.' Then the door slammed and he was gone.

I blow out a breath as I pack away my thoughts. My eyes scan the waiting area and the people sitting here, trying to work out where we are in the queue. I look at Josh again, his small legs dangling over the edge of his chair as he sits there eyeballing the little girl in a pink dress sitting opposite. She's making faces at him and I see him grin. He's a good natured kid with none of my hot-tempered ways in him, thank God. As Josh looks up and gives me one of his lopsided grins I hear a female voice call out, 'Josh Stevenson,' and watch him as he wiggles his bottom and slides off the chair. The bandage I've secured around his leg slips, revealing the cut, raw and bloody. Bending down to remove it, I help him as he hobbles towards the smiling, dark-haired nurse.

It's a nasty gash but Josh sits quietly while the doctor stitches. He's given a prescription for antibiotics, which means a journey to the hospital pharmacy. While we are waiting for the medication to be dispensed, a group of young white-coated doctors pass by in the corridor outside. They all have that shared air of confidence with their long strides, muted conversation and laughter, stethoscopes slung around their shoulders. A straggler runs to catch the group up. As he passes the entrance to pharmacy, something falls from his coat and skitters across the floor. I hear his footfalls as he returns to retrieve it. Bending forward to pick up what appears to be a pen, he glances our way and I suck in a deep breath.

'Lily?' He straightens up and frowns as he slots the pen into the top pocket of his white coat. 'Lily?' He repeats my name, walking towards me as if he wants to make sure he's not seeing things. I stand there in silence, too shocked to do anything but watch him approach. I never thought Zac Rayner could look any better but he does. He's filled out; he seems taller, his shoulders broader...and his face, that glorious face. His hair is longer now too, nudging the collar of his shirt, but it's still the same rich blond I remember running my fingers through. And then suddenly he's right in front of me with his all too sexy smile.

'It is you.' He grins. 'The hair colour confused me,' he says, frowning. 'How long have you been blonde?'

'Oh, a couple of years,' I say with a shrug.

'You're looking good.' He says running his gaze over my light navy suit and tan heels.

'Thank you.' I extract myself from past reflections and smile back. 'How are you?'

'Fine, just fine.' He turns his attention to Josh, giving him a grin. 'And who's this?'

'I'm Josh,' my son declares proudly, craning his neck to look up at this tall stranger. 'Who are you?'

'Josh,' I reprimand. 'Sorry.' I look up at Zac apologetically and wish I hadn't. Because I'm caught in the depth of those amazing blue eyes; eyes which now trigger warning bells in my head. *You've got a short memory,* a tiny voice niggles. *Aren't you forgetting what he said? About girls from your world not belonging in his. That you were...what was it? Ah, yes, amusement value. Good for a quick lay.* At the time he hit me with those awful words I would have done anything for him. Absolutely anything. But he didn't want me. I don't think he ever did. He was right... all I'd ever been was a distraction. If there was any satisfaction to be had it was that he didn't want Jess Hayden either. *Beware,* the voice insists, *you don't want to fall into the same trap again, do you?* Indeed, I don't.

'So,' he says with his eyes on Josh's bandaged leg, 'had a

bit of an accident, have you?'

'In and out of trouble all the time,' I say, ruffling my son's head affectionately while trying to ignore the way Zac's looking at me.

'I guess you're going to have some explaining to do to your dad when you get home.' He looks at Josh's wide eyed expression.

'I don't have a dad,' Josh says, shaking his head. 'It's just me and—'

'His father and I split a long time ago,' I explain, interrupting Josh and wishing he had had the sense to keep quiet. Zac nods, his gaze moving from Josh back to me. He is even more gorgeous than I remember but the voice in my head is calling out once more, warning me to be careful. Because beneath the lure of those light indigo eyes lurks an eighteen carat bastard.

'Josh Stevenson.' I hear a female voice call out my son's name and turn to see a young brunette in a blue tunic standing at the pharmacy counter with his medication in her hand, her eyes fixed on Zac.

'Thank you.' I step forward and take the packet from her. She isn't even aware of my presence or the prescription as it slips from her hand into mine, and I see her give Zac the kind of smile that definitely indicates some sort of past emotional entanglement. However, his cool reaction indicates she, like me, is very much yesterday's news. I begin to back away. It's time to leave, to escape back to the safety of my car.

'I must go, lovely to see you again, Zac,' I say with a departing smile, Josh's hand clutched firmly in mine. The woman holds him there with paperwork she obviously has a query about. It gives me the opportunity for a quick getaway.

After trailing through endless corridors we finally reach the car park. I settle Josh in the back of my car and belt him in. As I start the engine someone taps the driver's window. It's Zac, and as the glass lowers I'm ready for him. I know exactly what's coming next and although he still has the power to melt my bones, I'm determined not to end up as a stop gap between the end of his current relationship and the beginning of the next. Because I'm under no illusions that is all I'll ever be.

I brace myself as he treats me to one of his killer smiles. 'I'm glad I caught you...' he begins, 'it's great to see you again. I was wondering if maybe we could—'

'No.' I cut him off sharply, wanting to kill this conversation before it can go any further. 'Not after what you said to me...not after what you called me. Do you think I'm completely stupid? That I'd let you use me again? Do I look that desperate?' I realise my voice has gone up several octaves, probably because, despite my promise to myself to remain in control of this situation, his closeness is having its usual effect on me.

'You don't understand,' he says, leaning in, 'A lot has happened since I last saw you and it's made me realise I've done some bad things to people. All I want to do is have the chance to make it up to you.'

'You can, by leaving me alone,' are my parting words as I hit the button to close the window and slam my foot down on the accelerator, wheels spinning as I leave the parking space. Reaching the car park entrance, I stop and take a quick glance in my rear view mirror, expelling a relieved breath as I find he is no longer there.

When Pauli left I was too angry to cry. I was still furious he could simply up sticks and leave the area. I realised opening my mouth had been a crazy move, but at the time, in my usual reckless way, I wanted to hurt him the way he was hurting me but it had backfired badly. After a few days I rang him and left a message on his voicemail asking him to contact me. I wanted to apologise. I had to because an inner fear told me he was going to carry out his threat and simply walk away. When he failed to return my call I contacted his company and spoke to their personnel department. They were surprised when I mentioned Manchester because no one actually knew where he had gone. He'd simply given in his notice and left.

I decided to wait. Everything hinged on the end of the

month and whether the rent and Josh's maintenance money arrived. When the end of November came and I checked the bank account there was no promised transfer, confirming I was well and truly on my own. I tried to tell myself it was my fault for never knowing when to shut up. However, part of me wondered whether he had planned this all along. The bastard.

I spent Christmas with Rosie. She was very kind to me and I didn't deserve it really, seeing as I used her as a convenience the same way I did most people in my life. Her mum and sister visited too, and brought presents for Josh - a soft toy and a little jacket. They were sweet people but, despite their generosity, I labelled them fools; people born to be taken for granted. I wasn't like that. I'd been on my own since I left home at fifteen. I'd learnt to be a manipulator, to use every trick I knew to get what I wanted. And if I was to get out of this situation and leave Rosie and Brooklands Terrace far behind, I'd have to find my way back to the person I used to be.

With the arrival of the New Year I did a lot of thinking. Suddenly, Pauli's disappearance didn't seem the quite disaster I'd thought it was going to be. With no one to give me grief, my benefits and rent sorted, I was feeling positive, determined 2009 was going to be different. The first thing I did was to apply to be rehoused. I wanted to get away from Rosie who, since Pauli had left, seemed to be finding too many excuses to drop in to check up on me, often staying for hours. I began to resent the continuous intrusion; it was something I could do without. Anyway, we didn't need three bedrooms and I was hoping I might get a swap for a smaller house on one of the new build social housing developments in Exeter, which I had seen going up back in the summer. When I got the letter to say I'd been allocated a brand new two bedroomed terraced house, I did a little dance around the living room. Yes, 2009 was definitely going to be my year. I arranged to move on a day when Rosie was at work. I know it was mean but I did leave her a note and a bottle of wine saying I was moving out of the area and thanking her for being a good neighbour. It meant I left with a totally clear conscience and, of course, ensured there was no chance of her turning up on my doorstep.

The next thing I had to organise was getting some proper qualifications and a job. I enrolled on an office training skills course at the local college. They had a crèche where I could leave Josh – it was perfect. I learned to type, to use the computer, and by the end of the course felt both confident and ready for work. Once the course was over I began applying for jobs. With no experience I was at an immediate disadvantage, something that was pointed out in a few of the "unsuccessful" feedback phone calls I received. Then I got a break. One of those calls suggested I register with an employment agency for temporary work. They felt it would not only give me the opportunity to gain experience, I might also land an assignment which could lead to permanent employment. So I did, and six months after signing on with Workshop, its owner, Katya Ryan, got me this dream placement at Warner Webb, an up-market estate agents based in modern offices in the centre of Exeter. Their receptionist was about to go on maternity leave and I would be covering for a whole year.

From the moment I walked through the door I knew it was exactly the kind of place I wanted to work. The team was young and professional, the building light and airy with masses of glass and chrome and fresh flowers everywhere. Max Warner, the owner, was a strikingly handsome man in his late forties. With his thick blond hair and dark assessing eyes, the first time I saw him he reminded me of a great golden lion. He wore designer suits, a gold Rolex and smelled of expensive after shave. He interviewed me with Antonia Lang, their Admin Manager. Although he came across the perfect gentleman, something in his appraising brown eyes hinted that while he might wear a wedding ring, he wasn't averse to straying if the opportunity presented itself.

In the months that followed, working at Warner Webb taught me image was incredibly important. I therefore invested in good quality work pieces which, I hoped, made me look as professional as everyone else. I was determined by the time Sophie Lancaster returned from maternity leave, I would be equipped to find permanent employment...and perhaps that all important new man. As it turned out, I didn't even have to look for a job. A week before I was due to leave, Antonia called me in to tell me they would like to keep me on. They wanted to train me to use their new marketing software. I was offered a twenty hour a week contract working with the sales team where I would be creating brochures, mail shots and other publicity stuff. And...the rest they say is history.

As I drop Josh back with Sonya, I check my watch and realise it's already ten-thirty. Today Max and Nick, Warner Webb's Sales Manager, are going out to visit a new client and Max has asked me to go along. As "Queen of Brochures" as he laughingly calls me, he feels it's time I got to see the real thing and he's selected this particular house because, he says, it's an exceptional property and we're very lucky to be the agency chosen to market it. I smile as I reach my destination, park my car and take the stairs from the multi-story to the street. I'm about to get my second throwback moment today; first Zac and now this. You see, the house is in Lynbrook, the village where Jess Hayden once lived. Privileged. Middle class. She had an irritating inbuilt air of confidence. She also had Zac and that made me hate her even more. The first time I saw him I wanted him so very, very much. Of course, I had no qualms about taking him from her. All's fair in love and war as they say. But then he dumped me, and okay, although I now know he wasn't to be trusted, I was pretty sure she was behind it all. She didn't get away with it though. You see I'm very much an eye for an eye girl so I made sure she got what was coming to her.

JESS

It's the last week in October and I'm back in Lynbrook for half term. I've already handed in my notice at St Helens and will be leaving at Christmas. After the shock of being left a small fortune in Leo's will, I sat down and had a heart-to-heart with Rufus. He already knew about my plans to leave Oxford and find a job teaching in a local village school. But the arrival of the money has changed everything. It's made me realise although I love teaching, it's given me the ability to change my life. I can put my career on hold for a while and take time out to do things once completely out of my reach. I can travel to places I've only ever dreamed of or maybe use part of my inheritance to set up a project. I have no idea what exactly it's going to be, only that I want to do something useful with the money.

The estate is still being wound up. I've appointed Roo to liaise with Elliot McIntyre, and he'll be looking after all my interests from now on. I've already had some of the money transferred to into my account and it's enabled me to buy something I've always wanted: my own horse. He's a gorgeous Palomino Arab cross called Caspar and is currently stabled at George Selby's place, Manor Farm on the edge of the village. I've been taking him out every day, which has given me an opportunity to really get to know him. I still ride in Barnfield Woods along the river bank and all the old familiar pathways. These places can't help but bring back memories of Talún and that long ago summer we spent together. Fragments of it run through my head like an old movie. For a long time afterwards I was angry. I couldn't believe what he had done, leaving the way he did. Although it wasn't just me he hurt; George and his wife Ellie, who became his surrogate parents when his mother disappeared, suffered too. Roo wanted me to get rid of the ring Talún gave me but, perversely, I insisted on keeping it. I hung it on a chain around my neck for a while as a warning to myself against falling for good looking liars. Time mellowed my anger and it now sits on the third finger of my right hand. A beautiful delicate thing, it deserves to be seen. The old saying "time's a great healer" is a good one. The anger's gone, along with the pain. I only hope wherever he is, Talún is settled and happy.

I can't believe it's been five years since I left Lynbrook for Exeter University. My father Rufus Hayden still runs the Black Bull Inn, the main watering hole and social hub in our quiet village. Not only is it a great pub, it also boasts an award winning restaurant. The other morning we were chatting over breakfast about the arrivals and departures there had been during that time...and there have been quite a few.

One of the biggest changes is the loss of Harry and Sally and I know how much dad misses his chef and star barmaid, who married and left to manage their own pub in Dorset. Bella Fielding, whose parents run the village shop and post office, has taken Sally's place behind the bar. She juggles her bar work with her day job as a teaching assistant at Lynbrook Primary. I don't know her well, but dad says she's been a great replacement for Sally. They have a common bond in their dislike for a particular set of new arrivals to the village.

Three years ago part of the rectory gardens were sold off and two large barn conversion style houses built. This saw the arrival of Jensen Lebeq and Felix Black, a couple of well-heeled wide boy finance men and their glossy wives. The village has become quite used to seeing them speeding past in their huge SUVs. They book regular Sunday lunch tables in the Bull's restaurant, usually arriving with an entourage of noisy friends filling the car park with their Range Rovers and Audis. My father walks a difficult path. He dislikes their ilk but he's never been one to turn business away and, of course, they do spend an incredible amount of money. Jensen and Felix's wives, Georgina and Danielle, have totally embraced the country thing. They can often be seen walking their newly-acquired Labradors while decked out in their Hunter wellies, Barbour jackets and Christy trilbies. Most of the locals view them as a harmless irritation. As far as they are concerned, they're an inevitable addition to village life after the way programmes like *Escape to the Country* have relentlessly advocated the benefits of rural living. Right from the start Bella dubbed them "The Witches" because, she said, their black and auburn hair colouring reminded her of Cher and Susan Sarandon in the *Witches of Eastwick*. It was also a derogatory term as the pair can be quite obnoxious at times. 'But what about the blonde?' I asked her, remembering Michelle Pfeiffer. 'Oh, don't worry, she'll be along soon,' she predicted confidently.

Later that morning I drive up to Manor Farm to take Caspar out. I look in on George and Ellie Selby, discovering he's already left for the day and she's in the middle of baking.

'Morning Jess, back for the holidays?' she asks, pushing her hair from her eyes with the back of a floured hand.

'Just the week.' I tell her, 'but I'll be here permanently from December.'

'Ah yes, George did mention you were coming home. Are you looking forward to being back?'

I tell her I am and that although I'm going to miss the children and my work colleagues, I'm quite excited about the future and the new challenges to come. We exchange a few words, then not wishing to hold up her dough pummelling session, I agree to call back for tea, cake and a chat later.

Ben is waiting in the barn. His face lights up as I arrive and he immediately heads for the loose box where Caspar is waiting. He's twenty-two now, a large, gentle lad with mild learning difficulties who adores horses. When I first came to Lynbrook I helped him improve his reading. *Black Beauty* was the first book we read together. He's a good, reliable worker and six months ago George gave him total responsibility for the small stables where people like me pay an annual fee to keep their horses.

'Morning Jess,' he says, giving me one of his famous ear-to-ear grins as he leads Caspar over to me.

'Morning Ben,' I respond, as I struggle with the chin strap of my riding hat. Then slotting my foot into the stirrup, I haul myself into the saddle. Ben stands there silently, alternating his blue gaze between me and the horse.

'You okay?' I ask, feeling there's something on his mind he probably wants to share. But he's very shy and often needs help.

He nods, reaching out to stroke Caspar's nose as he looks up at me. Colour floods his cheeks and then he smiles. 'I just wanted to say...well, I'm glad you're coming back to stay.'

'Thanks Ben, me too,' I say, and suddenly I realise it's true. I'm coming home and I can't think of any better place to be.

LILY

'God, this house is gorgeous. I had no idea it would be quite so grand,' I say, and I'm making these comments before we've even stepped through the front door.

'Told you.' Max grins at me.

Over the years I've been with the company we've become good friends. My original assumption that he was philandering husband material was totally wrong. I had no idea, you see, about her. Davina Warner is a cold, career driven woman who runs a chain of high class boutiques throughout Devon and Cornwall. There's one of her boutiques in Exeter – *The Style Loft*. It's the sort of place where the price tags are discreetly turned over, an automatic indication you'll need to take out a small mortgage to afford even the cheapest item. Their luxurious home, *Bay Heights*, sits high above the Teignmouth Road, although Davina is rarely there. She's either in London, where they have an apartment, or flying to Milan or Paris to check out new collections. Max Warner, I soon discovered, was a lonely man, one who probably loved his wife before her obsession with clothes took over and pushed him out of her life. So if he keeps a mistress - and I'm sure there is one hidden away somewhere - I don't blame him.

Max has developed a soft spot for me. 'I know exactly where I am with you, Lily,' he told me once. 'You take the time to listen and you're always honest.'

Honest? Me? I smile at the memory. He has no idea. Actually I like him too. Without him giving me a chance, I might never have been where I am today – a working mother making her own way in the world.

I bring myself back to the present and see a plain, dark-haired woman is standing to one side and holding the front door open for us. Surely she can't be the owner of this place.

My silent question is answered immediately as we are invited into a large marble-floored hallway with a sweep of stairs to the right, where a thin, immaculately dressed woman is making an elegant descent. She's wearing navy trousers and an apricot silk shirt and her jet black hair is pulled back into a chignon, accentuating her high cheek bones. With pearl studs in her ears and a three strand choker at her throat, she looks like the mature version of everything I've ever dreamed of being. Reaching the bottom step, the woman, who I already know is called Mrs. Tremayne, all but glides across the floor towards us.

'Mr. Warner, so pleased to meet you,' She gushes and extends a beige-tipped hand towards Max in a way which convinces me he's expected to kiss rather than shake it.

Max introduces Nick and me, and then we're taken through to the drawing room. We sit and she explains her husband died three years ago and she has now met someone who not only shares her love of horses but has asked her to marry him. It's time to move on she tells us. 'There are too many memories here,' she says, dramatically, spreading an expensively ringed hand across the base of her throat. 'Tomaso and I plan a fresh start, somewhere new.'

'We have several fabulous properties on our books, Mrs. Tremayne,' Max tells her, keen to capitalise on the situation.

'Oh no, Mr. Warner,' She gives a slow shake of her head. 'We're planning to relocate to Italy. Tuscany to be precise.'

Watching her moves, I know this woman can produce a command performance when the situation arises. I'm beginning to like her style because I can see she has both

Max and Nick hanging on her every word. After offering us coffee and chatting about the property while we drink, she then takes us on an extensive tour of the house, grounds and the equestrian facilities. It's quite clear all her money has gone into horses as every room in the house looks tired. In fact, the whole place needs totally updating. Already I'm dreaming about what I'd do if it were mine. What's the matter with me? None of the other properties I've been involved with have had this sort of effect on me. But then, I guess it's because I've never actually visited any of them; this is the first.

Within a week, Nick's team have done their stuff and from the information provided I've drafted the brochure for Max to okay. Usually Nick would do this but as it's such a special property, this time the boss is getting involved. When the brochures have been printed I sneak a copy to take home. I've never done this before but somehow it seems I've become totally obsessed with this house.

'Now, if only I could get myself a lottery win,' I tell Sonya later, as I show it to her over coffee when I call in to collect Josh.

'Or a rich husband.' She grins.

'Well, that's not going to happen any time soon, is it?' I laugh as I slip the brochure back into my bag, 'Not in a million years.'

'Guess you'll have to stick with the lottery then,' she says, as Josh appears in the doorway with Sonya's son, Bailey.

'You had a good day?' I ask as she disappears into the hall to retrieve his coat. Josh nods silently then looks across at Bailey. I sense a conspiracy. 'What?' I say.

'I was naughty,' he bites his lip. I look up and catch Sonya's expression as she comes back into the room.

'What's he done?' I ask. After all, whenever Josh is involved in anything there's bound to be damage.

'Oh, there's nothing broken.' Sonya smiles and shakes her head, making her ponytail dance. 'Although you may find he doesn't want any tea.'

'Josh?' I transfer my gaze to him.

'Bailey and I...' he hesitates, 'we...'

'Cupcakes,' Sonya interrupts, shaking her head as she smiles at my son. 'I baked and iced a batch of cupcakes and very foolishly left them on the kitchen worktop. When I was upstairs, Bailey and Josh decided to help themselves. To four each.'

'Cupcakes?' I say, giving his hair a ruffle as I help him slip his arms into his coat. 'Come along, trouble, let's get you home.'

JESS

Today, the sun is streaming through my bedroom window as I wake. Deciding to make the most of the morning, I arrive half an hour early for my ride with Caspar. I drop in on the Selbys first, where George is finishing off his post-breakfast mug of tea. The moment I walk into the kitchen I sense something is wrong.

'Morning.' I look at him then at Ellie, who is standing in front of the Aga with her back to me.

'Jess.' She turns, her tight expression quickly rearranging itself into a smile. 'You're early this morning.'

'Yes, well it's such a lovely morning, it's a pity to waste it. Everything okay?' I ask, looking from one to the other.

'Everything's fine. Spot of tummy trouble, that's all.' George rubs his stomach and winces as he finishes off his tea. 'Ah well, time I wasn't here,' he says, eyeing the kitchen clock. Retrieving his jacket from the back of his chair, he pulls it on. 'I'll be back by one,' he says, not even looking at Ellie as he disappears out of the door.

'Just having one of his off days,' Ellie says with a shake of her head as the kitchen door closes.

'It's not the beginnings of an ulcer, is it?' I ask, wondering whether running the farm is becoming too much for him.

'Oh, good heavens no.' She waves a hand at me as she moves towards the kitchen table and begins to clear away the breakfast things. 'It's simply a bad bout of indigestion.

That's the problem when you get to our age,' she explains, 'the things you like sometimes don't like you. And then there's the EU paperwork he has to deal with. It's enough to upset anyone's system.' She manages a smile as she begins to load crockery into the dishwasher. However, the reassurance in her words don't match the uneasiness I can see still lingering on her face as she straightens up and closes the washer's door.

I feel totally helpless. I've known George and Ellie for six years. They're tough, resilient folk. They looked after Talún when his mother disappeared and I'm aware his leaving without as much as a goodbye hurt them deeply. However, the pain they went through then isn't what's happening now. This is very different. And no matter how much they're trying to hide it from me, there's definitely some sort of problem.

'I guess I'd better go, see how Caspar is.' I mask my anxiety with a quick smile. The last thing I want is to make Ellie feel I'm intruding into their privacy. I want to help, but until they decide to share anything with me, all I can do is keep a watchful eye on them.

LILY

I might have known Zac would find me. I think he must have read my lapel badge when I was talking to him in pharmacy, damn him. Thank God he didn't turn up at the office asking for me. That would have triggered far too many unwanted questions. I've carefully scripted my past into a neat, believable story and the last thing I want is someone coming along and turning the whole thing upside down. No, at least Zac had the decency to be discreet. He was across the road from Warner Webb's when I left for lunch today.

'Lily.'

I curse under my breath as I recognise his voice. In a public place he has me at a disadvantage. Quickly, I turn and smile as if nothing in the world is wrong.

'Zac.' I watch as he catches up with me, determined he's

not going to coerce me into doing anything I don't want to.

'Look, I'm sorry to intrude on your lunch hour,' he says, stopping a few feet away, 'but could you spare me a few minutes?'

'Zac,' I raise a hand in protest, 'just go away will you?'

'Lily, listen, please?' There's a strange desperation in his voice as he blocks my attempt to leave, 'I'm trying to do the right thing here. Besides, you won't have to put up with me for much longer. I'm leaving the UK for good. I've a medical job lined up in Canada. I'm flying out to Toronto in the spring.'

'Not joining Daddy in his clinic? He will be disappointed.'

'Ah.' He purses his lips and studies his feet for a moment. 'Well, that was the original plan...but I messed up big time.'

'No doubt there was a woman involved.'

'Dad's new partner's wife.'

'Oh dear, got your fingers well and truly burnt then.' I can't resist a satisfied smirk.

'Look.' He ignores my jibe. 'All I want is to make things right with you before I go.'

'I'm not sure I understand you,' I say. 'How can you possibly make things right? I've moved on. I have a life, a job, I'm happy. I don't need anything you think you can give me to make up for the way you treated me in the past.' I pause for a moment. 'Or is it you're looking for something from me? Forgiveness, maybe?' I tilt my head curiously. 'Don't tell me Zac Rayner has suddenly developed a conscience.' The accompanying laugh sounds harsh, but I can't help the bitterness I feel. I shake my head, needing to get away. 'Honestly, you're wasting your time here. You want some advice? Go find the next casualty on your list. I'm sure it's a very long one.'

He gives me a sad, reflective smile and sighs deeply as he turns to go. Then he hesitates and I brace myself for yet another attempt to persuade me out to dinner, or some equally unwanted offer. Instead, he simply says, 'Look, I'm here until the twenty second of April. If you change your mind about seeing me, just phone the hospital's main switchboard and they can bleep me.'

I walk away, not even bothering to say goodbye. I hate to say it, but seeing him like this today has left me with another reminder of what I was to him: a cheap fix for his ego.

JESS

I never thought I'd want to see Leanna Tremayne again. The last time we were face to face she was very drunk and accusing me of stealing Talún from her. At the time they had been having an affair and I was horrified to think he could be involved with someone old enough to be his mother. Since the days Talún warmed her bed, there have been a string of other young men, mostly employees. But now she's really hit the jackpot. A thirty five-year-old Italian called Tomaso Abbatelli, who is a member of his country's equestrian team. Where she met him is a mystery, but he has all the right attributes: money, looks and no doubt great staying power between the sheets.

Her plan to sell Lynbrook Hall and move to Tomaso's homeland has met with a mixed reaction. None of the locals particularly like her. She has a reputation for being pretty abusive to staff and still rides through the village as if she owns it. However, there's an old saying, *better the devil you know*. What sort of devil is coming in her place is anyone's guess and that's what is beginning to worry people around here.

When I heard the Hall was on the market, the cottage in Barnfield Woods didn't cross my mind. It was Talún's childhood home, the place he lived with his mother, Cesca, before she mysteriously disappeared. While he was still working for George he lived in the cottage during the summer months, and during the time we were together it was our secret meeting place. After Talún left, George secured the doors and boarded up the windows and that's the way it has remained for the last five years. It was only when, quite by chance, I asked George whether he had any

47

future plans for it that I discovered it didn't belong to Manor Farm at all. What was even more perplexing was the question seemed to trigger George's newly-acquired worried look – the one Ellie insisted was down to a combination of EU paperwork and bad food choices. Then it hit me. Of course, it was the mention of the cottage that had clearly upset him. Both he and Ellie had never forgotten Talún and it probably held memories for them. Which meant its fate, once the Hall was in new hands, was bound to concern them. As I had the money I wondered whether I could persuade Leanna to let me buy it separately. You see, I too can't bear the thought of some incomer arriving and deciding to raze it to the ground. Because I think I might have a use for it...if she decides to sell, of course.

As I turn into the long sweep of tree-lined driveway leading to the Hall I realise that, although I'm a villager, this is the first time I've actually been beyond the gates. To my left I can see extensive stabling and paddocks, and then a slight bend in the driveway reveals the house. I never thought it would look like this: warm, honey-coloured stone walls under a matching tiled roof. With its windows catching the morning sunlight, it's breathtakingly beautiful and I feel as if I've been caught in a time warp. My car seems out of place, totally alien in an environment more used to elegant carriages and their occupants.

As I reach the front of the house, the driveway sweeps round in a huge circle. There is an ornate fountain in its centre, which I notice is not working. Adrian McKenzie the Hall's head gardener is always complaining to Rufus about trying to juggle priorities with the meagre budget allocated for the upkeep of the estate. Seeing this, it's clear water features aren't high on the list. I park up and head towards the front door. Tugging on the wrought iron bell pull I hear its sound echoing deep within the house. Moments later the door opens and Leanna's housekeeper, a small neat woman dressed in navy, is there with a polite greeting and a request to enter. She takes me through to the drawing room where the woman herself is sprawled elegantly on a sofa, reading a copy of *Country Life* with a small, white Shih Tzu curled up next to her. Seeing me, the dog jumps down to make my acquaintance. As I bend to give its ears a friendly rub, she consigns the magazine to a small table next to her.

'Take Cassie away, will you, Monica?' she says, in her usual clipped tone, 'and bring some coffee.'

Leanna Tremayne seems a world away from the wild-haired harridan who managed to fall over and land with her face in the communal dogs' bowl outside the Bull all those years ago. Today she's immaculate, beautifully made up with not a hair of her luxurious black chignon out of place...and she's smiling.

'Jessica, please take a seat.' She indicates the sofa opposite with a flash of long painted nails.

Maybe this won't be as difficult as I thought, but you never know. With the possibility Leanna might still hold a grudge, I'm wise to be wary.

Monica arrives with the coffee almost immediately. She sets the tray down, serves us both and leaves. Settling back, Leanna takes a sip from her cup and looks at me thoughtfully.

'So, what can I do for you?' she asks.

'It's about the sale of the Hall,' I tell her as I add sugar to my coffee.

'Not planning to make an offer, are you?' She gives me an amused smirk.

'Not for the Hall...' I smile, leaving my sentence hanging.

'Ah, the cottage.' She nods, understanding.

'Yes, it's not mentioned in the sale particulars.'

'Are you surprised?' She shrugs. 'It's a hovel. I'm guessing the new owner will simply demolish it and plant more trees.'

'Would you consider selling it to me?'

Leanna leans over and places her cup and saucer next to her discarded magazine.

'I don't understand the attraction,' she says, settling herself back on the couch with the kind of expression that

49

says she thinks I'm mad. 'After all, it's not exactly filled with warm memories, is it?'

'I'm sure I don't know what you mean.' I call her bluff. As far as I'm aware, only George, Ellie and Rufus were aware of what happened back in the summer of 2007.

'Oh, come on, this is me you're talking to. Talún was always about new conquests. Until you arrived in the village I was the longest relationship he'd had.'

'What makes you think he had any interest in me?' My response is immediate, keen to damp down on the direction this conversation is taking.

'Because I saw the way he looked at you. He never could hide his feelings.' She gives a slow smile. 'And the fact you were off limits made the game all the more interesting. He loved a challenge. However, in the end, like the rest of us, you were simply... discarded.'

Ouch! That hurts, and I can feel from the heat growing in my face I'm not going to be able to bluff my way out of this.

'Talún was extremely fickle where women were concerned,' I agree, as I carefully pick my way through this verbal minefield, not wanting to ruin my chances of securing the cottage. 'He was also generally careless with people's feelings. Yes, I admit I was involved with him and Rufus did try to warn me but...' I hesitate, wanting to draw her in, to make her believe I'm feeling like a complete loser, 'I was young and foolish then. I know better now.'

'I'm glad you do.' She smiles, and I guess she's probably feeling pleased about reminding me I got my comeuppance for stealing him from her.

'I hear you have a new man in your life.'

'Tomaso? Yes, he absolutely adores me,' she says in a voice full of breathless passion. 'We're due to be married in Venice next month.'

I nod as I lean forward and slide my cup and saucer onto the small table next to me. 'Getting back to the cottage,' I say, 'is a deal possible?'

Leanna fingers her pearls for a moment then looks at me with one of her calculating smiles. 'I still don't understand why you want it, but yes, I guess I would be amenable if the price was right. Had you an amount in mind?'

'Well. I pause thoughtfully. 'I was thinking maybe ninety thousand.' I've already taken a look at the place and I know anyone making a purchase with a view to demolishing and rebuilding will have a difficult task. The cottage is surrounded by woods and accessed down a narrow track bordered by mature trees, making it virtually impossible to bring heavy equipment to the site. It's not a prime location either but I've done my homework and I know land prices in this area are at a premium.

'Ninety thousand?' Her eyes widen. She looks surprised, but is that because I've offered too much or too little?

We sit in silence for a moment as Leanna considers my offer. 'Ninety thousand?' she repeats, tilting her head thoughtfully and I get ready for disappointment. I can tell by her expression she's going to screw me down on this sale. 'It's a little on the low side,' She eventually informs me, 'maybe if we could nudge things up a bit...'

'Nudge things up?' I brace myself for the impact of what I'm sure will probably be an extortionate sum of money. I knew it. She's been playing with me all along and I'm guessing she's a *revenge is a dish best eaten cold* type of girl, and this is payback for the night outside the pub when she had the whole village as an audience. I make a mental note of the maximum amount I'm prepared to pay, cross my fingers and pray.

'Yes.' She has another reflective moment then smiles across at me. 'Make it one hundred and twenty thousand and I think we have a deal.'

'One hundred and twenty thousand?' I mentally punch the air. I was sure we were looking at far more than that. I consider the amount thoughtfully, then with an air of defeat, nod and confirm we do indeed have a deal.

'Wonderful.' She gets to her feet and to my surprise extends a hand. 'Thank you. You know I hadn't given the cottage a thought. One hundred and twenty thousand is quite a nice little bonus for a derelict hut and some scrubby woodland. What do you plan to do with it?'

'Do it up and move in.'

'You mean demolish and rebuild.' She corrects me. 'Jessica you can't possibly be planning to live there. No one can, it's—'

'I can.' I interrupt with a smile, 'And once I've finished you won't recognise the place.'

'Well, I wish you good luck because I think you're going to need it. Oh and if you're looking for a local builder...' She moves over to the fireplace, picks up a small card from the mantelpiece and hands it to me. 'He called two days ago when I was out. He's just arrived in the village. Might be exactly what you're looking for.'

'Thank you.' I take the card and scan it before slipping it into my pocket.

Leanna walks me through to the front door and we say our goodbyes. I hand her Roo's business card to give to her solicitor. Then I wish her the best for the future and walk away. I have the cottage and the land within budget. It's mine, really mine!

As usual on a Friday evening the bar is packed. The restaurant is busy too, every table booked for Rufus's Thai cuisine night. It's nine days since my trip up to the Hall. Roo reports Leanna's solicitors have been in touch and if all goes well the property should be mine just before Christmas.

The Hall's head gardener, Adrian McKenzie, arrived with the gardening team about half an hour ago with news there has been a steady stream of potential buyers looking over the property during the last week, including a lottery millionaire. It's anyone's guess how this will eventually play out and currently the village seems to be holding its breath. George arrives on the end of Adrian's update and takes his drink off into the corner, where he sits gazing gloomily into the fire. I so want to tell him my good news and bring the smile back to his face, but I can't, not yet.

Tonight it's the usual mix of farmers, Hall staff and villagers. Bella and I have worked non-stop, serving drinks and taking orders for bar meals. Then just after nine thirty everyone seems settled and we get a chance to breathe for a while. In this moment of calmness, Bella slips between the drinkers, collecting glasses up from the tables while I load them into the washer. As we finish and settle back together, the door opens.

'Oh...My...God.' Bella's mouth drops open. 'It can't be.'

I look in the direction she's nodding but all I can see are a sea of heads.

Adrian, who has just arrived at the bar with a collection of glasses ready for another round, frowns at both of us then turns to look where Bella's gaze is firmly fixed. 'Who are you talking about?' he asks. 'The tall blond guy over there talking to the Blaketons? That's Thor.'

'Thor?' Bella and I chorus together.

'No, not here surely?' Bella gasps, her dark eyes wide with excitement. 'I thought he lived in LA. Do you think he's been looking at the Hall? My God!' she gasps, 'how amazing would it be to have *him* living here in Lynbrook.'

'What are you wittering about woman?' Adrian rolls his eyes impatiently. 'That's Krister Sorenson, he's a builder.'

'But I thought...' I see disappointment in Bella's face.

'Chris Hemsworth? Aye, you're not the first to notice the likeness. It's where he got the nickname Thor from.' Adrian grins, his teeth white against the redness of his beard. 'However, the man's Danish not Australian.'

'Krister Sorenson. Where have I heard the name before, I wonder, and then it comes to me. The card Leanna gave me. I called him over a week ago, asked him to ring back so we could set up a meeting. Well, he might have just dropped in for a drink but if not, I need to take him somewhere quiet to talk. The last thing I want is George's natural curiosity to bring him over to the bar to see what's going on. That really would wreck everything.

'Well, whoever he is he's bloody gorgeous,' I hear Bella say, just as this six-feet-two blue-eyed blond pushes through the drinkers and leans on the bar.

'Adrian,' he nods a greeting. The tone of his voice and his accent send small shivers along my spine. Bella's right, this man is magnificent...and he does bear a striking resemblance to the Australian film star.

'What can I get you?' Bella's there immediately, elbowing me out of the way with her welcoming smile, brown eyes full of mischief as her black corkscrew curls bounce around her shoulders. She's obviously keen to make an impression.

'Ah.' His shoulders lift and he frowns, confused. 'I have not come for drinking. I am looking for Jess Hayden.'

'I'm Jess,' I say with a smile, which eclipses Bella's, noticing her disappointed expression as he swings his gaze from her and focuses totally on me. Adrian clears his throat and nudges his empty glasses towards Bella, forcing her to turn her attention to his order for another round of drinks.

'I was expecting you to ring so we could set up a meeting,' I say as casually as I can, realising how difficult those deep blue eyes are making my concentration.

'I have been out of the area for a few days. Also I have a cottage in Church Lane. Very close. I thought it was better I come here to see you to talk about your requirements. I have brought a portfolio of my work for you to see,' he says, and I notice a broad leather strap diagonally crossing his chest, which indicates a man bag of some sort. I'm aware Bella is eyeballing both of us as she busies herself with Adrian's order. Her curiosity is probably going into overdrive over what exactly his *portfolio* might be.

'Right.' I pause for a moment, trying to think what to do next.

'It is a problem?' He pushes himself off the bar. 'Shall I come back another time?'

'Oh no, no, please, don't leave. We can do this now,' I say, turning quickly to Bella. 'Can you hold the fort for a while?'

Bella, in the middle of pulling her next pint, locks her hand over the pump handle, looks at Krister dreamily, then at me, and says, 'What? Oh yes. Why? Where are you going?'

'Somewhere a little more private.' I emphasise the word

private, trying not to laugh at her open-mouthed expression as I raise the hatch. 'Would you like to come through?' I say to Krister, who grins and immediately slips behind the bar.

'Won't be long,' I say to Bella with a wink as I go, causing Adrian to almost lose the mouthful of beer he's just taken. Her eyes are on both of us as, pulling his man bag over his head, Krister follows me into the passageway behind the bar and up the stairs to our lounge.

The meeting is over in half an hour. I hand over a set of plans, which have been drawn for me by an architect friend of Rufus's, and Krister shows me photos of his past work. He's been in the UK for eight years and has built in villages before. What he's done is great, and exactly what I'm looking for. We agree to meet up at the cottage as soon as the keys are in my possession. I have my builder...another step in the right direction.

TALÚN

When I enter the breakfast room this morning, Marcus is already there, his grey head bent in concentration over his morning newspaper.

'Lynbrook, isn't that your old neck of the woods?' He asks as I walk over to the breakfast counter to check out the assortment of food our housekeeper, Marianne, has laid out.

'Yes, it is.' I swing around to look at him, puzzled. 'Why?'

'There's a piece in here about the sale of Lynbrook Hall,' he says, pulling off his glasses and patting the paper. 'It seems to have got the villagers in a bit of a lather.'

'Really?' I say, as I finish filling my plate and join him at the table. 'Leanna Tremayne, who owns the place, was never well liked. I would have thought they would all be glad to see the back of her. What's the problem?'

'It seems there's a dispute going on about a farm which belongs to the estate.'

'I wasn't aware the Hall had a farm,' I say, wondering if some journalist has been fed the wrong information. 'There's a stud but I don't remember there ever being a farm.'

Slipping his glasses back on, Marcus returns to the paper and scans the details once more. 'Well,' he says with a glance across the table at me as he continues, 'it seems the Hall has been in the Tremayne family for several centuries. The Selby's have been tenant farmers since the early 1700s and it appears no one was aware of the fact until the estate came onto the market recently.'

'Neither was I,' I say, placing a napkin over my knees and picking up my fork, ready to slide it into the yellow softness of Marianne's delicious scrambled eggs. 'I thought George Selby owned it,' I add, remembering how he had promised to sign over the farm to me when he became too old to run it. My inheritance, he'd said, as long as he and his wife, Ellie, could still live there. And all the time it was never his to give... he'd merely wanted to hold me there as an insurance policy for his twilight years, the devious old devil.

'Well, that's the thing,' Marcus replies, tearing me away from my thoughts. 'It doesn't. And George Selby can't afford to buy Mrs. Tremayne out. So it looks as though he's going to be evicted.'

I shake my head, thanking Marianne as she arrives with fresh coffee and pours me a cup. 'But surely the new owner will make arrangements to re-lease the farm to George, won't he?'

'One would have thought so, except...' Marcus hesitates, 'it appears Mrs. Tremayne is on the verge of accepting an offer from a large business syndicate. They want to put their own manager in to run it. It seems they feel George is rather, shall we say, past his sell by date.'

'Oh rubbish,' I say, watching Marianne pour coffee for Marcus. 'George is one of the most competent farmers I know. Old? He's barely past sixty. Besides, he has three hundred years of farming in his blood.'

'Well,' Marcus lowers the paper and looks over the top of his glasses at me, 'that doesn't mean much in the great scheme of things, therefore unless a miracle happens....'

'What's this about a miracle?' I look up to see Anna has joined us. In open neck shirt and jodhpurs, she's obviously on her way out to the stud.

'Trouble at Talún's old village,' Marcus says, showing her the article as she slips behind him to look over his shoulder. Anna's pale brows butt together in concentration as she reads. She finishes, raising her eyes to mine. 'Was he a friend?' she asks.

'Yes, I guess he was,' I say, not wanting to get drawn into any lengthy conversation about my past life. No one has ever known the truth about Lynbrook, the people I left behind or the fact I disappeared without saying goodbye to anyone. Not even Fliss. It's my very own dark secret.

'Wouldn't you like to help him?' Anna's voice breaks

through the thick fog of my memories.

'Help? How?' As soon as the words have left my lips I want to bite them back quickly. They invite the sort of suggestions I'm not going to like and don't particularly want to get involved in.

'Well, you could buy the estate.'

My worst fears are realised. 'I don't think so,' I say with a shake of my head, my words coming out rather more forcefully than they should have. 'I've absolutely no interest in returning to South Devon. Besides,' I add dismissively, 'knowing Leanna Tremayne, she'll be asking a ridiculous price for the place.'

Anna nods, releasing a soft breath. 'Ah well, it was just a thought,' she says, leaning in and dropping a parting kiss on Marcus's cheek. As she straightens up she gives me a thoughtful look. 'Don't forget you've a ten o'clock appointment with the locum vet.' Then, seeing my frown she reminds me, 'Giles is on holiday for three weeks, remember?'

I nod and watch as she leaves the room, wondering why I have the feeling the subject of Lynbrook and the sale of the Hall is by no means closed. When Anna gets the bit between her teeth...

Sure enough, just after lunch as I'm closing the door to my office and about to leave for a meeting with Niall Collins, our stable manager, Anna materialises out of nowhere, clutching several sheets of paper.

'Ah Talún, glad I caught you,' she says, in the kind of voice that pulls me to an immediate halt. 'I won't keep you long. I've got something to show you.'

Noticing the sheaf of papers she's holding, I voice my immediate thoughts. 'About the Hall, is it?' I'm aware I sound impatient but I really don't want to go down this road. She stops, expels a deep breath and awards me the sort of exasperated look an adult gives when dealing with a difficult fourteen-year-old.

'Sorry,' I say. 'Of course.' I open my office door and show her in. Lodging myself on the edge of my desk, I wait, arms crossed, knowing by the way she watches me as she seats herself I must look incredibly defensive.

'Yes, it is about the Hall,' she admits. 'I simply thought you might like to see these details.' She leans forward in her seat and holds the papers out to me. 'I'm not hassling you, honestly. Just take a look. Please?'

I take the sheets from her. White, A4, the information printed from her office computer. The fact she's gone as far as to not only look for this online but print off a copy of the sale details means it's caught her interest. If it had been a non-starter we wouldn't be here having this conversation.

'It's a beautiful property,' she prompts, as I begin to read the details under the picture of the main house. 'Looks as though it could do with some updating though.'

I nod silently as I flip over the first page and see photos of familiar rooms. Anna has no idea I could walk through this house blindfolded. For four months I was in a relationship with Leanna Tremayne, a woman nearly twice my age. Yet another dark secret no one here knows about.

I give the sheets a thorough read. Niall is always caught up with yard business so won't be aware I'm running late. 'You're right,' I say with a nod, as I hand them back to Anna, 'it is lovely and yes, it could do with a makeover.'

'And?' She looks as me expectantly, like a child desperate to be granted its dearest wish.

'And... it's not for me. I told you, I have no wish to return to South Devon. You know I've always followed my mother's mantra – it's all about the present and looking to the future, not returning to the past.'

'Talún, you can't abandon George.' she says, in a tone which indicates for some reason he's become my responsibility.

'What do you mean?' Suddenly I feel uncomfortable. Anna knows something. How, I have no idea, but as I said before, when she gets the bit between her teeth...

'It was George you worked for when you were there, wasn't it?'

'What makes you say that?' I ask. Her question fills me with unease. It looks as if her interest in the Hall has gone far beyond a print out of the estate agent's details.

'Because Manor Farm is the only farm in Lynbrook isn't it?' I was right, she has been rooting around.

I rest against my desk uncomfortably, not knowing what to say. Old sins cast long shadows. The truth is about to come out and there's nothing I'm going to be able to do to stop it. My heartbeat starts to pick up and I damp down on the panic I'm beginning to feel. Eventually I'm back in control. I clear my throat and find my voice. 'Yes,' I say, expelling a heavy breath. 'It was.'

'Then you must help him.' She leaves her seat and settles herself next to me. 'Talún you can't sit back and let him and his wife be evicted. Please, buy the Hall. Make it the project we talked about.'

'I can't, Anna.' The panic is back, I feel it in the tone of my voice. Taking a deep breath, I revise the sentence. 'I mean, it's pointless. I have no plans to return.'

'Something painful happened there, didn't it?' She looks up at me, her eyes soft with understanding. 'Please, you know you can confide in me.'

Yes, of course I can. If there's one person who has empathy and consideration for other human beings it's Anna. My widowed grandfather chose well when he married her. She has all the attributes needed to support him: an amazing knowledge of horses, an ability to get the best out of the staff both on the estate and in the house, and a kind, compassionate nature. But if I am going to open up to her there have to be limits.

So I tell her about my life with George and Ellie and the real reason I came looking for my mother's family. But I don't give the reason a name. Telling her about Jess would only send her off on another investigatory mission and I can't handle that; it's a part of my past which is firmly under lock and key.

Once I've finished she folds her hands in front of her and looks at the floor for a moment before raising her wise grey eyes to me.

'A badly broken heart.' She nods quietly. 'From the first day you arrived I guessed you hadn't told us everything.'

'The thing is,' I reply, 'I acted in a completely selfish

way. I walked out on George and Ellie without as much as a goodbye. I left while they were sleeping and I never bothered to contact them to tell them I was okay. I even threw away my mobile. I wanted to disappear completely. I realise I probably put them both through hell. Which means I'm not sure what their reaction will be if I turn up on their doorstep after a five year absence, even if I am there to rescue them. George would most likely take a twelve bore to my backside,' I add, making a feeble attempt at humour.

'You don't have to go back there if you don't want to,' she says, giving my arm a reassuring pat, 'but, after all you've told me, we really must help them. And as for what happens to the Hall, well we can discuss that at a later date. The most important thing is the initial purchase. All I need is for you to make arrangements to transfer the necessary funds as and when I need them, and I'll do the rest.'

'There is a possibility Leanna might not want to play ball,' I say. 'She has a reputation—'

'Ah, but reputations are made to be broken, don't you think?' she interrupts as she opens the door to leave. 'Believe me, she'll be putty in my hands.'

DECEMBER 2012

JESS

Well, this is it. Farewell to Oxford. I give the city one last look as I head towards the motorway with the last two years of my life stowed safely in my VW Beetle. I have loved my time here and I shall miss my year ones and all my teaching colleagues, many of whom have become good buddies. However, Leo's money has made me realise I have a new destiny to fulfil and in order to do that my life needs to take a completely different direction. Who knows? I may return to teaching someday in the future, but right now I'm heading back to the village and I'm planning to simply chill out and enjoy Christmas with family and friends. Then once the tinsel has been taken down I'm going to meet with Krister again and firm up details on the cottage. The sale is almost complete, as is the winding up of Leo's estate. I've decided to keep part of the property portfolio; a prudent decision Roo tells me as it means a guaranteed regular income. Now my man of business – a title which I gave him and which made both of us laugh – he is liaising with Leo's solicitor to sort everything out for me. There's more good news as he's due to return to the Exeter office in the New Year, which means I shall be able to have regular lunch meets with him. It will be like old times. Well, not quite. There is one absentee - Talún who, I realise, hasn't crossed my mind for a while.

In those early days after his disappearance, Rufus rented me a flat in Exeter. I couldn't face staying in the village, knowing he wasn't around any longer. I did come home for Christmas but it was tough. Part of me was convinced the Season of Goodwill might see him returning from wherever he had been and moving back in with George and Ellie. It didn't happen and, in the end, I decided to cut short my stay in Lynbrook and spend the New Year in London with Roo. Easter was difficult too, but I muddled through, avoiding the farm completely. In the summer of 2008 I persuaded Roo to go backpacking around Europe. The village was the last place I wanted to be for eight whole weeks. It was too much of a temptation to think *this time last year...* I simply couldn't handle it. During my first year at uni my work was fine. It was the emotional stuff that got complicated. Talún's grandmother's ring was my talisman. Hanging around my neck, it was a reminder of my determination never again to let any man make a fool of me. However, although I'd decided to lock my heart away, breaking someone else's was a completely different matter. I had regular dates but whether they were decent guys or not, I ditched them when they no longer appealed. It was Roo who eventually took me aside quietly to tell me not only how destructive I was becoming but where it would eventually lead.

By the end of the second year I'd got my life back together again. I volunteered to go overseas during the summer break and worked in a school in Uganda teaching English. I returned completely energised, finished my final year and then went on to complete my DipEd in Reading. This included a practical teaching placement at St Helen's over the border in Oxfordshire, where I was eventually offered a permanent place. And now here I am, cruising down the M4, at the beginning of yet another new and exciting phase in my life.

LILY

If there's one time of the year I don't mind being a mother, it's Christmas. Josh gets so excited. Prompted by Sonya, we've had to write a letter to Santa. This year he wants a Lego JCB as he and Bailey seem to have caught the Lego bug. I've watched him at play when he's at Sonya's and he's very quick at working out how to fit the pieces together. I like to think his smartness comes from me. Certainly there was nothing quick about Pauli, although he did organise himself into getting an HVG licence. However, thinking about it, I guess it was a means to an end. I know he had a responsibility for his loads both at the beginning and end of his journey, but it also meant he could spend most of the day sitting on his backside. Yeah, I decide, that was definitely the pull.

Tonight I'm taking Josh into town to see the lights and look around the Christmas Market. This is probably the first year he'll really be able to take everything in and enjoy it properly. Sonya's going but we've no plans to meet up. Her husband will be there too, and it's times like this which makes me all too aware of my single mother status and wish for things I haven't got.

Leaving the house, the glitter of frost is already forming on the roofs of cars and I'm glad we're both well insulated against the cold with our coats and scarves. Josh has extra protection from a cute knitted hat pulled snugly over his ears.

As soon as we arrive on the Cathedral Green and he spots the brightly lit huts of the market, he's tugging on my arm. I'm pulled in the direction of a cabin selling soft toys. Among the items on display is a green dragon with horns, a red tongue, a long tail and wings. Sonya's always telling me how lucky I am because Josh never cries for or demands anything. No, I smile as I watch him, why should he need to get into a strop? He's much more subtle. My little man simply stands, hands clasped in front of him, and gazes longingly at the dragon with his wide, angelic eyes.

'How much?' I ask the stall holder as I lift it from the display.

'Eight fifty,' she says, blowing on her mittened fingers and giving Josh a smile. As I'm about to find my purse to pay for it, a hand reaches around me and takes the toy. I swing round, startled, only to find Max standing there, wrapped in a black cashmere coat and grey scarf.

'Let me get this for him,' he says with a smile, his long fingers wrapping themselves around its small felt body.

'Max, no,' I protest, trying to grab the dragon back. But he simply laughs and moves it out of reach.

'I insist,' he says, smiling at the stallholder who is still busy blowing on her fingers. 'In fact I want to.'

I give in graciously. It's pointless arguing with my boss.

He always gets his own way with things and now is no exception.

'It's very good of you, thank you,' I say, as Josh looks on in bug-eyed amazement.

Money changes hands and then Max hands the dragon to Josh.

'Thank you,' he says, his face breaking into the kind of adorable smile that fractures the hearts of everyone he meets.

'Max,' Max prompts. 'My name is Max.'

'Thank you, Max,' he says, looking up at what, in his small world, is a giant human being. He studies my boss seriously for a moment and then switches his concentration to the dragon. 'I love it. I'm going to call it Toofless.' He announces gazing adoringly at his new possession.

'Ah.' Max smiles, understanding. 'You've seen *How to Train Your Dragon*, then?'

'Yes.' My son gives a serious nod as he continues to gaze at the newly christened Toofless. 'But he's black and mine is green.'

'It's probably because your Toofless is still in his summer coat. You need to cuddle him, keep him warm,' Max suggests, and Josh smiles. Squinting up at him, he says, 'Are you my mummy's friend?'

'Max is my boss,' I explain. 'He owns the company where Mummy works.'

Josh nods and turns his attention back to his toy. He pulls out part of his scarf and wraps it around the fabled beast, then cradles it against him. I continue to watch as he begins the kind of one way conversation with it only small children are capable of.

'I had no idea you were coming here this evening,' I say, turning back to Max, wondering if Davina is anywhere around.

'Oh, I was at a loose end,' he says. 'Davina's in London, staying over with some of her fashion friends tonight.'

He looks downhearted and suddenly I feel angry. Max is a good man and deserves a better deal in life than a wife who's never there. However, I've no idea of their history, who's to blame for their current situation, and I tell myself it's none of my business. All I know is Max is a kind hearted guy who should have had kids of his own. You can see it in the way he's looking at Josh now.

'Would you like to join us?' I ask. It seems rude to abandon him after his generosity.

'That would be good.' He smiles, and not for the first time it strikes me what an attractive man he is. Once again I find myself coping with a total alien feeling - of sorrow for someone who seems to have everything he wants in life, but not the things he needs.

Half an hour into our walkabout, Josh is feeling tired and, without warning, Max bends down and lifts him into his arms. Josh really enjoys this as he is raised above the crowd and can see things he normally wouldn't be able to. I can hear the excitement in his voice as he chatters away to Max, his small arms wrapped around his neck, one hand clinging to Toofless.

An hour later Josh is asleep, his small head resting on my boss's shoulder. The dragon has been safely slipped into Max's coat, its pointed green face peeking out from under the pocket flap. Together we head to my car and Max hands Josh over, kissing the top of his woolly-hatted head almost reverently. Once I've secured my sleeping son in the back, I turn back to Max to thank him.

'It was a great evening,' he says as he extracts the dragon from his pocket and hands it to me. 'Having someone to spend time with made all the difference...Josh is amazing.'

'Yes, he is,' I say, 'and so are you. I reach up and gently touch his cheek. Thank you.'

Max folds his fingers around my hand and moves it to his lips. I feel the warmth of his mouth against my skin. He looks at me and smiles, then drops my hand and leaves, striding off into the night without a backward glance. A strange feeling of sadness engulfs me and it's all I can do not to cry. What the hell's the matter with me? I don't do tears.

TALÚN

How quickly Christmas comes around. This year has been no exception. Last week we had the staff dinner here in the ballroom. It's a chance for my grandfather to say thank you to everyone for their hard work during the year. Anna, with a team of helpers, organises everything and everyone has a really good time. There was a kid's party too, because at Hawkeswood Estates no one gets left out. I always enjoy the staff dinner. It's informal and lively, unlike the more serious event taking place this evening.

Tonight Amberleigh is hosting its New Year's Eve Ball, another annual Hawkeswood tradition. Neighbours and business associates are invited to a lavish evening of music and dining. The driveway is lined with a few million pounds worth of expensive vehicles and for the last hour I've been standing here with Marcus and Anna, welcoming our well-heeled guests. But beyond the sumptuous buffet and chilled champagne lies another purpose: an opportunity to network and talk business.

Tomorrow will be the start of a new year, one I'll be greeting with slight hesitancy. Because Lynbrook Hall is finally mine. Anna pulled off a miracle and stole it away from the business syndicate who were planning to turn it into a conference centre and corporate events venue. Well, if I can be pleased about anything it's that I've saved the village from khaki-clad, gun-toting paintballers rampaging through Barnfield Woods. And, of course, George will be able to sleep at night without the worry of being evicted. Anna is completely taken with this house and wants us to work together on the refurbishments needed. We're pulling in some high end interior designers to give us their thoughts on the Hall's transformation and she plans to project manage the whole thing. I'm fine with this arrangement; happy to help from a distance and fund the necessary work, but I'll never set foot in Lynbrook again. No way. Once the revamp is completed I'll put the place up for rent.

JESS

'I can't believe Christmas is over. Seems like only a couple of days ago we were decorating this room and getting ready to celebrate.'

I nod in agreement, watching as Bella, her neck wreathed in tinsel, stretches up to reach the last few green and gold decorations suspended from the huge tree in the corner of the bar.

'I mean, it seems like weeks ago I was on a beach in Ibiza and now look at it.' She nods towards the window at the dusting of snow in the car park. 'I hate this time of year,' she adds, backing up her thoughts with a frown and a shake of her head. 'Christmas over, awful bloody weather. The hedgehogs might have got it right you know; there's something to be said for hibernation.'

'There are always the sales in Exeter to cheer you up,' I offer hopefully. Bella is a girl born to shop and a day at the sales should be enough to banish the January blues.

'Please, don't mention the word sales...' she begins, making me regret my choice of topic. 'Have you seen the state of George lately?'

'George has been out of sorts for ages,' I say, remembering the day I called up to the farm to take Caspar out and wondering what connection it has to the January sales. 'And now you mention it, yes, he always seems to be looking pretty miserable lately. When I asked, all Ellie said was EU paperwork and rich food were taking their toll on his digestive system and stressing him out.'

'Not as much as the sale of the Hall is,' she replies, revealing her train of thought, a connection which confuses me even more.

'The Hall?' I'm totally lost here. 'I don't understand why— '

'Because Manor Farm belongs to the Hall. He's their tenant.' She interrupts, pushing a wayward curl back from her face.

'What? That's rubbish.' I shake my head. 'Someone who used to work for him told me he owned it.'

'Well they were mistaken.'

'How did you find this out anyway? Who told you?'

'George,' she says, unwinding the tinsel from around her shoulders and dropping it into the large cardboard box I'm holding out to her. 'This miserable phase of his started when it went on the market. I thought it was because he was worried about who his potential new neighbour might be, and he is, but not for the reason I was thinking. He told me last night he's likely to be evicted.'

'Surely not,' I say, as I seal the lid of the box and stack it with the others, ready to be stored upstairs. 'The Selby family have farmed there for nearly three hundred years without any problem.'

'That's because the Hall has always belonged to the Tremaynes.'

'But surely the new owner will be happy to simply renew the tenancy.'

'Well, I think George was hoping they would. However, the last he heard Leanna was about to accept an offer from some company who want to turn the Hall into a corporate events venue. They plan to keep the farm and put their own manager in to take over from George.'

'Can they do that?'

'Well, George went to see Mrs. Tremayne and she told him the new buyer's solicitor has looked at the original agreement and says he can.'

'Oh hell, poor George,' I say. 'I bet she enjoyed delivering that piece of news. After all, he was never one to hold his tongue about her high handed ways in the village, and things got worse when Talún was—'

'The gypsy who used to work for George, you mean?' Bella says, as she spots a decoration she's missed. She wasn't here five years ago...she has no idea what happened. 'They were lovers weren't they? A funny pairing don't you think?' she rolls her eyes, crossing over to the box and peeling back the tape. 'Still...'

'What?' I watch her as she slips the decoration, a glitter

covered snow flake, back into the bag with the others before resealing the box.

'Well,' she says with an innocent shrug. 'With her husband shut away in a care home, maybe she was desperate... or she just fancied a bit of rough. You know, like Lady Chatterley.'

'Talún was no Oliver Mellors,' I say, perhaps a little too fiercely.

'Of course, you must have known him.' She tilts her head slightly, waiting for me to elaborate.

'Yes I did, and he wasn't the way you think he was.'

'Close were you? There were rumours....'

'I expect there were.' I interrupt with sigh, wondering who she's been talking to. 'And that's all they were, Bella. Rumours. We were friends, just friends.'

'Was he the one who told you about George owning the farm?'

'Yes.'

'Jess, I don't want you to think I'm intruding.'

'I don't.' I say, seeing her worried expression, aware she feels she's upset me. I give her an encouraging smile, 'Look, if you really want to know how it was, yes, I knew him and whatever you've heard has probably been airbrushed and photo shopped until it doesn't bear any resemblance to the truth. This village is notorious for gossip, what they don't know they have a habit of making up.'

Bella nods thoughtfully. 'I'm sorry.' She reaches out and gives me a soft hug, 'Mum got it off someone who came into the shop ages ago when we all heard you were coming back for good.'

'No worries, I'm amazed I'm such a local celebrity,' I joke, hugging her back, glad this seems to have put an end to her curiosity. Bella is one of the good guys and it's natural she's curious but it's ancient history and has no place here, in the present. 'Right then,' I say, looking at the boxes, 'let's get these decorations back into the storeroom, shall we? We've a pub to open.'

LILY

'We've been invited where?' I take my concentration from my computer screen and look up at Max.

'The Exeter Abode. Used to be the Royal Clarence Hotel. You know the one; white fronted, faces the Cathedral.'

'I know it.' I nod, remembering. I've had drinks in the Champagne Bar there on a couple of occasions when my significant other happened to be someone who could either afford it or was keen to impress.

'The new owner wants to treat Nick and me to dinner as a thank you for our part in helping persuade Mrs. Tremayne to turn down the Galaxy Holdings offer in favour of theirs. I've managed to blag you an invite. A table has been booked for eight-thirty tomorrow evening and Nick will pick you up from home at seven forty-five.'

'Ah so I get to meet the legendary Anna Hawkeswood at last.' I say, aware Max is full of admiration for this woman's diplomatic skills in her negotiations with Leanna Tremayne.

'Anna won't be there. It's her grandson, he's the new owner.'

'Oh.' I sit back in surprise. This is news to me. 'Really?'

'Yes, I think Anna said his name is Torin. She stepped in to deal with the purchase because he's been abroad on business. He's back and has arrived to tie up a few loose ends and sort out the lease on Manor Farm.'

I give a disinterested nod. Dinner at The Abode will be a Friday evening bonus. I had nothing planned; now it's all about what to wear.

Picking Josh up from Sonya's, I negotiate a sleepover for tomorrow night. Luckily, her husband who works as a security guard at the Drake Centre in Plymouth is on nights this week, so there's no problem having him stay. Sonya is an angel. She adores Josh and sadly I sometimes think she'd make him a much better mother than I do.

Having sorted sleeping arrangements, the next most important thing is deciding what to wear. Once we've had our evening meal and I've given Josh his bath and tucked

71

him up, I spend time checking through the contents of my wardrobe. Smart and sexy is the order of the day and there in the corner is the very thing I'm looking for - my knock 'em dead little black dress and a pair of wonderful red Louboutins.

Friday is busy and by five-thirty I'm really looking forward to the luxury of reaching home and being able to get ready without having to think about anyone else but myself. As I sink into my hot scented bath, my mind drifts away to dreams of a different life, one of carefree luxury. My visit to Lynbrook Hall is to blame, it's resurrected a crazy longing for a lifestyle so out of reach. I really should get a grip on reality. Maybe these feelings are an omen though, an indication I should buy myself a few lottery tickets, maybe. Once I was the kind of girl who wasn't frightened to take chances, but that was before Josh was born. Although I'm not the loving, tactile type of mother Sonya is, my son is a responsibility I don't take lightly.

By seven I'm ready: nails a glossy red, face with a slight dusting of makeup and my blonde hair woven into an elaborate French braid, courtesy of Chloe next door who works in a local salon. And the dress looks absolutely amazing. How I've changed from the woman Pauli left behind. I laugh as I catch a glimpse of myself in the mirror. He probably wouldn't recognise me if we passed in the street today. Not that I'd want him back, oh no, my tastes in men are far more sophisticated. As I'm slipping on my coat, I hear Nick's Audi pull up outside. Grabbing my bag and keys, I leave the house.

Nick gives a low whistle as I slip into the passenger seat and fasten my seat belt. 'Very nice, Lily.' He follows up with an appreciative wink.

'Thank you, you don't look so bad yourself,' I tease. And he doesn't. Nick scrubs up well. Tonight he's in a dark navy suit and has managed to persuade his unruly brown hair to behave itself for a change. 'Do you know much about Anna Hawkeswood's grandson?' I ask as we drive. 'Is he married?'

'Not any longer.'

'Divorced?'

'No, Max said he lost his wife and baby daughter in a tragic accident a few years back.'

'No one since?'

'Why?' Nick takes his eyes from the road for a second and grins at me. 'Thinking of bagging him for yourself, are you?'

'Me? No just curious,' I laugh. 'Oh come on, this guy must be seriously rich. He'll be way out of my league. Besides,' I add, 'he might be a cross-eyed hunchback.'

'I doubt that very much.' Nick shakes his head and laughs.

Leaving the car in a nearby car park, we make our way through the streets towards the hotel. A cold wind whips around us as we cross the Cathedral Green and I pull my coat around me, burying my face in my scarf.

Nick gets a friendly greeting from the manager as I know this is a place where he and Max regularly bring clients for lunch. He arranges for our coats to be taken and then shows us through to the Champagne Bar. There among the other drinkers, Max is deep in conversation with someone in a dark suit with his back to us. I get the impression of long legs and broad shoulders as he leans against the bar. At a guess I'd say he's a good six feet tall, maybe more, and although I can only see the back of his head, I notice how the curl of his thick, dark hair wraps itself attractively around the edge of his shirt collar. I like what I'm seeing and hope when he turns around his face will match the rest of this interesting package. Max leans around him and waves out to us. He turns and I come to a sudden halt, Nick nearly running into the back of me. My hand goes out to the bar to steady myself and I realise my mouth has gone completely dry.

'Are you okay?' Nick's hands are on my shoulders, supporting me.

'Fine. Damned Louboutins,' I say, grabbing at my left foot and the first plausible excuse, while in front of me Anna Hawkeswood's grandson stares at me, a look of bewilderment on his face.

'Lily?' he says. 'Lily Stevenson?'

And now I realise Max must have misheard Anna. Because this guy's name isn't *Torin*, it's Talún, and when I knew him way back his surname was Hansen. I feel I'm in some sort of weird dream, because how the hell has a penniless gypsy become the new owner of Lynbrook Hall?

TALÚN

I had no idea my journey back to Exeter would see me running into a face from the past. I couldn't stop looking at her over dinner; there was so much I wanted to ask her. She looked completely different. Her hair is blonde, quite a change from the rich dark red it used to be. She wears it slightly shorter too, and coupled with her clothes, it makes her look more sophisticated. Max Warner referred to her as a very valuable member of his sales team but from their body language I'd say his interest goes way beyond proud employer. In the five plus years since I last saw her, she's not only got herself an education, she's also worked her way into a good job. It has me wondering how much is down to Max and what exactly their relationship is.

She seems shy, embarrassed even, as our eyes meet and I'm rewarded with a nervous smile. I guess seeing me has resurrected the memory of the last time I saw her – the night of Jess Hayden's party. All my fault of course, I was very drunk. I took advantage of her, something I've always regretted and it cost me Jess...although after what happened only days later, I realised maybe she wasn't as honest with me as she claimed to be. After all, it didn't take her long to replace me. The night I found her in that club holding onto another guy as he kissed her told me I'd made a complete fool of myself. I saw it all then: I, the poor traveller's son, had been nothing more than a summer distraction. And now here she was, hooking up with someone else. A middle class chinless wonder Rufus would no doubt approve of. The realisation I'd not only lost her but had been tricked pushed me into leaving Lynbrook. I was angry then but I guess after all this time I should thank her. After all, I discovered my family and had a moment of rare happiness with Fliss and Emily. Something I hope to find again someday.

'Penny for them.' I look up and see Lily is watching me.

'Sorry,' I say, reaching for my wine glass. 'A lot on my mind at the moment.'

'Yes, I can imagine,' she says, before Max takes her attention away, threading an arm around her shoulder as he leans in to discuss dessert options. The thing is, I really want to see her again and I think the feeling is mutual. I notice the curiosity in her face. She's probably thinking where's he been? How has he become so rich? And I've questions for her too, but first I need to apologise for what I did that night.

Dinner is a pleasant affair and it's clear the three of them get on well together with their light hearted banter. Max is charming but then he would be – I am, after all, the client and have just earned him a huge commission on the sale of the Hall.

All too soon the evening is over, chairs are pushed back and we're preparing to leave. As we reach the foyer and our coats are brought, I can see it's raining. Nick, who has driven Lily here this evening, slips his on and disappears to get the car, and Max excuses himself and heads for the gents. It's my one and only opportunity to speak to Lily so I have to be quick.

'Can I see you again?' I ask. 'I'm here for another twenty four hours. Maybe dinner tomorrow evening? That's unless of course you...' I indicate the direction of Max's departure and she looks at me and laughs.

'He's a great boss and a good friend, nothing more. However, I'm not sure how he'd view my seeing one of his clients socially, especially someone like you who has just shelled out several million pounds on a purchase. But...' she gives me a wide smile as I help her slip on her coat, 'as long as we're discreet, I'd love to have dinner with you.'

'Wonderful,' I say, and really mean it. I watch as she slips her hand into her bag, pulls out a pad and pen and quickly scribbles down her mobile number.

'If I don't answer, leave a message and I'll call you back,' she says, handing it to me before reaching up to kiss my cheek. 'and thank you for a lovely evening.'

As I push the folded piece of paper into my pocket, I hear the blare of a car horn and see a red Audi has pulled up outside.

'Till tomorrow then,' she says with a final wave and disappears out into the night.

'Everything okay?' Max asks as he reappears, watching as Nick's Audi pulls away.

'Sure,' I nod. 'It was great to see Lily after all this time.'

'Ex-girlfriend, was she?' He eyes me curiously. 'You know, before you moved away?'

'Oh no. We went to the same school, that's all,' I say. 'Lovely to catch up with her though and to discover she's doing so well.'

'Yeah, she's a great girl.' Max squeezes my shoulder and gives me a meaningful smile as he turns to leave. 'I'm very lucky to have her.'

LILY

I lean against the door of my flat and close my eyes. What a night! So many questions are flying around my head. I can't believe Talún Hansen, or should I say Hawkeswood, is the new owner of Lynbrook Hall. On the way home I pumped Nick for more information. I like to be ahead of the game and intelligence gathering is always useful. Sadly, it appears he has already told me everything he knows about our mysterious Mr H. Of course, asking Max anything is a bit of a no-no. There was a lot of weird body language going on at the table this evening, like he was the alpha male in the group and I was his personal property. Maybe he was trying say 'keep it professional Lily, don't stray into dangerous territory'. After all, he is a very important client who has spent one hell of a lot of money to secure the Hall. Tomorrow when I turn up for work I'm sure Max will expect me to tell all. So I'd better sort out some plausible responses. School is the safest choice and it is, after all, a truthful answer. I might eventually have to come clean about my dinner date too. I've a good relationship with Max and I don't want to sour it by keeping secrets from him, but I'm not going to reveal all unless it's absolutely necessary.

And now as I push myself away from the door and slip out of my coat, I'm heading for bed. Not that I'll get much sleep. I'll be too busy working out all those questions for tomorrow night.

TALÚN

I have just visited Richards, Knight and Varley. I remember they were the solicitors used by George on the few occasions he required legal advice. I told a rather surprised Theo Knight, who is George's solicitor, that I was representing the Hawkeswood family. My visit was to let him know, because of their long tenancy, Hawkeswood Estates have decided to gift the ownership of the farm to him and Ellie. I handed over a letter with the details and asked him to contact our solicitors as soon as possible to get the transfer underway. As I left the building I felt a great sense of achievement knowing I'd set things right for two special people who had done so much for me.

Returning to the car I slip behind the wheel and sit for a while, trying to work out where to take Lily for dinner this evening. Having made a decision I pull out my phone. I've already added her number to my phonebook and as I call her I wonder whether I'll get her or a voicemail message.

'Hi.' It's her; she sounds breathless as if she's been running and I can hear a hum of activity in the background.

'You okay?'

'Yes, I'm at the gym. I gave myself an early lunch break,' she explains.

'Great, you're able to talk then.'

'Yes,' she replies, as I hear the wheeze of an automatic door closing.

'You still on for this evening?'

'Looking forward to it. Where are we going?'

'I thought we'd drive into Plymouth. Have you ever visited The Dome?'

'Gary Rhodes' restaurant you mean? Yes, once, with Max and the team to celebrate Nick's birthday. I'd love to go there, but could you do something for me?'

'Sure.' I'm curious now, wondering what she's about to ask of me.

'Would you book a window table overlooking the sea?'

'Oh, I think that can be arranged.' I smile, up for the challenge. I get the feeling I'm really going to enjoy this evening. 'I'll pick you up at seven thirty,' I say. 'You'd better give me your address.'

'I... um... live in a new development at Exeter Quayside. Newlyn Place?'

'Don't worry, I'll find you, I'll key it into my Sat Nav.'

'There's a small car park facing my block. Give me a call when you arrive.'

'I will. I'll be driving a white Lexus.'

'Great...' I can still hear her breathing but it's softer now, more relaxed. 'I'm really looking forward to catching up. It's been a long time, Talún.'

Yes, it has. I think as I end the call, my mind fixed on the apology I need to deliver.

LILY

Just when you think everything's going to plan it all goes completely tits up. Be quiet, I reprimand myself quietly, didn't you do enough swearing when you got the phone call? Sonya's son Bailey is unwell, an upset stomach, meaning she can't have Josh for the planned sleepover. Oh hell! What am I going to do? I'm in freefall for a moment, fingers touching my temples, desperate to clear my thoughts. The ring of the doorbell intrudes. Moving towards the door, I pull back the catch and open up to see Chloe standing there in her pink leggings and bright red angora top. As usual, she's got a mouthful of gum.

'Sorry to bother you,' she says, halting her chewing and

78

giving me a smile which makes the jewelled stud above her upper lip sparkle. 'I was just curious about how everything went last night...you know... on your important dinner. Hair okay, was it?'

For a moment everything seems to be in slow motion as I only half listen to what's being said, my mind still running through alternative babysitting options. Then the whole world comes crashing back and I take a deep breath.

'Yes, yes great,' I say, clinging to the door. 'Look, I'm sorry Chloe, but you've caught me at a bad time. Can we chat tomorrow? I'm due to go out in less than an hour and Sonya has called to say Bailey's ill and she won't be able to have Josh. I need to find another baby sitter...like now.'

'Not a problem,' she says, kick starting her chewing once more. 'I'm free tonight, I can do it for you.'

'You can?' I want to hug her but she's so thin I'm sure I'll fracture something if I do.

'Sure, seven-fifteen okay? I can settle your little man in with a bedtime story. Then he won't miss you when you go.'

'Chloe, you're a star, thank you so much!'

'No probs.' she gives me a little wave. 'See you in a mo then.'

Chloe and Josh are firm friends. Since she moved in last year he's got to know her well. She cuts his hair and from the way they interact she's someone else who would make a far better parent than me. Actually, I think anyone would. I still hate the restrictions motherhood has placed on me. I wasn't cut out for this. I want my life back, to feel I'm more than just a cook...a cleaner... a wiper of snotty noses. How sad is it that I enjoy the time I spend at work more than I do being with my son? It's not normal, is it? I should look forward to coming home, curling up on the sofa and reading my beautiful blue eyed boy a story, but I don't, not at all. He's a responsibility, one I'll never walk away from, but sometimes I find myself thinking of all the things I could have done with my life, things which are now never going to happen, and I feel angry because Pauli is out there having his freedom and the life he wants. I hate him.

With this resentful thought I push myself away from the door and go to find Josh. He'll be really excited he's going to spend the evening with Chloe and I realise I need to get a grip and look on the bright side. After all, for one evening I get to slip into Cinderella's shoes and go to the ball. Or in this case The Dome, so I need to make the most of it.

JESS

I had lunch with Roo yesterday. It's lovely to have him back working in the Exeter office. We got together in our favourite Italian not only to celebrate my purchase of the cottage, but for him to hand over the keys. There was also another special moment later when I collected the brand new black Mazda MX5 I'd ordered. However I did feel a pang of regret saying goodbye to my reliable old Beetle convertible which had kept me mobile for nearly six years. This, I told myself, was the last of the big spends: the cottage, the horse, and the car - now it was time for me to draw a line under 'me' spending. No more extravagance.

This morning I arrived at Manor Farm a little after nine. As I reached the back door I could hear someone inside weeping and for a moment I hesitated, wondering whether I should walk away and go straight to the stables instead. However, I've known both George and Ellie for a long time and my natural instinct was to see whether I could help. Opening the door slowly, I was immediately hit by the warmth of the room and then I noticed George sitting at the table and Ellie leaning over him, her arms around his shoulders. Both were in tears. This looked to be an incredibly private moment and immediately I knew I shouldn't be there. As I began to back out, however, Ellie looked up and saw me. I bit my lip. 'Sorry,' I whispered, 'I'll come back later.'

'No,' Ellie left George and crossed over to where I was standing. Wiping the tears from her face with her fingers she smiled. 'Come in, please. It's good news.'

'But you're both crying.' I frowned as I look from one to the other.

'With relief...and happiness.' Her smile widened as she pulled a hankie from her apron pocket and began to dab at her eyes. It was then I noticed the letter on the table in front of George.

'It's a miracle.' He said picking it up and showing it to me, 'A bloody miracle.' Then without warning his tears returned with a vengeance.

'It's about the farm.' Ellie said, pulling me over towards the Aga and lowering her voice. 'There were problems...ownership problems. It wasn't ours.' I nodded, not wanting to admit Bella had already told me this. 'It belonged to the Hall and this fancy company made an offer which Mrs. Tremayne accepted. They had plans to put their own man in to manage here. Then this other party put in a bid and Mrs. Tremayne accepted their offer. So there we were again, not knowing what was going to happen to us until this morning when we got this letter in the post from our solicitors. It appears the new owner has given us the farm.'

'*Given* you the farm?' I was amazed. Manor Farm must be worth the upper end of a six figure sum. Why would anyone be that generous?

'I'll find out more when I see the solicitor this morning,' George said, interrupting my thoughts. I looked across and noticed his tears had now morphed into the same excited smile as Ellie's. He shook his head, still unable to believe his luck.

'Any idea who the Hall's new owner is?' I asked, curious to discover the identity of this benefactor who would soon be living among us.

'Can't read the signature on the bottom of the letter my solicitor sent,' George said, squinting through his bi-focals, 'but it's on Hawkeswood Estates headed paper.' Pulling off his glasses he looked up at me. 'I know the name. Yes,' he nodded, 'they farm a huge part of Norfolk. Big suppliers to the supermarkets.' He gave a puzzled shake of his head. 'It doesn't make sense though, why would they buy a manor

81

house in Devon?'

Why indeed? I left them both, still wondering at their good fortune and the reason behind it. As I headed for the stables, I decided I'd Google *Hawkeswood Estates* later and find a little bit more about them - that's if Bella hadn't already heard the news and beaten me to it.

FEBRUARY 2013

JESS

Today I'm meeting Krister at the cottage. Bella's been badgering me for days about coming along under some pretence or other. She's been working hard on chatting him up when he drops in for a drink but suddenly things seem to have come to a halt. I suggested she ask him out but strangely, although Bella prides herself on being a twenty first century girl, she's quite traditional about romance. She figures as she's worked hard at getting his attention, it's only fair he's the one to do the asking. But, for whatever reason, Krister is simply not playing ball. So currently she's not sure what happens next and thinks my meeting might be just the opportunity to get him on his own. While I'm quite happy to help her snare this six feet two Viking, it's not going to be while she's bouncing around like a demented poodle as I'm trying to talk to him about my plans.

It takes ten minutes to reach the small parking area in the woods just above the cottage. First to arrive, I sit behind the wheel and wait for Krister, taking a moment to look around this once familiar spot. When I was here last the trees were in full leaf, but now everything is brown and bare and through the latticework of branches I can see the pale walls of the building. I take a deep breath, pulling myself away from the need to reminisce. I live in the present, the past is gone and memories do have a habit of distorting the reality of what has been. I was almost nineteen, savvy in many ways, totally naïve in others. Good looking, with a 'give a damn' attitude and a bad reputation, Talún lived by his own rules and broke most of everyone else's. The naïve half of me, ever the great optimist, thought love could change all that. I was wrong.

Gazing at his grandmother's ring on my right hand, I wonder if he hadn't left, whether I would still be wearing this. If I'm honest with myself, probably not. Rufus always said leopards don't change spots. And on the night of my party, Talún proved him right and my world fell apart. Despite my eventual decision to give him another chance, maybe his leaving was for the best. It spared me any future heartache, but it was unbearably painful at the time.

A tap on my window makes me jump and brings me out of my deliberations. Krister is staring in at me, all untidy blond hair and sexy smile. I understand Bella's passion. This really is one hot man.

'Sorry,' I say as I slide out of the driver's seat, noticing his man bag draped across his hip. 'Miles away.'

He simply smiles and follows me as we make our way down the muddy path towards the cottage. As I enter the porch I remember the key used to live under a loose floor tile. Today, however, I have it firmly in my hand. Unlocking the door, I slowly lift the latch and push and suddenly we're there, stepping into a world which has remained closed and in semi-darkness for almost six years.

The ceiling is laced with cobwebs and as we enter dust motes rise, caught in the light which filters through the boarded up windows and the open door behind us. I hesitate as something scurries across the floor a few feet away.

'Rats?' Krister says, immediately activating the torch he has pulled from his bag.

'It's probably a mouse.'

'You are not scared?' Blond eyebrows lift at my calm statement. 'I thought most women went crazy when mice were around.'

'Not this one.' I laugh. 'Shine the torch over here.'

He does as he's asked and I trip the light switch on the wall. Immediately the room is bathed in artificial light.

'There is still electricity here?' Krister looks surprised.

'No, George had it disconnected before the place was boarded up. I had it reconnected last week. Don't panic, I've already had an electrician in to check everything.'

He nods and looks around the room. The place is bare and I remember how George arranged for a second hand furniture firm to dispose of everything a couple of months after Talún had left. Now there is just faded paper and paint, tired carpet on the floor and a layer of dust everywhere. Krister pulls the drawings I have given him from his bag and we go on walkabout, discussing details of the changes I want to make to this cottage. Eventually we reach the room which was once Talún's bedroom. Tiny slivers of memory of our nights together here dance into my mind as I step through the door: the warmth of his breath against my skin, the silky thickness of his hair, the way the morning sun's warmth through the gap in the curtains would wake us. I close my eyes, take a deep breath and they're gone. I wait silently while Krister makes notes and then thankfully we head for the bathroom and I force myself to concentrate on his views about maximising the limited space. At the end of our meeting, as he folds up the plans and slips them back into his bag, he's smiling.

'Yes,' he says with a confident nod. 'All of this I can do for you, no problem.'

'Fantastic.' I am totally over the moon; thoughts of Talún Hansen and our long ago summer love affair suddenly fading as the excitement of knowing my project is underway kicks in.

TALÚN

I'm nearly home and most of my journey has been spent thinking about Lily. It was good to see her last night and to catch up on what's happened to us since we last met. I could see by the look on her face during our pre dinner drinks in the bar she was dying to find out how I had morphed from penniless traveller's son to multi-millionaire. Once the meal was underway, I decided to let her ask me questions first. I glossed over my reason for leaving Lynbrook with half-truths. I told her I had discovered my birth certificate when I was sorting through some of my mother's things and as I was going through a difficult time at the farm I decided to leave to find her family. Everything after that was fairly straightforward: the discovery I belonged to a well-heeled family, my return to university, my work at the stud and my marriage to Fliss. I couldn't avoid mentioning the accident but she seemed to understand how it still affected me. Quickly she moved the conversation on, asking me about my plans for the Hall.

'Max took me there when he first visited Mrs. Tremayne. I absolutely loved it.' She smiled and scrunched up her shoulders like a small excited girl. 'It's a real dream home...so beautiful.'

Talking about Lynbrook made me think of Jess. It brought back hazy memories of the night when Lily and I sat together drinking wine and giving each other moral support after being thrown out of her party. I vaguely remember her telling me how awful Jess was. How her warm, soft hearted personality was a smokescreen for the hard, spiteful creature she really was. The kind who got a kick out of playing with people's feelings and breaking hearts. The alcohol, coupled with the misery of finding her talking to Zac Rayner - someone she assured me she no longer wanted anything to do with - when I arrived was what had finally caused me to seek refuge in Lily's arms. A kiss was one thing, though what happened after that was inexcusable. The time had come to apologise.

'Before we go any further,' I said, resting my cutlery against my plate, 'I need to say something.'

'What?'

'I'm really sorry for what happened that evening in the cricket pavilion.'

'Talún, that was more than five years ago.'

'I know, but it was wrong. I was totally out of order.'

She laughed. 'I think you were just a little drunk actually, and besides, I didn't exactly fight you off, did I?' She hesitated as the waiter arrived to clear away. As he disappeared she cocked an eyebrow at me and smiled. 'Now I guess you want to hear what I've been up to all these years.'

I ordered another bottle of wine and listened and while we waited for our main course she took me on her journey from a life on benefits to her current job working for

Warner Webb.

Listening to her story, I wanted so much to give her a hug and tell her what a fighter she was. That she should be proud of the success she'd made of her life. However, although it was great to discover how well she'd done, what happened later left me with more unanswered questions.

When I dropped Lily off at the end of the evening she thanked me for a wonderful time, kissed my cheek, slipped from the car and left without looking back. I sat for a moment enjoying the lingering aroma of her flowery perfume, hoping when I returned in a few weeks we could meet up and do it all again. Next time, however, there would be no sad stories. I wanted an enjoyable evening with good company and wine. I fired up the engine then stopped, realising I should make sure she reached her front door safely before I left. Twisting slightly so I could watch her, I waited as she headed towards the middle door of six in the modern red brick terrace which fronted the car park. An outside light was burning to the right of the front door and as she approached it I saw movement upstairs and a small blond head appeared through the curtained window, lifting his hand to wave at her. She didn't see him and he hesitated for a moment then disappeared as she slipped inside, closing the door behind her. I drove away, confused, because during our whole evening together there had been no mention of a child.

I run his image through my mind once more as I reach the main gates of Amberleigh. A blond boy, too big to be a toddler but not yet old enough for school. It seems Lily is keeping secrets...

LILY

This morning as I sit in front of my PC, typing, I'm thinking of Talún, who by this time should be well on his way back to Norfolk. I still can't believe what he told me: that he is the grandson of a millionaire and the sole heir to an international food business. How things change. We're so far apart now. It's not just the distance between Exeter and Norfolk, it's the social thing. I'm amazed at how he's adapted to his new life of wealth and privilege. You would never believe he once worked on a farm. He's even better looking than I remember, if indeed you can improve on a guy whose parents were obviously gene pool royalty. Sadly attractive dark haired men don't float my boat, but I definitely wouldn't mind the money.

When we said goodnight he told me he'd be back in a few weeks, something to do with the purchase of horses, and he would like us to meet up for dinner again. I'm hoping maybe we can keep our friendship going. I'd love to visit Lynbrook Hall once the work has been done and...well, here I know I'm wishing for the impossible...maybe even get a trip to Norfolk to see his grandfather's place. Amberleigh, he said it was called. He told me he doesn't plan to move into the Hall. Instead, once the work is done he's going to rent it out. He does, however, plan to continue to run the stud there, so hopefully as he'll be here on a regular basis, maybe there's a chance we can keep in touch.

I give a sigh as I rest my elbow on the desk. Ah well, a girl can dream.

JESS

It's true what they say out here in the country: February is a month which can have a nasty sting in its tail. After a mild end to January, the first part of this month saw Arctic winds whipping through the woods and across the fields. However, with March knocking on the door it's suddenly much, much warmer. That means today I'm in early spring gear - a thick sweater and body warmer - for my morning's ride. I emerge from the wood into my favourite place, Barnfield Steps. It's a small open area surrounded by trees where the water rushes over a haphazard row of exposed grey rocks before continuing on its way towards the village. Here, where the river curves to the left, the outside bank drops gently away to meet a small gravelled shore beside which a huge grey slab of rock is wedged. It provides both a vantage point to watch the river and a place to relax.

I lead Caspar to the water's edge and let him drink, and then leaving him to crop grass I settle myself on the flat surface of the boulder, take off my riding hat, unzip my body warmer and sit for a moment, watching the sun's rays playing across the surface of the water. Time never touches this peaceful oasis buried deep in the middle of the wood and although the river still brings back memories of my summer with Talún, time, it seems, has exorcised his ghost.

Aware of Caspar's sudden snort, I take my gaze away from the rush of water over rocks to see he's stopped cropping grass. His head's up and he's looking towards the wood. A moment later I hear the sound of approaching hooves and a female rider on a big black emerges from the treeline.

'Good morning,' she calls out as she approaches. I'm immediately aware of the brown monogramed Kingsland vest, the Italian riding hat and the sleek shine on her finely muscled mount, all of which indicate this woman has money: lots of it.

'Hi there,' I respond and as she reaches me, I slip from the boulder and walk out to meet her.

'I don't suppose you could tell me where I am, could you?' she says, adjusting her gloved hands on the reins. 'I'm new to the area and have to confess, completely lost.'

I look up into warm grey eyes, tiny wisps of blonde hair escaping from under her black KEP riding hat. 'Where are you heading?' I ask her.

'Oh, Lynbrook Hall.' A warm smile follows this revelation. 'I'm Anna Hawkeswood,' she says, sliding from her horse's back and offering me her hand.

An actual living, breathing Hawkeswood, no wonder she's kitted out so expensively and sitting astride high-priced horseflesh. Having checked out the Hawkeswood website I found disappointingly it focused totally on the business. There was a shot of Marcus but other than the one photo of this handsome grey-haired man, I have absolutely no idea how many other members of this farming dynasty there are. I'm guessing as she's probably in her late fifties she's either a sister...or maybe even his wife?

'You do exist then.' I smile back. 'The villagers were beginning to wonder—'

'Oh yes, I'm very, very real,' she interrupts, amused.

'Don't tell me you're relocating from Norfolk.'

'You know about the Hawkeswoods?' Do I detect a little unease in her voice?

'Only that they farm a huge amount of land there and have business connections in the UK and on the continent as suppliers of ...well, almost everything to do with food.'

'We have quite a famous stud as well,' she informs me. 'The Anna McNeil Stud.'

'Yes, I have heard of it. So, I gather you are, or were, Anna McNeil?'

She nods, then her gaze moves to Caspar. 'I can see you have an eye for good horseflesh. He's stunning.'

'My pride and joy,' I say, glancing at my beautiful Palomino boy. 'Are you planning to continue to run the stud at the Hall?'

'I'm not, but my grandson will be. He's the new owner. The facilities there are state of the art. Unlike the house...' Her voice trails away accompanied by a roll of her eyes.

'I think Leanna lived and breathed horses. I don't expect the house had seen a lick of paint in years.' I sound deliberately vague as I'm not about to admit I was there recently, negotiating the purchase of the cottage and saw how tired the whole place looked.

'Well, that's all about to change,' she tells me as she moves forward to allow her horse access to the water, 'because I'm here to project manage the Hall's facelift. It's my grandson's first venture into property development. We had initial discussions with a selection of interior designers but what we've arrived at are his vision and his choices. He felt it needed a woman's touch to bring it all together but didn't want a designer on board. So,' she smiles, 'here I am.'

'There's obviously not another Mrs. Hawkeswood to

take up the challenge then?'

'No, only this one.' She laughs.

Suddenly her mobile buzzes and she reaches into her jacket and excuses herself as she takes the call. From the one way conversation I overhear, it's obviously something to do with the work going on at the Hall.

'Sorry,' she says, slipping her mobile back in her pocket, 'looks like I'm needed – the carpenters have arrived. Can I trouble you for those directions?'

'Of course.' I relay them to her and watch as she carefully remounts and swings the black's head around.

'Well, it was lovely to meet you....'

'Jess, Jess Hayden.'

She nods and smiles. 'Are you here often, Jess?' she asks.

'Most mornings,' I confirm, gazing out across the water then back at her.

'No doubt you and I will see each other again then.' She says, and with a final wave she's gone, riding off into the trees.

MARCH 2013

TALÚN

Anna is back for the weekend and reports everything is going well with the refurbishment of the Hall. As I join her and my grandfather for dinner this evening, she's chatting to him about the plans for the equine facilities there. It seems since I've been gone Leanna has lavished money on her horses. Six more loose boxes, a five furlong gallop, a covered horse walker and a combined ménage and pool. The arrival of a new stable manager two years ago saw the facilities being run as a small business enterprise. Leanna was happy to sell us the existing stock but, after checking them out, Anna suggested it would be better if we purchased new. She also wants to expand the business, offering more services such as remedial work with problem horses, and physio and fine tuning for competition, services which mirror the facilities at Amberleigh. To do this, I remind her, we will need to employ more specialist staff.

When Marianne has finished serving, Anna continues her report by telling us how the house is coming along. She seems to have got the sub-contractors eating out of her hand but then it's no more than I expected. She's good with people, a great motivator, and it appears she's been talking to the Hall's head gardener, my old drinking companion Adrian McKenzie.

'Now the Hall is under new ownership, Adrian's keen to have a bigger input in what goes on in the gardens,' she confides with a smile, as Marcus tops up her wine. 'You don't mind do you?' She glances across at me obviously seeking my approval.

'Not at all. Actually I'm surprised he's still there,' I say, as I help myself to vegetables. 'After the way Leanna treats her staff I thought he would have been long gone.'

'You know him?' She looks across at me curiously.

'Yes, and he knows his stuff.'

'He likes a tipple too. Took me for a drink at the Black Bull one evening to meet the locals.'

Hearing her mention the pub means she's probably met Rufus Hayden. Has anything been said I wonder? Of course not. After all, why would a penniless gypsy who's been absent from the village for years rate as a topic of conversation? However...

'You haven't mentioned my name to anyone, have you?' I feel a little pathetic asking this but all the same it's something I need to know. I realise Anna's not an empty headed woman, she's very discreet, and asking this makes me sound as if I have something to hide – which, of course, I do.

'Of course not.' She frowns as she reaches for her glass. 'I accept you want to choose your own moment should you decide to reacquaint yourself with everyone. They're a great bunch of people though. I especially like Rufus; he's an excellent pub landlord. The villagers are very fond of him. And then there's his...'

Before Anna can say any more, Marianne enters the room to inform Marcus there's a call for him. As he disappears I seize the opportunity to put an end to this conversation. I don't want to hear any more about the residents of Lynbrook, especially Rufus Hayden, who made it clear I was the kind of scruffy mongrel he wanted kept as far away as possible from his daughter.

'Anna, I'm sorry,' I say, 'but I'd rather we didn't talk about Lynbrook if you don't mind.'

'Still difficult for you, is it?'

'Yes, even after all this time, I'm afraid it is.'

'It's more than a broken heart, isn't it? Something really painful happened. Is that why you don't want to live at the Hall when it's finished?'

'Lynbrook is the past,' I say, ignoring her question. 'My life is here at Amberleigh. I have no wish to be anywhere else. I've played my part, saved George and Ellie and, yes, I will go and see them once the refurbishments are complete. I'll look Adrian up too. But I was never really close to anyone else. I doubt most of them even remember me.' Another lie. Of course they do.

Anna gives a silent nod but I know from her expression this is unfinished business as far as she's concerned. She's a woman who never lets go until she's got to the bottom of things. However, by that time I'll have devised a strategy to send her off in another direction. I thought helping George and Ellie out would be easy. Anna said she would handle everything and all I'd need to do would be to transfer funds and provide a signature when required. Unfortunately, things have become far more complicated. I felt I had an obligation to visit in person to deliver the deeds to George's solicitor, to be part of the process because I owed them both so much. And, of course, if I had sent someone else I would never have run into Lily. I'm organising a trip soon to visit a breeder just outside Okehampton to look at stock for Lynbrook. I'll be stopping over in Exeter again and I want to catch up with Lily for dinner. Hopefully it will be an opportunity to find out more about that small face at the window.

JESS

It's a fortnight since I met up with Krister at the cottage. Following our meeting he's made another visit and has been busy putting his quote together. Now, just as we open for lunchtime drinking, he's arrived carrying a brown envelope.

'No hurry,' he says, politely declining a drink as he's rushing to get to a meeting with a potential client. 'Give me a call when you're ready. I have already checked out with the Council's local planning department and your project does not require planning permission, just building regulations. Don't worry,' he says to my obviously worried look, 'I can deal with all of this... that's if you want me to do the work,' he adds with a grin.

'Thank you,' I say, suddenly realising this whole building process is far more complex than I thought.

Rufus joins me at the bar, nodding a greeting to the departing Krister. 'Well,' he stares down at the envelope, 'go on then, I know you're dying to see what's inside...and so am I,' he adds with a grin. Slowly, I insert a fingernail under the flap and ease it open.

Rufus had suggested I ought to get two more quotes for comparison, but no one I spoke to was interested. It was either too small a project or they were booked up with jobs well into summer. And for me it's important to get this underway as soon as possible.

Removing the folded sheets and opening them out, I scan through their contents until I reach the last page.

'Well?' Rufus asks as he leans on the bar, his dark eyes watching me closely.

'See for yourself.' I hand over the paperwork. 'What do you think? You're the expert.'

'Flattery will get you everywhere.' He laughs as he takes it from me and begins to check methodically through each page. When he eventually reaches the end he looks at me and he's smiling. 'Well,' he says, 'it's pretty thorough, and all in all I think you've got yourself a great price.'

'Really?'

'Really.'

'We're good to go then.' The news my project has moved another step towards becoming a reality is wonderful news.

We're so engrossed in our conversation we don't see George enter.

'And what are you two plotting?' he asks, eyeing the papers in Rufus's hand suspiciously, as he arrives at the bar and pulls off his cap.

'It's Jess's project so I'll leave her to tell you,' Rufus replies, as he folds the quotation and slips it back into the envelope, quickly handing it to me just as Adrian and two of the gardening staff arrive. He moves down the bar to serve them, leaving us alone.

'What's all this about a project then?' George shoots me a curious frown as I select a glass from the rack above my head and begin to fill it with his usual half of best bitter.

'I've bought the cottage in the wood,' I reply matter-of-factly, as he roots around in his pocket for change.

'I see,' he says, as he watches me ring the money into the till. He takes a moment to savour a mouthful of beer before slowly wiping his mouth with the back of his hand. 'And you thought that heap of old rubble was worth rescuing, did you?'

'It's not a heap of rubble,' I protest, a tad annoyed at having this sort of label hung around my new venture. Of course, George would never have made the diplomatic corps. He has a habit of telling it like it is. I honestly believed he had some attachment to the cottage, but since then I've realised my mistake. It was all about losing the farm. Still, I'm not about to let him rain on my parade. I do think the place is worth my time and effort, and from the plans I've had drawn up it's going to be fabulous when it's finished.

'Sorry Jess, just teasing.' He reaches out and pats my hand. 'I should have known.'

'Known what?' I frown and then I realise, 'Talún? You think I bought it because of him?'

'Well, didn't you?' His voice trails away and he gives a confused shrug before taking another mouthful of beer.

'He's gone, George,' I say, slightly irritated his name has surfaced in our conversation. 'We've all moved on. Yes, it took a while to get over him. But I'm older and smarter than I was then. No one could ever change him. I simply failed to see it at the time.'

'Is that what you believe?' I find myself the subject of his close scrutiny again. 'Don't you realise what your arrival did to him? He dumped Leanna almost straight away and stopped chasing women. You brought about those changes in him. He wanted to be different... for you.'

'Not enough though. Aren't you forgetting what happened on the night of my party?'

'He said he was drunk and he made a terrible mistake. He was very upset about the whole thing.'

'Well that makes two of us,' I bite back, remembering the way in one single, drunken moment he completely destroyed any chance of our future together.

'Lass, I don't know what happened or why he decided to

leave in such a hurry but up until the moment he disappeared, as far as Ellie and I were concerned, he was planning to wait for you to come home.'

'Has it ever occurred to you he might have left the village with the mystery woman from the cricket pavilion?'

George gives my suggestion careful consideration before shaking his head. 'I don't believe that's what happened, Jess.'

'Well, it's the only sensible conclusion I've come to. Now please, can we stop this conversation? There's no point dredging up the past.'

George swallows a final mouthful of beer and sets the glass on the bar. 'Yes, of course, lass. I'm sorry.'

'Same again?' I reach for his glass with a forgiving smile. I have to confess this conversation has unsettled me. Buying the cottage seems to have dredged up all sorts of issues from the summer of 2007. Even though I thought the past was firmly behind me, it seems as though I'm going to have to grow a tougher skin.

'Better not.' George shakes his head. 'I'm collecting a batch of calves from Tiverton later.' Pulling his cap from his jacket, he slots it onto his head as he turns to go. 'Oh, by the way,' he says, stopping for a moment to look at me. 'Those plans of yours for the cottage. If you've got the time, maybe you'd like to drop by. Ellie and I would love to see them.'

LILY

I received a text message from Talún this morning. He's coming down to Exeter next Tuesday and he wants to take me out to dinner. It's just the opportunity I've been waiting for and a great excuse to go shopping for something really special to wear.

JESS

Today I'm visiting the kitchen suppliers with Krister. When we discussed kitchens and bathrooms and all the other choices I had to make, he was adamant this was the place to come. So here we are, pulling up outside a double fronted unit on a business park just east of Exeter.

'If you're having an Aga, min blomst,' he tells me, 'you need to give it the kitchen it deserves.'

'I think we have, haven't we?' I counter. 'We've already agreed on two designs from the brochure. So we're there, aren't we?' I frown at him suspiciously. 'I hope you're not going to try persuading me into buying anything ridiculously expensive as you did with the bathroom.'

'Jess, always you are in the driving seat. It's your money and for you to decide. Yes, sure, we have two designs in mind. I'm only saying it is good to keep your options open. Who knows, you may see something else you like better.'

It's true of course. It's fine to sort through brochures, but seeing the real thing is completely different and yes, he's right, I could well end up changing my mind...just as I did with the bathroom.

'Excellent.' He looks pleased. 'It is good you have an open mind. I—'

'Krister,' I interrupt, as we reach the automatic doors of Eclipse Kitchens, 'what did you call me just now? Min something or other?'

'Min blomst? It is a Danish word, a compliment. It means *my flower*.'

I smile. I rather like the thought of being his flower. Krister is growing on me. His English, although perfectly pronounced, brings something completely new to the language, especially the way he structures his sentences, which sometimes makes me laugh. He tends to stumble over the odd word too and he loves to discover something new, particularly the occasional rude word which Bella is all too keen to introduce him to. She winds him up all the time and Krister, a total innocent not used to our English ways, gets completely taken in only to find himself on the end of a grand leg pull. He's very quickly got wise to her though and has, to the amusement of the locals, got his own back once or twice. She's gradually drawing him out of his shell and it looks as though this might be the way to get that coveted date she's after. As for me, well Krister is a good friend. He's been remarkably supportive, guiding me through the whole project, including navigating me through a minefield of rules and regulations.

Pulling his faithful man bag over his hip, he pulls out a folded up plan, one we've been working on together and which should ensure the best use of the space allocated for the kitchen in the new open plan downstairs area. He also delves into its depths and pulls out a brochure, which contains the style choices I've opted for.

'Hi, Roland,' he says, greeting the approaching salesman. 'This is Jess Hayden. Remember I told you about the cottage I was working on for her? Well, we've come to talk kitchens...and of course your best prices.'

LILY

He's picking me up in half an hour. Once more, Chloe's doing the honours. Somehow I feel although Josh looks forward to sleepovers with Bailey, he's more settled at home. When I told him Mummy was going out for dinner this evening and Chloe would be coming around to babysit, he was so excited. He kept chattering about some story she'd read him last time round. The good thing is it means I now have someone other than Sonya when I need a free evening.

Talking of Sonya, she's been quizzing me about Talún. I've told her he's an old school friend I've run into – no lies there – and that he's done well for himself and we're just catching up on old times.

'And?' She pushes for more.

'And nothing.' I laugh, trying not to smile. 'He's a friend, Sonya, and he lives in a world completely different to mine. He's extremely wealthy.'

'Well, make the most of it, girl.' She gives me a sly wink.

'It's not like that,' I say. 'Yes, he's very good looking but definitely not my type.'

'If someone was rich I think I could overlook whether he was my type or not. Just think of the life you could have.'

I agree, forcing a smile, because I know how much I covet the lifestyle Talún now has. But if there's the remotest possibility of it happening at all it definitely won't be with him.

As I slip on my brand new midnight blue Max Mara dress - something that's left a hefty dent in my credit card – all I'm hoping for tonight is a continuation of our friendship; nothing more, nothing less.

Fastening my earrings, I hear the sound of the doorbell followed by voices. Oh God, I hope it's not the awful woman from number nine. Lately she seems to home in on me for the most pathetic of reasons. I've been waylaid in the car park several times with requests to sign petitions or give to the latest charity she's supporting. Coming to my door, however, is a step too far. I brace myself as I come down the stairs, ready to give her short shrift. However, as I near the bottom, it's a male voice I hear beyond the closed lounge door. My hand trembles slightly as I reach for the handle as I realise who has arrived. How the hell has he discovered where I live?

Taking a deep breath, I push open the door and enter the room. Chloe is standing there with a glazed expression on her face, watching Josh chattering to Talún as he shows off his latest piece of Lego. He smiles as he asks my small son a question and listens attentively to his response before turning to greet me. His eyes scan me from head to foot and I can see from his expression he likes what he sees.

'Lily,' he smiles, 'you look lovely, but you've been very naughty...' he switches his attention back to Josh, 'keeping secrets from me.'

For a moment I'm lost for words, my brain totally numb. Quickly I recover and smile. 'Ah,' I say, as the words begin to form in my head. 'I was going to tell you about Josh over dinner this evening.' It's a lie, of course, but what else can I say?

Chloe, still bug eyed from her encounter with my 'to die for' dinner date, suddenly comes to life and crouches next to Josh. 'Ah, right, time for bed, young man,' she says cheerfully as she lifts him into her arms. 'Say goodnight to—'

'Talún.' He completes the sentence and smiles, his eyes fixed on my son.

'Goodnight Talún,' Josh says as he wraps his arms around Chloe's shoulders. 'See you soon.'

'I hope so,' he says, and as they disappear from the room he turns to me. 'Ready?' he asks. Anything but, I think, pushing my face into the semblance of a smile. Oh God! He's going to want some answers now, what the hell am I going to tell him?

JESS

I've begun to meet regularly with Anna at my spot in the wood. She says after the flatness of Norfolk she has come to appreciate the surrounding countryside, particularly Barnfield Woods and the river which flows through it. She has an amazing knowledge of horses and has asked if I would be interested in putting Caspar out to stud once the Hall's facilities are up and running. She tells me although she is going to be instrumental in setting up additional services so the Lynbrook Stud can run more commercially, her grandson will be taking charge.

I am interested in the enigma who will soon be joining us, but Anna immediately made it clear although he will be a regular visitor to oversee the stud, he has decided to rent out the Hall. She told me one of the empty cottages is currently undergoing refurbishment as a crash pad for Lynbrook visits. I'm really curious about him but I don't know Anna well and I don't want to seem as if I'm snooping. Anyway, it's not as if he's going to be a new addition to the village, merely someone who drifts in and out for business purposes.

Anna, on the contrary, has begun to embrace village life. This evening, accompanied by Adrian and the gardening team, she's making yet another visit to the pub. I remember the very first time she walked through the door, the surprise on her face when she discovered I was the landlord's daughter. She had a wonderful evening and was welcomed by all the locals, including George, who thanked her for the farm. I heard her tell him her grandson plans to come and see him as he was the one who made the decision to transfer the deeds. I guess as he's the new owner he feels it's only good manners to do this. The more I learn from Anna about how the Hawkeswoods run their business, the more impressed I've become. They seem to be good people and a breath of fresh air after Leanna Tremayne.

Now Anna has now moved away from her seat with the gardeners and is at the bar chatting to Krister. When he mentions the work he's doing on my cottage, she wants to know why I've not told her about it.

'Because we only ever talk horses,' I remind her and Krister laughs. 'But if you'd like to see it, I can take you there tomorrow.'

'It's a deal,' she says, and we agree to meet at Barnfield Steps at eleven.

TALÚN

The evening I'd planned to have with Lily at The Dome has been soured slightly. It seems I have intruded into a part of her life she obviously wanted kept private: Josh. My own fault I guess; my curiosity got the better of me. As soon as she walked into the lounge I could see I'd made a serious error of judgement. It meant if I wanted to get her to open up I had to plan my conversation very carefully. So I worked hard to keep our evening's chat as light and friendly as possible. Unfortunately, it didn't work. Our normal relaxed way with each other had completely disappeared. She looked tense and her stilted responses and inability to make eye contact told me she was uneasy and on edge.

'Look, I'm sorry Lily,' I apologised, as we're waiting for our main course to arrive. 'I honestly didn't mean to intrude. When I dropped you off the other week I saw Josh watching you from the bedroom window. You hadn't mentioned anything about having a child and I thought....'

'You thought what?' She lifted her eyes to mine and there was that unease again.

I leaned on the table, linking my fingers and resting my chin against my knuckles, remembering the conversation I'd had with the baby sitter. 'Well, that he might be mine.'

'Yours?' I saw shock mingle with confusion as she stared across at me. 'He looks nothing like you.'

'No, but now I've seen him, I can tell you he has the same bright blue eyes as my grandfather. And my mother was blonde as a child. I've seen photos.'

She took a deep breath then pulled her napkin from her lap. 'I'm sorry,' she said, on the verge of tears, as she dropped it onto the table and got to her feet. 'I'm not feeling very well. Would you take me home please?'

LILY

Be careful what you wish for, isn't that what they say? I must admit I was panic stricken when I found Talún had already arrived and was busy chatting to Chloe and Josh. I didn't want this to happen. I knew damn well if he was aware I had a child he'd be asking questions. I had deliberately closed the door on my old life. I'd moved to Exeter and surrounded myself with new people who knew nothing about me. But this evening changed everything. I felt trapped. He wasn't Josh's father but the last thing I wanted was to have to answer questions about who was. It completely screwed me up and I felt the most sensible thing to do was to abort the evening there and then.

We travelled in silence all the way back to Exeter. During the journey I worked out what I was going to say to him and when we pulled up into the car park and he killed the engine I was ready.

'Lily...' he began, but I reached over and gently placed my finger against his lips. I planned to do all the talking and I wanted to make it short and simple.

'No, Talún, please listen,' I insisted. 'It's been great to see you again after all these years and I want to thank you for your hospitality. But this is where it ends.'

'I've made a complete mess of things, haven't I?' He sounded miserable and I could see the hurt in those unusual golden flecked eyes of his. 'I shouldn't have intruded, neither should I have been so insensitive, asking you if he was mine,' he said with a shake of his head.

'So, why did you?'

'Because when I asked your babysitter, she told me he was four and a half. Work it out, Lily. September 2007? Ring any bells?'

'Well, he's not yours,' I snapped as I unbuckled my seat belt. 'His father was a waster who didn't bother to hang around. Okay?' I felt tears threatening and the need to get away as quickly as possible. I shouldered the door open and taking a lung full of cool night air, I quickly escaped.

I ran across the car park. I didn't look back. As I slotted my key into the door, I heard the engine of the Lexus fire, saw its headlights dance across the buildings and then he was gone. I stood for a moment, looking out across the silent car park, feeling numb. All my hopes and dreams of staying friends with him and all that could bring were in ruins.

Naturally, Chloe was surprised to see me. I made the excuse I'd come home early because I'd developed a migraine and felt sick. She made coffee and we sat and chatted. She wanted to know all about Talún and I told her I was at school with him, he is now very rich, lives in Norfolk and has just purchased an expensive local property from the agents I work for. I tried to sound casual when I told her we probably wouldn't be seeing each other again but as I heard myself say those words the reality of my situation came back and made me want to cry. Chloe simply put her arm around my shoulder and declared I should go to bed as I was clearly still unwell. I pulled some money from my purse to pay her, but she wouldn't take it. I followed her to the door, thanking her again and apologising once more for messing up her evening. Then I climbed the stairs and after checking on Josh, undressed, fell into bed and sobbed.

JESS

As we ride into the clearing on this frosty Sunday morning I see Anna is smiling. It appears she likes what she sees.

'I love it already,' she confirms, gazing at the pale walls in front of her. 'The wood store has seen better days though,' she says, indicating the dilapidated lean-to attached to the cottage.

'Yes, I think Krister has already has something in mind for that,' I say, securing Caspar's reins to a nearby tree.

'It seems to me Krister figures a lot in your life, Jess,' she teases, 'and not just as your master builder.'

'He's become a great friend,' I tell her, anxious to stamp on any romantic ideas she may have about us. 'I thought when he arrived, what's a Dane doing setting up in an English village? But he's settled in well...just as you have.'

'Me?' She looks surprised then begins to laugh. 'No way.'

'Yes you have. The locals are fond of you already. And you got invited up to Manor Farm for tea and a tour.'

'That was a wonderful day. I adore Ellie, she's some baker.'

'Yes she is,' I agree, as I extract the key from my jacket and move towards the porch. 'One thing's for sure, George will never go hungry.'

I hear Anna laugh as she follows me in through the open door. She stands for a moment in the dimness, shafts of light filtering through the cracks in the boarded up window. I reach up and flip the switch, flooding the empty room with light. The walls have been re-plastered and there are bags of cement, plus a few empty crates and items of builders' equipment stored in one corner. I outline my plans, the internal changes and the jewel in the crown: the conservatory.

'There will be a patio too. I'll be able to sit out on a summer evening with a cool glass of wine,' I tell her, already visualising myself doing just that. The more I talk about this place, the more my enthusiasm grows. I can't wait to shop for furniture.

'Who lived here before?' she asks.

'Cesca and Talún.'

'They worked for George?'

'Yes.'

'A married couple? '

'Mother and son.'

Anna nods. 'Did you know them well?'

'Cesca was gone by the time I arrived in the village. I knew Talún, though. He lived here during the summer months,' I say, gazing around the room and suddenly feeling those unwanted memories return once more.

'Did you know him well?' she asks, eyeing me with a curious smile.

I draw in a sharp breath and shrug. 'We were friends. I remember he cooked me a meal here once. It was a lovely warm summer evening and we took our wine outside. There was a bench and a table. He'd made them himself.'

Anna nods. 'Are they still here?'

'No, when he left George had everything taken away.'

'And what exactly happened to Talún? Did he move away?'

'In a manner of speaking.' I clear my throat, wondering why I'm finding it difficult telling her about him. It's almost six years...I'd closed the door on the past, healed my pain and moved on. But it seems conversations with Bella, George and now Anna are slowly prising it open again and all sorts of long forgotten things are beginning to spill out. I see his face, those unusual green eyes with their amber flecks, his dark hair spilling untidily around his shoulders. Memories of very first morning I met him come flooding back. Ellie asked me if I'd ride up to the cottage to drop off the lunch he'd forgotten. There was the sound of someone chopping wood as I arrived. I slid from the saddle and it stopped. Then suddenly there he was, bare-chested and beautiful with that intricate sunburst tattoo sitting just below his left shoulder.

Nervously, I reach up to push a strand of hair behind my ears as I recall the moment I saw him for the first time up close. I relive the powerful ripple of attraction which passed between us and expel a deep breath. Anna watches me quietly, her eyes following the path of my hand as my fingers tangle in my hair.

'He simply left,' I say with a shrug, as my eyes scan the empty room and then settle on hers. 'He took his things from the farm and from here and disappeared one night without saying goodbye to anyone. He even threw his mobile away. George and Ellie were devastated. After Cesca left they took responsibility for him; he was like a son to them. He left them a note saying he felt there was nothing left for him in the village and it was best he moved on.'

I fall under Anna's grey-eyed scrutiny again as she shakes her head. 'After living here for so long, it must have been something deeply distressing for him to do that, don't you think?' she says quite pointedly, before she pauses to think for a moment, 'A love affair gone wrong maybe?'

'Who knows?' I give a vague shake of my head. 'He was a very private individual. Personally, I feel both Cesca and Talún never really lost their transient ways. George told me they arrived here with a group of travellers when Talún was five. His mother left with another group thirteen years later and never returned. Maybe she sent word and he joined her.' For some reason I sense something deeper than general interest. 'Why do you ask?'

'Oh, just curious.' She gives a casual shrug. 'Were you upset when he left?'

'I think we all were. And shocked, of course.'

'I can imagine,' she nods thoughtfully, 'Sorry, I'm being incredibly nosy, aren't I? And rude. That's it; no more questions, I promise,' she apologises and turns her attention towards the stairs. 'Let's get back to our tour, shall we?'

'Come and see the kitchen first.' I coax her towards the back of the cottage, glad this topic has run its course. 'I still haven't settled on a colour. Perhaps you could give me some advice.'

LILY

What a difference a day makes. Yesterday evening I felt the world had come to an end and now... well, I have a plan that just might change the rest of my life. Last night when Talún began asking me about Josh I reacted angrily. My son is a private part of my life and I don't want anyone intruding there. Exeter has enabled me to create a new life for myself. I know how fragile this existence is and the last thing I needed was anyone asking awkward questions. So naturally, as soon as he mentioned Josh I freaked out. All I wanted to do was get out of the restaurant.

Now this morning, as I'm taking a shower my mind runs over the conversation we had last night. I suddenly realise the implications of what he said and how easy it would be for him to reach that conclusion. After all, the night I spent with him was only weeks before I conceived Josh with Pauli.

I turn off the water, my mind in overdrive. I remember the expression on his face last night; he was really taken with my lovely blond boy. Josh is quite the little communicator. He's bright and curious and once he's been introduced to someone he chats on for hours. He has a lot of appeal too, such a sweet face and those big blue eyes. So what would be the harm in making Talún's wish come true and giving him a son to replace the daughter he lost? And in exchange I will get the life I've always dreamed of. I'm just beginning to feel this might work when a brick wall looms. Although I have a contact who could produce a new birth certificate with dates reflecting a September conception, I realise the first thing his well-heeled family would demand would be a DNA test. And there's no way I can fake that. The whole idea is dead in the water. Damn!

TALÚN

I'm back in Norfolk now and getting on with my life. However, I still can't get Josh's face out of my mind. Lily hit the panic button during our meal in the restaurant and

I'm sure she's hiding something. Okay, he looks nothing like me, but his eyes are exactly the same shade as Marcus's. And as for the colour of his hair, well, I've seen enough photos since I've been living here to know my mother was blonde as a child. He seems such a sweet boy and I hate to think she's spent the last four and a half years struggling to bring him up on her own. I so want to take this further but I know it's total madness. I tell myself I have to be sensible and put it all behind me. But doing that makes me feel totally empty. Seeing him and learning how old he was, I suddenly felt this great surge of hope. That out of the misery and loss of the past two years had come something fresh and wonderful. But it was not to be and I will simply have to learn to live with my disappointment.

APRIL 2013

LILY

For a week now I've tried to turn my back on this lunatic idea I've had about persuading Talún to accept Josh as his. The thing is, no matter how much I think he wants it to be true, it's not enough. The fact is there's no way Josh and Talún are ever going to have a compatible DNA test result. It's a complete non-starter.

It's lunch time and, as I've a deadline to meet on a brochure, I decide to grab a sandwich from the deli across the road. As I collect my lunch and leave, I catch sight of Zac coming towards me.

'What are you doing here?' I ask, instantly suspicious.

'Going to lunch,' he says, and draws in a tired breath. 'Look, give me a break. If you hadn't noticed, this is the direct route from the car park to the Red Lion.' He points down the road.

'Off to meet another victim, are you?' I can't resist the question, wondering if by any chance Jess Hayden's back on the scene.

'No, I've a day off and I'm heading there for a drink and a bite to eat. On my own.'

And then it suddenly hits me. Although I've researched DNA tests on line, who better than Zac to ask about the subject in detail. He says he owes me, so... God, I sound really desperate, don't I? Why oh why can't I let go of this? It's insane.

'Look, I'm sorry, I didn't mean to snap.' I apologise, 'It's been one of those mornings. Would you mind if I join you?' I push my lunch into my tote and try to banish my work deadline from my mind. 'I could murder a drink.'

I settle in a corner table by the window while he orders drinks at the bar. He returns with a large glass of wine and a bottle of lager, a menu tucked under his arm. As I scan down the food on offer he leans over and tells me lunch is on him.

I thank him as I reach for my wine. During the time I've been sitting here alone I'm beginning to realise impetuous me has propelled herself right into this without any proper preparation. What do I say? How do I even broach the subject? Oh well, there's no choice. I'm here now, so I'll just have to see where the conversation goes and grab the opportunity when, or rather if, it arises.

'So how are you and that lad of yours?' His voice barrels into my thoughts as he tilts the bottle to his lips.

'We're both fine. What about you? All packed and ready?'

'Not quite.' He gives a grin. 'Looking forward to it, though.' He leans back in his seat and regards me for a moment. 'Okay,' he says, 'time to come clean, Lily. What exactly is it you want?'

'Want?' I try to cover my confusion, wondering what kind of response I should give. If I simply say "I need your advice about DNA testing," he'll be asking why. He won't play ball, I know he won't. However, I just might have an idea; a toe in the water to find out exactly how the land lies.

'I don't want anything,' I say, as my gaze locks with his. 'We happened to run into each other. I had a rubbish morning, I was rude, felt bad about it and decided to join you for a drink. I thought it would be an opportunity to catch up. Seeing you the other day made me wonder where all the others had got to. Those twins for instance...Felicity and Miles?'

'Kermit and Miss Piggy, you mean?' He gives an amused laugh. 'Well, last I heard they were both working abroad. A real couple of Noddy heads they were,' he says, swigging back another mouthful of lager.

'Is Roo still about?'

'He is. Working as a lawyer based here in one of his father's practices.'

'And what about my nemesis?'

'Jess, you mean? God knows? Teaching small sprogs somewhere, I would imagine.'

'You never sorted things out with her then?'

'After that night at Lynbrook? No. Anyway, do you think I'd want her back after she'd been with him?' Zac's handsome features bunch themselves into an angry frown. 'Troublemaking bastard.'

I nod sympathetically, hearing the grievance in his voice. Jess really did mean a lot to him but he didn't take their relationship seriously at the time. He was playing around behind her back with other girls, including me. So if he lost her, he really only had himself to blame. But Zac has an ego the size of the o2 Arena and would never ever dream of taking the blame for things which happened as a result of his actions.

'Bloody hell! The number of times I wished I'd given him a good hiding...or got someone else to,' he admits, as he takes another swig from his bottle and sets it on the table.

'He's still around you know.' I ease this piece of information into the conversation.

'Is he?' He gives me a slow smile, making me wonder if he's thinking of resurrecting his plans for revenge.

'Oh yes, and no longer a gyppo. He's rich.'

'Really? Won the lottery has he?' I can see from Zac's dismissive expression he doesn't believe me.

'Not quite. He left Lynbrook and found his mother's family. Have you ever heard of Hawkeswood Estates?'

He nods. 'One of the UK's biggest farming businesses'

'Well, turns out he's Marcus Hawkeswood's grandson.'

'What?' His eyes widen in surprise as he pushes himself upright. I've definitely caught his interest him now. 'You're having a laugh.'

'No, straight up. He's just purchased Lynbrook Hall. In fact he's been to the office on several occasions. I've even been out to dinner with him.'

'Dinner?' He blows out a breath and then his eyes narrow as he eyes me suspiciously. 'What are you playing at Lily?'

'I want the kind of life he can give me,' I say quite unashamedly. 'And you know me, Zac, if I see an opportunity I go for it.'

112

'Like you did with Leo Hayden you mean?' He smirks. 'That was definitely a bad move. The man was a control freak and a complete shit. I thought you had more sense.'

'I'm not complaining,' I argue, not wanting to admit any failure. 'After all, he spent a fortune on me.'

'Until you decided to enlighten Jess about the identity of her real father.'

'Yeah, well, I rather let my temper get the better of me.' I shrug uncomfortably. 'This time it's different. Talún's not some creepy middle-aged man. He's good looking, a real catch in the marriage market.'

'Marriage market? You're hoping it goes that far are you?' He lets out a snort of laughter. 'Oh, Lily, be sensible, if he's related to a family like the Hawkeswoods, you're the last person he'd be interested in. '

'Maybe,' I give him a teasing smile, 'but I have collateral...'

'What sort of collateral?'

'Josh.'

'Is he Talún's then? '

'He seems to think he is, but no,' I shake my head, 'Josh's father left when he was a baby and I've not seen him since.'

'And you were hoping to pass him off as the Hawkeswood's great grandson?' he says, tapping his index finger against his bottom lip thoughtfully. 'Ooh, slight problem eh?'

'A bloody big one.' I agree trying to ignore the way Zac's smugness is beginning to get under my skin. 'His family are loaded. A DNA test is the first thing they will ask for. Brilliant idea but it fell at the first hurdle. A pity there's no way around it.'

Zac sits back for a moment, his expression caught in a frown as if he's considering what I've just told him, 'Actually there might be.' He tells me, as a slow grin surfaces, 'The downside is if you were ever discovered it would mean a long spell behind bars. But hell,' he runs a hand through his blond hair and laughs, 'Let's take a chance and dance with the devil shall we? I'll be setting things right by helping you achieve your heart's desire. And me? Well it would be the best leaving present ever; getting one over that piece of trash.'

'So what's the plan?' I ask. I have absolutely no idea how or indeed if you can falsify a DNA test but I'm interested in finding out.

'All in good time,' he says, nodding towards the menu. 'First let's get lunch sorted, shall we?'

I opt for lasagne and he heads to the bar to order and get another round of drinks. As I watch him flirting with the barmaid doubts begin to creep in. Can I really trust him after what he did to me all those years ago?

JESS

Today I'm taking Rufus, George and Ellie up to see the cottage. I didn't want any of them on site until the whole project was completely finished. I gave Anna a tour yesterday and I could see from her delighted expression and complimentary comments that between us, Krister and I have brought about a brilliant transformation to this old derelict cottage.

Adrian has been an absolute angel, sorting out the small garden in his spare time. The result, I hope, as the summer months arrive, is a proper cottage garden, a riot of lupins, hollyhocks, delphiniums, phlox and peonies. He's laid out a rose bed too, plus a small herb garden, and around the patio he's arranged stone tubs and filled them with pansies. Oh, and I have a water feature as well. It's all totally amazing. I hope today's visitors will be as impressed as I've been with what's been achieved.

We pull into the small newly tarmacked parking area and I lead my guests down the narrow path towards the cottage, past the post lights Krister has had installed. Triggering at dusk, it will mean the pathway is constantly illuminated at night. We take time looking at the garden, which brings comments from green fingered Ellie. As we reach the cottage I point the out the new cedar wood structure which replaces the old lean to and houses the green plastic heating oil tank. In the covered porch the cracked floor tiles have been removed and replaced, while above its apex a new block of stone has been inserted into the wall with the year 1854 carved into it. This, the date it was built, is something I discovered in the deeds of the property along with the fact it started life as a gamekeeper's cottage.

I reach the door and unlock it, stepping inside and standing back to allow my guests to join me. Everyone is wide eyed with surprise: Rufus because he's seeing the reality of the plans for the first time and George and Ellie because they remember how it used to be. Spring sunshine spills in through newly fitted windows, revealing a room full of warm colour.

'Well,' Ellie says, 'I never would have thought it could look like this.' She shakes her head, stunned by the transformation.

'Come and see the kitchen,' I say, leaving the men behind. As we emerge into what is the new kitchen diner, she does a double take. 'What have you done here?' she asks.

'The lounge has been partitioned off into a separate room creating this kitchen diner. And this,' I proudly announce, 'is my new baby.'

Her eyes light up at the sight of the yellow Aga.

'The colour's not to everyone's taste,' I remark, 'but I think it goes well with the new brick wall Krister created behind it, don't you?'

She nods, still lost for words, as Rufus and George join us, both with matching smiles of approval.

My little party follow me through the rest of the cottage, taking in the furnishings and fabrics. They admire the changes to the bathroom, which now has a modern suite and shower cubicle, the black and white tiling replaced with warm beiges and browns.

Downstairs I settle them in the new conservatory while I make coffee.

'Amazing,' George says, helping himself to a biscuit. 'If this is what the Viking can do then he'll have people

115

queuing up. He's a bloody miracle worker.'

'Language, George.' Ellie frowns at him as she adds sugar to her coffee, then turns to me and smiles. 'It's a grand little house, Jess. Are you planning to rent it out?'

'Oh no, I'm going to live here,' I say.

'Are you sure you really want to after...you know?' She eyes Rufus nervously and it's George's turn to frown.

'It's not the same,' I reassure her as I look around the room. 'This place is different now. It's fresh and new and I know I'm going to be very happy here.'

LILY

I'm beginning to wonder whether Zac has been winding me up. Since our lunch at The Red Lion, I've heard absolutely nothing. A week has passed since he left me, promising to get in touch with a friend who owes him big time... someone who in his words 'would be willing to take care of the DNA test'. Annoying bastard that he is, he's fed me the possibility of fulfilling my dream and then simply disappeared. To add to my frustration he's not answering his mobile and the messages I've been leaving remain unanswered.

Just as I'm about to head off to lunch, I hear my ring tone and his ID appears on my mobile.

'Lily, how are you?' he asks, in his best buddy voice.

'How the hell do you think I am?' I hiss down the phone, wishing I wasn't sharing an office with the rest of Nick's sales team and he could feel the full force of my frustration.

'Tsk, tsk,' he rebukes me, 'no need to lose your temper, darling.'

'I am not your darling,' I say through gritted teeth. 'Where've you been? You promised to come back to me by the weekend. It's been over a bloody week.' My last rather loud retort has heads turning curiously.

'For God's sake, calm down, Lily,' he says, blowing out an angry breath. 'It's not my fault my contact has been away sunning himself in Sharm El Sheikh.'

'You could have told me, not just left me wondering what the hell was going on.' I've lowered my voice but I get the feeling two sets of interested ears are still tuned in.

'Look, I'm about to go to lunch. I'll speak to you later,' I say, and abruptly end the call. Damn him, if he's going to start messing me about I might as well forget the whole bloody thing. Grabbing my bag and coat, I leave the office feeling I want to kick something. Hard. Then, as the automatic doors open to let me onto the street a hand reaches out and grabs my arm. It's Zac; he's been waiting outside for me all the time, damn him. 'Let go of me,' I say, as I attempt to shake him off.

'Calm down, will you?' he says, wrapping his arm around my shoulder and moving us down the street as if we're a loved up couple.

'Stop it!' I push him away, furious at being manhandled.

He pulls me to a halt and spins me around, resting his hands on my shoulders. 'Will you behave?' He shakes me gently. 'I've got some important news for you. Come on.' And grabbing my arm, we head towards the Red Lion.

An hour later I return to the office fizzing with excitement. Karl Weston is an ex-uni friend of Zac's who works for a DNA testing laboratory in Bristol and apparently owes him a huge favour. I don't want to begin to think what that means but it's obviously something serious if it can persuade him to fake a set of results. I'm still being kept in the dark about what exactly is going to happen after samples have been taken, but maybe it's better I don't know. Once I've convinced Talún Josh is his, I'll phone Karl and get him to despatch the kits. I take a deep breath as I return to my desk. Now for some devious planning...

JESS

I'm sitting by the river with Anna. It's a beautiful morning. May is nearly here and in another month, sadly, she'll have returned to Norfolk and I won't be able to share time with her. Over these few months she's become a close friend and this morning I've been hearing about her life. She grew up in an army family, frequently on the move. For a long time her father was based in what was then West Germany and she boarded over here, returning to her parents for the holidays. Her love of horses came from her mother, who was an accomplished rider. This meant she learned to ride almost as soon as she could walk. As an adult she qualified as a vet and eventually met and married Kevan McNeil, a horse breeder based just over the Welsh border.

'He was such a wonderful caring man,' she says, and I can see by her expression as she gazes out across the river that in her mind she's reliving her time with him. 'I never thought I would lose him after only ten years of marriage.' She turns back to me, a deep sadness in her grey eyes. 'A brain haemorrhage,' she explains, 'one moment he was there, full of life, the next moment gone. He lived for his horses and I felt I should continue his work. So I remained in Wales and eventually opened the Anna McNeil Stud.'

'And how did you meet Marcus?'

'At a breeder's convention twelve years ago.' She laughs. 'The last thing I was looking for was another husband. In the end I guess it was inevitable, we were two sad souls who came together. Even after all those years he was still grieving for his wife. It seems we had both buried ourselves in our work and, ironically, it was the thing that brought us together. Six months…a whirlwind romance, and now I feel really blessed.' She looks across at me and smiles.

'That's good,' I say. It's great to have a happy ending and I have come to like Anna very much, as has everyone else in the village.

'And what about you? How has your life path been? I gather you've not always lived in Lynbrook.'

I find myself wondering whether I want to divulge my past. However, Anna has been so open with me she deserves to hear my story… well, certain parts of it.

'No, I came here just under six years ago. It's rather complicated. Rufus wasn't always my father,' I begin, 'he was my uncle. It wasn't until I was eighteen that the truth came out and I came back here to live with him.'

'Where did you live before?'

'About twelve miles away in small seaside resort called Milton Bay.'

And so I begin to unwrap my life, first enlightening her about my social butterfly mother, Diana who Leo divorced when I was thirteen, and how life was before I arrived in Lynbrook. I tell her Leo was a bully and a control freak and how his foolish fascination with a girl we had as our lodger caused the destruction of our family. On the positive side I tell her about Amber, the woman who is the nearest thing I have to a real mother, and, of course, about my surrogate brother, Roo, who has always been there for me. Rufus, she is aware, has been my rock. I deliberately leave out what happened with Talún – after he cropped up in conversation the other day at the cottage, it would cause far too many difficult questions. I then give a brief resumé of my uni days, my teaching life, ending with my decision to return home.

When I finish she's quiet for a moment, as if taking time to absorb all I've told her. 'Leo sounds like a pretty damaged individual,' she says. 'I know you said he decided to stay up in Scotland but has anyone heard anything from him since?'

'He died last August. Heart attack.' I say to her surprise. 'Rufus and I attended the funeral with Roo and Amber flew in from Majorca. Only five of us there at his funeral. A sad reflection on his life, don't you think?'

'Five?' she queries, and I realise I haven't mentioned Elliot McIntyre.

'Leo's solicitor. He came down from Aberdeen to read the will.'

'Don't tell me he left his money to the lodger.'

'No, he left it to me,' I say with a smile. 'The solicitor said during his time in Scotland Leo had become a changed man, one who wanted to make up for the pain he'd caused both Rufus and me. He left my father his classic Porsche.'

'Well, that must have come as a surprise.'

'It did. Neither of us could believe it.'

'Oh, Jess.' Anna reaches out, wrapping her arms around me. 'You've been through so much, you poor girl.'

'Actually, a rich girl,' I say with a smile as she releases me. 'Leo left me three and a half million pounds.'

'Heavens! So that's how you were able to give up teaching and come home?'

'Yes.'

'And what are your plans now?'

'Well, I've bought the cottage and restored it and ...' I hesitate. I haven't told anyone this yet, not even Rufus, but it sort of brings my story full circle. 'Krister has found some land in Dark Lane with outline planning permission for housing. We want to build eight terraced homes there. I'm putting up the money and he'll do the rest. They will be eco homes: energy efficient, environmentally friendly and available only to local couples or families. Locals are priced out of the market around here and I aim to help more of them to stay and put down roots.'

Anna regards me quietly for a moment. 'What an amazing project to be undertaking,' she says, eventually finding her voice, 'If there's anything I can do to help...

'Actually, there is,' I say, hoping she'll be receptive to my request. 'Dark Lane borders the Hall's grounds and if we could purchase a small area of land from you, we could extend our build to another four houses.'

'Well,' Anna smiles, 'obviously I'll have to clear it with my grandson but I don't think it will be a problem. In fact, I think he'll be rather taken with the whole thing. I can't wait for you two to meet.'

I may be wrong but I have the sudden feeling Anna may be lining me up as potential girlfriend material for her mysterious grandson. From brief conversations with Adrian I understand he's single and nudging thirty but he doesn't know much more. I smile, not wanting to spoil the moment. However there's no way I'm ending up in Blind Date territory with Anna playing Cilla Black.

TALÚN

This morning I picked up a text message from Lily. She apologised for leaving me the way she did and spoiling our evening. She says she wants to see me again about something important. I try not to think it might be anything to do with Josh; that would be too much to hope for. No, it's probably she feels we parted badly and wants to make amends. So tomorrow I'm returning to Exeter to see her. I'm staying at The Abode and have booked a table in the restaurant for eight thirty. Now it's all about being patient and waiting until then to find out exactly what this is all about.

LILY

Well, today is the day. Talún will arrive in Exeter this afternoon and I'm meeting him for dinner at The Abode. Ever since he texted me to confirm, I've been in a complete fug. I want this so much, yet I'm aware it's a potential house of cards with the possibility of chaos and collapse. I'm really focused on what I have to lose rather than him finding out the truth. I know I'm breaking the law, but hell, it's not as if I've seduced him or lied to him about the way I feel in order to get what I want, is it? No, Zac told me to look at the whole thing purely as a business deal. He gets the son he wants and I get the life I deserve, simple as that.

Thanks to Gav, one of Pauli's mates who does a great line in forged documents, I am in possession of a new birth certificate for Josh, which shows his date of birth as 9th June instead of 10th July 2008. And where once there was Pauli's name listed as the father, there is a blank space. Comparing it with the original birth certificate, it looks totally authentic. So now I have this in my possession I should be feeling confident, shouldn't I? Well actually, no, far from it. You see it's suddenly occurred to me that breaking this kind of news in a restaurant is a totally inappropriate place. If anything should go wrong...I take a deep breath and focus. I need a slight change of plan.

TALÚN

I'm sitting at the bar waiting for Lily to arrive. I check my watch. Eight-forty five; she's late, very late. As I finish off the last of my whisky, my mobile, which has been resting on the bar, vibrates. I pick it up. It's her.

'Talún, I'm sorry, I don't think dinner at the hotel is a good idea,' she says, her voice calm but a little shaky.

'You do still want to see me though?' I try not to sound too desperate but I don't want to have come all this way for nothing. This was, after all, her request and not mine.

'Yes, of course. It's...well I think it might be better if you come here. I just feel I need somewhere more private for what I have to say.'

'That's fine, it's not a problem. I'm on my way.' Somewhere more private? This can only mean one thing, can't it? I have a son. A beautiful blond, blue eyed son.

LILY

Great, he's coming here. I feel far more secure. If things go wrong and I end up in tears, at least I'll be blubbing in the privacy of my own home. But that's not going to happen, is it? Pull yourself together, Lily, I tell myself. You can do this. I check my face in the mirror then go to sort out some music from my small collection of CDs.

By the time I hear the doorbell ring I'm feeling quite relaxed, probably because I've already had a couple of glasses of wine. I go to the door to let him in and I can see from his expression he has an idea about why I asked him to come back. I take his coat and show him through to the lounge. We settle ourselves comfortably on the couch and I offer him wine.

'Only one glass,' he says with a smile. 'I'm driving, remember.'

'About the other evening...' I begin as I reach for the bottle and begin to pour, but straight away he hijacks the conversation.

'My fault,' he says, as he takes the glass from me. 'I

stepped over the line, stomping all over your personal life with my size tens.'

'The thing is,' I take a sip of my wine and place the glass back on the coffee table, 'well, I don't know quite how to say this, but...' I leave the sentence hanging.

'He is mine, isn't he?' Our eyes meet and I can see immediately how desperate he is for this to be true. He wants Josh as badly as I want the life he can give me.

'Yes, Josh is yours,' I confirm, biting my lip and summoning up my best tearful expression.

'So I'm the waster who didn't bother to hang around?' A smile hovers on his lips but in his eyes I see the shimmer of tears.

'I'm sorry.' I apologise, realising although I'd been referring to Pauli, the comment is tailor made for this situation too.

'That's okay.' He nods, 'The most important thing is I'm back. For good.'

I'm glad,' I say, watching as he fights to hold back tears. I'm embarrassed. Men don't cry; it's just not done. 'I felt terribly confused when I first saw you,' I continue. 'Things are different now. You're rich, you have money and the last thing I wanted to do was come right out and land something so life changing on you. You might not have believed me. You might have thought I was just some gold digger trying to get lucky.' I clear my throat, aware of the truth in those words. I take a breath and continue. 'After all, Josh doesn't look anything like you.'

'I told you before, I can see both my grandfather and mother in him.' He looks at me, his expression eager. 'Can I see him?'

'He's not here this evening. Sleepover with my childminder's son. He'll be around tomorrow though.' I summon up my acting skills, give a well-timed sniff and reach for a tissue from the box on the coffee table, eager to support him in this emotional moment.

'You'll never know,' he begins, wiping away tears which have suddenly returned, 'after I lost Fliss and Emily, I couldn't see the point any more. For months I simply existed. It was Anna who persuaded me to buy Lynbrook Hall to help a friend keep his farm. If she hadn't, I never would have met you again, or found out about Josh.' He smiles, clears the moisture from his eyes and reaches out to take my hand.

'But now you have,' I say, giving his fingers a gentle squeeze, 'and I hope you'll stay for a few days. Get to know him.'

'Yes.' He wipes his eyes again and smiles at me. 'I'd like that very much.'

JESS

Today, Anna has invited me up to the Hall to have a look around. I'm interested to see what she's done to this beautiful old house. I approach the Hall along the winding driveway where the horse chestnut trees are now in full bloom. I love the late spring, it's a warm, bright time of year and everything looks amazingly fresh and green. Ahead, I can see the house and as I pull up and park up near the fountain Anna is there waiting.

Getting out of the car, I'm greeted with a kiss on the cheek before she loops her arm in mine and guides me up the steps towards the front door.

'We'll have the tour first,' she says, 'then back to the pub for lunch perhaps?'

I nod in agreement. 'My treat though,' I insist. After all, I'm feeling quite privileged to be here this morning, sneaking a peek before anyone else.

For the next hour she steers me from one room to another. While most of the work is painting and cosmetic repair, there's a revamped indoor pool and sauna and a new cinema room. But it's the kitchen that has me holding my breath.

'Did you design this?' I ask, looking around in total awe.

'No, Leanna's cook Naomi is on a retainer waiting to begin work when the Hall is occupied once more. I was so pleased I could persuade her to stay. I got her involved with the design and purchase,' she adds, 'saved me the headache of sorting it out. My grandson set aside a hefty budget and, as you can see,' she said with a sweep of her hand, 'Naomi spent most of it. Now then,' with another wave of her hand she shepherds me back towards the main hall, 'let me show you the bedrooms and the bathrooms.'

As we're half way up the stairs her mobile warbles and she stops, retrieving it from her trouser pocket. 'Ah, it's Marcus,' she says with a smile before lifting the phone to her ear. I step back down into the hall to wait, not wanting to intrude on her private conversation. Watching her, I can see from the expression on her face and her anxious tone there's a problem. Moments later she pockets the phone and joins me at the foot of the stairs.

'I'm sorry, Jess, I'm afraid I'm going to have to abandon the tour this morning. Marcus needs me back in Norfolk urgently. A family emergency.'

She walks me to the car and gives me a hug. 'I'll call you as soon as I'm back,' she says, trying to mask the worry I can see in her face. There's some sort of crisis at home but exactly what, I have no idea. I only hope it can be resolved easily.

TALÚN

I thought I knew the art of diplomacy but I guess there was never going to be an easy way to break the news about Josh. Even more of a shock must be the fact you plan to marry his mother and bring them both to live at Amberleigh.

And now all hell has broken loose. Marcus is furious with me, summoning reinforcements by calling Anna back from Lynbrook. But as much as I understand my grandfather's concerns about what I've done, I have to make him realise I have been given a second chance for happiness. It might not have come about in the conventional manner, but there's no way I'm going back on the decision I've made.

Well, who would have thought it could have been so easy? Talún's gone back to break the news to his family and I'm sitting here celebrating in the Red Lion with my mentor. Zac is all smiles because he can now leave the UK for his new life in Canada, happy in the knowledge he's been instrumental in getting one over on someone he totally detests. And me? Well, I am really excited at the prospect of the new life I'm about to embark on.

Talún stayed for nearly a week. I managed to get a few days off and during that time the DNA test was completed. 'I want a reputable company,' I insisted, plastering on a serious face, 'it's important we do this right.' Talún, of course, was one hundred percent behind me.

'I'll leave you to organise it,' he said, his distracted gaze focusing on my son with the kind of longing in his eyes I'm beginning to get used to. 'I'd really like to take Josh out, if that's okay with you.'

'Of course,' I nodded in agreement, eager to get rid of him, 'it's important you two get to know each other.' By this time Josh was really beginning to take to Talún and the thought of swings and an ice cream was greeted with excitement and lots of hopping from one foot to the other. As the door closed on both of them, I found my bag and the business card Zac had given me and called the laboratory where Karl worked to arrange for two testing kits to be sent by express service. Well, no use hanging about, was there? The sooner he took up his responsibilities as Josh's father the better.

The two kits were delivered by courier and we did the test at mine with Sonya present. The express service meant we got the results in two days. Talún was over the moon. This time he didn't cry. Instead he kissed me and hugged Josh. We then had the job of sitting Josh down and explaining to him.

'But I wanted Max to be my daddy,' he said, his little face creased with disappointment. I thought it might upset Talún but he simply smiled down at him and shrugged.

'It's an enormous thing for him to take in,' he said gently. 'I gather he's talking about Max Warner, your boss.'

'Yes,' I said, 'we went to the Christmas market back in December and he was there. He bought Josh a stuffed toy dragon. It goes everywhere with him.'

Talún squatted down beside Josh. 'How would you like your own pony?' he asked.

'A pony? For me?' Josh's eyes were like saucers.

'Yep, and I'll teach you to ride as well.'

Suddenly he had a captive audience as Josh instantly forgot Max and began asking questions about this potential pony. My boy's new father skilfully moved the conversation on, telling him about Amberleigh where he lived and his new great grandmother and grandfather who had a huge farm with tractors. As soon as the word 'tractor' was mentioned, Josh was hooked.

'I'd like to thank you,' I say, raising my glass to Zac. 'It went like a dream.'

'No more than I expected,' He replies, sitting back and nursing his bottle against his chest, a smug grin on his face. 'Couldn't happen to a nicer bastard.'

'And that's not all,' I say, revealing something I have carefully hidden from view since I joined him, 'because when I told him he couldn't have Josh without me, well he asked me to marry him.' I smile, displaying my three carat, square-cut diamond solitaire engagement ring.

Zac is rendered speechless for a moment. 'Bloody hell, Lily,' he says, finding his voice as he leans across the table and grabs my hand. 'You've really reeled him in, haven't you?'

'You better believe it,' I reply, unable to resist a self-satisfied smirk. 'And Josh and I are off to meet the family this weekend.'

'No doubt you and the new grandchild will be welcomed with open arms,' he says, relaxing back in his seat with a smile and a shake of his head, as if he can't believe I've accomplished so much.

'There was one dodgy moment,' I admit. 'He told me his

family would need to do a background check on me.'

'And?'

'I persuaded him that could see some unwanted people resurfacing. My old man, for starters. I think I did a good job convincing him if he got wind of my good fortune he'd be the kind of unpleasant parasite we'd never get rid of. So he told me to leave things with him and he'd sort it.'

'What do you think he'll do?'

'He's done it. Told them he's already undertaken his own investigation and that everything is okay. You see he's so desperate to have Josh he'll even lie.' I laugh. 'And the family haven't challenged anything he's told them, can you believe that?'

'Like taking candy from a baby.' Zac salutes me with his bottle and takes another swig.

TALÚN

Anna arrives back late afternoon. I'm with the stud vet who has arrived to check one of the pregnant mares when my mobile rings to let me know she's home. It leaves me a couple of hours before the brown stuff hits the fan. Of course, they're bound to think asking Lily to marry me was a crazy move. Yes, I've lied about the background check but it's not as if she's a complete stranger - I was at school with her. Okay, she comes from a poor family but she's smart and streetwise and she's done an amazing job bringing up Josh on her own. I'm counting on Anna's help in all this. She's a fair minded woman and is aware of the dark depths I sank to after the accident. I'm hoping she'll calm my grandfather and make him understand.

Anna and Marcus are already in the dining room when I arrive. They both look up as I enter. Anna's smile is warm, which gives me hope, but he simply nods uncomfortably and watches as I take my place at the table. I have trouble with this as in all the time I have known him he's always been fiercely supportive and protective of me. But now, understandably, he is not. I have shaken the foundations of his business empire. I'm proposing to bring a fait accompli into his world; a son and fiancée who are complete strangers. Of course, it's bound to make him uneasy.

Dinner is a quiet affair. We seem to be tip-toeing around each other and I'm guessing their plan is to broach the subject of Josh and Lily in the drawing room once the meal is over. Therefore, we limit our talk to business. I update Anna on what's going on at the stud, Marcus talks about staffing levels and his farm shop manager's ideas for new lines. There is also talk of a new food venture, which the marketing department are currently investigating. Finally, the meal is over, plates are cleared away and Marianne is asked to serve coffee in the drawing room.

Although May is only a week away, today has been chilly and there's a cheerful fire burning. I follow them into the room. Marcus and Anna seat themselves together on one of the couches and I settle myself in a chair opposite. Marianne arrives and sets a tray of coffee down on the small table in front of us all. This is new territory for me. Usually I slip away after dinner to return to some unfinished business at the stud or settle down to a film in the cinema room. Tonight will be different; very different.

'How is work at the Hall progressing?' I ask Anna as she pours and hands round the coffee.

'Very well. The builders have been brilliant. They're working on some external issues but I think another week and they will have finished. Once they've gone we'll need to talk about your plans for the place,' she says, settling herself back beside Marcus. 'In light of your news, do you now plan to live there?'

'No, this is my home,' I say, 'and I was proposing to bring Lily and Josh here to live.'

My grandfather helps himself to sugar and then sits back, slowly stirring his coffee before taking a sip. 'Now then,' he relaxes slightly and manages a smile, 'before we get into any further discussion, I think you'd better bring Anna up to speed on your situation.'

And so I go over my story once more, telling Anna I was

with Lily for six months, but we eventually broke up. Anna immediately asks whether this was my reason for leaving Lynbrook. I nod in agreement, aware although it's not true, it gives credence to my story of having a proper relationship with her. I dread to think how they would react to learning Josh is the result of a one night stand with someone I hardly knew. The truth is, I care about Lily but we're not in love, nor are we are likely to be. If anything, I guess we're friends and marriage is merely bringing us together to raise Josh. Maybe this partnership is the best way. I've had two shots at love, one all consuming passion, the other steady and gentle. Both ended badly and left their scars. It's not a road I'm keen to travel again.

I tell them about the DNA testing and produce the results and the birth certificate. I also tell them what a wonderful boy he is with his great grandfather's blue eyes and his grandmother's gentle nature. At the end of my speech I'm waiting for my grandfather's response.

'There is the question of Lily's background,' he says, returning his empty cup to the tray. 'What have you done about that?'

'Don't worry I've already had everything checked out.' I confirm, handing him the official looking report I created and had typed up by an office services company back in Exeter. 'Apart from the odd parking ticket there's nothing to be concerned about,' I tell him confidently as I watch him scan the contents. 'Besides she's not a stranger, we were at school together. After giving birth to Josh she went back to college, got qualifications and has been working in Warner Webb for four years. Max Warner called her an exemplary employee. He'll be more than willing to give a reference regarding her character.' I assure them, 'She's raised Josh on her own too. He's a lovely child and a great credit to her.' Heaven help me. I know I'm probably heading for the fires of hell after this elaborate piece of fiction but I have to do this, there is no other way.

I field various questions from them, not able to glean anything from their closed expressions. Eventually Marcus looks at Anna then at me.

'Can you leave us for a moment?' he asks.

'I'll wait in the library,' I tell him as I get to my feet. After returning my empty cup to the tray, I leave the room hoping I've done enough to convince them both.

Twenty minutes later, Anna's head appears around the door and I follow her back to the drawing room. She seats herself back beside Marcus, who sits there quietly, leaning forward, his hands clasped between his knees, staring at the floor. Eventually, with a deep sigh, he sits back. Then with a glance at Anna he delivers his verdict.

'Anna and I have discussed this issue thoroughly and in light of what you have just told us and the paperwork you have produced, we have decided we would like you to bring Lily and Josh to Amberleigh to meet us.'

I'm totally stunned. After my heated discussion with him yesterday and the way he looked at dinner, I never expected this. I'm guessing Anna, always the peacemaker, has had a hand in this.

'Thank you,' I say, totally overwhelmed. 'I know this whole situation is most unconventional but I think when you meet them you're going to love them as much as I do. They're very special and I believe this could be a new beginning for me.'

'A new beginning for us all, I think,' Anna says, reaching for Marcus's hand and squeezing it gently.

LILY

Talún picked us up early this morning. He was driving a black Range Rover with tinted windows and I asked him if he'd changed the Lexus. He simply grinned and said this was just one of the many cars they had at Amberleigh.

'How many are there then?' I asked, curious.

'Oh, six or seven. They're pool vehicles for the estate and the stud. Marcus and Anna have their own cars and I've an Aston Martin. I simply thought the Range Rover would be more comfortable for Josh to travel in. There's a DVD player built into the back of the passenger headrest and I've brought some movies I think he'll enjoy.'

He did too; it kept him quiet for a lot of the journey and he slept for the rest. As for me, well, I guess I was nervous although I wasn't about to bombard Talún with questions about his grandparents. Instead I asked general stuff about the estate and what exactly he did at the stud. He talked about his university days, of how his mother's disappearance had caused him to throw away his first opportunity to get his degree. Amberleigh changed all that. He went back and achieved a first class honours in his BSc in Equine and Agricultural Management. So as well as handsome, he's clever too and, of course, he has shedloads of money. And as for sex, well there was a time when, in order to survive, I had to do stuff I'm not especially proud of with men who made my flesh creep. Leo Hayden was one of those, although he never got to touch me in an intimate way. Thank God I didn't end up going to Scotland with him. No, even if Talún doesn't have the same effect on me he seems to have on females generally, he has looks and a great body. When the time comes for us to get it together I'll simply close my eyes and think of Zac. Ah, if only he hadn't been such a bastard, what a life we might have had together. But it is what it is.

After a break for lunch just outside Reading we resumed

our journey, reaching Amberleigh by late afternoon. Well, if I'd been in awe of Lynbrook Hall, I was totally gobsmacked as we turned in through high black gates and headed down a tree-lined driveway bordered by parkland...and deer! When I asked how big the house was in comparison to Lynbrook, Talún told me there were nine reception rooms and thirteen bedrooms. There is also a large indoor pool, sauna, gym and cinema room. All the creature comforts required for an affluent lifestyle. I just know I'm going to love it here. Eventually the house came into view and he's right, it's enormous and could swallow up Lynbrook several times quite easily.

As we pulled up I could see two people - a man and a woman - coming down the elegant sweep of steps from the front door. This was it. Although Talún had tried to convince me they were looking forward to meeting me, I was under no illusions they probably thought I'd trapped him into this marriage. Which, of course, was pretty much the truth of the matter.

I think I sussed Marcus out as soon as I met him. After all, men are a pushover, aren't they? There aren't many who don't respond to a little flirting. I didn't wheel out the charm straight away though. I was quiet as Talún made the introductions and we shook hands. Anna, however, was a completely different kettle of fish. I felt her grey eyes on me, taking everything in. If there was going to be one person I'd have to watch, sure as God made little apples it was going to be her. Eventually she smiled and stepped forward, drawing me into a hug and a waft of expensive perfume as she welcomed me to Amberleigh, saying she hoped I'd enjoy my stay.

Josh was the star of the show. His small boy chatter and winning smile went down well. Before I knew it he had slipped his tiny hand in Marcus's and was accompanying him into the house. Talún smiled as he watched them go then busied himself with extracting the luggage from the boot of the car.

'Shouldn't you be leaving that for the servants?' I asked as I watched him.

'We don't have servants here, Lily. We have staff.' Anna smiled as she corrected me, but I could see from her expression I'd made a huge blunder and she wasn't best pleased. Apparently, Downton Abbey this was not. I made a note to take extra care. The last thing I wanted was to create a bad first impression. Once I'm Talún's wife, however, things will be very different.

TALÚN

It's been a brilliant weekend. I think Josh has bonded really well with Marcus and Anna. His incessant chatter and tactile way, wrapping his small arms around their shoulders and kissing them both goodnight before Lily took him up to bed, has won him a place in both their hearts.

'He's a lovely child,' Anna says with a smile as she watches them leave the room. 'He asks so many questions and he's full of fun, never grumpy. Everyone here adores him already.'

'And Lily?' I ask. 'You like her too?'

'I think she's a little overwhelmed by it all,' Anna replies with one of her quiet smiles, and I get the feeling something has happened I don't know about. 'But I'm sure she'll settle in well once she's here permanently,' she reassures me.

I see Lily again on our way to breakfast the next morning. As she comes along the landing towards me, Josh is holding tightly onto her hand. Despite being hugely excited about the pony I've chosen for him, he's still clutching his toy dragon.

'I couldn't get Josh off to sleep last night,' Lily says, explaining her absence after last night's dinner. 'Ended up reading to him until well after nine and then...well... I felt absolutely bushed so had a bath and an early night.'

'Marcus was looking forward to another game of backgammon with you too.'

'Ah well, I can make up for lost time when we move in,' she says with a smile.

'Have you enjoyed your weekend?' After Anna's comments last evening it's important for me to find out exactly how Lily feels.

'Me? Yes of course. There's such a lot to take in,' she rolls her eyes, 'and it's going to be a completely different life but,' she adds, 'I know I'm going to absolutely love it.'

LILY

I'm back home at last and it looks as though Marcus and Anna have given the nod to us moving there. I think the weekend went pretty well although I've mixed feelings about Amberleigh. It's a great place and my room, well, it was to die for. A walk in wardrobe, sunken bath and gorgeous four poster bed! Yes, I felt really spoilt. But I don't think it could ever feel like home. Not with Anna there. She's so nice to the servants... and yes, I am going to call them servants. Bugger her! Because that's what they are. How the hell is she going to let them know who is boss when she treats them all like old mates? It's not the way to do things... well, not my way anyhow.

Yesterday afternoon Marcus showed us over the stud. The horses scared me a bit, but dressing up in tight jodhpurs appealed to me. The girls looked very sexy. Which brings me to another issue. There are a lot of attractive girls there, meaning rather too much temptation for my husband to be. What makes things worse is he seems to have taken a leaf out of Anna's book, you know, the way he is with them... just a little too friendly for my liking.

On Saturday morning while Anna kept Josh entertained, Talún took me to visit the Tindersley Hall Hotel, about twenty minutes away from Amberleigh. He'd booked an appointment with the wedding planner there and said he'd leave me to discuss my requirements while he went to meet a client. It took me completely by surprise. I didn't know what to expect and I thought, what if I don't like it? A bit of a difficult one that, as he was footing the bill. But I needn't have worried, it was fabulous. An old red brick manor house set in beautiful grounds and facing a lake with woods beyond. Natalie, the wedding planner, was really attentive, taking me through all the different package options before showing me around. The place is to die for and when Talún turned up to collect me I could see by his smile he was pleased I was happy with his choice. I couldn't stop talking about the things we'd discussed. I've another appointment booked to see her to finalise choices once Josh and I have moved here – it's going to be such a special day. It made me realise my dream is suddenly becoming a reality...so exciting!

On a more sobering note, tomorrow is going to be one of the most difficult days of my life. I have to see Max and explain what's happened between me and Talún...and, of course, I'll be handing in my resignation. I dread to think what he'll make of it all and I'm not sure why I should care about what he thinks. I'm moving on, and up, but I still can't help feel slightly uneasy about it all.

JESS

Anna's returned. I got a text saying she'd be arriving back at the Hall later this evening. I thought it strange she'd also asked me to come up to finish off the tour tomorrow morning. Surely she had better things to do than spend time showing me bedrooms and bathrooms. I'm wondering if there's an ulterior motive, something specific she wants to talk to me about, and whether it has anything to do with her emergency trip back to Norfolk last week.

LILY

Max is furious.

'Talún is Josh's father? Are you for real? How the hell has this all come about, Lily?' I sit in his office holding my breath as he paces backwards and forwards in front of me. 'Well?' he whips around to face me, his face filled with anger and something else...pain.

'It was at a party five years ago. It was only the one

136

night. We were both drunk. By the time I realised I was pregnant he'd left the area. No one had any idea where he had gone.' Well, it's half the truth I think, as I stare brazenly back at him.

'And now he turns up, every inch the rich playboy and you present him with a son. Very convenient Lily.'

'What are you casting me as? Some opportunistic gold digger?' I try to sound indignant but really I'm feeling panicky. Max is no one's fool and I wonder whether there's some hidden knowledge he has about me I'm not aware of. He runs his fingers through his hair and moves over to where I'm sitting, lodging himself on the edge of his desk.

'No of course not.' He shakes his head, pushing his knuckles against his mouth as he lets out a deep breath. 'I guess I hate the feeling of you and Josh not being here anymore.'

'We can always come back and visit,' I try to sound upbeat as I reach out to stroke his arm. 'After all, it's not as if I'll be living abroad.'

'Are you sure Josh is his?' he says. 'I mean, he doesn't look anything like him.'

'Absolutely,' I confirm with a nod. 'Talún arranged for a DNA test to be carried out, the result was positive.'

'I just can't get my head around it.' He's running fingers through his hair again and I know this is a sign of some pent up emotion he's trying to keep a lid on. Pushing himself off the desk, he reaches for me, pulling me up into his arms. 'I'm going to miss you both, every single day,' he says, looking down into my face as I see his eyes begin to mist with tears. 'Please, don't lose touch.'

'I won't,' I whisper back. 'I promise.' Another lie.

He kisses my cheek and lets me go. The intimacy of the moment vanishes and we're back in our respective roles once more.

'We'll talk more tomorrow,' he says as he shows me out. 'Sort out the details.'

I nod silently and leave, and as his door closes I realise although I'm going to have the most amazing life, I'm going to miss Max more than I ever expected I would.

I've just finished my tour of the Hall. The bedrooms and five bathrooms are fabulous. Each one has a different theme, from Victorian roll top to sunken tubs, with swathes of Italian marble on the walls and floors. A fortune has been spent here by Anna's grandson and, sadly, he'll never get to enjoy any of it.

'So much attention to detail,' I say, as we make our way downstairs, 'and yet your grandson doesn't plan to live here.'

'There's a possibility things may change,' she tells me, and just when I'm expecting her to expand on this statement she says, 'are we up for lunch at the Bull?'

'Only if I'm still allowed to pay,' I insist.

'All right,' she says, giving in without a protest with an expression which indicates her mind is elsewhere.

'Anna, are you okay?' I ask, noticing she's looking quite pale.

'I'll be fine,' she says, giving my arm a squeeze. 'Something has happened and I'm simply in need of company and a sympathetic ear, that's all.'

It's a lovely warm May day and Rufus picks a table for us out on the covered patio area overlooking the cricket field. He's made up a jug of Pimms and serves us with a glass each as we check out the menu. Eventually Anna begins to open up to me.

'It's about my return to Amberleigh a few days ago,' she says, lowering her menu.

I wait for her to continue, wondering whether she's about to tell me there are problems with Marcus's health. Maybe he's just been diagnosed with a heart condition....'

'It's my grandson,' she interrupts my thoughts and I'm relieved at least Marcus is okay. 'He was married to Fliss, a lovely girl, and they had a baby, Emily. Then the most awful thing happened. They were travelling home from ours one evening and there was a crash...a deer hit the car. Fliss was driving, she lost control, and the vehicle collided with a tree and turned over. My grandson survived. Fliss and Emily were killed. That was two years ago and he's been adrift ever since.'

'I'm so sorry, Anna, how awful,' I say, trying to imagine what he must have gone through.

'The thing is,' she takes a sip of her Pimms before continuing, 'he's met this young woman he had a relationship with long before he met Fliss. It turns out he had a son by her.'

'One he never knew about?'

She nods. 'I returned home because this has huge implications for us and Marcus wanted my help and advice. My grandson organised a DNA test which proved positive and he has accepted responsibility for the little boy...Josh. I persuaded Marcus we should invite them to stay for the weekend. My grandson was so pleased and Marcus and I, well, we both decided to have an open mind about it all and welcome them.'

'And..?'

'The little lad's a delight, full of life. A really sweet child.'

'But it's his mother you have reservations about.'

Anna nods. 'I'm afraid I do. I did try really hard not to have prejudices. I realise she's come from a poor background and yes, she's a hard working mother and the child is a credit to her parenting skills but...there's something about her that worries me. I guess I was so used to Fliss. She was such a kind-hearted, affectionate girl. Very tactile too. This one, well she's got no warmth about her at all. In fact, I find her slightly arrogant. She seems to have bonded with Marcus though, even plays backgammon with him. He's really taken with her...thinks I'm an idiot.' She expels a deep sigh. 'Towards the end of her stay she began openly disagreeing in front of everyone with things I said. In fact, I found her petty and quite spiteful.' She shrugs and smiles. 'Pathetic, isn't it, letting some young woman get under my skin?'

'But she's not just some young woman, is she? She's the mother of your grandson's child.' I reply, reaching across the table and giving her hand a comforting squeeze. 'I expect you were hoping she'd be like Fliss and you'd get on amazingly well. Maybe she felt uncomfortable, you know, big house, rich people. Give her another chance. I'm sure when she's spent more time with you, she'll be completely different. After all, what's not to like?'

She smiles, amused, and I'm glad I've cheered her up. I'm not sure what to make of her grandson's new woman but I'm hoping all this is simply a storm in a teacup. From what she's told me about life in Norfolk, they seem a close knit family and I would hate someone to come in and spoil that. However, in defence of the girlfriend, I'm guessing meeting someone as calm and confident as Anna, might have been slightly intimidating. In a new and completely foreign environment, it's possible it could quite easily have triggered the wrong sort of reaction.

'So, I guess your grandson will be supporting her and the child...Josh...from now on,' I say, moving the conversation on.

'Oh my dear, things are far more serious than that. He's asked her to marry him. They're engaged.'

I nod, taking in this new information. I can see why she's a little concerned. Everything is happening far too quickly. I only hope everything works out for Anna's grandson but worryingly his situation has a definite feel of being caught on the rebound.

TALÚN

I'm missing my new family already and can't wait to be with them again. Lily called to say she's given in her notice at Warner Webb. Max has very generously allowed her to leave after a fortnight instead of a month. Two weeks. It seems a lifetime away. With my grandmother back in Lynbrook, Marianne and I have been sorting out the accommodation for my new family. I've allocated Josh his own suite of rooms, which Lily will be able to redecorate and choose new furnishings for once she's here. As this whole situation has been rather thrust on my grandparents, out of respect we've both decided to keep to

140

separate rooms until the wedding. We have talked about when and where and she wants to be married at Christmas. We've agreed on St. Swithin's, in the village. She also says she wants to plan her own wedding without any assistance from Anna. I think she finds her a little scary and maybe thinks she might take things over and push her into having something she doesn't want. I hope she changes her mind, my grandmother is a calm, supportive woman and the last person who would try and muscle in on anyone else's project. Weddings, even basic ones, are expensive these days. I want her to have a really special day and the budget I've allocated reflects that. I set up an appointment for her at Tindersley Hall Hotel and she's already had an initial consultation and is due to see them again once she moves here.

And now it's all about waiting and being patient for them both to join me. I know this whole thing is slightly irregular but I'm sure the three of us will have a good life together. I've been given a second chance at happiness and to hell with the circumstances. I'm grabbing it with both hands.

LILY

Today is the first day of the rest of my life. And what a day! I'm saying goodbye to everything I've known. It's like shedding a skin. I've disposed of my furniture, paid all my utility bills and rent and, as they say, I'm outta here. I had a farewell night out with Sonya and Chloe, plus the inevitable leaving do with members of the Warner Webb team. They'd managed to get a temp in to cover my job until they could recruit a replacement, so I was busy with her for most of the week.

I dreaded the end of the day because there was one person I was going to hate saying goodbye to: Max. I knew my leaving had upset him. I was so surprised he had reduced my notice to a fortnight, saying it was a personal gift to enable me to join Talún earlier than planned. But ever since then he'd been very quiet and seemed to have been avoiding me. I now realise his generosity at letting me go early is because I've hurt him badly and he wanted me gone as soon as possible. As five-thirty arrived and people began leaving for the day, I was treated to a barrage of hugs and good luck wishes. Nick was the last to leave and as the front door closed behind him, Max appeared in his office doorway shrugging on his coat. Closing the distance between us, he stood there for a moment, gathering his thoughts.

'This is it then,' he said, looking at me sadly. 'I can't believe you're going.'

'It was bound to happen eventually,' I told him. 'If Talún hadn't turned up I probably would have met someone else.'

'True, but he'd probably be from around here and you wouldn't be leaving me.' His voice wavered and he looked absolutely wretched, and then, quite unexpectedly, he threw his arms around me, pulling me into a fierce hug. 'Don't you *dare* forget me, Lily.' I felt his choked whisper against my ear. 'And remember, if you ever need anyone I'll always be here.'

'Thank you,' I said, and as he broke our embrace I began to feel quite emotional. I needed to get a grip, this wasn't like me. The way this big man looked so vulnerable and lost, tears gathering in his eyes, really affected me. I knew I had to do something before this all spiralled out of control.

Taking a deep breath, I smiled and reached up to give him a quick peck on the cheek.

'You're very special, Max.' I said, as I breathed in his expensive cologne and gradually brought my emotions under control. 'Thank you for all you've done for me. I'll never forget you.' Then I snatched my bag from the desk and fled, not daring to look back.

TALÚN

Lily and Josh have been here for three weeks now. Josh has settled in really well and all the staff adore him. Lily, however, is a different matter. Part of me is feeling very protective of her. Our lifestyle at Amberleigh is worlds away from her nine-to-five at Warner Webb and the life of a single mother she's been used to. I wanted to give her space, to let her find her feet and settle in but we've already run into a few problems.

It began as soon as we arrived. Anna had lined up a temporary nanny for Josh but unfortunately, Lily wasn't at all happy with this arrangement. She didn't say anything to Anna directly but told me this was our son and she should be the one to decide who looked after him. I understood how she felt but pointed out the fact Anna was only trying to help. However, as far as Lily was concerned this wasn't help, it was all about Anna taking over. Although we've already advertised for someone permanent, Lily wanted Anna's choice gone straight away. She insisted she'd look after Josh in the meantime and do the interviews for the new nanny on her own.

As Josh was learning to ride I suggested it would be a good idea if she too began lessons at Amberleigh's riding school. Living in a rural community, I told her, riding is a must, and although at first she was reluctant she eventually agreed. I hoped it would provide a distraction and stop her from constantly complaining about Anna's so-called interference. Her progress hasn't been as good as Josh's - he seems a natural - but Jason, her instructor, seems quite pleased with her. However, any chance it would ease the animosity towards Anna turned out to be a false hope.

The next issue was over clothes. One of the first things she asked for when she arrived was a clothes allowance. I know she's fashion conscious and it's great to see her looking good so I arranged a credit card for her right away. She began making regular trips into Norwich with Ralph, our driver, returning loaded with bags and boxes. I know this has not gone unnoticed by Anna but to be fair her only comment has been "your money, your business". Lily, however, insists although Anna never says anything, what she calls her disapproving looks are as bad as any verbal criticism.

Then Lily made an appointment to visit a bridal

couturier in London, to look at wedding dresses. Despite having told me the new nanny was due next week, an hour after she left a tall thin homely girl with short brown hair arrived complete with luggage. Thea McGovern assured us today was her agreed start date. A call to the agency also confirmed this had been the day agreed with Lily. It therefore fell to Anna to put her morning's work on hold to sort out the new arrival. On her return Lily checked her diary, admitted she'd got the date wrong and apologised to Anna, who simply shook her head and walked away.

Finally, this morning I took Lily to look at cars. Apart from my Aston Martin, Hawkeswood Estate runs a fleet of Range Rovers. Marcus and Anna are happy with this and see no need to change the brand. After some consideration Lily decided to test drive an Evoque. However as soon as we walked into the showroom I knew straight away by the expression on her face she'd changed her mind. The salesman was very helpful, persuading her to sit behind the wheel as he explained its main features. However, when she eventually vacated the car she took one last look at it before telling me, 'Actually, I think I'd prefer an Audi.'

Once she saw the Q7 nothing would persuade her from having this huge SUV. I did argue for a smaller vehicle but when she threw Josh's safety into the argument I knew I was onto a loser. I only hope Anna will understand. I rub a tired hand over my face. Two women under the same roof are turning out to be damned hard work. But it's early days yet and I'm not a quitter. Things will eventually settle down, I'm sure.

LILY

I have my car and I love it. I had to fight to get it though. Talún and interfering Anna had definite choices in mind; not that he'd force anything on me but, well, the moment we walked into the Audi dealer and I saw this huge impressive white vehicle I knew it was exactly what I wanted.

'It's far too big, Lily.' He stood pursing his lips

thoughtfully as he gazed at it. 'The Q5 would be better,' he said, nodding towards the smaller blue vehicle next to it.

'The thing is,' I said with a sigh, pushing my face into its most serious expression, 'I need to feel Josh is safe when he's travelling with me. This might look like a bus but behind the wheel I feel we'll both be secure.' I emphasised my determination, stroking my fingers along the paintwork as I gave him my best "pretty please" look.

He caved in immediately. It appears I've only got to mention concern for Josh and he'll jump through hoops. Oh yes, he'll do anything for me if it concerns his boy.

Over dinner he raised the subject of my newly acquired, soon to be delivered baby.

Anna looked up from her meal, eyebrows raised in surprise, as she glanced first at him then at me. 'But I thought we'd agreed on the Evoque,' she said with a frown.

'Change of plan,' my wonderful fiancé said, smiling across the table at me. 'Lily says with Josh on board she feels safer behind the wheel of the Audi than the Evoque and, well, I'm inclined to agree.'

Anna never mentioned the subject again but I knew she wasn't happy having her authority challenged. Although she was friendly with me when all the family were together, if I was on my own she gave me a wide berth. I hoped she's learned a lesson - that unlike the saintly Fliss, who probably did everything she was told, I'm someone with a mind of my own. A few days later the witch went back to Lynbrook and her supervision of the Hall's refurbishment. Free of her influence around the place, I felt I could relax, but it turned out I was wrong.

Yesterday I went for my Tuesday morning riding lesson. I still can't resist posing in front of the mirror with my gear on. I have to say I look and feel amazing. Who would ever have thought jodhpurs could be so sexy? All the other girls in the yard wear ankle boots but once I'd seen the knee length ones I had to have them. White shirt and green quilted body warmer complete the look. Oh, and my hair's tied back into a fat plait, courtesy of nanny Thea. Well, at least she's good for something other than child minding.

I've been allocated a short blond guy called Jason, who Talún tells me is the best riding instructor they have. This morning when I turned up at what is called the riding arena – a big indoor barn really – I noticed Josh over in the corner with his instructor, Lauren Goodyear. My son is totally smitten with his new pony, Liquorice, and all I'd heard about was Lauren. On my first visit here I had noticed the number of attractive young women working in the stables. Lauren, with her short dark curly hair and easy smile was definitely one of the prettiest.

'How long has Lauren been here?' I posed my question to Jason quite innocently. He looked down the far end of the indoor riding arena where she was holding onto the pony's head as she chatted to Josh.

'Oh, about three years I think.' He looked back at me with a grin. 'Nice girl, a good choice for Josh too. She's got a lot of patience, knows how to handle kids.'

After a general discussion about what we would be doing in today's lesson, I fastened my riding hat and he helped me mount the chestnut he had earmarked for me. He made a few adjustments to the stirrups and then just as I was about to move off, Talún arrived, waved out to us both and headed over towards Lauren and Josh. I sat for a moment watching, annoyed he hadn't come over to see me first. He reached Josh and made a fuss of the pony before beginning a conversation with Lauren. They laughed together, obviously sharing a joke. It seemed a harmless gesture but as he turned to leave he leaned towards her, cupped his hand around her shoulder, and whispered something in her ear. She paused for a moment, checked her watch and then nodded. Immediately I was suspicious. What were they up to? Was he seeing her behind my back?

'She seems to get on well with Talún,' I remarked as I watched him walk away.

'Oh yes, they're great mates. Everyone thought after Fliss died they might get together,' Jason said with a grin as he watched Lauren resume her lesson with Josh. 'But it never happened. Still it's all water under the bridge now,' he added reassuringly. 'Because he's marrying you, isn't

146

he?'

'Yes,' I agreed, my eyes fixed on this new threat. 'Of course he is.'

JESS

Anna's back again. She returned to Norfolk for a couple of weeks, asking Krister to supervise the work on the Hall in her absence. We make arrangements to meet at our usual place by the river. It's mid-May now and so much warmer, with huge swathes of bluebells beginning to cover the floor of the wood; a colourful contrast to the multi-colour patchwork of green in the trees above. I'm at my usual spot, perched on the large flat boulder overlooking the river. It's a sunny morning and already there's a sparkle on the water as it tumbles over the rocks. I watch Anna's approach. She lifts a hand and waves a greeting as she emerges from the trees riding a beautiful grey stallion, obviously another acquisition for the Lynbrook Hall Stud.

Joining me on the rock, she sits for a while, immersing herself in a stillness broken only by the rush of the river. I break the silence, eager for news. First the horse; he really is a beautiful specimen.

'Ah, the gorgeous Achilles,' she says, watching him affectionately as he crops grass beside Caspar. 'Yes, he arrived yesterday. He's my grandson's horse. He absolutely adores him.'

It suddenly occurs to me Anna has never actually mentioned her grandson by name. 'Do you realise,' I say, amused, 'in all the time we've talked together, you've only ever referred to him as "my grandson"?'

The moment I ask the question I detect a slight panic behind her calm, controlled exterior. I watch as she takes a breath then looks across at me and allows herself a smile. 'Ah well,' she gives an amused laugh, 'there's a good reason for that. It's Marcus, you see, the same as his grandfather. I simply wanted to avoid confusing you.'

'Well, how about we call your husband Marcus and your grandson Junior?' I suggest, making light of the situation, still not sure what she's told me is actually the truth.

'Junior.' She shakes her head and laughs. 'Makes him sound like a small boy in short trousers, doesn't it? But if it's easier for you, then Junior it is.' We both laugh.

'So has Junior's fiancée moved in?' I ask with a grin.

'Yes.'

'Any better?'

'Not really, but difficult as it is, I've made myself promise not to interfere.'

'There are still issues then?' I hesitate for a moment. 'Sorry,' I say, 'it's none of my business really.'

'Don't be silly.' She reaches over and gives my arm a reassuring pat. 'It's lovely to have you to talk to. You know, *really* talk to. You listen, you don't pass judgement and well, you're so sensible.'

I accept her compliments, feeling rather embarrassed. Rufus is always telling me I'm twenty-four going on forty. An old head on young shoulders is his description. Well, that may be true now, but when Talún left me my sensible self rather fell off the wagon. It took Roo several months of patience and hard work to persuade me away from the destructive path I had taken.

'It's all down to taking a leaf out of Roo's book,' I tell her, as his face looms in my mind. 'I had a bad emotional experience when I was eighteen and he helped me get through it. Through him I learned a lot about calmness and common sense.'

'Yes you told me,' she nods, 'when you discovered Rufus was your father.'

'No, it was something completely different. I fell in love that summer. Passionately in love. But things went badly wrong. I won't go into detail but let's just say we parted and I never heard from him again.'

'You loved him very much?'

'Totally. Even at eighteen I instinctively knew he was the one. We were so good together...' my voice trails off as I look out over the water, memories of those days returning, 'but sadly it seems my judgement was flawed.'

'I am sorry, Jess.'

'Yes, so am I,' I respond, aware ever since my return unwanted memories of Talún seem to be slowly filtering back into my life.

TALÚN

Anna went back to Lynbrook a week ago. The house is nearly finished and a few more horses have been delivered to my fledgling stud. This includes Achilles, seventeen hands of fabulous grey horseflesh purchased last year from a friend of Anna's who lives in Shropshire.

Lily, as usual when Anna's not around, is much happier. I know she finds it difficult, seeing my grandmother as some controlling matriarch. However, this is so far from the truth. If only she could understand running a large house, a stud and all the other one thousand and one things she does to support my grandfather is a responsibility she takes very seriously. Trying to reason with Lily only seems to end in tears with accusations she is the victim in all of this. Something that began as a petty domestic issue has gradually spiralled out of control and is beginning to affect everyone here. Lily will never make peace with Anna and that means one thing: we can no longer stay here. The only alternative is to return to Lynbrook, the one thing I had hoped to avoid.

LILY

Thank goodness that awful woman has gone back to her bloody building project. At least now she's no longer here I can do what I like. Actually, I need to take another trip to London. The couturier has received a new delivery of dresses which she's anxious to show me and I need my hair cut. Gone are the days when I booked into my local salon. Today I'm a regular customer of one of the top celebrity hairdressers. I might have to pay a small fortune but...well...Talún can afford it and besides, he likes me looking good. Lately, however, I have a sneaky feeling he's taking more than a casual interest in my spending. He doesn't actually say anything, rather it's the expression on his face, the way he sucks in a breath very gently, or the slight lift of his eyebrows when I show him my latest purchases. I swear he's beginning to morph into Anna! So to get him off my back, the other day I took Josh out and bought him a whole load of new clothes. Obviously, the first thing he wanted to do was to take Talún to his room to show him. I let them have their moment together but did sneak a look through the partially open door. The rapt expression on my husband-to-be's face as Josh showed him his incredibly expensive new trainers was priceless. It seems my son is the perfect distraction when I need to keep the world spinning the way I want.

While Talún was away in Ireland looking for stock for the stud at Lynbrook, Lauren had an accident...or rather one of her pupils did. No one is sure why the girth on Justin Danvers' saddle hadn't been secured properly. Niall Collins, the stable manager, had to call for an ambulance and the nine-year-old was taken off to hospital with a badly fractured right arm. Lauren was horrified and couldn't imagine how it had happened. She always checked the girth, she said. Obviously not well enough otherwise she would have discovered what I had done.

As Anna was away in Lynbrook, I used her absence to my advantage. Over breakfast with Marcus the next morning I briefly mentioned what had happened. I was calm and careful with my words as I explained she was Josh's instructor and after the accident I no longer felt confident letting her have responsibility for him. He was very non-committal but said he would look into it.

Then, just before ten, Justin's mother phoned Marcus to complain. She'd had a call, she said, from another concerned mother, and although she understood it was an accident she didn't want Lauren teaching her son any longer. Two of her friends also had daughters being looked after by Lauren, she told him, and they would be approaching Niall to ask for a new instructor. I was listening behind the breakfast room door and as soon as I heard Marcus put the phone down I walked through into the hall to join him. He looked very concerned as he told me about the conversation he'd just had. Her husband was an important client, he told me, and news of the accident was already spreading.

'Ah well, let's get it over with,' he gave a resigned sigh as he fished his car keys from his pocket. 'It's a shame, she was a damned good instructor.'

Of course she was, I agreed silently. But she was also an unwanted temptation for my husband to be so she had to go.

TALÚN

Returning from Ireland, I've walked into a storm. Lauren sacked, and Anna waiting in my office for me with the kind of expression that says she needs to talk to me urgently.

'Close the door please,' she says quietly as I walk in and drop my wax jacket over the back of my chair.

'Is it about Lauren?' I ask as I lean against the desk, waiting to hear what has happened in my absence.

'No, unfortunately that's done and dusted,' she says with an annoyed huff. From the look on her face I can see she's none too pleased the decision to fire Lauren was taken in her absence. 'Marcus sanctioned her dismissal. But what else could he do? The news was spreading like wildfire.' She waves a frustrated hand. 'We'd had an angry Mrs. Danvers on the phone and as you know, her husband, Philip, is a crucial part of your grandfather's export business. Besides, the parents of other children Lauren taught were ringing up and demanding new instructors. We were in a difficult situation.'

'And where is she now?'

'I have no idea. Niall sacked her four days ago and she left immediately.'

'I need to speak to her,' I say, pulling my mobile from my jacket pocket and skimming through my phone book to find her number. 'Something's wrong here. You and I both know Lauren was one of the most safety conscious instructors working in the riding school'

Anna's hand reaches across and gently closes over the phone. 'It won't achieve anything,' she says with a shake of her head, 'and besides, we all make mistakes, Talún. None of us are perfect. I'm as saddened as you are, but we have to leave it and move on.'

'So, what did you want to talk to me about?' I ask, as I slip my phone back in my jacket and perch myself on the end of my desk. 'Ah, of course, Lily.'

'Talún, please,' She shakes her head, 'I don't want to fall out with you over this, but—'

'What has she done this time?'

Anna walks over to the window and stares out into darkening grey skies which herald the approach of rain. 'Everyone has tried incredibly hard to welcome her, to ease her into her new life,' she says quietly. 'However...'

'Get to the point please.' I have never raised my voice to Anna before but having a first class riding instructor and great friend sent away in disgrace has resulted in this anger I'm currently feeling. Had either of us been here, the outcome could have been so different. And as if that were not enough, now I'm about to hear my wife-to-be's latest failings.

Anna turns calmly and props herself against the window, folding her arms and watching me. She's about to open her mouth to speak when I interrupt.

'You don't like her, do you?' It's a statement rather than a question and, as they say the best form of defence is attack, I'm getting in first. 'You never have. Ever since she arrived here, you and everyone else has given no thought to what's she's been through. Five years on her own, first carrying Josh, then giving birth, and afterwards the hardest part of all, raising him as a single parent. She's done a damn good job and if she feels like going out and being extravagant, as you love to call it, well it's not a problem. As far as I'm concerned she deserves every penny she spends on herself.'

'It's not just the spending.' Anna pushes herself from the window and walks around to where I'm still leaning against the desk. 'There are other issues.'

'What other issues?'

'Her attitude towards the staff here. She's becoming very high handed. Only two days ago she had a very public spat with Joyce in the laundry room. Apparently a dress had not come back from the dry cleaners on time.' She raises her hands. 'Hardly Joyce's fault, was it?' When I fail to comment she continues. 'Meals have become another fractious area. Food is either under cooked, over cooked, sauces are too salty, too bland. I've lost count of the number of times she's sent her meal back with Marianne and requested something different.' She shakes her head. 'This isn't just about us. You may feel we're not giving her enough support but, believe me, she's a difficult individual for anyone to get close to.'

'Especially you.'

'Especially me, and believe me, I have been extremely patient with her.'

'Your problem,' I say, pushing myself off the desk, 'is you're comparing her to Fliss and that's not fair. Their backgrounds are entirely different.'

'Talún, you are so wrong. Like everyone else here, all I wanted to do was welcome her and help her settle in. But somehow I get the feeling it's not what she wants.'

'What does she want then, Anna?' I demand, feeling it's about time we got all this out into the open.

'Quite simply, I don't think Lily likes her role here. In fact, I'd go as far as saying she wants to be the one in charge and giving the orders.'

'Well, she spent four years at Warner Webb with no problems. Max told me she was an exemplary employee.'

'Max Warner was probably wrapped around her little finger.' She shakes her head and smiles. 'Just the way she has you now.'

'Me? That's a crazy accusation. I told you, I'm trying to make up for what she went through.'

'In the worst possible way. You've over indulged her and cut her far too much slack, Talún, and you're gradually losing control.'

153

'Oh rubbish,' I snap, annoyed she's talking to me as if I have no idea what I'm doing. Anna shakes her head and looks away. 'What?'

'Talún, you need to take a step back and really look at the situation.'

'The situation?' I say. 'Which is what exactly?'

'The obsession with shopping, her neglectful behaviour with Josh—'

'She does not neglect Josh,' I cut across her words angrily. 'She's a good mother.'

'So that's the reason Thea is the one who's with him all the time, is it? Why he's suddenly taking all his meals in his room. Poor girl, she never gets a break. And I know I said I wouldn't interfere in your money matters but I think you ought to be aware—'

'Enough!' I raise my hand. 'I don't want to hear any more of this constant criticism. I'm beginning to feel it might be better for everyone if we left and made our own lives somewhere else. It's obvious to me living together has become impossible. You and Lily will never find common ground—'

'Not from lack of trying on my part,' she interrupts, but I choose to ignore her and continue.

'Once Lynbrook Hall is ready, I'll arrange to move us there. I think it's for the best, Anna.'

'No, Talún. You belong here.' I can see from her shocked expression my decision has upset her. '

'Yes I know I do, but if we're to have peace in the family, I have no choice.'

LILY

I think something has happened between Anna and Talún. They were both unusually quiet over dinner this evening. He did ask me whether Josh would be having dinner with us but I made the excuse he'd been out with Thea all day visiting the Dinosaur Adventure Park at Lenwade and was dog tired. Personally, I think now Thea is in charge, the less we see of him the better. I like my life as it is, child free

154

but with "mama moments" when it suits me. He's got a fantastic life and he's happy, so my conscience is totally clear. I did suggest that it might be a good idea if Talún checked on him after dinner and perhaps read him a story if he's still awake. He's becoming even more the doting father and I'm keen for this to continue. I know he's already smitten, but I want this father-son bond water-tight. It's not only about Josh either. If anything – heaven forbid - should go wrong I want to be able to guarantee my future too. When I suggested a pre-nup, Talún said he'd think about it. I'm hoping he doesn't ask Anna for her thoughts because I'm sure she'll probably persuade him it's a bad idea. I'm desperate to secure a financial deal because if things go wrong I need to come out of this smiling.

Once the evening meal was over, Anna returned to the stud to check on a mare that was about to foal and Marcus left for one of his many committee meetings in Norwich. Which left me alone with Talún, and I couldn't wait to find out what had been going on.

'Have you two had words?' I asked, as Marianne finished clearing the table and left the room.

'Why do you ask?'

'There was a definite atmosphere during dinner, you hardly spoke, or made eye contact. Is it something I've done?'

'Of course not.' He brushed away the suggestion as if it was a ridiculous notion. 'I've come to an important decision, that's all and I think it's come as a bit of a shock to Anna.'

'What sort of decision?' I said, chewing my bottom lip nervously. Had there been a row over my spending, I wondered. Or had she been telling him I wasn't paying Josh much attention these days? No, if Anna was shocked about anything, it was probably because Talún had done something totally out of character. And then he told me.

'I want us to move to Lynbrook Hall,' he said with a smile, 'once the renovations are complete.'

'You want us to go back to Devon? Honestly?' I felt a smile spreading across my face as he nodded.

'Things simply aren't working out here the way I thought they would. I think we need our own home.'

I looked at him not daring to speak. Although he's making light of it, I can see the tension in his face. It's obvious they've had an argument over me and he's come down firmly on my side. I want to punch the air. Not only will I be getting away from interfering Anna, I'm going to be moving into my dream home.

'I've already chosen the furniture.' I hear him telling me, 'but if there's anything you don't like, we can get it replaced.'

'No, no I'm sure I'll love everything,' I said, getting to my feet and walking around to where he stood with his back against the window. I hovered for a moment, excitement fizzing through me, and then threw my arms around his neck and kissed his cheek.

'Hey!' He prised my hands away. 'I think I deserve a bit more than just a peck, don't you?' he teased, tilting his head and giving one of those smiles that seem to affect every other female but me.

So I obliged, summoning up all my long-buried talents. I clung to his shoulders and delivered the kind of kiss that would make him believe I was beginning to feel something for him. Sadly, any excitement stirring in me had nothing to do with the man whose arms I was in. It had more to do with being the new mistress of Lynbrook Hall. As my fingers teased through his thick, dark hair he deepened the kiss and I wrapped my body around his, playing it like a professional. However, as he rocked me gently against his hips and I felt his arousal, I realised I may have taken my acting talents a little too far. Quickly, I pulled away from him but his eager hands reached for me again. I fussed with my hair and was all breathless embarrassment. I didn't want this; not yet. Maybe once we were living at Lynbrook, but I couldn't handle any thoughts of intimacy with him, not under this roof. No, here I was going to be squeaky clean. I had enough disapproval to cope with from Anna already.

'What's wrong?' I felt the warmth of his hands on my

shoulders and looked up to see him observing at me with a mixture of curiosity and concern.

'I don't know.' I took a step away from him, breaking our contact once more as I gathered my thoughts. 'It's just...' I began, 'well, I'm trying so hard, but living here I can't seem to relax, to let myself go.'

I found myself pulled into his arms again as he whispered into my hair, 'I know it's been difficult for you here but once we move things will be very different. I want you to be happy, Lily. You and Josh are all that matter to me.' He pulled back to look at me and I managed a smile.

'I know you do,' I said, 'and we will be. Now,' I patted his shoulder, 'hadn't you better go catch our son for his story?'

'I'm on my way,' he said, and planting a kiss on my forehead disappeared out of the door.

TALÚN

I thought leaving Amberleigh would be easy. I guess I was so wrapped up in co-ordinating with Anna, making sure the builders had vacated the Hall and everything was ready that the enormity of it didn't hit me. Currently I feel like a man hanging on a rope which is gradually slipping through his fingers because, suddenly, the magnitude of what I've decided to do has hit me like a wrecking ball. Returning to the house is one thing and I'm really looking forward to seeing what Anna's done with the stud, and getting on with building the business. The village, however, is another issue.

Today Anna and I are having lunch to talk about the best way for me to take up my new life in Lynbrook. After our recent disagreement she seems to have come to terms with my decision and we're at peace with each other once more.

'Has anyone mentioned me while you've been there?' I ask as a waiter serves our main course. I know I've asked this before but crazily it's something I still need to be sure about.

'No.' Anna shakes her head. 'But that's not to say you've ceased to exist in their minds. By the way, you must make a point of seeing George and Ellie,' she tells me as she twirls pasta around her fork. 'Transferring the deeds to them is one thing, but you need to put in an appearance.'

'I will but I'll need to be careful. I don't know how they'll react to me just turning up and once I've gone George will be straight down the Bull meaning news of my return will be everywhere.'

'Perhaps we need a different strategy then.' She says as I top up her wineglass, 'How about inviting everyone to a party at the Hall?'

'A party? Are you serious?'

'Absolutely. I can't think of a better way to meet the villagers and as I'm going to be in Lynbrook anyway I can organise the whole thing for you.'

I know Anna loves planning and today is no exception. 'We can have a huge marquee on the rear lawn and a hog roast and music...' she says as she begins to count each item off on her fingers.

'Hey, hey,' I stop her mid flow, 'slow down. It's a great idea but I think it might also give you another opportunity.'

'Opportunity?'

'To involve Lily. Get her on board. Let her help you with the organisation.'

'Talún, no,' She shakes her head. 'It simply won't work.'

'Then why not hand the whole thing over to her. As it's her new home, why not let her make all the arrangements.'

'Are you mad? She has no idea about budgeting.'

'Nevertheless, I'd like this to be her baby. Her first big social event as mistress of the Hall.'

Anna gives in graciously. I can see she's less than happy but in her usual good mannered way she accepts my decision and even offers help if she's needed. Soon, I think, all this hassle will be over. But I know the sacrifice I'm making is huge and leaving Amberleigh, a place I've grown to love, will be the most painful thing that's happened to me since the loss of my wife and daughter.

LILY

Talún must have taken leave of his senses. He's been talking to the witch and between them they've come up with the idea of a party at the Hall to announce our arrival. I was really keen on the idea, until I learnt the guests would be the villagers. I mean, I really don't want these people wandering all over my house. I understand the reason he wants this is because of his history there, leaving without saying goodbye to anyone, but I'm sure he could have found a different solution without inviting the whole damned world into our new home. Now I'm being expected to socialise with God knows who and plaster on a welcoming face. If it had been left to me I would have made a list of a few of the most important locals and invited them around for dinner instead. Worse still, he asked me if I'd like to coordinate the event – with Anna on hand to help if I need her. Of course I declined. If she's so keen to have the world and his dog invited to Lynbrook Hall then she can organise it all by herself.

JESS

It's the last week in May Anna and I are meeting for the final time. I feel quite sad her work at the Hall is now over and she'll be going back to her stud in Norfolk. She's promised to keep in touch and says she'll be coming down regularly to see how grandson Marcus is getting on with his equine projects. It's three weeks since she delivered the news about him deciding to bring his fiancée and small son here to make their home. She was very upset when she told me, but I persuaded her it was for the best. They need their own home; a place to settle and expand their family. Josh is due to start school in September and no decision has been made on where yet. I suggested he'd probably end up pre-prepping as a day pupil at my old school - St Ursula's – which is a few miles away. I tried to reassure her it was a great place and was sure he'd make a lot of new friends there.

The day has been kind to us. A beautiful morning, all blue skies and fat white clouds. The wood is at its best too, lush and green with the sound of birds everywhere. She emerges from the tree line on Achilles and I watch the huge grey pick his way down the slope towards this small open area with its arc of gravelled shore and the slab of rock which has become our eyrie.

'Everything ready for your big day?' I ask as she joins me.

'I think so.' She nods, looking exceptionally pleased with herself. 'But I couldn't have done it without all the local support I've had. Your father was fantastic; we simply sat and discussed numbers and menus and he did the rest. And then there's Adrian; the flowers he's organised are simply amazing. I've been overseeing the return of the Hall's staff too, and I'm proud to be handing over not only a beautiful house but a wonderfully supportive team.'

'I'm glad,' I say, 'it's a great start for them.'

'Yes,' she says with a thoughtful smile, her grey eyes meeting mine, 'I just hope... well, I realise my grandson is big enough to be in charge of his own life but it doesn't stop me worrying about him.'

'I'm sure he'll be fine,' I reassure her, knowing her concerns relate to the woman he plans to marry. 'And you can be sure the locals will welcome him and his fiancée, just as they have you.'

We talk for a while longer, mostly about my eco house project. Krister is working on the plans with a new architect he's found. Once they have finalised the draft designs I'm meeting them so they can run through their ideas with me.

'Junior is very interested in your building project,' she tells me. 'I think it might be a good idea for both of you to chat with him at the party. Remind me to introduce you.' She pats my knee then pauses as if having a "what's next?" moment. 'Ah, yes, I completely forgot, about our last lunch. One-thirty at the Bull, wasn't it?'

Mention of this has me checking my watch and I realise

I need to be going. We've organised a surprise for Anna and I have to get back to the pub, like now.

'Yes, that's right. Ooh sorry, have to go,' I tell her as I slip from the rock. 'I have a thousand and one things to do before then. See you later,' I call over my shoulder as I cross to where Caspar is cropping grass.

Rufus and I both wanted Anna's stay to end on a high and I think the village did her proud. She arrived dead on one-thirty, thinking it was just the two of us for lunch, only to find Rufus had closed the restaurant to the public and set out a lavish buffet in her honour. She was totally overwhelmed by not only the gesture, but the number of people who turned up to wish her a safe journey home.

'I'll be back in a week's time with Marcus,' she promised, as we said our final farewells in the car park. 'The rest of the family will be travelling down on the morning of the party.'

'We'll have a great day,' Rufus assured her. 'If there's one thing this village is good at is celebration.'

'Celebration,' she repeated with a thoughtful nod, suddenly appearing distracted. Then as quickly as it arrived she seemed to shake it off, her smile returning. 'Yes, of course, we're going to have a wonderful time.'

Watching her drive away, I asked Rufus if he had noticed her sudden change of mood.

'I realised after I'd said the word celebration maybe I'd committed a bit of a faux pas,' he said. 'I forgot, she's very close to her grandson. She's going to miss him, isn't she?'

'I guess she is,' I agreed, having a strange feeling that wasn't what had upset her. It was something else; something completely different.

JUNE 2013

TALÚN

We're leaving today and I'm putting on a positive face. I'm going back to a place where they remember me as a long-haired farm hand with an easy smile and a way with women. Not exactly the image Marcus Hawkeswood's grandson should be connected with. I have no idea what awaits me there but whatever this evening brings, I know with my grandparents and Lily by my side, I'll be fine.

Before I left I walked up to the churchyard to say my farewells to Cesca, Fliss and Emily. Since Lily and Josh's arrival my visits have become easier. It's as if their presence has put everything into perspective. I've a future to look forward to now and my memories of the past have become warm ones, all the pain has gone. As I ran my fingers along the edge of their headstones I hoped their spirits understood this was my opportunity to begin my life again. I'm only sorry it has to be so far away.

We stopped for lunch at a pub just south of St Albans. Josh, released from his booster seat, bowled out of Lily's Audi none the worse for his long journey. He was bright eyed and excited, wanting to know if Liquorice had arrived safely and was being looked after in his new stable. I told him he not only had a brand new stall but a new groom, Sadie, to look after him. Thea emerged from the back of Lily's car and joined us. Lily made a great choice when she employed her; she's everything a nanny should be: patient, kind and totally devoted to Josh.

Lily on the other hand, has been very quiet. I think the closer we get the more she's beginning to realise exactly what moving into Lynbrook Hall means. At Amberleigh she was free to come and go as she pleased: a life with absolutely no responsibilities. Now things are about to change dramatically, although Anna tells me there is a great supportive staff in place to help her.

We both watch as Thea takes Josh off to the play area

where he makes a bee line for the slide. It seems to be the appropriate moment for me to discover what's wrong.

'Lily, are you worried about our move Lynbrook?' I ask, hoping she'll open up to me.

'No, why?' she says, fixing her pale blue eyes on me curiously as if she wonders why I would ask such a question.

'You've been very quiet, and that's not at all like you.'

'I am a little concerned, I guess,' she says, running her fingers over the wood grain of the table before her eyes meet mine again.

'If it's the management of the house,' I begin, but she cuts me off.

'No, it's not. It's just...' she hesitates, '...I'm not sure how to say this. The last thing I want to do is cause a rift between us before we've even moved in, but....'

I wait as she gathers her thoughts, wondering what she's about to say.

'Well, you're going to think I'm insane for asking this, as I know we're moving in together but...the thing is, until we're married I'd prefer to have my own room.'

'If that's what you want, Lily, then that's okay, it's not a problem,' I respond, masking the disappointment I'm feeling. I thought setting up home on our own would bring us closer but of course it's alien territory for both of us. The last thing I want to do is put pressure on her. 'Look,' I say gently, reaching to take her hand, 'I do understand this is a strange situation. We've come together because of Josh but I do hope in time things will change between us. The wedding isn't until Christmas so we've plenty of time. And it's important you feel comfortable with our situation as you settle in.'

'Thank you,' she says, and I see her eyes fill with tears.

Pulling her hand away from mine she finds her handkerchief and begins to mop her eyes. Now I'm feeling really bad. It makes me wonder whether we should have stayed at Amberleigh and tried to make things work with Anna. Instead, I'm plunging her into a whole new situation I'm not sure she's ready for. It's hardly surprising the

163

thought of sharing a bed with me for the first time is a step too far. On the surface it seems nothing fazes her. But having to cope alone bringing up a child, she's had to develop a hard shell against life's knocks. Seeing her vulnerability for the first time, I feel incredibly protective.

'Lily, please. Don't worry, we're going to be just fine,' I promise her, reaching across the table once more to cover her hand with mine.

'Why are you two holding hands?' a little voice interrupts, and I look to see Josh has arrived back with Thea.

'Mummy's having a chat with Daddy about our new house,' she says, hastily slipping her handkerchief back in her bag. 'I was a bit worried about getting lost. It's such a big place.'

'Don't worry, Mummy, you stay with me,' he replies confidently, slipping his small hand in hers and bestowing one of his sunny smiles. 'We'll be fine.'

'Do you know what?' She bends towards him and ruffles his hair. 'That's just what Daddy said.'

LILY

We arrived at Lynbrook just before five. The last time I was here was with Max and Nick. Everything looked dull; the trees were bare and there was little colour in the gardens. Now on this sunny afternoon the whole place resembled a mini Chelsea Flower Show. Anna and Marcus were there to welcome us and we were introduced to Jeanette Russell, the house manager she'd hired. A mature, dark haired, business-like woman in her fifties, she looked as if she knew what she was about. I don't think there'll be any problem handing everything over to her. After all, this is her world and I'm sure she won't want me under her feet.

Josh was tearing around wanting to explore everywhere and I had to ask Thea to calm him down. The first thing he wanted to do was to see his pony. Talún talked him out of it, saying there was going to be a big party and there was no time.

'Am I coming too?' he wanted to know.

'No darling, this is for big people,' I told him. I could see he was not only dog tired, he wasn't happy at being left out of something he thought was going to be new and exciting. He was just working himself up for a good bawl when Anna appeared by my side. For the first time ever I wanted to throw my arms around her shoulders and hug her.

'Come with me,' she said, stretching a hand towards him, 'I've a surprise for you.'

Wide eyed and curious, he halted his tears immediately and went with her, Thea following in their wake.

'I think he's about to get a grand tour of his rooms,' Marcus, who had been talking to Talún while this was going on, smiled. 'And ice cream afterwards of course.'

'He'll love that.' I gave Marcus an acknowledging smile. 'Rooms?' I queried.

'Yes, his bedroom, a playroom and nanny's quarters.'

I was stunned. 'Oh,' was the only thing I could manage to say.

'Now Anna has taken charge of young Josh,' he said, 'perhaps I can show you over the house.' He checked his watch. 'We've plenty of time, our guests aren't due to begin arriving until eight.'

And so off we went and, I have to say, Anna had done everything exactly to Talún's instructions. At least that's what I gathered from the way he sang her praises as we moved from room to room. Eventually we came to my suite. Marcus opened the door and I walked in to the most beautiful room I had ever seen. Decorated in pastel colours, it had an enormous bed and delicate, feminine furniture. Through a connecting door there was a huge en-suite bathroom with a huge free standing bath and loads of white marble. I loved it. It was then I realised there were no wardrobes. When I mentioned this he simply smiled and walked over to a door in the far corner.

'There are no wardrobes in your room,' he said, 'because you have a walk in closet, exactly the same as you did at Amberleigh.'

Oh my! It was amazing. There were rails and racks and

drawers, and to my surprise my clothes were already there. It was then I remembered the van carrying our luggage hadn't stopped for lunch with us.

'Thank you,' I said, losing my head for a moment as I threw myself into Talún's arms and kissed him. 'I love it.'

'I hope you two will be very happy here,' Marcus gave us both an amused smile, observing the way we were wrapped around each other.

'Oh, don't worry, we will be,' Talún said, giving me a hug. I was grateful he was keeping up appearances. I was also relieved he didn't seem too disappointed about my request for separate beds here until we're married. I really don't want to get into anything too intense with him before I have to. Of course, he'd do anything for me; absolutely anything. He's honourable and caring, characteristics most women would kill to have in a partner. However, for me, they're the two worst weaknesses a man can have.

JESS

I'm almost ready for our big night out. Bella has come over and we've got ready together. Although she's only twenty-two she seems to have had a lifetime of different jobs, hairdressing being one of them. It's been a real blessing having her here today to help me change my look.

'For the life of me, I don't know why you want to do this,' she grumbles, as she carefully works the straightening tongs through my unruly blonde hair. 'It's absolute sacrilege.'

'I fancied a completely different look for this evening, that's all,' I say, as Rufus leans around the doorway, sees us and gives a thumbs up.

'See?' I say as he disappears, 'my father likes it.'

Outnumbered, Bella gives an indignant huff and continues with her work.

With hair done, nails follow and soon we are dressed. I've opted for figure hugging white lace while Bella's in floaty yellow silk.

'Now we're ready,' she gives me a secret smile, watching

as I pour us a glass of wine each, 'I can tell you my news. Krister's asked me out,' she says, looking like the cat who's got the cream. 'It's taken a while and I had to work damned hard but I got there in the end.'

'Brilliant news, well done you.'

She laughs and we high five.

'I guess he'll be partnering you tonight then?'

'Yes, I'm meeting him there...and he's seeing me home.' As she finishes the sentence her expression saddens. 'You don't mind do you?' she asks, surveying me closely.

'Of course not, I'll be fine with Rufus.'

'I feel bad you don't have anyone.' She takes a sip of wine and shoots me a thoughtful look. 'You know, I honestly thought when you were seeing Krister about doing up the cottage something was going on between you two.'

'Absolutely not. You'd already staked your claim.'

'But if I hadn't, would you have been interested in him?'

'Wrong flavour.' I shake my head.

'So your preferences are what? Strawberry or vanilla?' she giggles.

'It's my way of saying I prefer dark haired men to blonds.'

'Was he dark then?'

'Who?'

'Your lost love.'

'I haven't got a lost love,' I insist.

'You don't date, Jess. You want to know what I think? You're pining.'

'Oh come on, be sensible! I've been back in Lynbrook for what...seven months? No more than the blink of an eye and besides, look around you. Where's there any home grown talent, eh?'

'Very true.' She acknowledges my comment. 'But I'm good at picking up vibes and I definitely think there was someone; it ended badly and you've never really recovered.'

'Why are you making a drama out of this, Bella?' I can hear the agitation in my voice. I'm annoyed she's holding onto this topic like a terrier with a bone. A subject too close to the truth for comfort and one I need her to drop at once.

'Because friends shouldn't have secrets from each other.' She gives me a forlorn smile. 'Don't you trust me?'

'Of course I do,' I say, and mean it. We really have become close since I arrived back in Lynbrook and we began working together at the Bull. But there is a limit to how much of my private life I'm comfortable sharing with anyone. Look,' I tell her, 'I'm not trying to hide anything okay? Yes, I had a bad romance a few years back and it took time to get over it. But at the moment being single is right for me. However that's not to say should the right man come along....'

'As long as you're sure...'

'I'm absolutely positive, now drink up.' I nod towards her glass, pulling the bottle from the ice bucket and offering her a top up.

TALÚN

Anna has done a fabulous job with the Hall. It's almost as if I'd been here overseeing all the work myself. Everything is exactly how I wanted it. Remembering the place from Leanna's days, it feels very different. Gone are all the heavy wallpapers and old furniture. Instead, we've achieved a balance of retro and modern, and something else...a home, which despite its size is warm and welcoming. Somewhere that is beginning to make me feel leaving Amberleigh might not be quite as difficult as I first imagined.

After our long journey, a relaxing bath has done wonders for me. In fact currently I'm feeling a little more at ease about meeting my former neighbours at this evening's party. A knock reveals Anna at the door. Wearing her favourite colour, turquoise, she gives my pale linen suit the once over and nods. 'You'll do,' she says with a teasing smile.

'Is Lily around?' I ask, realising we need to be together to greet guests.

'When I looked in on her she was nearly ready. She

looked tense. I guess it might be a bit daunting for her, meeting such a large group of new people. Obviously she wants to look her best. I've told her we'll be in the drawing room. We've a good half hour before the guests arrive,' she says, hovering at the door, 'enough time for a celebratory drink. Jeanette has organised some champagne.'

'Lead the way,' I say as I join her. A couple of glasses of bubbly should be just the thing to settle any remaining pre-party nerves.

LILY

I am not in the best of moods. My hair wouldn't play ball and took ages to style, my mascara smudged and my dress was creased. I had to find someone to take it away to iron and then had an unreasonably long wait until it was returned. I gave the young girl - Alice - a good talking to. Has she no idea how important this evening is for me? Obviously not, as she simply looked at me like I had two heads and scurried off. Well, she's not going to be here long if she continues to play dumb and insolent. I'll definitely be having a word with Jeanette about her tomorrow. I want professional people here, not Anna's charity cases from the village.

Anyway, after all that stress, I'm ready and taking a final look at myself in the mirror. I have to say this is definitely a knock 'em dead dress and goes well with the Valentino heels. Yes, red is definitely my colour. I'm looking great and I don't think *Lady* Anna will have any reason to find fault with me, although knowing her there's bound to be something not to her liking. Well, to hell with her. This is my house thank you very much and I don't have to suffer her upper class disapproval any longer. Even Marcus, who I used to get on well with, is beginning to grate on my nerves. Thank God they'll both be on their way back to Norfolk by this time tomorrow.

I check my watch and realise I should be in the drawing room having my pre-party glass of champagne. As I reach the end of the corridor I pause for a moment, realising I've forgotten to look in on Josh. Ah, well, I expect Thea's got him sufficiently distracted with the huge plasma screen in his room. He'll be so busy choosing which DVD to watch I don't think he'll miss me at all. I'll do my penance when I see him tomorrow at breakfast, I promise.

JESS

Well, we're here, and as Rufus's four by four makes its way up the drive I can see everything is looking fabulous. As we reach the house I notice the fountain at the head of the driveway has been brought back to life and is now vigorously spewing water. To the left of the main house I can just make out the top of a huge white marquee...and then there are the flowers. Adrian and his team have worked a miracle.

Colin Jeffries, one of Adrian's gardeners, is on parking duty and waves us into a vacant space in a roped off area among the trees. From there we follow the gravelled pathway which leads around the side of the house to the huge white marquee. Rufus has scrubbed up nicely this evening. Bella and I have persuaded him out of his much-loved t-shirt and jeans and tonight he's wearing green chinos and a cream linen shirt. As we approach the main entrance to the marquee I can hear live music, and in a small tented area to one side I see food prep underway while Dominic and two of his junior chefs look after the hog roast. The Bull is closed tonight, Rufus having donated the services of his dining room staff to Anna for the evening. It's great to get the village all together for a big social event and this is one I'm really looking forward to. While Rufus checks with Dominic on how everything is going, we're joined by Adrian, who emerges from the tented interior, a glass of beer in his hand.

'It's full house in there,' he says with a grin. 'I've just come out for a breather.'

'You've done wonders with the gardens,' I say, which brings a delighted smile to his face.

'Aye, it's great to have a proper budget at last,' he says,

170

taking an admiring glance at his handiwork. 'Makes all the difference.'

'Have you met Junior Hawkeswood yet?' Bella asks.

'Junior? Is that his name? No, really?' He stifles a laugh.

'His name is Marcus, the same as his grandfather,' I interrupt. 'The Junior tag is something Anna and I invented to avoid confusion when she was talking about them.'

'Ah, I see.'

'So have you seen them?' Bella's back on the interrogation trail.

'No, but I did see the cars arrive. A dark blue Aston Martin and a white Audi.'

'Very mysterious, isn't it?' Bella chirps up. 'I can't understand all the secrecy. I mean, why didn't he just move in like other folks do, then drop into the Bull for a pint?'

'What like Leanna did, you mean?' Adrian arches an eyebrow. 'They're not like us, Bella. I doubt you'll see either of them much, only out riding or driving through the village.'

'At high speed, like the Witches, you mean?'

Adrian frowns and again explanations are due. 'Georgie and Danielle.'

'Oh they're in there at the moment,' he hikes a thumb towards the marquee, 'necking down the champagne while their husbands are chatting to a couple of the other upwardly mobiles from Albany Close.'

I feel Rufus's hand on my shoulder as he joins us, also keen to compliment Adrian on his work. 'Right then girls,' he says, 'let's go and join the party, shall we?'

Leaving Adrian, we enter the marquee where groups of villagers congregate, glasses in hand, chatting. Some tap their feet or move their shoulders to the music coming from a five piece group performing on a small stage to the far left. The atmosphere here is warm and relaxed and if feels like the start of a great evening for our new arrivals.

Rufus appears with drinks and we circulate, taking the opportunity to catch up with our neighbours. It's mostly small talk, although there's a lot of interest in my house building project. By eight thirty the marquee is pretty full. Rufus gets caught up with Bella's father talking golf and then suddenly I see Krister squeezing his way past people, looking for us. I wave out and he arrives looking totally edible in thigh hugging black jeans and an open neck fitted white shirt, which shows off his pecs to great advantage.

'Wow!' says Beth, as he reaches us

'Wow!' I echo in agreement.

He brushes a hand through his thick blond hair and grins, all boyish embarrassment.

Suddenly I feel a touch on my shoulder. It's Anna looking amazing in turquoise chiffon.

'Caught up with you at last,' she says with a smile. 'And Krister's here too...good. Can I borrow them for a moment?' she asks Bella and Rufus, who has just returned, 'I want to introduce them to my grandson. He's very interested in their eco build.'

Leaving my father and Bella to chat, Anna weaves a path through the assembled crowd and suddenly there's an open space where I see an older, distinguished grey haired man who must be Marcus. Anna introduces him then leans into me and whispers, 'Junior's chatting, I'll just go and find him.' As she leaves, Marcus smiles and steps forward to shake my hand.

'Pleased to meet you. Anna has told me what a good friend you've become to her while she's been here,' he says, before greeting Krister. Marcus chats about the Hall and is obviously proud of the way Anna has managed the whole project. 'And you two are about to embark on a building venture of your own, I hear.'

At the mention of our collaboration, Krister becomes quite animated. 'Ja,' he says, giving me a grin. 'Jess and I are going into partnership. The planning is through. Now we are putting our team together for the building.'

'Anna mentioned it in passing and I know it's something my grandson will definitely be interested in. He's...ah,' he says, looking over our shoulders, 'I think I can see my wife returning. Looks as though she's found him. '

Krister and I both turn at the same time. Everything seems to happen in slow motion. The crowd parting as Anna comes towards us. People are turning and smiling. At first I feel I must be hallucinating, that the tall, good looking, dark-haired man following her is, like Krister, the mirror image of someone else. However, as he reaches me it's apparent from the expression on his face he's no doppelganger. He is the real deal and the nightmare is confirmed when Anna steps to one side and says, 'Jess, Krister, I'd like you to meet my grandson, Talún Hawkeswood.'

TALÚN

As Anna felt it might be a good idea for me to meet with George and Ellie separately, she asked them to arrive slightly earlier than the other guests. I was waiting in the library for them and spent a good deal of time pacing and working out not only exactly what I was going to say, but wondering how they would react. And then the door opened and in they walked behind her. They've both changed in the time I've been absent. Older, a little more worn down by life. George is almost totally bald and Ellie's thick auburn hair is peppered with grey.

As Ellie saw me her hand went to her mouth, eyes wide with shock while George simply stood there stunned. It was Anna who broke the silence by explaining the situation and introducing me as her grandson. She then told them that as the new owner of the Hall it was me who had the deeds for the farm transferred over to George. With a meaningful look in my direction she said, 'I'll leave you to chat,' and left the room.

Ellie took a deep breath. Her hand slowly traced a path from her mouth to the base of her throat as her eyes began to well up with tears. She looked at George, then at me, and said, 'Talún why didn't you phone? Just one call to say you were safe and well. It would have stopped all the worry, all the distress. Were we not worth bothering about once you'd found your new rich family?' Anger quickly replaced the tears and she hastily wiped away the moisture from her eyes with a handkerchief pulled from her pocket. I'd never seen her that way before but I guessed mingled in with the anger there was the hurt and pain I'd also been guilty of causing. I needed to explain. I hoped when they'd heard me out they would not only understand what drove me away from Lynbrook but also find some way to forgive me.

'It wasn't like that,' I began defensively. 'I thought...well...'

George stepped forward and put a comforting arm around Ellie. He pinned me with a hard stare and blunt as ever, growled, 'Well boy, it's time to stop your thinking and talk. At the very least we deserve an explanation.'

They did, and I was about to deliver it; to make things better if I could. Giving them the farm seemed so inadequate. It meant nothing if I'd lost the respect of the two people who had taken responsibility for me when my mother disappeared. 'Yes, you do.' I agreed. 'Let's sit shall we?' I indicated two chocolate leather couches over by the large Edwardian fireplace. When we were settled and facing each other I began.

George sat back and crossed his arms over a paunch, which appeared to have doubled in size since I saw him last. Ellie, her auburn waves still as unruly as ever, sat straight and tall, knees together, hands clasped, waiting expectantly.

Quietly I began my story. The pain of discovering Jess with someone else, which had prompted me to decide to leave the area. The discovery of my birth certificate in my mother's things as I packed, the reason I'd headed for Norfolk. I also told them about Cesca, how she made it back home gravely ill but had sadly died. This made Ellie retrieve her handkerchief and dab her eyes. She'd had a special bond with my mother and no doubt it felt as if she'd lost a daughter. I told them of my life with the Hawkeswood family, my marriage to Fliss and the loss of her and our baby, which had Ellie reaching for her handkerchief yet again. When we got to the present and my discovery of a son, I deliberately skimmed over the detail. They didn't need to know about the circumstances. It's not something I'm particularly proud of, but I feel the consequence of that night – Josh – is a blessing. After so much pain in my life, I told them, I felt I've been given an exceptional gift and a chance to begin again.

'Can I just say,' I told them as I finished, 'I'm extremely sorry. But at the time I was full of pain. I loved Jess so much and I couldn't have stayed here seeing her bring other boyfriends home. There wasn't a choice. I had to leave. I admit I was selfish, you'd done such a lot for me and I treated you very badly. But I hope we can make a fresh start now I'm settling back in the village.'

I sat back and waited. They'd let me tell my story without interruption and I was expecting questions.

It was Ellie who broke the silence. 'But I don't understand,' she said. 'Jess came back for you. She spent months holding onto the hope you'd return.'

'No, she didn't want me anymore,' I argued. 'I went to Exeter. I found her in a club in the arms of someone else. A tall gangly guy with blond hair.'

'We never saw anyone like that. In fact, I don't think she ever brought anyone home.' Ellie gave a vigorous shake of her head. 'Mind you, she did move away from Lynbrook after the first Christmas. Rufus said it was too painful for her to be here so he was renting a flat for her in Exeter. She was here during the holidays though, but her friend Roo was the only one we ever saw her with.'

'Well, whatever happened, it's in the past now, isn't it?' I said, knowing even if what they said was true, Jess was now simply a memory from the past, nothing more. 'I'm here to settle down with my fiancée and son,' I explained. 'We're planning a Christmas wedding and I'd like you both to be there.'

'We will be,' Ellie looked at George and they both nodded.

George pursed his lips, nodded, and blew out a deep breath. 'I think with the shock of seeing you here I completely forgot something important. He got to his feet, his eyes moistening. 'It's about the farm...' he began.

'It was the right thing to do,' I interrupted him, as I pulled myself upright. 'The *only* thing to do.'

'I'm sorry I lied to you.' He brushed away his tears. 'Somehow I always thought you'd go and we didn't want that to happen, did we Ellie?' he said, looking at her.

Ellie shook her head in agreement. 'No, we hoped it would persuade you to settle down in the village. Raise a family.'

'Well, now I'm here doing just that.' I wrapped my arms around both of them and we hugged. 'It's so good to be home,' I told them. 'I was concerned about coming back, which is why Anna organised the purchase and refurbishment of the Hall. I needed time to get used to returning to a place which has such sad memories for me.'

Ellie stared at George and a strange look passed between them. When she turned back to face me there was something I couldn't read in her eyes. 'Talún I think there's ...'

She never finished her sentence. I saw George frown and shake his head as if to stop her. Then there was a knock and Anna appeared in the doorway.

'Sorry to interrupt,' she said, looking at George and Ellie, then me, 'but if you've finished there are a couple of people I'd like you to meet.'

'Sure, I think we're all done here,' I said, and they both nodded in agreement.

We walked through the house and out onto the terrace before making our way across the lawn to the marquee. Once inside, Anna organised a drink for both of them. I eventually caught sight of Lily. Marcus had been looking after her but now I could see she was seated at a table in the corner with two expensively dressed thirty-something women; a redhead and a brunette. I had been concerned she might find this whole thing overwhelming but from the way they were laughing together she seemed to have made friends already. After seeing the Selbys I was feeling upbeat about my arrival. It looked as if things were going to work out well here after all. Anna joined me again and I noticed George and Ellie, with their glasses of champagne, deep in conversation with the vicar and his wife. Although the place was packed, Anna managed to negotiate her way through the crowd. I finally caught a glimpse of Marcus up ahead. He was talking to a couple with their backs to us. The guy was tall with shaggy blond hair, the woman slim and dressed in white, her hair a slightly darker shade than his, falling thick and straight down her back. Marcus spotted me, waved out and they both turned towards us as we approached. I frowned. The woman's face, with its pale arched brows and dark brown eyes was familiar. But the hair was all wrong. Then I caught the expression on her face as she saw me clearly for the first time. Anna stopped, smiled, introduced me and then identified them.

'These are the eco-developers whose project I was telling you about,' she said, obviously pleased she'd united like minds. 'Krister Sorenson and Jess Hayden.'

I took one look at Jess and although my first instinct was to turn and walk away, it was impossible. I felt all sorts of emotions stirring, anger being one of them, but I needed to rein it in. I'm different now, not the traveller's son she had a fling with nearly six years ago. I remembered the Selbys' words only moments ago in the library but I didn't believe a word of it. Spending months holding onto the hope I'd return? No way. It was all smoke and mirrors. Lily was right all those years ago when she told me Jess's warm, caring manner hid the liar she really was. Well, she might have my grandmother fooled but not me. Not anymore.

JESS

Standing beside Anna, Talún acknowledges both of us with a nod. The only thing betraying his surprise in seeing me here is a slight widening of his eyes. Then he completely dismisses me, turning instead to Krister to ask him about the project. Anna frowns, obviously baffled by his behaviour, and when he suggests they take their conversation elsewhere I can see anger mingled with disbelief as she continues to watch him. Krister automatically looks across at me, confused as to how to deal with this. To diffuse the situation I merely take a mouthful of champagne and with a lift of my shoulders say, 'It's okay, go, you're the brains behind this,' and I watch as they walk away.

'I'm so sorry, Jess.' Anna says, obviously embarrassed; Marcus hovering behind her looks equally unhappy. 'That was totally uncalled for and not like him at all. I can't think what got into him but I will definitely have words later. The least he can do is apologise.'

'Oh, no please...' I protest, trying to play things down. The last thing I want is to have to face him again. 'I'd be pretty useless anyway. Krister is the builder, he's the one Talún really needs to talk to.'

'Even so,' Anna says, 'his lack of manners was—'

'Has anyone seen Talún?' a voice interrupts, and ice cold fingers touch my spine. Memories of words spoken years ago as we faced each other in the hallway of my home in Milton Bay come crashing back: *You're a bastard Jess, Leo's not your father...'* Please no, it can't be...

'He's chatting to a local builder here about a project,' Marcus confirms, then turns his attention to me. 'Maybe Lily could keep you company while the men are otherwise engaged,' he suggests helpfully. 'Lily, this is Jess...' is as far as he gets. I turn to face my nemesis. Her red hair is now blonde and she's back to being the glossy creature she was under Leo's patronage. It doesn't take an Einstein to work out why she's here. Another hammer blow hits me.

'Oh my, it's you,' she says with a smirk, her left hand going to her throat. The huge diamond on her engagement finger confirms my first fears. She is Talún's fiancée. The one he rediscovered after a five year absence. And they have a child. My mind is in freefall. Suddenly I need air.

'You two know each other?' Anna looks curiously at both of us.

'Oh well, it was a long time ago. I hardly recognised you,' Lily says, dismissing me as if I'm yesterday's news. 'You look so ...different.' She casts a disdainful eye over me before turning to Anna with a smile. 'When you see Talún, can you tell him I'm off to show Georgie and Danni over the house?'

I watch her depart, all swaying hips and self-confidence. Marcus, keen to break the uncomfortable silence surrounding Lily's departure, offers to get us both another drink. I thank him but refuse, saying I need to find Rufus. I can see Anna is curious about my connection to Lily but she's getting nothing from me. I'll leave that to the soon-to-be Mrs Hawkeswood. At this very moment I don't care what lies she decides to tell her. I simply want to get away.

On my way to find Rufus I come across Bella, who tells me Dominic has asked her to find Anna because the food is ready to be served.

'You look a bit peaky, are you feeling all right?' she asks, dark eyes scanning me curiously and probably seeing more than they should.

'I need some fresh air, that's all. Champagne's gone straight to my head.' With her hand on my arm she steers me purposefully out of the marquee. Across the lawn there is a small cluster of trees, an ornate bench set beneath them. We reach it and she plonks me down. 'Stay there and don't move.' It's a command rather than a request.

I sit for what seems an eternity, watching the day fade and the shadows lengthen. People who have been standing outside the marquee drinking and chatting filter back inside, probably to join the queue for food. I look around at this beautiful house and its grounds and can't believe all of it will soon belong to Lily. What justice is there in the world, I wonder.

My thoughts then stray back to the moment I first saw Talún. He seemed worlds away from the twenty-two-year-old I'd once known. Now there is a polished quality about his good looks. Expensively dressed, the thick dark curl of his hair touching his collar, he looks every inch the Hawkeswood heir. Although his expression had been completely bland as we were introduced, there was no mistaking the hostility mirrored in the depth of those green eyes as he looked at me. For a moment I wondered what had prompted his anger. Then I realised it was probably because he didn't expect to find me, an embarrassing reminder of his past, still living in the village. Well, he needn't worry; I'm no gossip. Anyway, as far as I'm concerned the past is dead and buried. I think the village is big enough for both of us. And I doubt he'll be calling into the Bull for a pint at any time.

Caught in my thoughts I don't see Bella approaching. She sits down next to me, shaking me out of my memories. 'Here, I brought some food for both of us,' she says, handing me a plateful of bits and pieces. 'Hope you don't mind, but I passed on the hog.' She gives a little shudder. 'I can't deal with whole dead animals. Poor pig,' she says, holding a mini vol-au-vent between her finger and thumb before devouring it whole.

'Come on, what really upset you in there?' she asks, as she picks up a giant prawn and begins to peel it. 'Was it Danielle and Georgie's new best friend?'

'Who?'

'The tarty blonde in red.'

'Tarty? Did you think she looked tarty?'

'Jess,' she says in a tone which makes her sound like her mother, 'you don't have to be wearing cheap clothes to be a tart. What angered me most was how patronising she was to Rufus's staff, clicking her fingers to get a waiter over for another bottle of champagne for her and the Witches. Thank God I'm not working today or I might have accidentally spilled something over that glitzy dress of hers,' she says with a wicked grin.

'Then you would have been in trouble.'

'Why? What's so special about her?'

'She's Anna's grandson's fiancée.'

'You're joking. What *is* he doing with someone like her?'

'They knew each other way back. They had a child together.'

'A child? How old?'

'Four and a half,' I say, remembering the age Anna had mentioned. As soon as the words leave my mouth it hits me. Why the hell didn't I make the connection before?

'You've gone a funny colour again,' Bella remarks, another prawn hovering at her lips.

'It's nothing. Sorry,' I shake my head, staring at my plate of uneaten food and feeling quite nauseous. 'I don't think I can eat this. In fact I think I'd like to go home.'

'Oh Jess honey, poor you,' I hear Bella's sympathetic words and feel a comforting arm cradle my shoulder, 'Right, you sit there quietly while I find Rufus and get the keys.' she says, releasing me and getting to her feet, 'I'll have you back to the cottage in no time.'

She leaves me, running across the lawn. Putting down my plate, I lean forward and rest my head in my hands for a moment. As if things couldn't get any worse. Not only is Talún back with Lily as his wife-to-be, but I now realise the extent of his betrayal. Whether he knew about this child or not, it was conceived at the same time he was with me. Rufus was right all along; I should never have let him touch me. Suddenly I want to cry, to get rid of all the pent up anger seeing him again has created. I look up to see Bella returning and damp down on my need for tears. They will come all too soon, in the darkness of my room, when I'm alone.

LILY

Well, what an evening. Fancy running into Jess Hayden. Such a dull and pasty thing in that white lacy dress she was wearing and whatever has she done to her hair? I guess I shouldn't be surprised, she never did have much in the way of style. But then spending your day at the beck and call of small noisy children doesn't exactly call for wearing high end fashion, does it? Luckily I am now able to indulge myself as I have Thea to run around after Josh. Anyway, enough of boring Jess. I have made two wonderful new friends. Yes, Georgie and Danielle – call me Danni – are a real find. Of course, they are nothing like me. They're older for a start. They've also been cushioned by their middle class upbringing, friends at boarding school who drifted into their comfortable marriages to two money men.

Looking at their husbands, one small and ferret featured with glasses, the other tall, pale and ginger, it doesn't take much to realise these weren't love matches. The girls married for money and lifestyle. It seems we are kindred spirits; sisters under the skin.

As I take them on a grand tour of the house there's a constant hitching of breath. I can see they are in total awe and envy as they admire Talún and Anna's handiwork. Obviously, I'm not going to admit I had nothing to do with all this. Instead I simply sigh and accept the compliments as they come. They are totally bowled over by the bathrooms and when we come to my room and see my walk in wardrobe their envy is complete.

'Ah,' Danni twirls an auburn curl around her finger and looks at me curiously, 'you don't sleep together then?'

'No,' I say in my most dignified way.

'Lily, this is the twenty first century,' Dark haired Georgie reminds me with an amused laugh. 'And your man is drop dead gorgeous.'

'The Hawkeswoods are a family with old fashioned ways,' I explain, happy to let Marcus and Anna take the blame for my celibacy. 'Talún and I may have had a child together but they...well...' I let the sentence hang so they can make of it what they will.

'Ooh, poor you,' Danni says, 'and another six months until the wedding, too. Still, you know what they say about *what the eye doesn't see.* If it was me, I'd simply wait till they'd gone back to Norfolk and then...' she rolled her eyes '...well, no one would be any the wiser, would they?'

'You're forgetting it takes two. Talún respects his grandparents, he would never do anything to upset them.'

'You are joking of course?' Georgie's laugh melts away as she sees my expression. 'Oh please, I'm sure you're persuasive enough to make him change his mind. And if not, well maybe we could...assist in some way?' She looks at Danni and a little smirk passes between them.

'Assist?' I say, pinning them both with a hard stare. 'I'll pretend I didn't hear that comment.'

Immediately they go quiet, all embarrassed smiles and

excuses. Of course they wouldn't dream of doing anything so outrageous, they tell me. It was a joke. I extract myself from this uncomfortable situation by moving our tour on to the east wing where the old swimming pool has been refurbished and a sauna and fitness room added. They return to their wide-eyed admiration and upbeat comments but I'm not fooled. Potential friends they may be but when Talún's around I'm going to have to keep an eye on those two.

JESS

For the next forty eight hours I've decided to stay away from the river. By then Anna and Marcus should have returned to Norfolk. I want to avoid meeting her because I know there will be questions. Questions I don't want to answer. Besides, she's probably already had Talún and Lily's version, which will make things even more complicated. This morning I take Caspar deep into the woods where the sun filters sparingly through the canopy of green overhead. The place reflects my mood. There's a quiet, shady atmosphere where I can find a little peace away from everyone. Bella hasn't mentioned anything about the Hall's welcoming party other than to ask if I'm feeling better. Rufus, however, is another matter. We chatted over breakfast the morning after and he was very vocal about our new arrival. He'd established a great friendship with Anna so discovering the identity of her grandson had come as quite a shock.

'How did you react when you met him?' I asked, knowing how his dislike of my ex- must have put him in a bit of a spot.

'I simply shook hands and welcomed him back,' he said with a shrug. 'I could hardly snub him in front of his family and the village, could I? What about you?'

'He gave me a silent nod and then ignoring me completely he began a conversation with Krister.'

'Arrogant arse,' he muttered, slapping butter on his toast. 'After all he did to you.'

'I think I understand his reaction,' I replied as I reached for the marmalade. 'I don't believe he's been entirely truthful with Anna about his life here. He didn't expect to find me still living in the village and it's caught him off balance. I gather you didn't run into his fiancée then?'

'What, the tarty blonde in the red dress?' he said, which made me laugh, realising he was echoing Bella's comments. 'I'm really surprised Anna approves.'

'I don't think she has a choice. There's a child involved, remember? And before you say anything, she told me DNA tests confirm it's his.' The painful reminder of this had me chewing at my bottom lip.

'What is it?' He paused, knife in hand. 'What's wrong?' And I knew I had to tell him. I wanted to keep it to myself but it was eating away at me so badly I needed to get it out in the open. Of course Rufus would be angry, very angry, but there was nothing I could do about it.

'You didn't recognise her then?'

'Should I have?'

'It's Lily Stevenson.'

'Ah, I thought there was something familiar about her. Of course, I only saw her on the one occasion when she came to the restaurant opening with all of you, and she did have red hair then.' He gave a low whistle. 'Well, she's really bagged herself the star prize there. And a child you say?'

'A four and a half year old child.'

I watched him mentally do his sums. 'My God,' he said, 'that means...'

'Yes, he was seeing us both at the same time.'

I didn't know what would come next. I believed he would, in the gentlest possible way, remind me how he'd seen the danger and warned me. And how that warning had gone unheeded. Instead he got up and reached out, pulling me into his arms. 'Oh Jess,' he expelled a heavy breath, 'what a bastard.'

'Isn't he just?' I tried to make light of it, 'Don't worry though, I doubt our paths will cross often. Anyway, from what Anna told me, he'll be making regular trips between here and Norfolk so I guess he won't be around a lot of the time.'

'No, but Lily will.'

'Given the condescending way she greeted me, I doubt I'll even show on her radar.'

'I saw her with Danni and Georgie,' he grinned, 'do you realise this means we now have our blonde and the trio is complete? We really do have our very own Witches of Lynbrook.'

I managed a smile, wondering whether Lily might have met her match with the delightful Danielle and Georgie. They may fool everyone into thinking they are simply wealthy airheads, but I recognise a couple of devious mischief makers when I see them.

TALÚN

It's been a difficult morning. I'm still getting over the shock of meeting Jess Hayden at our welcoming party yesterday. I never expected her to still be here in Lynbrook. It was no surprise to find her in good looking male company, of course. She's probably got him wrapped around her little finger just like she had me. I automatically snubbed her. After what she had done she deserved it. I was eager to talk about their project but deliberately directed any conversation towards Krister. Of course she brushed off my rudeness, saying he knew more about the project than she did, but I could see despite her calm manner I'd upset her. Krister and I discussed the plans for their eco-house development and I hate to say it but I actually found myself agreeing with Jess's sentiments. Too many locals have been forced out of villages as these locations become desirable and prices rocket. So giving them an opportunity to buy or rent is a first class idea and one which I support. He mentioned wanting to purchase some land adjacent to their site, which would enable them to have a bigger development. I already knew about this through Anna and was keen to help until he told me Jess is financing the whole project.

That killed it dead. I don't want anything to do with her. In fact, I intend to avoid her as much as possible while I'm here. Meeting Rufus was another tense moment but once introductions were over I made my excuses and disappeared.

I knew I wasn't going to escape this morning's inquisition. Thankfully, Anna waited until breakfast was over and Lily had left, saying she was planning to drive into Exeter for shopping and lunch with new friends Georgie and Danielle. Marcus followed shortly afterwards to have a chat with Greg, my newly hired stud manager, leaving me alone with my grandmother. Folding her napkin, she dropped it onto the table and got to her feet.

'It's a lovely morning,' she nodded towards the French doors, 'fancy some fresh air?'

Translated, that meant she wanted to talk to me privately about yesterday. I cursed Jess Hayden under my breath as I followed Anna out onto the terrace. Across the lawn the men had arrived to dismantle the marquee. I heard the cheerful whistling of one of them and wished for a moment I could change places with him. To be anyone else other than me at this moment in time, because I knew I was going to have to lie again. I didn't think Anna would approach Lily but I have had a quiet word with her just in case. As we walked she kept up a stream of small talk, telling me about the gardens and how much work Adrian had put into them. Finally we reached our destination: a small stone bench set into the wall on the eastern side of the grounds. A narrow gravelled pathway looped around a central water feature and I knew she'd chosen this location deliberately so we wouldn't be disturbed.

Settling ourselves comfortably, Anna linked her fingers in her lap and drew in a shallow breath. 'Now,' she looked at me thoughtfully, her eyes meeting mine, 'would you like to tell me what the problem is between you and Jess?'

It's three days since the Hall's welcoming party. By now, both Marcus and Anna should be back home in Norfolk so I've decided it's safe to take Caspar along our normal route through the woods.

Reaching the huge rock slab which serves as my resting place I dismount and, pulling off my riding hat, settle myself down, dangling my legs over its smooth, grey edge. Drawing a deep breath, I close my eyes and breathe in the warm, fresh morning air. It's a wonderful place for moments of quiet solitude. However, my peace is interrupted as Caspar nickers and swings his head towards the trees. Over the river's burble I hear the sound of a horse approaching and, grabbing my hat, I quickly slide from the rock. I know it must be Talún. Who else would be out riding in these woods? And the last thing I want is to run into him. Reaching Caspar, I swing into the saddle and ease him towards the shelter of the trees. There I sit, waiting for the mysterious rider to show themselves. Achilles emerges from the treeline opposite but it's Anna riding him, not Talún. Why is she still here? As she pulls up and dismounts, I ease Caspar out of the trees towards her.

'I thought I caught a glimpse of you,' she says, shading her eyes against the brightness of the sun. 'How are you, Jess?' she asks, her smile hesitant.

'I'm fine,' I say, as I dismount and lead Caspar towards her. 'And you?'

'A little confused,' she says, as we settle ourselves on the rock.

'You've spoken to Talún, I gather.'

'Yes.'

'Well then, there is no confusion. You know everything. And why did you tell me his name was Marcus?' I round on her crossly. 'Why did you lie?'

'I didn't. It's his middle name and he asked for his real identity to be kept from everyone. He wanted anonymity, to be able to meet the locals in his own time on his own terms. And as for knowing everything, I only have his side of the story,' she corrects me. When I fail to respond I hear her sigh, and then she's back again as relentless as ever. 'Jess, I'll be honest with you, Talún would not tell me why he's so angry with you. I wondered whether...'

'I'm sorry,' I interrupt, 'but I don't have anything to offer either. For me, the past is a closed door.' How typical of Talún to refuse to talk to Anna about me, I think angrily. But then what could he say without incriminating himself? All that cold superiority the other evening, treating me as if I was invisible. How dare he. Well, I'm not a vindictive person, but I can't let him get away with that sort of behaviour. While I'm not prepared to tell Anna anything, there is something else I can do that will take her straight back to Talún to demand answers.

'Oh dear.' I watch as she draws in a disappointed breath. 'Well, that rather leaves me to draw my own conclusions about how you, Talún and Lily fit together, doesn't it?'

'I guess it does.' I manage a cool smile. 'Although this,' I say as I slip his grandmother's ring from my finger, 'might help you with your deliberations. It's time I gave it back anyway.'

Anna takes the platinum band from my outstretched palm. 'He gave you this?' Her grey eyes widen with surprise.

'Yes, he said it belonged to Sesca's mother.'

'It did,' she confirms, 'Marcus wondered where it was. Apparently it's been passed down through the family to every Hawkeswood bride for over three hundred years.'

'All the more reason for it to be returned to him now, then.'

'Thank you.' She studies the ring once more, her pale brows pulled together in a frown before she slips it into the breast pocket of her shirt and buttons the flap.

We sit in silence for a moment. It's clear our conversation has run its course. As I told her, it's pointless stirring up the past. Talún is back in the village and although his behaviour angers me, somehow we have to learn to exist here together. I check my watch. 'I have to go, I'm afraid,' I say, 'I'm working a lunchtime shift at the Bull today.'

'I'm really sorry about all of this,' she says quietly. 'I hope it hasn't affected our friendship.'

'Certainly not.' I manage a smile. I'm very fond of Anna and there's no way I'm letting him be the reason for ending our relationship.

'Well, I won't say goodbye, that's far too final a word,' she says, leaning over and giving me a hug. 'Besides, I will be coming back so we'll catch up then. In the meantime we have each other's mobile numbers to keep in touch... or better still we could arrange a weekly Skype call.'

Promising to set up a regular weekend chat session, I slide from the rock and quickly cross the open space to retrieve Caspar. I swing up into the saddle and give her a final wave and then I'm gone, galloping along the woodland path. My final link to the past is now safely tucked into Anna's top pocket. I only wish I could be there to see Talún's reaction when she hands the ring back to him.

TALÚN

Anna has returned home in a strange mood. She barely speaks as we pass in the hallway and tells me she's going to pack. I ask her to stay for lunch, saying Toby, Thea and myself would love to spend some time with her before she leaves. Ignoring my request, she halts half way up the stairs. 'Where's Lily?' she asks.

'Not back yet.'

'Of course, she's with those two new acolytes of hers again isn't she?' She rolls her eyes.

'As a matter of fact she is,' I respond irritably, annoyed at her attitude. 'She's settling in and making friends. I thought that's what you wanted?'

She shrugs and continues her climb.

'Will you be staying for lunch then?' I call after her.

'No, sorry, I need to be on the road,' she says abruptly, and I realise her mood is because she's not happy with

Lily's absence from the Hall again this morning. I tell myself it's early days, she wants to indulge her love of shopping and spend time with new friends, which is fine with me. Jeanette seems to be firmly in control of the household, and as for Josh, well, he seems quite happy with Thea. In fact, he doesn't seem to miss his mother at all.

I catch up with Anna some time later. Her Discovery is parked outside the front door and Jeanette is in the process of arranging for one of the gardeners to stow her luggage in the boot.

'Have a safe journey,' I tell her, as I approach her for a farewell hug. 'I'll be up in a few weeks' time.'

'I'll keep in touch by phone,' she promises, as she steps back from me and begins fishing around in her top pocket. She pulls out a small circular object and hands it to me. 'I nearly forgot; I believe this belongs to you.'

I stare down at the ring and immediately understand the reason for her bad mood. This inflammatory piece of evidence will mean my silence is no longer an option. I swear under my breath. Damn Jess Hayden for stitching me up, and damn Anna for wanting to poke around in the past. Why couldn't she leave well enough alone?

'Now you have that in your possession, is there anything you want to tell me about your relationship with Jess and Lily before I leave?' she asks quietly.

I drag in a heavy breath and close my eyes. I'm up against the wall here. I can't possibly tell her the truth, instead I'm going to have to add to my growing pile of lies and deceit.

'Talún?' I hear Anna prompt, and realise she's still waiting for an answer.

'Okay, okay.' I raise my hands, wanting to calm the situation. 'I was seeing both of them at the same time. Are you satisfied now?'

'Totally,' she says, and her displeasure is evident. 'You disappoint me. I wasn't lied to but I wasn't told the truth either. I thought I could at least count on you to be honest, even if what you had to tell me showed a complete lack of moral standards on your part. Your anger the other evening when you first saw Jess... I'm guessing it was because you realised you were about to be found out, wasn't it?'

This is not like Anna. Such a personal swipe at me really hurts. But the Hawkeswoods are a highly respectable family raised on good manners and impeccable behaviour. What I've just admitted to has, in her eyes, been the eighth deadly sin – thou shalt not mess around with two women at the same time.

'Yes it was,' I say, feeling resentful as I watch her walk towards her car. I push my own untruths to one side as I try not to panic, wondering what else has come out of their conversation. 'But you should be wary of Jess, Anna. She's not what you think she is. No doubt she had a high old time telling you all about me,' I continue angrily, 'but you can rest assured there isn't a grain of truth in any of it. She's incredibly spiteful.'

'Well, that's very interesting,' Anna says as she opens the door and leans on it, 'because I didn't get a word out of her either. She simply refused to talk. You've got her all wrong Talún, you really have.'

She doesn't say any more, she simply slips behind the wheel and slams the door. The engine fires and the vehicle pulls away. I watch it disappear down the driveway until it's out of sight. Then I go indoors to find my son and his nanny and join them for lunch. I'm feeling murderous. I'm not letting go of this. How dare Jess Hayden put me in this situation with my grandmother. I don't give a damn about what Rufus might do to me, tomorrow I'm going to find his daughter and settle this once and for all.

The next morning after breakfast I try and work out the best way to get Jess on her own. I've already decided on the bait: the purchase of the extra land she's enquired about. Now I realise she is part of this eco-building team, there's no way I'm selling it to her. However, it will definitely act as an incentive for her to meet me. I have no idea what her movements are but I know Krister will. I find the business card he gave me and punch his number into my mobile. Answering on the second ring, I ask him if he can get a message to Jess at the Bull, telling him Rufus and I have history which would make things awkward if I turned up there.

'But you can catch her at the cottage.' He tells me, 'She is there most afternoons.'

'I thought she lived at the Bull?'

'Oh no,' he says, 'she moved out in early May.'

For a moment I think he means they're living together. 'So she's living with you now?'

'Me?' he laughs. 'No, we are not together in that way. Jess is my business partner. She is living in the cottage in the wood.'

'The one that belonging to Manor Farm?'

'It didn't belong to the farm, it belonged to the Hall,' he corrects me. 'She bought it from—'

'I know exactly who she bought it from,' I interrupt, my voice ice cold with rage. I thank Krister for his help and terminate the call.

I resist the temptation to kick something. I see it all now. Jess befriending Anna, using her in order to buy the cottage, probably for a knock down price. Nothing has changed. She's still a sly conniving creature, despite what my grandmother believes. This is partly my fault, of course. I should have taken more interest in the sale and made sure it was secure. Losing it is bad enough, but to think Jess Hayden lives there makes me even more determined to confront her.

I spend the morning with Josh and Thea. My first reaction was to drive there and confront Jess. I used to act on impulse but those days are long behind me and I've learned to curb my temper. What I'm about to do is very important therefore I need to plan this confrontation carefully. Because of this, I have a cooling off period with my son and his nanny. She's come with us to the riding stables today and leans on the barrier as Josh's new instructor, Lee, puts him through his paces. He's come on so well and I see such pride in Thea's homely features. She is absolutely devoted to him.

Lily disappeared after breakfast, saying she had to sort out some domestic issue. I asked her if she was coming down to watch Josh and she said she would once she'd finished with Jeanette. Sadly, she didn't materialise, and I'm guessing she's managed to get herself tied up with some other domestic issue. When we return to the house for lunch, however, Jeanette informs me Lily left around ten-fifteen but wasn't specific about where she was going. As we eat, Thea tells me she's planning to take Josh out to the Pennywell Farm Wildlife Centre for the afternoon. She's such an asset, totally organising Josh's life using her laptop to research places to take him. Today it's all about animals: pigs, donkeys, ponies and goats. He will love it. It reminds me I need to see Lily. When we were in Norfolk, Anna˙commented about his lack of contact with children his own age. I need to talk to her about organising a couple of days a week at a local playgroup. I know Georgie and Danni both have pre-school kids so maybe she's already spoken to them and has gone to check a few places out.

I've organised an estate Discovery for Thea's use today. As they leave I can see Josh's excited face as he waves me goodbye from the rear of the car. I'm about to return to the house when Lily's Audi arrives. As she gets out, I realise far from sorting out Josh's needs she's been seeing to her own as I watch her extract half a dozen designer carriers from the back of the car

'Hi,' she says breezily as she reaches me, 'am I too late for lunch?'

'I expect Naomi can rustle you up an omelette,' I say, one eye on her shopping. 'Exeter?'

'Plymouth.' She smiles as she steps past me into the house. 'So much more choice there.'

'Actually, I wanted to talk to you about Josh,' I say, following her into the house.

'What about him?'

'Do you remember Anna suggesting we get him into a playgroup?'

She stops and dumps her bags at her feet. 'No Talún,'

she shakes her head. 'I don't think that's a good idea at all. Besides, he'll be starting school in September.'

'September is nearly three months away.'

'Yes, but I think I'd rather leave things as they are for now.' I catch a slight tetchiness in her voice, realising she thinks Anna's been interfering again. Then just as I think she's about to argue her point she pauses thoughtfully. 'Actually, I have an idea,' she says, collecting up her shopping. 'It's Josh's fifth birthday next week. I know we're planning to take him to Legoland but I could organise a party here on the Friday. Georgie and Danni's two children could come and bring some of their friends. It would give me the opportunity to get to know more mothers and Josh would be able to meet and make new friends.'

'That's a great idea,' I say, pleased she's taking this interest. 'I'll leave it to you to arrange everything then.'

'I'm on the case.' She grins. As I watch as my wife-to-be and her shopping head for the stairs, I'm sure Anna is mistaken about Lily. She simply needs time to settle in and find her feet in this new world of ours. But she'll get there, I know she will.

JESS

It's just over a week since Anna left. I really miss her company and our daily meets by the river. Today Bella and I are doing our usual Friday evening shift together. It's just turned seven and there's a smattering of locals in the bar. All's quiet until the noisy arrival of Adrian and a small party of Hall staff. I realise they're much earlier than usual and from the angry expression on Adrian's face he's in one hell of a mood.

'Who's rubbed you up the wrong way then?' the ever curious Bella asks as she serves him his usual lager.

Rob Eames, one of the stable lads leaning on the bar next to Adrian, shakes his head. 'Don't go there, Bella,' he warns her, 'just serve the man his drink.'

Bella does as she's asked and we both watch as Adrian

tips back the glass and drinks deeply. Then placing his beer back on the bar he wipes his mouth with the back of his hand and says, 'The bitch fired me.'

'What's all this?' a voice says behind me, and I turn to see Rufus has joined us. 'You've been fired? Why?'

'Well,' he says after another mouthful, 'Talún's fiancée held a birthday party for Josh today. The Witches and their kids were invited and they brought friends of theirs who had bairns the same age. There were ten including Josh. Lily pushed the boat out: bouncy castle, a clown, it was all going well. And then the women decided to take themselves off to the pool and sauna, leaving Josh's nanny, Thea, in charge. Poor girl, she was overwhelmed, it was total mayhem. They ran riot in the gardens, trampled the flower beds and splashed about in one of the ponds, scaring the coy carp.' He shook his head. 'Absolute madness. I went crazy. Thea went to get help but when Lily arrived I swore at her and she sacked her for being incompetent and me because she said she wasn't having a foul-mouthed Scottish gardener working for her.'

'You don't work for her, you work for Talún,' Rufus protests. 'Anyway, you can't simply sack people, it's illegal.'

'Well, maybe it isn't if you tell someone you don't care and to stick the job where the sun doesn't shine,' he says.

'All the same,' Bella says, 'didn't Talún have the final say?'

'He's not here,' Rob chips in, 'he's up in Yorkshire looking at horses with the stud's manager.'

'He'll be in for a nice surprise when he gets back then.' Rufus gives a smug smile, his dislike for Talún even greater since our recent conversation.

'That doesn't help Adrian though, does it?' I remind him. 'You realise he's lost his home as well as his job.'

'You're more than welcome to come here,' Rufus tells him, 'rent free until you get yourself sorted.'

I can see Adrian's really touched by my father's gesture. Eyes filling with moisture, he shakes his hand and thanks him, telling him he's a life saver. He then chats with his colleagues about moving his things out.

195

'What will you do?' I ask him later, when everyone is settled with a drink and the discussion has turned to less fractious topics.

'W...ell,' he stretches out the word as he considers my question. 'I suppose I could start my own business. Buy a van, become a mobile gardener. I don't want to leave the area. All my friends are here.' He smiles and I'm glad to see he's beginning to put today's unpleasant events into perspective and think about the future. I'm not sure what will happen when Talún returns but even if he asked him I don't think Adrian would go back, not with Lily there. I also heard on the grapevine that little Alice Tanner was sacked the day after the party. Something about taking Lily's dress to get the creases ironed out and not getting it back to her quickly enough for her liking.

'Strange isn't it?' I say to him. 'Everyone thought Leanna was an awful employer.'

'Och, she's got nothing on this one,' he says with a slow shake of his head. 'She's a real piece of work. I have nae idea where the hell he found her or what madness made him decide to marry her but the way things are going there's trouble coming, and make no mistake about it. He can't see anything wrong with her. God knows what he'll make of it all when he gets home. Josh will really miss Thea, she was a great girl, looked after him brilliantly. The trouble was caused because those women were only interested in having a good time and necking down the champagne. They couldn't have cared less about their kids. Selfish bitches.'

As I listen to Adrian, I wish some part of me felt sorry for Talún's situation but I don't. I think I could have made my peace with him had it not been for Lily. What he did behind my back changes everything and it's something I simply can't forgive...or forget.

LILY

Talún is due back this evening. I'm not sure what his reaction will be when he gets home. I don't have any guilt over dismissing Thea. She's supposed to have been trained to look after children and she didn't do her job properly. I was looking forward to an afternoon of relaxation by the pool and getting to know some of the other women. Instead I got hauled out to deal with wrecked flower beds, wet children and a foul mouthed Scottish gardener. It was all too much. Well, I'm glad he's gone, Talún was far too familiar with him. I mean, how can you possibly manage staff when you treat them like a best mate? Ridiculous.

I'll have to get an agency replacement for Thea. Josh is inconsolable and has been quite difficult. He wouldn't stop crying and actually told me he hated me for getting rid of his *best friend in all the world.* In a few days he'll be over it, kids are like that, they bounce back. At the moment Jeanette's looking after him until I can organise the new nanny. God, I don't need this hassle! Everything was going so well...

I've already worked out what I'm going to say to Talún when he gets back. I'll put the blame on Adrian, tell him he upset Thea with his aggression and foul language and she refused to stay any longer. After all, he won't be here to say any different. Jeanette told me he'd already handed in the keys to his cottage which means hopefully he's well on his way to the Scottish border by now.

Everything's been sorted apart from the damage to the garden. I asked the gardeners to repair the ruined flower beds before Talún returned. However, they were particularly difficult, saying with one man down they were too short staffed. I daren't risk threatening them because they could easily down tools and walk out. The last thing I want is to make a bad situation worse, but I won't forget this in a hurry, damn them.

TALÚN

I've been away two days and I return to chaos. Adrian and Thea have gone and some of the flower borders look as though a herd of cattle have rampaged through them. Then there's Lily insisting she had no option but to sack Adrian after his abusive tirade - one which apparently was sufficiently awful to make Thea hand in her notice and leave straight away. Josh is very upset. When I looked in on him this evening I found Jeanette attempting to read him a story. He had, however, turned away from her and was lying facing the window, clutching his toy dragon, his thumb in his mouth. Seeing me, Jeanette smiled then closed the book and left us. I sat with him and chatted about where I'd been for the last couple of days, wondering if he might say something which would shed light on recent events. He moved onto his back and looked up at me, his pink, tearstained face indicating he was truly heartbroken. As he started to sob I reached out and pulled him into my arms. I told him everything was going to be fine and we'd find another Thea to be his best friend. I asked him if he'd like to visit the farm and see George – something I'd been planning to do with him. He nodded, sniffed and rubbed his eyes, asking if we could go tomorrow. I told him yes, but not until the afternoon, then maybe we could see the cows being milked. He liked that idea and I settled him down again, brushing the soft blond hair from his eyes and kissing him goodnight. It was as I left the room I realised I still had unfinished business with Jess Hayden. Mentally I scheduled it for tomorrow morning, right after breakfast.

JESS

Krister was in the Bull last night and mentioned Talún wanted to see me. When I asked him if he knew why, he simply shrugged. 'Something about the project I guess...the extra land maybe?'

'You could be right,' I responded, thinking what a nice gesture that would be, but knowing Talún I guessed it was probably something completely different. But what? An apology for his rudeness the other evening? Pigs might fly.

I'm still wondering about the reason he wants to see me as I return from my ride. Leaving Caspar in Ben's capable hands, I drive back to the cottage, stopping at the village shop on the way to pick up a few groceries. Carrying my purchases, I walk down through the wood towards the cottage, unlock the front door and let myself in. As I walk into the kitchen and deposit my bags on the worktop, I feel a sudden draught on the back of my neck. I turn, confused, as I was sure I closed the door behind me.

He's standing there, broad shoulders filling the doorway, his untidy dark hair curling around his collar. Dressed for riding in high black boots and jodhpurs, topped with a loose cotton shirt open at the neck, he looks as if he's stepped from the pages of some Regency romance. His green eyes watch me silently as I walk back into the living area to face him. I was so shocked at seeing him at the Hall's welcoming party I hadn't had a chance to study him properly. Now I realise when I knew him all those years ago, those wild gypsy looks that drew me were merely nature's work in progress. Five years have turned him into a spectacular man and instantly I hate the fact Lily is the one who has him. But then, be sensible, I tell myself, beauty is only skin deep. In reality he's nothing but a two faced liar.

'Krister said you wanted to see me,' I say curtly. 'Is that why you're here?'

He doesn't respond. Instead he walks in and looks around the room, taking everything in. 'I can see you've made a lot of changes,' he says. 'Got it for a song, did you?' There's a sarcastic edge to his tone I don't much care for but I'm determined not to let him needle me.

'We came to a mutually suitable arrangement, yes.'

'I bet you did.' He walks past me into the kitchen diner. 'Worked out well for you too, didn't it?' He turns to look at me, his expression icy. 'Befriending my grandmother. It got you exactly what you wanted. Very clever Jess.'

'This cottage had nothing to do with Anna.' I tell him.

'Rubbish,' he snaps back at me. 'It was part of the estate.'

'Yes I know it was, but—'

'No buts, you tricked her into thinking she was your friend. Still the same old Jess, lying and cheating to get what you want.'

He's moved closer to me, so close I can see the amber flecks in his hard, disapproving eyes. I realise the extra land's not going to happen, he's just here for some mudslinging. Well, I've got a pretty good aim too.

'Me a cheat and a liar? Well, that's great, coming from you.' Folding my arms, I stand my ground.

'What's that supposed to mean?'

'When we were together; always and forever you said. Did you say that to Lily too? You know if you hadn't turned up here with a four and a half year old son I'd never have known you were seeing both of us at the same time. '

'I didn't come to discuss the past.' He says dismissively, 'I came to tell you to stay away from my grandmother. You've got what you wanted and no doubt you're pleased but—'

'What the hell are you talking about?' I interrupt. 'I bought this cottage from Leanna weeks before your family put an offer in on the Hall.'

'I don't believe you.'

'I don't care if you do or not,' I say. 'It's the truth.'

'Your truth maybe. Like the twisted version of events you fed to George.'

'What are you accusing me of now?'

'You told George you came back for me.' He gives an indignant snort. 'Well, if that's true, it didn't take long for you to tire of the new boyfriend, did it?'

'What new boyfriend?'

'Tall, lanky, untidy yellow hair.'

'I have no idea what you're talking about. Anyway I thought you said you weren't here to discuss the past.'

'The club? Rococo's?' He carries on as if he hasn't heard me.

'You were there?'

'Yes, I was.'

'With Lily no doubt.'

He pushes out an angry breath and turns away towards the window.

I didn't want this sort of verbal entanglement, but he's

started it and I'm so angry at his ridiculous suggestions, I'm determined to finish it. I press the tips of my fingers into my forehead, trying to take myself back all those years. My mind is spinning and then a name surfaces. 'You mean Tristan Whittaker,' I say.

'Ah, it all came back to you in the end didn't it?' His smile holds no warmth as he turns back to look at me.

'But I wasn't with him, not in the way you think.' I look up into his angry, disbelieving face. 'Roo was there too. Tristan wasn't my boyfriend, he was—'

My explanation comes to an abrupt halt as Talún refuses to let me finish. 'I don't think I want to hear any more, Jess.' He dismisses me with an arrogant wave of his hand, 'The lies just pour out of you, don't they?'

'I am *not* lying.' Livid at his accusations, I push myself off the couch to confront him. 'I think you'd better go. I really do have better things to do with my time than listen to you and your unpleasant allegations.' I push past him, heading for the kitchen, but his hand wraps around my upper arm and he pulls me back to face him.

'Let...go...of...me,' I say as I attempt to shake him off, furious at being manhandled.

Our gazes lock for a moment and then he releases me. 'Just remember what I've told you. Stay away from my grandmother.' He issues a final warning then leaves, slamming the front door behind him.

LILY

At last we have a new nanny. Her name is Stacey and she was over an hour late; claims she couldn't find the house. I close my eyes, wondering what sort of idiot she must be, seeing she comes from the next village. I decided not to go back to the agency, too many uncomfortable questions would be asked and it's the last thing I need. Georgie said there was a local girl - a friend's daughter - who had looked after Darcy during the holidays. She sounded fine on the phone and because she came recommended I didn't see the need to interview her. The bonus was she was between jobs and could start straight away.

The reality of Stacey Beauman is altogether very different. She's nineteen and a fully-fledged human Barbie Doll. She has great cascades of peroxide blonde hair - mostly extensions I'm guessing – styled, if that's the word, to look as if she has just walked out of a wind tunnel. Her nails are long and painted shocking pink, and from the size of the boobs competing for limited space beneath her tight cerise blouse, I have a feeling Stacey and the surgeon's knife are already old buddies. When I quiz her about her connection to Georgie it appears her parents are clients of Jensen Lebeq.

'Jensen looks after my old man's money,' she says with a smile. 'He supplies slot machines all along the south coast – arcades, clubs, and pubs. Wherever they're needed. Makes a fortune. I don't really need to work,' she pauses to study one of her acrylic tipped fingers. 'I do fill in jobs like this instead. I like to have some sort of distraction.'

'Fill in?' I echo, as I begin to wonder whether Georgie has stitched me up. 'I'm looking for a full time nanny, Stacey.'

'Well,' she examines the nail again then looks at me and smiles, 'we'll see how it goes, shall we?' Pushing herself away from the pink BMW convertible she's arrived in, she says cheerfully, 'Right, how about showing me what's what?'

I show her over the house and find myself having to bite my tongue as she makes comments, obviously finding it lacking when comparing it to what she calls the Hollywood glamour of "Beaumont Towers". However, as we talk, I begin to get a better feel about her. She seems harmless, if a little scatty, and I decide she'll do for now, but I need to find another good quality agency pretty damned quickly.

Once the guided tour is over I run through my expectations of her role as Josh's nanny. Naturally, I'm basing her duties on Thea's and it's here we hit a huge problem. She's not prepared to live in. She sees herself more as a daytime supervisor, not someone getting involved in all aspects of twenty-four hour child care.

Damn! I realise I'm going to have to call on Jeanette again to plug the gap until I can sort out something more permanent. I introduce her to Josh and he is fascinated by her gravity defying hair. He keeps staring at it and smiling. Stacey calls him a "cute kid" and asks him what he'd like to do today. He tells her about his riding lessons and she's very enthusiastic, telling me she has her own horse at home. I leave her to take Josh down to the stables. I wince as I watch them go. The tight jeans I can just about cope with, but the cling film blouse and skyscraper wedges will have to go. I make a mental note to have words later.

TALÚN

I actually thought the day couldn't get any worse. All the way back from the cottage I was thinking how typical it was of Jess, always having to have the last bloody word. Of course, I didn't believe anything she'd told me. Just as Lily had said in the past, Roo would walk on hot coals for her. Yet another fool who couldn't seem to see her for what she really was. Well, I knew she was an accomplished liar and, if anything, our meeting this morning has deepened my dislike of her even more. The only satisfaction I had was that there was no way she was getting the extra land she wanted.

I arrived back at the stables to find Josh in the middle of his riding lesson. He waved out and shouted something I couldn't quite hear and pointed over towards the far corner of the ring. I turned to look and had to do a double take. 'What the...'

'It's the new nanny,' an amused voice next to me announced. I swung around to see Greg Martin leaning on the rail, his eyes fixed on the blonde in the tight shirt and jeans who had my attention.

'You are joking.'

'No, her name is Stacey and she's caused quite a stir here this morning.'

'I can imagine,' I said, as I handed over Achilles to a nearby groom. I made my way back towards the house, slapping my riding crop against my boot as I walked. I needed to talk to Lily. This had gone beyond a joke.

LILY

I have never seen Talún in such a temper. I don't know where he's been this morning but he came back spoiling for a fight. And boy is this some confrontation as we are both shouting. No doubt most of the staff will be quick to take tales of our argument back to the village where it will circulate for days.

'What possessed you to hire her?' he demands. 'She looks like a rock band's camp follower,' then to my frown, 'a groupie?'

'I plan to have words about her dress,' I assure him. 'She was late arriving and I needed her to take Josh for his riding lesson.'

To this statement he closes his eyes and shakes his head. 'And I suppose the candy floss pink BMW outside is hers.'

I nod. 'I'll get her to park it around the back with the pool vehicles. I assume she'll have use of the Range Rover you let Thea drive?'

'Well, Josh is certainly not being driven about in *that*.' He waves his hand in the direction of the front door. 'So, has she seen her room and been briefed her on her role here?'

'Ah...'

'Yes?' He sucks in an irritated breath.

'The thing is,' I grope for the best way to break the news, 'she's local and, well, she's only here during the day.'

'That's not a nanny, it's a childminder. Why didn't you go back to the agency?'

I make what I feel is a credible excuse. 'We needed someone quickly. Look, I'll get on to them tomorrow but interviews will take time to set up. In the meantime,' I say gently, trying to calm the situation, 'let's see how she gets on, shall we?' I take a deep breath. I think the worst is over but then the next moment I realise he's not finished with me.

'So who looks after Josh when she's not here? You?'

'Jeanette's offered to do it and I've agreed to pay her extra.'

Talún steps forward and takes my hands in his. 'Lily,' he says, 'you have to get a grip on things here. Jeanette is our house manager. She's already taking more than enough responsibility covering for your absences.'

'What's happening with Adrian?' I ask, deliberately switching the attention away from Stacey and my shortcomings. 'Have you seen him? I know you want him back. I thought you might have managed to talk him into returning. After all, you're pretty close to him aren't you?' His next words aren't at all helpful.

'It's too late," he says. 'I've already heard from the other gardeners he's currently living at the Bull and planning to start his own business.'

'Can't we promote one of the others?' I ask. 'After all, it's not as if gardening is rocket science, is it? So putting someone in charge should be fairly simple.'

Another sigh and he walks away, telling me to leave it with him, that he will sort it.

For the first time since we arrived here Josh has lunch with us. Stacey's left for the day, Talún advising her she won't be required until tomorrow. He tells me he's planning to take Josh up to the farm this afternoon to see the animals. Well, at least that should get him off my hands for a while. I have volunteered to bathe and put him to bed this evening though. You see I need to keep Talún sweet because there's something I'm about to ask him. Something I want that is very important - a mid-week break in London with the girls.

TALÚN

I think I've got our staff problems under control. It's pointless trying to get Adrian back so I've promoted Dave Wardell, his deputy, and asked him to recruit two new experienced gardeners. I have left Lily to organise the new nanny. Relieved peace is restored at the Hall, I turn my thoughts to this afternoon when Josh and I are driving up to the farm to see George and Ellie.

This is the first time I have been back to Manor Farm since my departure. The house is still the solid, warm, buttery stone building with matching tiles I remember, but I see the old stables have been replaced and there's a new Dutch barn. I take Josh around to the back of the house and into the kitchen, where the familiar smell of baking greets us.

I introduce Josh to Ellie and immediately he's asking questions about the things she's cooking and wants to know what they are and how she makes them. Having had his curiosity satisfied, we say our goodbyes and leave to find George.

George is in the new stable block with Ben. When we met at the Hall welcoming party, Ben was quite overwhelmed to see me again and I found myself the subject of a lot of man hugs. He's certainly filled out since I left; a gentle giant who has a special way with horses. I have no idea how he will react to Josh but find I needn't have worried because after experiencing yet another enthusiastic welcome, Ben squats down to Josh's level and immediately begins to tell him about the stable and the horses there.

'That's a beautiful gold horse.' Josh points to a Palomino, its head poking through the open top of the loose box in the corner.

'His name is Caspar,' Ben tells him. 'Would you like to give him an apple? I keep a few in the tack room. Then we can meet the other horses if you like.'

Josh nods then looks to me for approval. 'Is that all right Daddy?' he asks.

'Sure, 'I say, ruffling his hair, and then tell Ben, 'I'll be with George for a while.'

Leaving my son who is clearly smitten with the big golden horse, I seek out George, finding him in the milking parlour getting ready for the afternoon's session. He stops and we sit for a while, discussing farming matters and my fledgling stud.

'Josh is quite taken with the Palomino,' I tell him. 'Who does he belong to?'

'Jess.'

'She keeps her own horse here?'

'Yes. Paid for the new stable block, too.' George watches my reaction and laughs. 'No, she didn't rob a bank,' he jokes, 'Leo left her all his money. He was a well-to-do bloke by all accounts; owned a lot of property. She's a wealthy young woman now and doing a lot of good for the village.'

'And for herself,' I say, unable to halt my words in time.

'Talún.' George shakes his head. 'Don't.'

'I'm sorry George, but I can't forgive her for persuading Anna to let her buy the cottage.'

'She didn't buy it from Anna,' he says with a laugh. 'She bought it before you Hawkeswoods ever came on the scene.'

The news hits me hard after our row. I was so sure she was lying.

'She bought it for me,' he says, taking off his cap and running the back of his hand over his forehead to wipe away the sweat gathered there. 'When the Hall was put up for sale I realised everyone would find out I didn't own the farm, that I was just a tenant. It stressed me out and people, including Jess, began to notice and ask questions. She got it into her head I was bothered about what would happen to the cottage. Leanna had already jokingly said the new owner would probably demolish *the hovel*, as she called it. Jess thought it was of sentimental value for Ellie and me because it was where you and Cesca lived. So she went to Leanna and made an offer for it. Of course,' he laughed, 'when she told me, I had to put her straight. It was then she met Krister, asked him to do the renovations and decided to live there.'

I stand there silently not knowing what to say. I was wrong about her; she didn't groom Anna in order to get the cottage, it was already hers. I feel totally embarrassed. I let my dislike for her colour my judgement and my tongue run away with me.

'You haven't gone storming in there, have you Talún?' George eyes me curiously. 'Ah, I can see you have,' he says with a sigh as he slots his cap back on his head.

'Okay, I was wrong,' I admit reluctantly, 'but how am I to believe any good of her after what she did?'

'Don't you mean what you *thought* she did?' he says, pinning me with a stare.

'I know what I saw, and despite what she says there was no sign of Roo.' I say, feeling annoyed George should be taking her side.

'Well, if you're bothered about it...which I can see you are, why don't you ask him?' He suggests squinting at me from under the peak of his cap, 'He's back working in Exeter now. He's an honest lad, he'll tell you what really happened.'

'Will he? I'm not so sure.' Roo and Jess are joined at the hip. I'm under no illusions where his loyalties lie.

'Well at least think about it. I mean, after all this time, what reason would he have to lie?' He gives my shoulder a fatherly pat. 'Now then, how about giving me a hand to get the herd in for milking.'

That evening I took George's advice and gave his words a lot of thought. I remembered the morning after my fall from grace. I was on my way to the Bull to break down the door if necessary to get to Jess and beg her forgiveness. Roo intercepted me, calmed me down and gave me Jess's message. He told me she wanted to use her week away at uni to think things through and come to a decision about our future together. He seemed to think the outcome would be a positive one for me and promised to look after her. I saw myself clearly then, full of pent up frustration. On the one hand I blamed myself for my foolishness, getting drunk and sleeping with Lily. But I was also scared of losing Jess and I knew during her Fresher's week she'd been mixing with lots of new guys, ones who weren't penniless gypsies. So I'd ignored Roo's advice and gone to find her. I remember the place was packed and I'd only come across her by accident. Could he have been getting a round of drinks or maybe even taking a leak? I'd already made one mistake about Jess and the cottage. What if I was wrong about this too? George was right. I needed to talk to him and I knew just the excuse.

JESS

It's weeks since my confrontation with Talún at the cottage. I often see him riding through the village at a distance but luckily the Hall is far enough away to ensure our paths never cross.

Adrian has bought a second hand Transit van and started his gardening business. When I bought the cottage a parcel of one and half acres came with it. I've let him have the land at the rear as an allotment to bring on plants and he's wasted no time in erecting a small shed and starting work. He's already managed to get a few jobs. It's mostly lawns and general maintenance but it brings in a regular income. Of course he misses the camaraderie of the team but at least he's able to have regular evening meet ups with them at the Bull.

Adrian's departure from the Hall has turned him into a real gossip about what's going on up there – something he receives regular updates on from his old buddies whenever they meet for a drink. I think he thrives on the fact things aren't working well for Lily; there's an element of payback there.

'They've got this empty-headed creature up there looking after little Josh.' He tells us, 'Local girl, only there during the day. Jeanette, their housekeeper, covers the rest of the time. Lily pays her for her trouble, but I think she's beginning to get fed up. There's no let up from it. She's constantly needed because Lily's off gallivanting. Want to hear the latest?'

He teases us with this as yet unknown piece of information and Bella gives one of her *here we go* again sighs.

'Go on then.' I look at her and laugh. 'You're obviously dying to tell us.'

'She's only gone and taken herself off to a fancy health spa with the Witches.'

'Really?' At the mention of Georgie and Danni, Bella is all ears. 'Where?'

'Some flash hotel in London.'

I hate to imagine what Talún's reaction will be when the bill comes in. He's in for a rude awakening as he has no idea of Lily's extravagances. While she lodged with us, her whole life was one round of shopping and overindulgence, courtesy of Leo. However, those days are nothing in comparison to her current situation and the gold Amex card she no doubt has tucked into her purse.

LILY

I've had a wonderful break in London with Georgie and Danni. We've shopped till we've dropped and done some serious partying. The hotel beauty treatments have been absolutely amazing, I feel like a new woman. I'll definitely have to do this more often and I'm sure when Talún sees how beneficial it's been I'll have no trouble persuading him to let me come again. It would be nice to have a crash pad up here too; maybe I'll suggest it to him when we get back. All this pampering has got me thinking about my body. There are bits of me I definitely think could do with a nip and tuck. Giving birth to Josh left me with a slightly saggy stomach and thicker thighs. Georgie noticed it when we were using the hotel's pool. She told me about this great guy she goes to in Knightsbridge so I made an appointment and saw him during our stay...I'm booked in for my first Botox injections next week.

On Monday morning while I go to reception to settle the bill, Georgie and Danni, carrying all our shopping, have gone to collect Georgie's Mercedes from the underground car park. I agreed to treat them to this trip...well what else could I do? It's all part of the bonding process as far as I'm concerned. The Hawkeswoods are extremely wealthy and my generosity reflects this. However when I'm presented with the print out I'm sure they've got it wrong. It's far too much. I point out it was an inclusive package. The receptionist is very patient but I can see by her expression she's totally pissed off with me. She explains what I booked didn't include alcohol and on checking the bill I can see Georgie and Danni have been ordering champagne in their rooms and they've also added more expensive treatments to the spa package. I'm stunned, then angry. None of this extra spending was agreed with me first; no one asked they simply used my money as if it was their own. As I hand over my card to settle up I realise this won't surface until my credit card statement arrives at the end of the month. This means I've a few weeks to work out how to soften the blow once Talún discovers how much I've spent.

As I leave the hotel Georgie pulls up in front of me, both her and Danni are smiling. I realise if I raise the issue of their extravagance I run a risk of making myself or Talún look penny pinching - not the image I want to project. So I simply smile back, take the hit and tell myself the next time we do anything like this the bill is all theirs.

TALÚN

Lily's due back today and one of the things I need to speak to her about is where we are with the recruitment of the new nanny. We can't continue with this halfway house. It's not fair on Jeanette and as for Stacey, well I think she needs to be jettisoned as soon as possible. I've lost count of the number of occasions I've caught her chatting and had to remind her about her duties. In the end I decided against letting her have use of the Range Rover. Behind the wheel of her pink BMW she's a liability. She's accelerator happy and she's been spotted texting on her mobile while driving through the village, so there's no way Josh is getting into a car with her. This means she's confined to the estate and there's very little to do other than spend time at the stables where I know her sights are set on Richard Havers, one of the stable lads. She's a nightmare. She has to go.

This morning I'm hoping to close the door on one thing that's been bothering me. I'm doing just as George suggested and seeing Roo Cadwallader. My visit is quite legitimate: to discuss the pre-nuptial agreement Lily has persuaded me into organising. But I'm also hoping I'll get an opportunity to discover what sort of role Tristan Whittaker played in Jess's life.

The offices of Cadwallader, James and Carr are situated a few minutes' walk from the cathedral. Inside the reception area is decorated in pastel tones with lots of glass and chrome and abstract prints; an understated quality which tells me this is a successful modern practice.

Roo's PA greets me and takes me through to his office where he sits behind a huge desk of pale ash. His files are piled to one side and his gaze is fixed on his PC screen as he types. Jacketless, he looks quite casual for a lawyer. As we enter he looks up and I see he still has that quiet serious air about him. He watches me carefully with a calm measured gaze. As the PA leaves he gets to his feet and reaching across the desk offers me his hand.

'Talún, welcome.' He gives me a warm smile and I find myself in the grip of a firm handshake, 'Good to see you after all this time. Take a seat.'

I give him a brief summary of my last five years and he congratulates me on my forthcoming marriage. We then get down to business and he's warm and friendly as we talk and he jots down notes. At the mention of Lily, however, he lifts his pen.

'You know her?' I ask watching the gold nib of the Mont Blanc hover above the pad.

'Yes, as a matter of fact I do.' He nods and immediately goes back to his writing.

'And?'

He stops again and looks at me. 'She's local, that's all.' He says with a shrug and an expression which suggests he's wondering why I'm asking.

We continue; me stating the arrangements I want to make and him listing them. Finally we finish and I lean back in the chair.

He stops writing and quickly scans the A4 pad he's been making notes on, 'Is there anything else you want to add to this?' He queries with a quick glance at his watch, 'or are we done here?'

'I think we seem to have covered everything.' I confirm as I look up at his wall clock and see it's nudging twelve-thirty. No doubt he's eager to escape for lunch.

'Great, I'll get this drafted and sent to you,' he tells me, capping his pen, 'then we can make another appointment to finalise things.'

I thank him and push myself out of the chair, realising an opportunity to quiz him about Jess isn't going to happen.

'Before you leave,' he says, halting my departure, 'can I ask you something? Why did you come to see me? You could have gone to anywhere in this city for your pre-nup. But you not only chose my father's practice, you specifically asked for me.' He tilts his head curiously. 'Is there another issue you wish to discuss? Something more personal, perhaps?'

I acknowledge his query with a quiet nod before I respond. 'As a matter of fact there is. What can you tell me about Tristan Whittaker?'

JESS

It's Monday and I'm not on lunch shift at the Bull today. I have most of the day to myself, which means a relaxing breakfast and taking Caspar out a little later than usual. As always, Ben has him saddled and waiting on my arrival at the farm. Now, under the green canopy of Barnfield Woods, my mind is on the trip I'm taking with Krister next week. We're attending a two day exhibition on eco-friendly building being held at the Grange Country Hotel just south of Bristol. Krister is already quite knowledgeable, having met up with other developers and looked over their projects. This trade show will expand his knowledge. It will not only give him an idea of the latest technology available, he'll be able to make a decision on exactly what we want to incorporate into our houses.

I reach the river and my rock and, leaving Caspar to crop, I perch myself there and pull my phone from my pocket to scan through my calls. Despite being in a wooded area this place isn't a black spot so I know I'll get a fairly good signal. On checking, I find I've had a text from Anna. As is the case whenever she contacts me, her opening line is how much she misses our chats by the river. Today she has some exciting news...Marcus has been given a knighthood in the Queen's birthday honours. He has known for some time but now they've gone public and I'm the first outside the family to be told. She reminds me it's her turn to Skype at the weekend when she says we can have a proper chat. I text a short reply sending congratulations and as I slip my phone back into my pocket I'm suddenly aware I have company. I can hear a child's voice and as I look across the clearing I see a small blond-haired boy standing beside Caspar. I'm immediately on my feet and waiting for an adult to appear. When that doesn't happen, I call out to him.

'Hello.' He replies taking a quick look at me before switching his gaze back to the Palomino. 'What's Caspar doing here?'

'He's my horse. Do you know him then?'

'Yes,' he nods, 'Ben showed him to me when my daddy brought me to the farm the other day.'

'Did he?'

The boy gives a serious nod. 'He's very beautiful,' he says. 'Golden.'

'Yes.' By this time I've reached him and have crouched down so we're on the same level. 'He's called a Palomino.'

He makes several attempts to pronounce the word and then gives up, cupping his small hands over his mouth as he giggles. I'm warming to this small boy and his sunny disposition. 'Are you here with your daddy today?' I ask.

'No,' he says, 'he's out.'

'What about mummy?'

'No,' he shakes his head. 'She's out too.'

'So who is with you?'

'No one.' He lifts his shoulders and works his small mouth, looking confused. 'Stacey and Richard came here too, but I can't find them. They went in there,' he points into the trees, 'they told me to wait and be good. But they've gone and Liquorice ran away.'

'Your brother and sister?' I ask, wondering in the absence of his parents whether older siblings are supposed to be looking after him.

'No, Stacey is my friend,' he says, 'and Richard works for my daddy. Liquorice is my pony.'

'Right.' I nod as I take in all this information. 'Well, shall we go and look for them?'

The thought seems to worry him. 'What will happen if we can't find them?' he asks.

Instinctively I put my arms around him and give him a hug. I feel the warmth of his small body, his breath on my face as his fingers burrow into my hair. 'I'll tell you what,' I say as I release him, 'how would you like me to take you home?'

'It's a long way,' he says, pointing. 'All over there.'

'Don't worry, Caspar will take us,' I tell him, a comment that brings a look of wonderment to his face.

'I can ride Caspar?' he asks.' Really?'

'Really. He's big and strong and he'll get us home very quickly,' I reassure him. 'Now where is it you live?'

'In the big house.'

'The Hall? Does your daddy work there?'

'No.' He shakes his head seriously. 'It's our house.'

I feel a rush of shock as I realise who he is. 'Josh? Are you Josh?' I ask, and he nods. I'm wondering what irresponsible individual could have abandoned a small boy here like this. Talún and Lily are both out. What kind of parents are they to leave idiots in charge of him?

We make good time getting back to the Hall. Josh keeps up his chatter as he sits in front of me his fingers laced in Caspar's mane. I hold him tightly, one arm wrapped firmly around his waist. He's a curious child, asking questions about the things we pass on our ride and wanting to know all about me. Eventually we turn in between the two large stone pillars which mark the entrance to the Hall and I ease Caspar into a trot.

Arriving at the house, I slip from the saddle and help him down. He reaches out to pat Caspar, who snorts and turns his head in Josh's direction, bringing a bubble of laughter from him. It's clear he adores my horse and the feeling appears to be mutual. I secure Caspar to a nearby tree and we are making our way across the lawn towards the front door when a silver Mercedes appears, approaching at speed. Stopping in a cloud of dust and gravel, the vehicle halts a few feet away. I see it's Lily and her two cronies, Georgie and Danni. It's then I realise they've probably just returned from London. Lily bales out of the rear door while the other two women sit there with smug expressions as they settle themselves comfortably to watch.

'What are you doing with my son?' she yells at me. 'How dare you trespass here.'

'I found him in the woods,' I tell her. 'He was on his own.'

'Lies! Absolute lies! Do you think I'm some idiot? Where's Talún?'

'I have no idea. Josh?' I bend towards him. 'Where did you say your daddy was?'

'Gone out.' He looks up at his mother with wide, innocent eyes.

The sound of hooves coming up the driveway halts our altercation. I see a young man and a blonde girl approaching on horseback, leading a riderless black pony.

'Ah, there you are.' Lily shields her eyes with her hand as they reach us. 'Where have you been?'

'Looking for Josh,' says the girl, who I immediately recognise. She's wearing tight jodhpurs and an even tighter t-shirt over gravity defying breasts. 'We lost him in the wood. Spent ages trying to find him, didn't we?' She turns to her companion obviously seeking corroboration.

'Yeah, we did.' His fixes me with a surly glare. 'Ages. How did he get back here?'

Lily points a finger in my direction before telling them to return to the stables and giving the girl the rest of the day off.

'Well,' she says, watching them ride off before turning back to me, 'I hope you're satisfied. Your interference means they've wasted most of their morning in a pointless and no doubt anxious search for my son.'

'He was on his own by the river,' I insist. 'He said they'd left him there and told him to wait.'

My words see Lily turning her attention to Josh.

'Josh!' she waves a threatening finger at him. 'You know what happens to naughty boys who tell lies.'

He obviously does as he bites his lip nervously and tears begin to form in his eyes.

'He's not lying,' I intervene, infuriated that because she can't intimidate me she has decided to take her temper out on him instead.

'Keep out of this!' she shouts. 'You're nothing but a trouble making bitch.'

The words feel like a physical slap but I stand my ground. I am not going to give Lily the reaction she wants in order to provide her two awful friends with some cheap entertainment.

Reaching down, Lily snatches at Josh and hauls him away from me. He begins to cry and I can see from the way her fingers are locked tightly around his upper arm she's hurting him. I'm horrified at such cold, callous behaviour and suddenly I don't care about the consequences. As she begins to drag him towards the house I go after her, blocking her way.

'What's the matter with you? Why are you punishing him?' I demand angrily. 'He only told the truth. You need to haul those two back and ask them why the hell he was taken into the wood in the first place.'

Her eyes narrow. 'What are you talking about?'

'That's Stacey Beauman, isn't it?' I answer angrily. 'You must have been mad letting a flighty piece like her look after Josh.'

'What I do is none of your damn business. Who the hell do you think you are?' she snaps, and I realise things aren't working out the way she thought they would. This isn't the show she expected to give her friends. She thought her new found status and accompanying arrogance would be enough to intimidate me. But it isn't; I won't allow this small child to be bullied in such an awful way. Releasing Josh, she swings around and I sense her hand moving towards me in a blur. Remembering our confrontation the day I discovered Rufus was my real father, I should have anticipated this kind of bad tempered reaction from her. I move quickly to one side and avoid the slap just in time. Unfortunately, she's put so much force behind it she shoots forward and lands on her knees in the grass. I turn towards the occupants of the car to see their reaction. They're laughing and I see their relationship for what it is: a shallow thing built on Lily's wealth rather than any honest attachment. As I turn back, Lily is struggling to get to her feet, her dress hem caught in one of her heels. Despite her cruel behaviour towards him, Josh is trying to help her up.

'Get off me,' she shouts, and shoves him away. He lands on the grass and, rolling onto his side, begins to cry. Dodging around her, I rescue him, lifting him into my arms and backing away from her. And through all of this, none of us has noticed the approaching car and its driver who now stands a few feet away, watching us angrily.

TALÚN

The drive home from Exeter gave me time to think, to gather my thoughts. Although all those years ago I didn't know Roo - or Alex as he's asked me to call him - I believe what he told me this morning is the truth. Despite the cronyism Lily accused him of, I left his office believing he had given me a true account of the events which had taken place during my last week in Lynbrook.

Fate often deals us strange hands. If I had waited we would probably have still been together. But I didn't. I drove into Exeter that night trying to do the impossible: to track down Jess in the middle of a city filled with hundreds of new uni students there for Fresher's week. My luck, or rather misfortune was to find her. Tristan Whittaker had been the name she'd given me and at the time I suspected if she could remember him he must have left a lasting impression. He had, but for entirely the wrong reason. In Alex's words, he was a floppy-haired nuisance. The incident in the club I had witnessed happened as they were about to leave. Alex, stopped from intervening by Tristan's friend Nick, had to wait until he had given Jess a rather drunken kiss goodbye.

'He was harmless really, just a complete pain in the arse. Ironically, after that night he never bothered her again. The sad thing is, on our way back to the flat I asked her what her plans were when she returned home. She said she had decided to see you, to try and sort out your differences. A strange thing, fate.' He managed a smile. 'If you hadn't witnessed what you did in Rococo's you would probably never have discovered your birth certificate and gone to find your family, would you?'

'No,' I say, 'I guess not.'

We parted company then; he left for a lunch meeting and I headed for home. As I turned in through the stone pillared entrance of Lynbrook Hall I made a decision to draw a line under everything I'd heard today and begin my new life at peace with everyone, including, if possible, Jess. But that, unfortunately, was not about to happen. As I approached the house I could see Lily and another woman arguing, with Josh in between them. What the hell was going on?

As I got out of the car I recognised the Palomino and realised it was Jess. Then I saw the Mercedes and its gleeful occupants. Reaching it, I banged on the glass.

'I'd like you both to leave,' I said to a surprised Georgie, as the electric window lowered.

'Lily's luggage and shopping is still in the boot,' she said belligerently, as if that gave them a legitimate reason to remain.

'I'll pick it up later,' I insisted, in none too friendly a manner. 'Please go.'

As their car headed off down the driveway I closed in on the two women. Lily was now on her knees in the grass after an unsuccessful attempt to slap Jess. Josh was trying to help her up but she swore and pushed him away. He fell and straight away Jess was there, scooping him up and taking him out of Lily's reach.

'What's going on?' I demanded.

Lily turned. 'Thank God you're back,' she said, struggling to her feet and almost falling into my arms. 'Get rid of her will you?' she gestured towards Jess, 'I found her here trespassing on our property. Goodness knows what she was up to.'

'That's a lie and you know it.' Jess stepped forward, lowering Josh gently to the ground. He rushed over to me and clung to my legs, clearly distressed. Lily reached us and gently untangled him with a few calming words. Then Jeanette appeared and took him by the hand, leading him back into the house. Lily joined me again and I slipped a protective arm around her shoulder, allowing her to lean into me. I could still feel the angry tremors coming off her. 'Get off our property,' she shouted, glaring at Jess. 'Now.'

Jess ignored her, her eyes on me, clearly wanting to explain.

'Lily's right, I think you'd better go,' I told her. Although I did want to get to the bottom of what had happened, I realised having Jess there would only inflame the situation. It was clear Lily was so wound up there was no way I could hope to deal with this sensibly.

Jess raised her hands, gave a silent shake of her head and then left. We both watched as she mounted up and turned Caspar's head towards the drive. Kicking her heels into his flanks, she galloped off and was soon out of sight.

'Thank goodness,' Lily moved away from me and gave me a smile, 'you came back just in time. Where are the girls?' she asked, noticing the Mercedes had gone.

'I asked them to leave.'

'I wish you hadn't.' She complained irritably, 'Georgie has my luggage and my shopping in her boot.'

'I'll collect them later.' I offered, in an attempt to pacify her.

'Oh, but I've bought this wonderful new black Stella

McCartney dress. You must see it. I'll wear it when our Bennett's Orchard friends come to dinner.'

Although I was relieved she seemed to have suddenly recovered from her spat with Jess, her news was not welcome. 'When did you arrange this?' I asked. Entertaining these two awful women and their husbands was the last thing I wanted.

'While we were in London. They're coming Saturday week. It's my first dinner party. I'm so excited. Now then,' she grabbed my arm and tried to lead me towards the car, 'please, go and get my stuff.'

'I said later.' I wrenched away from her grip. 'It seems to have escaped you, but there is something a little more important than shopping and dinner parties at the moment. Or have you totally forgotten our son?'

'Talún I'm sorry, blame that awful Jess Hayden. I'm all over the place.' she apologised at once, reaching up to kiss my cheek. 'I'll go and check on him straight away.'

As I watched her leave I realised discovering the truth about Jess hadn't made anything better. It had made everything far worse.

LILY

As I walk away from Talún I realise I need to find out what really happened this morning. I'm not happy about Jess Hayden's accusations. If she's telling the truth, this has the potential to blow up in my face. I must sort it out before Talún starts asking difficult questions. I know he's already unhappy about Stacey looking after Josh so I have to work out a plan to steer him away from this incident.

Jeanette is with Josh in his room. She's changed him into fresh clothes but he still looks wary of me as I enter. Jeanette smiles, ruffles his head and leaves.

'Come and give your mama a cuddle,' I coax, kneeling on the floor and stretching out my arms. At first he seems reluctant and then he's here, pressing his small body into mine. After a moment's bonding I lean back, holding him at arm's length. 'Right young man,' I say in my best, caring mummy's voice. 'Shall we have a chat about what happened this morning?'

TALÚN

I follow Lily up to Josh's room and find them sitting together on the bed, chatting. She looks up as I walk in and manages a smile, running the palm of her hand over his forehead to brush the hair from his eyes.

'I think he's had a bit of an adventure,' she says, looking down at him with a fondness I thought had all but disappeared. She seemed so caught up in her new world of socialising and shopping and trips to London I was beginning to think she had abandoned her son. However, it seems after today's incident everything has changed and she's firmly back in her role of caring mother. And whatever happened to Josh this morning, he looks a lot less traumatised than he did earlier when Lily and Jess were laying into each other.

It's obvious I need to keep my family away from Jess. I can't have Josh upset and it seems Lily can't handle any contact with her without losing it completely. I've never seen such a crazy look in her eyes.

'I'd like to chat to Josh alone for a moment,' I say, and he looks up at me, chewing his bottom lip nervously.

'I don't think that would be a good idea. He's still quite upset.' Lily says firmly, and then turns to Josh who is sitting there, his eyes moving back and forth between the two of us uneasily. 'So Josh and I have decided we're going to forget about this bad morning we've had, aren't we?'

Josh nods solemnly.

'Instead, we're going to have some lunch with you and then Josh is going over to Bennett's Orchard with me to pick up my things from Georgie. And after that,' she taps him lightly on the nose, 'tell Daddy where we're going.'

Josh looks up with his bright little smile and says, 'To see butterflies and otters.'

'At Buckfastleigh?'

Lily nods and kisses his forehead. 'My treat,' she says,

brushing back his hair again. 'Because I missed him so much over the weekend.'

'Where's Stacey this morning?' I ask, noticing she doesn't seem to be around.

'She had some family emergency. I gave her the day off.'

'And have you resolved the issue over Thea's replacement yet?'

She shakes her head. 'I'm waiting for them to come back. Thanks for reminding me. I'll chase it up this afternoon. Now, let's all go and have lunch, shall we?' she gives Josh a smile, 'because we need to make an early start if we're to see all the lovely wildlife. '

LILY

Phew, got out of that pretty well, if I say so myself. The promise of this afternoon's trip seems to have guaranteed Josh's silence about this morning. And when Talún appeared it was fairly easy to persuade him I had everything under control. I need to bury this as soon as possible as it opens up all sorts of problems for me. The last thing I want is for Talún to discover Jess had been telling the truth otherwise - heaven forbid - I'll probably be asked to apologise to her! Anyway I need to have a good talk with Stacey. I can't have her going off on lover's trysts in the wood and leaving my son on his own.

Talún's query about Thea's replacement sent me into a bit of a panic because I've done absolutely nothing about it. So, in the privacy of the car before Josh and I left, I took the opportunity to call them. Unfortunately, they weren't very helpful. It appears Thea has turned her departure into such a massive drama they are refusing to place another nanny with me. Of course, I demanded to speak to the owner. When she came on the line I apologised and told her the abusive gardener who had caused the trouble had been dismissed. But unfortunately it didn't cut any ice. Of course she was extremely polite...well, as polite as you can be when you're telling someone you don't want their business. Hell, I thought, as I ended the call, I've been blacklisted. What am I going to do?

TALÚN

After lunch I wave Lily and Josh off and as I step back into the house I see Jeanette. Although I need to speak to Lily about the strange scenario which greeted me on my arrival home I'm sure Jeanette's sudden appearance, meant she had seen what was going on.

'Can I have a quick word?' I ask as I reach her.

'Is it about this morning?'

'Yes. I wondered what was going on.'

'Isn't that something you should be asking Ms. Stevenson?'

'Yes, I should but—'

'Then I suggest you do.' She says politely, 'What goes on between her and Jess Hayden is none of my business. I merely came out to rescue an extremely distressed child. However, there is one thing I would like to say.'

'Yes?' I wait expectantly.

'Get rid of that awful girl. She's doesn't have Josh's interests at heart. Thea took Josh everywhere, they had such fun together. This one only wants to hang around the stable... and not for the riding,' she says. 'Am I painting a clear enough picture for you?'

'Perfectly.' I thank her and head for the stud. Jeanette's words trigger memories of Stacey down at the stables with Josh and one groom in particular, who always seemed to be hanging around while they were there: Richard Havers. Maybe it's time to have a word with him. First though, I call into Greg Martin's office. If there's anyone who would know what's going on, he will.

Armed with some interesting facts about his movements, I go in search of Richard and find him in the yard, rubbing down Summer, a bay mare I had purchased for Lily. Looking at the horse I realise she has shown absolutely no interest in her; in fact I don't think she has even bothered to come down to take a look. Richard straightens up as I reach him, curry comb in hand.

'Afternoon, boss.' He gives me a smile. A good looking, dark-haired twenty year old, I can see how he would appeal to Stacey.

'Richard.' I nod, settling myself on a nearby pile of straw bales. 'I understand from Greg you took Summer out this morning.'

'Yes,' he looks at her and pats her neck fondly. 'She goes like a dream.'

'Where did you go?'

'Oh, across the fields and down through Barnfield Woods.'

'Anywhere near the river?'

He hesitates as if he's working out what to say next.

'The truth Richard, please.'

'Yes, I rode by river,' he says hesitantly. 'Nowhere near the water though.'

'Did you go on your own?'

He heaves a breath. 'No, I was with Stacey Beauman.'

'And Josh was with you?'

'Yes, he was, but it wasn't our fault.'

'What wasn't?'

'Stacey said he'd be okay. He's a good boy. He does as he's told. She left him in a safe place.'

'A safe place?' I nearly explode. 'You leave a five-year-old in a wood on his own and you call it a safe place?'

'We weren't planning on being very long,' he says, and I hear the panic in his voice.

'Doing what exactly?'

Colour seeps into his cheeks. 'We wanted to be alone.'

'Why didn't you ask her out on a date? That's what normal people do.'

'Yeah, well I didn't.' He looks at the ground, his face twisting with annoyance. 'Probably because my parents wouldn't want me involved with a girl like her,' he says, releasing an angry breath.

Stupid kid, I think, and then remember what I was like at his age. 'And when you came back you found Josh was missing?' I prompt.

'Yeah, and we panicked. Stacey said you'd kill her if

anything happened to Josh. We split up, spent God knows how long searching through the wood, calling for him. We found Liquorice but Josh had gone. We rode back to the house as quickly as we could to get help. Stacey said Ms. Stevenson was still in London and you'd gone out, so we thought we could sort it before you both returned. When we got back to the house we could see Ms. Stevenson had already arrived. Josh was with them and she was in the middle of a row with Jess Hayden.'

'Over Josh?'

'It looked like it.'

'But you didn't tell her you'd left him on his own?'

'No. Stacey told her we'd lost Josh in the wood. It wasn't a lie...not really. Ms. Stevenson thought...well, that Jess had taken him without trying to find us. She was really angry she'd interfered. She told Stacey to take the rest of the day off and me to get back to the stables.'

'So she didn't ask what you were doing in the wood?'

'No,' He gives a heave of his shoulders. 'She seemed...I don't know...more interested in having a go at Jess. Well, when you think about it, she was to blame. If she'd left him where he was we'd have found him, wouldn't we?'

'Yes, you might have,' I agree. 'Face down in the river, perhaps?'

'Well, I...' Richard blanches at my accusation. It's obviously something he's not even considered. 'You're going to fire me, aren't you?' he stammers.

'Not this time.' I realise I'm being more tolerant than I ought to be but I know I was there once, driving George mad with my relentless pursuit of females. For that reason I'm going to give him a chance. 'But cross the line again and you're out, understand? '

'Thank you, I won't let you down,' he says, visibly shaking as he blows out a long breath. He thinks he's got away with a slapped wrist, but I haven't quite finished.

'You're right, you won't,' I tell him, 'because for the next seven days I'm transferring you to mucking out duties. Report to Greg first thing.'

He accepts his punishment with a nod. 'No more than I

deserve, I guess,' I hear him say as I walk away. Now to deal with the lovely Miss Beauman.

Returning to the house, I call her at home and tell her not to bother to turn up tomorrow because she's fired. She tells me she doesn't care, she hated the job anyway and slams down the phone. Then I phone the agency in London. Apparently, Lily has already called them and they won't entertain sending anyone to replace Thea. When I ask why I am shocked at what I hear from the owner. Thea didn't resign, Lily sacked her. I'm appalled Lily could lie to me like this and when she returns and Josh is in bed she's going to have some explaining to do.

I decide to spend some time in my office browsing the internet. I'm interested in the eco-build Krister and Jess are planning. The cottages on the site could do with updating and bringing into the twenty-first century. I want to turn them from draughty living quarters to comfortable, cost effective places. I check out a few sites and e-mail off enquiries and then out of the blue I see one site is exhibiting at a local eco technology exhibition. It's being held at a hotel south of Bristol and looks like a busy two day event including demonstrations and seminars. One phone call and I'm booked in for the two days with a room and dinner reservation for the first night. I'm about to call Krister to ask if he'll be there when I hear the front door slam. The patter of small feet indicates Lily and Josh have arrived back from their visit. I meet them in the hall, catching Josh up in my arms and swinging him around, keen to find out how his afternoon has gone.

'Did you have a good time?' I ask as I carry him through to the drawing room and set him down. He shakes his head, clearly upset. His small mouth is set in a disappointed pout, tears threatening.

Jeanette appears as if by magic. I'm sure she has some sort of telepathic link which tells her when she's needed. She looks at both of us and then turns her attention to Josh. 'I've a special surprise for your tea,' she tells him, and taking his hand, leads him out of the room.

'What happened?' I ask Lily as she kicks off her heels and falls into one of the couches.

'I am so glad to be home,' she says, as if she hasn't heard me. She stretches back into the softness of the leather and closes her eyes. 'What an afternoon.'

'Lily,' I persist, 'what happened?'

'Well, we went to Georgie's to collect my luggage and shopping,' she replies with a sigh, her eyes still closed. 'We got talking. Josh was playing with Georgie's daughter, Darcy, and...well the time just slipped by.'

'So you didn't take him?'

'No.' She pushes herself up and stares at me. I notice her cheeks are flushed and her eyes seem blurred as if she's about to cry.

'You were over the limit,' I say accusingly, leaning closer and catching a distinct waft of alcohol on her breath. 'You couldn't take him because you'd drunk too much at Georgie's. Bloody hell, Lily, how could you?' It's the first time I've ever raised my voice or sworn at her but from what's gone on today I've had enough. I'm only glad Jeanette and Josh are far enough away not to have heard me.

'Talún, please don't shout. Stacey can take him tomorrow.'

'Stacey no longer works here. I fired her earlier.'

'What?' Surprise morphs into anger as she gives me her full attention. 'Why, for heaven's sake?'

'Because Stacey and Richard abandoned Josh in the wood to get up to God knows what.'

'Has that lying bitch Jess Hayden been speaking to you?'

'No, Richard has. He confessed.'

Lily takes a deep breath. 'I had no idea,' she says with a shrug. 'They came back when Jess was kicking off here. I questioned them and they denied her version and...'

'Well they would, wouldn't they?' I interrupt. 'Anything to save their sorry hides.'

'Have you sacked Richard?'

'No. Stacey was a nightmare. Richard is a good stable

lad and I don't want to lose him. But don't think he's got away with it. He'll be mucking out the stables for a whole week.'

'Well done, it's all sorted then,' There's a sarcastic edge to her voice as she pushes herself up off the couch. 'Now if you'll excuse me, I need to get my things from the car. Grabbing her shoes she heads for the door but isn't quick enough to stop me intercepting her.

'We're not quite finished here. There's the matter of a replacement for Stacey.'

'Oh, right...yes.'

'The agency said you'd already phoned. And they had told you it would be better if we looked elsewhere for a nanny.'

'Oh.'

'Yes, oh, Lily, why didn't you tell me you'd sacked Thea?'

'I...well,' her mocking attitude vanishes. Instead her teeth graze her bottom lip nervously as we face each other, 'it was chaotic.' She raises her arms above her head as if to emphasise her frustration. 'Thea should have been in control and she wasn't. Then I had that bloody awful Scotsman having a fit because of the damage they'd done to the garden.'

'In control? Of ten children?'

'Well, she's a nanny. It's what's she's trained for, isn't it?' she says, looking at me as if I'm a complete idiot.

'No, it isn't.' I shake my head. 'Anyway, where were you and the other mothers while all this was going on?'

She's worrying her lip again and I get the feeling she's working out how to limit the damage, because I know from Jeanette exactly where they all were at the time.

'By the pool.' Her eyes meet mine, her voice quite calm, 'As I told you, I thought Thea could handle it. Obviously I was wrong and perhaps I shouldn't have sacked her. But I did and we have what we have.' Her comment ends with a shrug.

'Then I suggest you go online and find a reputable company who will provide us with a nanny for Josh.'

'Fine,' she says, meeting my challenge with a defiant tilt

of her chin as she levers on her shoes. 'Right, I'll do that.' And she leaves the room, slamming the door behind her.

I help myself to a whisky and stand, looking out of the window across the lawns. I'm incredibly angry with Lily and there will have to be changes. Handing your child over to be looked after by a nanny is one thing; abandoning responsibility altogether to go chasing after retail heaven and eternal youth is absolutely selfish and irresponsible. When I met her in Exeter she seemed different – totally grounded and committed to Josh. She made it clear I couldn't have him without her and the price I had to pay was marriage - a small sacrifice for being able to claim my son. And after all I'd been through I had never wanted anything so much in my life. I thought this was going to be a new start and a chance for happiness. I didn't love her but I was sure we were the type of people who wanted the same things and would make a good partnership. It's not happening and we haven't even got to the wedding. She's not only proved how thoughtless she is, she's also deliberately lied to cover things up. I could see my anger scared her and I hope this is a turning point in our relationship. She has to learn that living in this house comes not only with privileges but responsibility as well.

LILY

Bloody hell! I thought I had everything sorted. That Talún was far too busy with his horses to be bothered with my daily goings on. I had my whole support team in place until Josh's birthday meltdown happened. Georgie and Danni recommended Stacey Beauman. Why do I get the feeling they were having a laugh at my expense? When I think about it, no one in their right mind would employ a girl like her. But I was desperate, and I thought although she looked a bit suspect I'd give her the benefit of the doubt. Well now I've paid the price for my stupidity. I can see I'll have to tread a careful path. He was quite frosty with me over dinner and disappeared afterwards to spend the evening with Josh, reading to him and telling him -

according to Jeanette who overheard him chatting - that he would take him to see the otters when he's back from this seminar he's booked himself onto. He did actually mellow slightly when he returned to the drawing room, where I was flicking through the latest copy of *Vogue*. Deciding to try and calm things down, I pretended to be interested as he explained the reason he wants to attend. It's another project for the estate, upgrading the cottages to make them more eco-friendly. I did try to pay attention, but eventually it all went over my head. I then made a very rash promise; I said I would spend the next couple of mornings with Josh down at the stables, something I hoped would bring the smile back to his face. And then later, as I made my way up to bed, I realised I'd fouled up big time. Because on the second morning I need to be on my way to London, where I have an appointment for my Botox injections. I do realise after my rather extravagant long weekend and the row looming over the bill it might be wise to cancel and rebook in a few weeks' time. But no, after the dreadful day I've had and the verbal battering from my husband-to-be, to hell with it. I deserve this last treat. After this, I promise I'll become a totally reformed character.

JESS

The Grange Country Hotel is everything I expected it to be. Solidly Victorian and ivy covered, it is surrounded by lush green parkland and a perfect setting for this particular exhibition and conference. As we arrive I can see a multitude of white canvas pavilions set to one side of the main building. Krister tells me these are where the exhibitors can be found and once we've checked in we'll have a wander before going into lunch. Tomorrow, presentations on new breakthrough technologies will be held in the main conference hall. As all this will be terribly technical, Krister has suggested I spend a relaxing morning in the hotel's spa before lunch, and then home. Well, I'm definitely up for that.

Once we've gone through registration and have been issued with ID badges, I find I'm actually looking forward to seeing what's on offer After forty-five minutes of browsing, chatting and collecting business cards and brochures, we're about to head for the dining room for lunch when I see a familiar figure emerging from the Connaught's Underfloor Heating pavilion.

'What's he doing here?' I nod towards Talún.

'The same as we are of course.' Krister replies with a shrug, 'I heard he is planning to upgrade the cottages on the estate, were you not aware of this?'

'Anna did mention it a while back,' I say with a reluctant nod, realising the sight of him has dredged up my anger, remembering our last meeting at the Hall where he dismissed me like one of his hired hands.

'So this is why he is here, doing what we are doing.' Krister confirms, 'Look, I know you two are not the best of friends at the moment but—'

'Best of friends? What are you talking about?'

'Bella told me how you found Josh in the wood and took him back to the Hall. Lily was rude to you, yes?'

'Very. Stacey and Richard lied. They deliberately abandoned Josh. He was near the river when I found him. Anything could have happened and I was cast as the bad guy. I didn't expect Lily to believe me, but Talún wouldn't even give me a chance to explain. He simply demanded I leave.'

If it makes you feel better I have heard he sacked Stacey Beauman and his stable hand has been punished.'

'It doesn't. He was very rude. In fact he's an arrogant pig.' I say with feeling.

Krister crosses his arms and studies me for a moment. 'And is Talún bothered you feel this way?' He asks, 'Does he care? I think maybe not. So to me you are wasting your time with this anger.' He shakes his head, his beautiful blue eyes observing me sadly, 'you see in the end this hurts only one person: you. You are my very good friend and I do not wish to see this happening.'

'It won't,' I assure him, 'but thank you for your wise

words. Now then, let's get some lunch and talk about what we've seen so far, shall we?'

Dinner is seven-thirty for eight. Krister's room is just down the corridor from mine and a knock on the door at seven-twenty-five announces he's here to collect me. Dressed in a soft collarless green shirt and beige chinos, his hair still damp from the shower, he looks every inch the dream date. I'm sure he'll be turning female heads in the dining room when we arrive.

The lift takes us down to the ground floor and opens with a whisper of parting doors just off the reception area. From there we make our way to the bar and I settle myself on a high stool while Krister orders wine for me and a beer for himself. Taking our drinks to an area of comfortable seating in the lounge, the waiter follows us with the menus and wine list. We spend time deciding what to eat and are still not sure whether we'll go with Italian or New World for the wine choice. Eventually we toss a coin and the Australian Shiraz wins. In no time at all we're being shown to our table on a covered terrace overlooking floodlit gardens. It's a magical, warm summer evening and the food is wonderful.

While we're waiting for the sweet menu to arrive, I leave to find the ladies cloakroom to freshen up. Leaning on the basin and checking my make-up I'm feeling relaxed, due partly to the wine we've consumed over dinner. On my way back to the table I'm so busy thinking about tomorrow morning's visit to the spa, I accidentally collide with someone who's just stepped out of the lift. Knocked off balance, I manage to steady myself against the wall. I feel a strong hand grip my shoulder and hear a voice apologising and asking me if I'm okay. My bag, which has fallen to the floor as a result of the impact, is handed back to me. As I straighten up I find myself looking into a familiar face...

'Jess?' For a moment Talún looks confused. 'What are you doing here?'

'Attending the exhibition with Krister, of course.' I say, slipping my bag over my shoulder, 'He's in the dining room waiting for me and we're about to order sweet, so if you'll excuse me.'

I manage to unwrap myself from his grasp but as I step away, he says, 'Before you go, there's something I need to say to you. It's about—'

'Sorry, I have to get back to Krister.' I cut him off as I back away. I don't want to hear anything he has to say. Not now, not ever.

TALÚN

I thought I might run into Krister while I was here but I never expected him to bring Jess with him. He told me she was putting up the money but had no input into the building. So why is she here with him at this exhibition? The thought of them together makes me feel uneasy, especially seeing the way she looks tonight; with her hair pinned up and a soft blue dress clinging to her curves. Is something else going on I don't know about? That Bella Fielding doesn't know about? I stop myself mid-thought, wondering why I care at all. Jess was so rude to me back there when I bumped into her but then I realise it probably has to do with the other day up at the Hall. Tonight I wanted…needed…to apologise but, predictably, she's not in the mood for listening.

I reach the dining room and the head waiter shows me to a corner table by the window. It's quiet here and just the place to observe what's going on. As I drink my first glass of red I scan the room and eventually find them out on the terrace. He's leaning across the table and saying something which makes her laugh. I skip the starter and as my beef bourguignon arrives I see their empty sweet plates being taken away. Moments later, a waitress delivers cups and a cafetière to the table. They seem to linger a long time over the coffee and I'm just coming to the end of my main course when I see Krister call the waitress over to sign off their food tab. They stay a while longer finishing off the wine and then I see them both get to their feet. By this time I'm ready to vacate the dining room too, and follow them out at a discreet distance. By the time I reach the foyer they are already in the lift and the doors are closing. I watch the floor indicator stop at three, the top floor, and then head for the stairs. As I reach the landing and push through the fire door I see them both halfway down the carpeted corridor. Jess is rummaging in her bag for her door swipe. Finding it, she brandishes it at Krister who laughs and takes it from her. The next moment there's a muffled shriek from Jess as they both disappear into the room. The door closes behind them confirming my fears, that Krister and Jess are up to something behind Bella's back.

As I turn to leave I hear a door open and Krister appears. He laughs as he wishes her goodnight, telling her he'll collect her for breakfast at eight-thirty. I see him walk off, disappearing around the curve of the corridor, then a door shuts noisily. In the following silence I'm left feeling embarrassed. How could I think something was going on between them? I've done it again, believing the worst of her when I'm supposed to be trying to mend fences. I pause for a moment as a crazy thought enters my head. Now she's on her own it would be the perfect time to talk to her. No, my sensible voice argues, it's a stupid idea. Remember her reaction when you collided outside the lift? But my reckless self insists from her unsteadiness in the corridor she's had a few drinks, meaning she'll be relaxed and more receptive to me. The wine has mellowed me too and I'm in a "what the hell" kind of mood anyway, meaning my sensible self stands no chance. Releasing my hold on the fire door, I enter the corridor and make my way towards her room.

JESS

Thank goodness Krister managed to catch me in time as we fell through the open door of my room. We almost landed in a heap on the floor. Too much red wine for both of us, I think, stifling a giggle. I drop my bag on the bed and kick off my shoes. I'm about to head to the bathroom to clean my teeth and get ready for bed when an unexpected knock brings me back to the door. I stop and turn around, wondering whether during our tangled entry Krister has dropped something and has come back to retrieve it. I scan the floor but there's nothing there. Wondering what he wants, I open the door.

My shock soon gives way to annoyance as I discover not Krister but Talún standing there. 'What do you want?' I ask. My relaxed self has fled; I'm full on irritable and angry because it's clear he's followed me here.

'A moment of your time, that's all,' he says quietly. 'Can I come in?'

'Certainly not,' I tell him, knowing he's the last person I want anywhere near me. 'Anyway, I can't think of anything you could possibly want to say to me.'

'How about sorry?'

'Sorry? Why should you be sorry for anything?' I say sarcastically.

He gives a sigh. 'Because I've made a complete hash of things.'

'Yes you have, now go away.' I try to close the door but he wedges his shoulder into the gap to stop me.

'Jess, please. Just hear me out, will you?' His tone is even and gentle, reminding me of the old Talún I knew and I hesitate, not sure what to do. It's at that precise moment I remember my conversation with Krister about the dangers of holding onto my anger. 'All right,' reluctantly I relax my hold on the door, 'but when you've finished I want you to leave, is that clear?' He nods his head solemnly.

As he's about to start, I hear the lift arrive, ejecting a noisy group of people onto my floor. I glance around the door and see it's several of the male exhibitors who have spent most of the evening in the bar drinking. Their loud laughter carries down the corridor as they approach. The last thing I want is to be found here in an open doorway with Talún looking as if I'm having some sort of secret assignation. I have a nanosecond to make a decision. Feeling there's no other alternative, I haul him into the room.

'Thank you.' He looks relieved and gives me one of his familiar heart-stopping smiles. I try not to react, putting the way my heart picks up a beat down to the wine. I blow out a deep breath, determined to strengthen my resolve. He's been rude and arrogant ever since we first met. He lied, he broke my heart and the sooner he's said what he has to, and leaves, the better.

'You've got five minutes, then I want you gone, understand?'

He nods and seats himself on the end of the bed, lacing his hands in his lap. Bending slightly forward, he is silent for a moment as if he's gathering his thoughts.

'So what were you saying?' I prompt. 'Yes, it was something about you making a mess of things, wasn't it?'

'A complete mess.' He looks up and nods, fixing me with his green gaze. 'Which is why I want to begin by apologising for laying into you the other day about Tristan. I wasn't being very fair.'

'Why this sudden change of heart?' I eye him suspiciously. 'Are you drunk?'

'Of course not,' he says, 'it's simply that we're neighbours in a small community and I don't want to have this atmosphere between us anymore. Please, will you accept my apology for being such a brute?'

A brute? I consider his words for a moment. He's right, of course, we can't continue like this. Pride has to be swallowed; differences put to one side. I might not like what has happened with him and Lily but there's nothing I can do about it. And as Krister so rightly says, holding onto anger can be such a destructive thing, constantly eating away at you. My eyes meet his and there's a warmth there that was missing on the night of the party. The wine is beginning to have a mellowing effect too and coupled with my Danish friend's advice echoing in my brain, pushes me into agreeing. Without even realising I've done it, I nod, even managing to work in an accompanying smile.

'And then there were my accusations about the cottage.' He gives an embarrassed shake of his head. 'It took George to put me right. He gave me a good ticking off, which I fully deserved. Forgive me, Jess, I seem to have been wrong about so many things.'

The thought of the small, rotund farmer waving a reprimanding finger at Talún amuses me. That hard, arrogant stance he greeted me with the other evening seems to be gradually evaporating and he's almost back to being his old self.

'And there's something else.'

I'm wrenched from my thoughts as I hear his words. There's more? Wondering what can possibly come next, I settle myself next to him.

'Remember the morning when you found Josh in the woods and brought him back to the Hall? I was rude to you. Lily was almost hysterical. Asking you to leave seemed the easiest way to calm her down. But I could have been a little more gentlemanly about it,' he says contritely, rubbing a tired hand over his jaw.

'It doesn't matter,' I reassure him. 'Josh's safety was the most important thing.'

'Richard confessed, you know. He admitted he and Stacey had abandoned Josh to be alone together. Needless to say, she is no longer at the Hall and Richard is earning his penance shovelling manure for a week. I won't have anyone compromising Josh's safety.'

I manage a smile, pleased Talún has dealt with the problem. 'No,' I agree, 'and I hope you find a better nanny for him. He's a beautiful boy.'

'He is,' Talún nods in agreement. 'I'm very lucky to have been given another chance.'

'Yes, Anna told me about Fliss and Emily. It must have been a terrible time for you.' The words are out before I can stop them. I realise my error as a sudden sadness fills his eyes. Instinctively I reach out and cover his hand with mine, angry with myself for being so tactless. 'Now it's my turn to say sorry,' I whisper, 'I didn't mean to disturb your ghosts.'

He gives a silent nod, squeezes my hand and smiles. Moments later, as I slip my hand from his I see the memory has gone, and he's back in the present once more. I ask him how he found his family in Norfolk and hear about his mother's death and his return to education. Five minutes expands well beyond thirty as we talk about Amberleigh and his hopes for the stud he's developing at the Hall.

'Heavens, is that the time?' he says, as he stretches and gets to his feet. 'I think we'd both better get some beauty sleep, don't you? Thanks for giving me the chance to settle our differences, Jess.' He reaches for my hand, cupping it between his warm palms. 'I hope things will be better between us from now on.'

'I hope so, too,' I smile, wondering whether I should tell him he needs to thank Krister for bringing all of this about.

'Before I go,' he says, as I follow him to the door, 'there is one last thing. The land you wanted? It's yours.'

For a moment I'm stunned. It means we can build those four extra houses. As my senses return, I find a voice. 'Oh my goodness, Talún, thank you so much. Have you a price in mind?'

'No,' he says, shaking his head. 'It's a gift...from me. It's the least I can do after...'

'A gift? No way.' I interrupt him. 'I insist on paying you market value.'

'Jess...' Warm hands cup my shoulders as his dark serious eyes meet mine. 'Take it...please.'

He seems to loom over me, tall, broad shouldered and far too close for comfort. I breathe in the familiar aroma of sandalwood mingled with his unique masculine scent and my whole world tilts.

'Well, if you insist,' I manage breathlessly, locked into his green gaze.

'I do.' Caught in the same spell I seem to have fallen under, he hesitates for a moment and before I have time to react, he bends his head, and his mouth covers mine in a warm, possessive kiss.

LILY

Talún left yesterday morning for his conference. He plans to stay overnight with another full day after, which luckily means he won't arrive home until early evening. That means he won't be back before I am. I was glad to see his mood had lightened with my promise to spend time with Josh. It felt almost as if our argument had never happened – what a relief, I was really beginning to worry. My first morning without Talún went well. I took Josh down for his riding lesson and stayed to watch. I was terribly bored but my mood lightened considerably by the arrival of Georgie with Darcy just after eleven. It was such a lovely day we had lunch in the garden and cracked open a bottle of our favourite bubbly while the kids played.

And now it's just past seven-thirty am on day two, and I'm driving through the village on my way to pick up the motorway for my journey to London. Up ahead, there's a jeans-clad figure walking a black and white dog. As I get nearer I realise it's Jess's friend, Bella Fielding and Krister Sorenson's border collie. With the school having broken up for summer she's not working at the moment. My brain does a sudden somersault as it occurs to me this girl could be the answer to all my problems.

As I reach her I slow down, lower the window and lean out, giving her a good morning greeting. She stops and eyes me warily, no doubt because she has Jess Hayden's warped view of me imprinted on her brain.

'Can you spare a minute?' I ask, and wait for her to cross the road to reach me. 'Bella, isn't it?' I give her an encouraging smile.

'That's right.'

'You work at Lynbrook Primary, don't you?'

'Yes...and?'

'I need help to look after Josh until he starts school in September. Are you interested?'

'I might be,' she says with a shrug, tugging at the dog's lead as he attempts to investigate something in the hedge. 'Depends what you're paying.' I catch a glint of avarice in her dark eyes.

'Well, I was thinking of, say, five hundred and fifty a week.' I tell her. Having already looked into this I'm aware it's around the base rate for a nanny from one of the best colleges. Of course it's an outrageous amount to pay a mere teaching assistant, but I've run out of options and Talún won't mind. After all, when it comes to Josh, it appears money is no object.

Her eyes widen and it seems she's taken the bait. 'Jeanette sorts his breakfast and puts him to bed after his evening meal,' I continue, 'all I need is someone to fit in between those hours, say nine to four-thirty.'

'Make it six hundred and fifty and we have a deal,' she says, adding, 'You're offering the base rate and I've a Teaching Assistant's Certificate, which means I'm qualified to look after kids ...not like useless Stacey Beauman.' She gives me a cocky grin.

'Okay.' I grit my teeth, hating the fact this girl is smarter than I thought and I've been out manoeuvred. But the fact is I need her...desperately...and she damn well knows it. 'Can you start Monday?' I ask, smiling through my annoyance.

'Monday will be fine,' she says chirpily. 'See you at nine then.'

I notice her in my rear view mirror, standing there watching me as I drive away. I try not to feel too aggrieved, after all it's Talún who will be covering the bill. With one huge problem out of the way I'm free to concentrate on London, my appointment and maybe time for a little shopping. I turn on the CD player and the sound of Bill Withers' *Lovely Day* fills the car. Yes, it is, I say to myself...a bloody beautiful one.

JESS

Daylight peeks through the curtains as I open my eyes. Turning on my side I check the bedside alarm: seven-thirty. As I become fully conscious, memories of last evening come flooding back. I shouldn't have let him kiss me, but at least I had the presence of mind to stop what was happening before we got to the point of no return. Now as I lie here I feel troubled. The way he threw open the door and left made me realise my actions had upset him. Or maybe he was embarrassed, who knows? He can't have been thinking straight. Neither could I, come to that. Blame the wine, an inner voice niggles, but I know what happened had little to do with the alcohol and it's something I find deeply unsettling.

I stretch and throw off the covers, ease myself out of bed and walk over to the window to see what the weather is doing this morning. As I pull back the blinds I hear the throaty purr of a car engine passing beneath my window. Someone has obviously decided on an early departure. As I watch the midnight blue Aston Martin exit through the parkland, I wonder whether the events of last night or some home emergency have caused Talún's decision to quit the exhibition early.

TALÚN

Kissing Jess was arguably the stupidest thing I've ever done. I couldn't stop myself, though. She was so close and I wanted her so very much. It made me realise nothing had changed. What we had that summer, however fleeting, is still there and her closeness hauled it back to the surface again. The way she responded I'm sure she felt it too, although at least she had the sense to eventually push me away. Realising what we'd nearly done, I beat a hasty retreat from her room. I was too embarrassed to face her this morning. As soon as I had showered and dressed I knew the only thing I could do was leave.

I need to keep away from this new and dangerous temptation. Jess and I may be at peace with each other but I have to remind myself it's my son who is the focus of my life now. And of course that goes hand in hand with my commitment to Lily. I know we're going through stormy waters at the moment and it's not going to be easy to change her habits, but for Josh's sake I have to keep trying to mould us into a family.

I'm still thinking about Josh as the Aston slips between the Hall's high stone entrance pillars. I drive straight to the stables, hoping to catch his morning riding session. I remember Lily has promised to be there with him too. As I get out of the car I catch sight of Greg crossing the yard. He waves out and heads towards me.

'Thought you weren't due back until this afternoon,' he says.

'I cut it short, got all the information I needed yesterday.' I make my excuses. 'Thought I'd check on Josh before I go up to the house, see how he's getting on.'

'Josh hasn't been here this morning,' Greg says with a shake of his head.

'But Lily promised to bring him down while I was away.'

'She came with him yesterday, but I haven't seen them this morning and I know the Audi's been missing since early on.'

Although I'm annoyed about Josh missing today's lesson, I think I know what's happened. Despite me saying I'd do the trip to Buckfastleigh, she's decided to take him herself this morning. 'It's okay,' I tell Greg, 'I think I know where she's gone.'

When I eventually park up, sure enough, the A7 is missing. But as I walk in through the front door, to my surprise Josh comes belting down the hall.

'Daddy, Daddy, we're cooking. Come and see!' he shouts excitedly.

I grin, amused at the delight in his small face. He's got chocolate around his mouth and down the front of his t-shirt. Despite this, I swing him up into my arms and he curls comfortably into my shoulder, chattering about what he's been doing in the kitchen.

'I think Naomi plans to cook you too,' I tease, giving him a playful tickle, which makes him squeal. 'A chocolate Josh,' I tell him, showing him the state of his face in a nearby mirror. As we arrive in the kitchen I lower him to his feet in time to see our tall, blonde chef pull a large batch of chocolate muffins from the oven.

244

'Are they cooked?' He asks, running around the table to join her.

'Yes, and they are very hot,' she warns him. 'But when they have cooled down you will be the first to have one as you were such an excellent little helper.'

She smiles at me as she begins to place them one by one on a cooling rack.

'So, Josh has been helping you this morning, has he?'

'Yes, and he's been very good.' She looks down at him and smiles. 'We made the mix together and he had a taste to make sure it was all okay, didn't you?'

He gives a confirming nod, solemn and wide eyed as he continues to watch her, his small fingers wrapped around the edge of the table.

'It looks as if you gave the t-shirt a taste too,' I say to him. He glances down, pulls out the front and inspects it, a serious frown on his face.

'No worries, the washing machine will soon sort it all out.' I hear a voice say and turn to see Jeanette has joined us.

'He's had a really enjoyable morning,' she says, ruffling his hair, 'haven't you?'

Josh nods. 'I like cooking,' he informs us all with a grin.

'I see Lily's car is missing. Do you know where she's gone?'

It's a simple enough question but I notice it's one which makes both women look slightly uncomfortable.

'Can I have a word, Jeanette?' I nod towards the door and we leave the kitchen. I lead her towards the drawing room and close the door. Asking her to sit, I settle myself opposite before asking, 'Where is Lily this morning?'

I see her discomfort. She doesn't like being the meat in the middle of this contentious sandwich. Eventually she takes a deep breath and says, 'London. She's gone to London for the day. She said she would be back later this afternoon.'

I thank Jeanette and she leaves. I walk over to the window to look out at the garden, sculpted lawns and borders full of colour. I feel a crisis brewing. No doubt Lily

245

is on another of her expensive shopping trips. For a while I understood her actions, aware of her love of clothes and a background which, until we met, had denied her the ability to indulge herself. But now it's affecting everything in this household. She wanted so badly to be mistress of this house and yet she's still leaving the management to Jeanette. We haven't organised a replacement nanny and the staff are being roped into look after Josh when she's not here. And although they love him and he's no trouble, it's not what they've been employed to do. It's not fair on them or him. Tonight when she returns I plan to sort this out once and for all.

LILY

I'm back earlier than I anticipated so I stop off at Georgie's to show her the new Max Mara dress I've bought for this coming Saturday's dinner party. Well, I'd sort of gone off the Stella McCartney and I need to look my best, don't I?

I discover her at the rear of the house, relaxing on a sunbed by their pool, all expensive shades, oiled skin and the tiniest yellow bikini.

'Lily.' She eases herself up from the sunbed and with a swing of her legs she's sitting and looking at me over the top of her Chanel sunglasses with a smile. 'You look fabulous, darling. I can see such a difference.'

'Yes, I feel like a million dollars,' I say breezily, 'although,' I touch my face, 'as you can see there is some slight bruising.'

'Oh, make-up should take care of that.' She says as she pulls off her sunglasses and stares up at my face. 'Actually, I can hardly see it. Any more trips in the pipeline?' she asks, cocking her head curiously.

'Well...'

'You naughty girl, there are, aren't there?' she teases me as she gets up and slips on a short white robe. After retrieving an empty glass from the low table by her lounger, she heads for the small poolside bar. There she pulls another flute from the rack and pours us each a glass of sparkling wine from a bottle nestling in a glass ice bucket.

'Yes I am,' I admit, as I take the proffered glass. 'I want everything to be perfect for the wedding.'

'A nip and tuck somewhere? Or new boobs maybe?' she prompts, before tipping back her glass.

'I'm still deciding,' I tell her and laugh. Little does she know at the moment I'm bracing myself for the fallout when the monthly credit card bill lands. After today's clinic visit I'll need to lie low for a while and take my foot off the spend accelerator. In order to get back into Talún's good books I'm definitely going to have to reprise my Good Mama role too and spend more time with Josh.

After another glass of wine and giving Georgie a glimpse of my new dress for Saturday, I leave for home. All in all it's been a good day, one which can only get better.

TALÚN

It's nudging five and from the landing window I see the Audi as it approaches. Pulling up outside, Lily gets out, hauls a large, shiny cardboard carrier from the back of the car and makes her way towards the house. I'm half way down the stairs as she breezes into the hallway, calling for Jeanette to bring coffee into the drawing room. I see Jeanette arrive and Lily's purchase and her jacket are thrust into her hands. Pausing in front of the hall mirror, she admires her reflection, teasing out her hair with her fingers. Then she disappears and moments later I hear a door close. I meet Jeanette as I near the bottom of the stairs. 'I'll take the coffee in when it's ready,' I tell her.

By the time Jeanette appears with a tray of coffee and biscuits I'm ready for what I have to do. I am furious that, despite her promises, she has once again taken herself off to spend money. Balancing the tray in one hand, I open the door and close it carefully behind me. It shuts with a loud click. She's made herself comfortable in one of the chairs. Shoes kicked off, she's curled up with a magazine. Her back is to me so she has no idea I'm not Jeanette.

'Leave it on the table,' she says, without looking up.

I place the whole thing down with a heavy thud, making the crockery rattle. She slaps the magazine shut and wheels around. The intended rebuke never leaves her lips, it morphs into an 'O' of surprise as she sees me standing there.

'Talún.' She manages a nervous smile. 'You're back. Did you get all the information you needed?'

I move around to stand in front of her. Ignoring her comment, I ask her where she has been.

'Me? Oh, out and about.' She gives a carefree shrug.

'You promised to spend time with Josh this morning.'

'I know, but something came up and I had to go out. Anyway, Naomi was brilliant, she held the fort.'

'She's a cook Lily, not a babysitter.'

'Yes I realise that and it's one of the reasons I went out...to find a new nanny.'

'I see. And did you?'

'Yes. She starts Monday. You know her, I think. Bella Fielding?'

'The barmaid from the Black Bull?'

'That's only a part time job.' She rolls her eyes impatiently. 'She works at Lynbrook Primary as a Teaching Assistant. She'll work from nine to four-thirty for six fifty a week, which although more than Stacey got is well below what we were paying the agency for Thea.'

Actually, I'm aware of Bella Fielding's full time job, supporting the village school's reception class. She seems an excellent choice and I'm pleased Lily has sorted out the problem. However, as I'm about to congratulate her, something else catches my attention.

'What have you done to your face?' I ask, leaning over and caging her in the chair.

'What do you mean?' She touches her cheek nervously. 'Nothing, why?'

'I can see bruising.' I lean closer, catching a whiff of alcohol. 'And you've been drinking again, haven't you?'

'What's this?' she says, 'The Spanish Inquisition? I stopped off at Georgie's on the way, if you must know. I had a couple of glasses of sparkling wine. It's not a big deal.'

I step back as she pushes herself out of the chair and runs an impatient hand through her hair.

'You didn't answer my original question,' I remind her quietly. 'Where have you been all day?'

'London.' She purses her lips, her expression surly.

'Why?'

'I changed my mind about the Stella McCartney and I was desperate for something to wear for this Saturday's dinner party. You do remember Georgie and Danni are here with Jensen and Felix? And yes,' she waves away any potential criticism, 'Naomi does know about it. I'm not quite as negligent over my duties here as you would like to believe,' she adds sharply.

'So a new dress required a trip up to London, did it?' I persist, determined to get to the bottom of what she's been up to all day. 'Come on Lily, what was the real reason?'

'Well,' she takes a calming breath. 'I was chatting to the girls while we were away and they mentioned this great clinic they go to.'

'Cosmetic surgery?'

'Hardly,' she snaps irritably, 'just a few Botox injections.'

'Botox? Why? There's nothing wrong with your skin.'

'Well, that's what you think. Georgie and Danni—'

'Are having a great time persuading you to spend money you don't need to.'

'Talún,' she says, hands on her hips, ready to do battle, 'you said when we first met you intended to make up for all the years I'd struggled on my own. You said you wanted me to be happy, and *this* ...' she indicates her face, 'makes me happy, okay? Now, if you've finished,' her hand goes to her temple, 'I have a bloody awful headache and need to lie down.' And with that she grabs her shoes, pushes past me and leaves.

'You canna be serious, Bella!'

Rufus is out on a jolly with his golfing buddies this evening and has left me in command of the good ship Black Bull. First I looked in on Dominic and his team in the kitchen, then Jake the Restaurant Manager, making sure there were no problems. Reassured everything is as it should be, and we were on course for another well organised evening, I returned to the bar only to be met by the Scotsman's loud protest.

'What's going on?' I ask, my gaze moving from one to the other, Bella smiling as she pulls him his usual pint and Adrian looking as if he's about to spit out a mouthful of feathers.

'What's going on?' he almost chokes, looking at me indignantly. 'This crazy Sassenach,' he waves a finger at her, 'has gone over to the Dark Side.'

'The Dark Side?' I repeat, looking curiously at Bella.

'He means I'm going to be working for the Hawkeswoods, looking after Josh during the summer holidays,' she says, sliding Adrian's drink towards him across the bar and taking the note he offers her.

'So what happens about your job here?' I ask, annoyed she has taken it into her head to abandon us. Bella and I are friends and I would have thought this would have been discussed with Rufus or me first, before it became public knowledge.

'It won't affect my work here,' she says as she hands Adrian his change. 'My hours are nine to four-thirty. I'll still be available for my evening shift.'

'So, Talún made you an offer you couldn't refuse?' Adrian asks, somewhat calmer now as he takes a mouthful of beer.

'It was Lily, actually. She stopped me on the road this morning when I was walking Finn. Offered me an *amazing* amount of money to look after Josh for the summer. I already knew Stacey had been given the big heave-ho so I'm guessing she was desperate to plug the gap. And who better than me?' she says with a slight lift of her shoulders. 'After all, I'm not only a qualified Teaching Assistant, I'm responsible for the reception class, which is where Josh will be in September. It's probably what she had in mind when she decided to ask me.'

Adrian scoffs. 'Don't kid yourself Bella, that wee bairn rarely crosses her mind.'

Ignoring his remark, I notice Bella has gone quiet. She nibbles nervously on her bottom lip as her brown eyes meet mine. 'I'm sorry, I didn't think it would be a problem. You're not angry with me, are you?'

'Should I be?'

'Well, I know you don't exactly get on with Lily. I don't want—'

'Who does?' Adrian interrupts with a growl. 'The woman's a bloody head case.'

'I don't want you thinking...' Bella raises her voice slightly, obviously annoyed at Adrian's interruption, 'that this is anything other than me taking advantage of an opportunity to earn some extra money. You're still my friend, Jess. I've no loyalty to anyone at the Hall. It's simply a summer job.' She blows out her cheeks before continuing. 'Look, I've not said anything before, but my mother has people from the Hall in her shop all the time. No one likes Lily, they say they can't trust her. One moment she'll be fine, the next she'll be screaming abuse at staff. She's a real harpy.'

'Well, as long as you're aware of the dangers,' I warn her, before adding, 'Actually I've already met Josh and he's a really sweet child.'

'Now that's one thing I'm not going to disagree about,' Adrian says. 'He's a great wee chappie. You'll have a fine old time, Bella.'

TALÚN

I'm not sure why Lily invited this dreadful quartet to dinner this evening. I think she was under the impression Jensen and Felix would want to talk investment opportunities with me. The thing is, all my money is managed back in Norfolk and I don't see the need to change. Particularly as looking at these two designer-clad wide boys, I know they'd be the last people I'd trust with a piggy bank, much less my finances. Jensen, long, lean and totally self-absorbed, is keen to tell me about his private box at Exeter Racecourse. Then his 'little side line' - a string of sports shops across the South West. Now he is currently setting up glamping sites – the next big holiday thing, he tells me. Felix, shorter and sharp featured with dark hair and glasses, is the more likeable of the two and he's into motor sport. He's actually done some rally driving, but Formula One is his passion. Although he can't always get abroad to watch, he makes sure he gets to Silverstone for the British Grand Prix every year. They also tell me they are both are keen squash players and are learning to scuba dive. 'When do you find time to work?' I ask with a laugh.

'Work?' they echo, and laugh in unison. 'Other people take care of business, we spend the money,' Jensen says. 'Don't tell me you get your hands dirty, old chap?'

Well, actually, this old chap does, and I tell him running a stud occasionally calls for some getting down and dirty moments. They both look horrified.

As the conversation drifts around the table I get the feeling these are four people whose existence is clearly centred on self-indulgence. Both Jensen and Felix have built businesses where other people create the wealth for them to enjoy. I listen to the women as they talk of health spas, shopping and the excitement of discovering a new eatery, either locally or in London, where they seem to spend an extraordinary amount of time. No wonder Lily finds them such kindred spirits.

As the sweet dishes are cleared away, Jeanette arrives and quietly tells me Anna is on the phone in my office. She says she is willing to tell her we have dinner guests and I will call her back tomorrow but I shake my head. I need to escape from this room and the claustrophobia of Lily's pleasure-seeking comrades.

I excuse myself, leaving the diners as they wait for coffee. Reaching my office, I close the door and pick up the phone. Anna's voice is a welcome sound after the banality of the evening. We exchange a few brief words, and then her tone becomes serious. 'Talún,' I hear her take a breath, 'my reason for phoning is because something has come up and it needs urgent discussion.'

My first thoughts are of Marcus. 'Oh don't worry, your grandfather and I are both fine,' she says, as if reading my thoughts. 'This is to do with business.'

'Actually, we have dinner guests and much as I'd love to abandon them...'

'Ah,' she interrupts with a laugh, 'no doubt you have the Witches and their warlocks with you.'

'We have.' I laugh, wondering how she knows. 'Can I catch up with you tomorrow morning?'

She pauses for a moment. 'Actually,' she says, 'it might be better if I come down to Lynbrook to talk to you. I could look in on Jess and Rufus at the same time. Would Monday suit?'

'Yes, of course.' This vague conversation is beginning to worry me. 'Anna, what is this about?'

'Go back to your dinner guests Talún, I'll speak to you on Monday,' she says, refusing to say any more, and then the line goes dead.

I return to the dining room. I hate mysteries and I wish Anna had been specific about the nature of this urgent business rather than leaving me to draw my own conclusions. I close my eyes. First the Botox incident, then spending the evening with the most brain numbingly boring people...and now this.

'Are you okay, old chap?' Jensen enquires as I return to

my seat, pick up my glass and drain it. 'Not bad news, I hope.'

'No,' I force a smile, 'just a family matter.'

I notice Lily is missing. She joins us moments later. Apparently she's been to check on Josh.

'Jeanette said Anna was on the phone.' She looks at me anxiously, 'Is everything okay?'

'Yes fine. She's coming down to see me on Monday. One or two estate issues to clear up that's all.' My casual lie is accepted. Lily joins the women in conversation again and I reach across the table for the white wine. As Jensen decides to entertain us with details of the beach condo in Cancún he and Felix are currently in the process of buying, I close my eyes, letting the alcohol anaesthetise my brain. The sooner this night is over the better.

LILY

When Talún leaves the room I take the opportunity to check on Josh. After our clash over the Botox I decided I'd better behave myself for a while. I've been the perfect hostess, organising the menus with Naomi and roping in a couple of the other staff members to wait table. I'm aware the credit card bill is imminent and I know I'm going to have to intercept and destroy it. If Talún sees what I've spent he'll go ballistic. Delaying its arrival will give me time to settle in to my new country wife role before he realises it hasn't arrived and requests a duplicate. Talún doesn't currently have a PA so Jeanette always leaves the post on his desk. It's simply a matter of checking each morning.

When I look in on Josh he is fast asleep, clutching his dragon. In the glow of the night light he looks totally angelic. He is a lovely child with Pauli's easy going, friendly nature. No wonder Talún loves him so much. If only I could, but I never wanted motherhood in the first place. It was an accident and then afterwards, when Pauli walked out, I felt trapped. I guess I've used my son ever since he was born. In those early days the only good thing I could say was because of him we kept a roof over our heads. And now? Well, he's my passport to this luxurious life. I wish there was a part of me able to feel some connection to him. To give him the warmth and loving he deserves. But I can't. So it's just as well my husband to be and the staff here more than make up for my shortcomings.

With one last look I leave quietly, closing the door behind me.

As soon as I return to the dining room and see the expression on Talún's face I know something bad has happened. At first I think maybe Marcus has had a heart attack. But then he says Anna will be arriving on Monday and the look he gives makes me realise it's probably got something to do with me. I wonder what the overbearing witch has got a problem with this time.

As coffee is poured I sit and listen to the conversations going on around me. Everyone is upbeat, Jensen and Felix chatting about a forthcoming golf tournament, Georgie talking about having a fancy dress party for Darcy's sixth birthday. Talún and I seem to be sitting on the edge of all this. I notice him reach for the wine again, casting yet another dark look in my direction. The white is empty but the red still half full. He fills his glass and sits playing with the stem, his laughter at the amusing story Felix is telling feels forced and phoney. He's been in this mood since the phone call and I'm now positive her visit is about me and it's something really bad. I could lose everything I have, including Josh, because I know the Hawkeswood family are so powerful they can take anything from anyone. Having Josh taken from me I can cope with, but I desperately want this house, this lifestyle. And to enable me to hold onto my dream, it means I have to become Talún's wife. But I need leverage; a strong bargaining chip which will mean there is no way they can get rid of me. Trying to dismiss my fears, I throw myself into conversation with Georgie and Danni, planning lunch at the Bull next week.

Our guests leave just after midnight. Talún finished off

255

the bottle of red and went on to share a couple of brandies with the two men. As I close the front door he is already half way up the stairs, holding onto the bannister, his steps slow and heavy. I follow him at a distance, hoping he won't turn around. The last thing I want is another row. On the landing I hesitate as he reaches his door then pauses to lean against the wall, his eyes closed. As I watch, quite unexpectedly it's there, the lightbulb moment I've been searching for. I step forward, a plan already taking shape.

TALÚN

I open one eye as light streams through a gap in the curtains. As I lie flat on my back I take a deep breath and swallow. My mouth tastes absolutely vile and I let out a soft groan. Taking to the bottle isn't a solution; what was I thinking? In my youth it was a coping mechanism I used to blot out my problems and push them into tomorrow when I was sure I'd be better placed to deal with them. I haven't done this for years, not even when Fliss and Emily died. Then it was all about working myself to a standstill and falling exhausted into bed each night. No, I've not used drink as an escape since the night of Jess's party and look what happened there. But last night my demons returned. I guess too many frustrating things collided: the row with Lily, my long drawn out evening with those awful people and the deliberate lack of detail in Anna's phone call. I stretch and look down, frowning. My last memory is of leaning against the wall outside my bedroom door. So how is it I'm now under the duvet without a stitch on?

I draw in a deep breath of surprise as red tipped fingers reach out and stroke my chest. Tousled blonde hair fills one corner of my vision. My first conscious thought is of Jess, but why the hell would she be here with me? Then everything becomes sharper as Lily leans over and plants a kiss on my cheek.

'Good morning,' she says cheerfully as her silk wrap slips off one shoulder, giving me a glimpse of soft, honey coloured skin.

'What are you doing here?' Surprised, I push myself up into a sitting position.

'Waiting for you to wake up,' she says, her fingers stroking my arm as she gazes at me with a smile.

'How long have you been in my room?'

'All night,' she shrugs. 'Don't you remember?'

'No,' I shake my head then as my thoughts clear, 'yes...'

'Sure?' She looks at me with a quizzical smile and when I fail to respond she decides to remind me.

'I followed you up the stairs. You looked so miserable and as you reached your door you simply stood there, leaning against the wall and, well...' she lowers her gaze for a moment, 'I couldn't help it. I walked over to you. I wanted you to tell me what was troubling you. I've been extremely selfish, Talún, and I needed to show you I do have a sensible, caring side. I put my arm around you, intending to help you into bed. I never realised what it would lead to...that we would—'

'What? You mean we slept together?' I finish the sentence for her, feeling confused. Why don't I remember anything? I run my hand over my forehead as I feel the beginnings of a headache.

'Yes,' she says gently, planting another kiss on my cheek. 'We did.'

I'm suddenly hit with an awful thought. 'It was mutual, wasn't it?' I ask. 'I mean I didn't try and—'

'You didn't do anything I didn't want you to.' She pauses and strokes my face as if remembering. 'In fact it was wonderful, quite wonderful.'

LILY

Phew! I can't believe my luck. He was obviously so damned drunk he hadn't a clue what had really happened. Oh, we spent the night together all right but there was definitely no sex. Our romantic tryst had me helping him into his room, out of his clothes and into bed where I eventually joined him. I then spent most of the night wide awake listening to him snore. Yes, a real night of unbridled

257

passion.

Of course, he's feeling guilty now; horrified his alcohol overload was to blame for us ending up in bed together and still not sure whether what he did was by mutual consent. He's insisting we still keep to our separate rooms until the wedding. I guess he's afraid something like that might happen again after he's had a few drinks. So sweet isn't he? Such a gentleman. I have to laugh. Still, the insurance I wanted is now firmly in my possession. Not that I'll need to use it, but simply having it there just in case feels very reassuring.

Today I've been in good wife mode. I've had a meeting with Jeanette asking her to update me on what is going on in the house. I've looked at menus for the week with Naomi and I've actually got around to taking a trip down to the stud. I spent half an hour watching Greg put Josh through his paces. I also did what Talún has been asking me to do for some time: take out Summer, the new mare he bought me. I'm not exactly enamoured with horseflesh but as it's going to be part and parcel of my new life and I'm currently doing penance, it had to be done.

This means at the end of my first day of perfect wife-to-be behaviour, I'm feeling pretty pleased with myself. With the arrival of the new nanny tomorrow Josh is a little apprehensive. I guess this is to be expected after the disaster we had with Stacey.

'Does Bella have angry hair, Mummy?' he asks, as we walk back from the stables.

'Angry hair?' I query, and then laugh, as I realise he means that wild peroxide mass of hers. 'No, darling, Bella has black curly hair. She works at the school in the village too, so she's good at looking after children. You'll have lots of fun.'

He gives a solemn nod and I watch as he contemplates my words before looking up with wide blue eyes and announcing, 'I think I'm going to like Bella, Mummy.'

'I think you will too,' I agree as we reach the house, my thoughts switching to Anna's arrival tomorrow and the reason behind it.

TALÚN

It's Monday morning and Bella arrives dead on nine, parking her black and white Mini just outside the front door. I've asked Jeanette to show her through to the drawing room to wait. Josh has just finished his breakfast and both Lily and I take him through to meet her. She gets to her feet as we arrive. Wearing jeans and a red '*I love Glasto*' t-shirt, she smiles and greets both of us, but she's soon crouching down to Josh's level, her concentration totally fixed on him. Since Lily told me she had hired her, I've made my own enquiries. I know she's friendly with Jess, works part time at the Bull and her parents run the village shop and post office. The fact she works at the school, looking after the reception class is a bonus as we both want Josh to start there in September. Yes, despite easily being able to afford private education, I decided it wasn't what I wanted for my son. And quite surprisingly, there was no argument from Lily, she was totally in agreement over this.

Josh seems to warm to Bella straight away and he's soon holding onto her hand and telling her all about his morning's riding lesson. Lily doesn't want to accompany us to the stables so the three of us leave her at the house and walk there to meet Greg. On our way I tell her about the use of the Range Rover and how Thea took him out for trips and shopping for clothes.

'I can issue you with a company credit card for purchases and Oliver Malone, my Estates Manager, will let you have any petty cash you need,' I tell her. 'I'll introduce you to him later so we can set up the necessary employment paperwork. Lily can brief you on anything else she thinks you need to know about looking after Josh.'

She nods and smiles, appearing to be happy with everything. She's bright and bubbly with an infectious laugh. Krister, I gather, is totally smitten and it's not hard to understand why. Already I feel relaxed as I see the way she interacts with Josh. I introduce her to Greg who says he will look after her and take her to see Oliver later. Thanking him, I leave them and make my way back to my office to catch up with work before Anna arrives.

LILY

Josh's first day with Bella went like a breeze. Jeanette took over once she'd left for the afternoon. I found him sitting at the table in his room having his tea with her and chattering away about his day. Tomorrow, he told us, Bella is taking him to see the otters, something neither Talún nor I got around to. It seems everything is going well with the new nanny. If only my own life was running as smoothly.

Anna arrived around eleven this morning. Talún appeared from the direction of the stables shortly afterwards. I ordered coffee and joined them in the drawing room. I felt like a third sock. I realise I have nothing in common with Anna. I'm not a business woman and I don't particularly like horses. Of course, she is always incredibly polite. She has manners and breeding and would never show anything but respect for me as her grandson's wife-to-be. What goes on behind those grey eyes, however, is another matter.

After coffee I left to get ready for my lunch at the Bull with Georgie and Danni, leaving them to discuss whatever it was she'd found it necessary to come all this way for.

As I came downstairs into the hall, ready to leave, I could hear raised voices behind the drawing room doors. Quickly grabbing my keys, I left. Whatever was going on in there sounded pretty bad. I fear the worst.

TALÚN

As soon as Lily leaves, Anna gets to her feet and walks slowly over to the French doors. She stands there silently for a moment, staring out across the lawn as if gathering her thoughts.

'Just tell me the bad news,' I say, eager to break the

silence. 'It's something to do with Lily, isn't it? What has she done this time?'

'Your credit card bill arrived.' She spins around to look at me. 'Talún, I know we're not exactly strapped for cash but Lily's still behaving like a lottery winner...and,' she levels a finger at me, 'before you go off the deep end, I fully understand your reasons for letting her indulge herself for a while. But—'

'Okay, enough,' I interrupt, raising my hands to stop her. 'I don't want to hear anymore, I'm already aware of the problem and I'm dealing with it.' I hear the irritation in my voice. It's because I don't like this intrusion. We're no longer living in Amberleigh. This place is my responsibility and I won't have any outside interference, not even from my grandmother.

Anna walks past me and retrieves her bag from a nearby chair. She slips her hand into one of the side pockets and pulls out a folded sheet of paper. 'Are you?' She asks quietly as she hands it to me.

'I don't understand.' Anger pulses through me as I scan the latest credit card statement. 'How did she manage to spend this amount of money?'

'It's the London Spa trip with Georgie and Danni that's done the damage, but I suppose it was to be expected as she covered the bill for all three of them.'

'All three of them?' I suck in an outraged breath, 'What the hell made her do that?'

'Here.' Anna offers me another three sheets. 'I got Marcus's PA to contact the spa and get a breakdown of the expenditure for each of them.'

'Marcus knows?' I close my eyes. If he's aware of this extravagance I'm in big trouble.

'Yes. It appears Lily's two friends went on a bit of a spending spree.' Anna takes a deep breath. 'Talún, I'm here to tell you that if you can't stop this, Marcus will step in and take control and the last thing you want is the embarrassment of him overseeing your day to day finances. Besides which, he has more than enough to do at Amberleigh,' she says sharply, before softening her tone.

'But it will happen, I promise you. Wealthy we may be, but he'll not stand by and see it so brazenly squandered in the way it has been recently. I should also add he's beginning to query whether Lily is the right sort of woman for you.'

'Anna. I don't care what Marcus thinks, I'm marrying Lily.' I hear my voice, strong, confident and totally at odds with the panic I feel inside. I don't even want to think about the consequences of my grandfather stepping in to end our relationship.

'But don't you see you can still have Josh. With Marcus's legal team, Lily wouldn't stand a chance of holding onto him,' she reassures me. 'Especially when I've seen the way she offloads him onto other people.' She cocks a curious eyebrow at me. 'I gather it's still happening.'

I ignore her question. Instead I tell her I won't be responsible for the damage it might cause if we go down that route. Because if there's one thing I know, Lily will not go quietly. She will go to the tabloids and they will dig up every sordid aspect of my past life. The fallout will be enormous. It will affect so many innocent people, and I can't let that happen. 'You have to give me a chance to sort this out myself first.' I insist, trying to hide the anxiety I feel. 'Tell Marcus I will do it,' I promise, gritting my teeth, absolutely furious I've been put in this position by Lily's thoughtless behaviour.

Anna takes a deep breath. 'Very well, but if you can't curb this spending by the end of August, your grandfather will take action.'

'It will be done.' I confirm, realising I sound more confident than I feel. At this moment all I want Anna to do is leave. She's right; having Marcus run my finances and control my spending would be totally humiliating. And, of course, there are implications for the future. I'm his only heir. One day I'll own Hawkeswood Estates, a multi-million pound international company. Or given the current circumstances, is he now planning to hand over control to a specially selected team instead, leaving me a powerless figurehead? It seems the ripples from Lily's behaviour could affect my whole future. I need to see her and put a stop to this. But first I need time alone, to think things through quietly and work out how to deal with her.

JESS

Since my return from the exhibition I haven't seen Talún at all. Having said that, I guess I'm not likely to. The Black Bull is hardly the place he'd drop into for a drink. It seems the same thing doesn't apply to Lily. I watch from the first floor lounge window of the pub as she follows Danni and Georgie across the car park towards the restaurant. They look like clones of each other with their Capri pants and t-shirts, huge totes, and lots of expensive bling. Bella would rock with laughter if she saw them. Thinking of Bella makes me wonder how she's getting on with Josh on this, her first day at the Hall. No doubt we'll hear all about it this evening.

Sometime later I go down to join Rufus in the bar.

'You've got a visitor,' he says, nodding towards the open door. I follow his gaze in time to see Anna getting out of her Range Rover. The passenger door swings open and I hold my breath. Talún? Surely not. I'm relieved when I see Adrian climb out.

'Anna, this is a surprise.' Rufus greets her with a hug as she arrives in the bar.

'I had to come down on family business and I couldn't leave without dropping in to see you all. I picked up this hitch hiker on the way,' she says with a grin in Adrian's direction, as she moves over to embrace me.

'Lovely to see you.' I say slipping back behind the bar, 'What are you having?'

'Oh, something non-alcoholic please...pineapple with ice?'

I pull Adrian his usual pint and then organise the fruit juice for Anna. They take themselves off into a corner and settle down to chat.

It's Monday so the pub is fairly quiet and when Anna comes over to talk to me, Rufus suggests we go up to the lounge, saying he'll take care of the bar.

We seat ourselves comfortably and I'm keen to start the conversation by updating her on the progress of my project with Krister. Contractors are already on site and the foundations excavated for the first two houses.

'Talún told me he's given you the extra land you wanted,' she says with a smile. 'It will make all the difference, won't it?'

'It certainly will. Four extra houses.' I pause thoughtfully. 'I did offer to pay but he insisted it was a gift. We've...um... sorted our differences and are friends again.'

'I'm glad to hear it because right now he could do with a friend.' She says pausing for a moment as if gathering her thoughts 'Look, I really shouldn't be saying this,' she begins, 'but—'

'Then don't,' I interrupt, sensing I might be dragged into things I want to avoid at all costs. We may both share an understanding of what happened all those years ago but after what we nearly did the other night I would think at the moment we're both quite keen to avoid each other.

'Jess, I feel so helpless. I've no one else to turn to.'

She's normally totally in control and her present state tells me it's something to do with Lily and that's definitely a no go area.

'Anna, I'm sorry, but it's not appropriate for me to get involved or comment about anything going on at the Hall.'

'Because of your past history with my grandson?'

'No.' I shake my head.

'Is it Lily?'

'No.' I hate lying, but what else can I do? I simply cannot get involved in their family problems, it's not appropriate.

'Marcus wants to postpone the wedding, you know.' She shakes her head in dismay. 'As time has gone on he's begun to have serious misgivings about Lily's suitability. I can't go into details, obviously, but my visit here today was specifically to talk to Talún about it. Needless to say, he won't listen.'

'Josh means everything to him. Maybe he's worried about doing anything to harm his current situation.'

264

'I've already told him Marcus won't let that happen.' It seems they've already been considering legal action.

'At what cost though?' I ask, fearing the consequences of trying to legally separate Lily from her son. 'Firstly, I don't think Talún would want Josh dragged through the courts. Secondly, your lives could be made extremely difficult. I'm quite sure if you attempted to take Josh away, Lily would make sure you had maximum exposure in the tabloids...for all the wrong reasons.'

At the mention of the media I see Anna blanch. From what she has told me about the family, the Hawkeswoods are very private people. Finding themselves on the front of every newspaper would be a nightmare for them.

She gets up and walks over to the window, running her hands along the ledge as she stares out across the village.

'God this is such a mess.'

'When I was with Talún,' I say quietly as I join her, 'the most important thing I learned was he does things in his own time and in his own way. Trying to force the issue will, as you've already discovered, only makes him dig his heels in. I know it's difficult but please, give him time to sort things out for himself. Just trust him; I know he'll make the right decision.'

Later as I watch her leave I realise my words of support are probably an empty gesture. Marcus calls the shots and if he doesn't want this wedding to go ahead he will stop it and there's nothing anyone can do about it.

LILY

Lunch was totally spoiled. Not only did I pass up on a trip to Exeter this afternoon, I had to turn down an offer of a girls' weekend in Guernsey in a couple of weeks' time. It's one of Georgie and Danni regular trips - a five star spa hotel and shopping. Double damn, I would have absolutely adored a mid-week break there.

There is, however, light at the end of the tunnel. Talking to the girls I'm beginning to see there might be a way around my current situation. They told me they both get generous monthly allowances. It made me wonder whether it might be a good idea to approach Talún about arranging this sort of thing for me. Now, on my way home, I'm working out how to pitch it to him. I'll tell him the card, with no spend limit, is easy to abuse. It means he might see it's partially his fault for giving it to me in the first place. I'll suggest he sets up a separate account for me and a regular monthly allowance. In the meantime I'll still keep a check on the mail each day so I can intercept this month's credit card bill. By the time a replacement copy has arrived my new account should be set up and although he'll be angry with me he'll realise with the new arrangement at least there's no danger of it happening again.

As I arrive at the house I see Anna and Talún approaching from the direction of the stables. Slipping from the Audi, I join them as she's getting into her Range Rover.

'Lily.' She gives me one of her well-mannered smiles. 'Did you have a good lunch at the Bull?'

How the hell did she know where I was?

'I called in to see Jess and Rufus,' she explains. 'I saw your car in the car park.'

I nod, deciding the comment isn't worthy of a response. Anything to do with the Haydens isn't worth bothering with as far as I'm concerned. How typical of her to have bonded with Jess and her father. Suddenly I can't wait for her to get into her car and leave. My wish is soon granted and Talún and I stand together watching as it disappears down the driveway.

'Is Josh around?' I ask, noticing the white Range Rover is missing.

'Bella has taken him to see the otters,' he says rather pointedly, resurrecting memories of my arrival from Georgie's when I'd drunk too much to make the trip myself.

'Well,' I brave it out with a smile, 'let's hope they have lots of fun.' Slinging my tote over my shoulder, I make a move towards the door.

'Lily, we need to talk.'

Taking a calming breath, I swing around to look at him. 'Actually, I need to talk to you too.'

'Good. I'll see you in the drawing room in five minutes,' he says, and I leave him standing there with a thoughtful expression on his face as he stares up at the house. Is he working out what he's got to say to me or wondering what I'm about to say to him? He always has a quiet air about him; he's slow to anger, easy going. Maybe I've got it all wrong and he wants a sympathetic ear because he's had enough of Anna and the way she seems to want to control everything, even down here.

Leaving my tote and jacket in my room, I make my way downstairs. Reaching the drawing room, I find he's already there. As he turns to face me I notice he's holding several sheets of paper in his left hand.

'What is it?' I look first at the papers and then at him, feeling confused and nervous at the anger in his face.

'Take a look and see for yourself,' he says, pushing them into my hand.

I look down and realise what he's just handed me. The room spins for a moment and then with a breath I manage a shaky response. 'Talún, I can explain...'

JESS

This is the part of the lunch shift I love: leaving the pub, driving up to George's and taking Caspar out for a ride. The world belongs to me until this evening when I'll find out how Bella's first day has gone.

As I enter Barnfield Woods sunlight dances in bright patches through the green canopy of the trees. A warm breeze completes this perfect afternoon and I'm heading for a place I haven't stopped in a long time; the falls. Since my return it's somewhere I've merely ridden by. But now Talún and I have come to terms with the past I feel able to visit our special place again.

On the way to pick up Caspar I dropped in to see how building work was progressing. Everything looks very business-like with a site office and Portaloo. Krister even has a professional advertising hoard announcing the construction of new homes. As I arrive I discover a large cement lorry offloading concrete down a chute while Krister's two general labourers busy themselves spreading it evenly through the foundation trenches. 'It's looking good,' My Viking said with a grin, and seeing our joint vision becoming a reality I nod, feeling a fizz of excitement.

I dismount and walk Caspar through the trees before tying him to a nearby sycamore. Stepping forward into the sunshine, I shade my eyes with my hand as I take in the familiar sight of the open grassy space in front of me. Beyond this, a waterfall tumbles over a grey outcropping of rocks, spilling into a deep pool beneath. And somewhere out there are stepping stones and a rock where we used to...

I come to a sudden halt. A familiar figure is already there, settled mong the rocks, skimming stones across the surface of the pool.

LILY

I had to get out of there. I couldn't cope any longer. I have never seen him so angry. Although I kept apologising, promising it would never happen again, he didn't seem to be listening. I even tried to tell him about my idea for a fixed monthly allowance - a foolish thing to do as it made things even worse.

'You told me you'd got a special deal for your spa break. I was aware of the cost but I had no idea I'd be covering the bill for all three of you.' He shook his head angrily, 'What the hell made you decide to treat those two freeloaders?'

'They're not freeloaders, they're my friends,' I protested.

'Do they ever pay for you Lily?' he queried as he began to pace back and forth in front of me. 'Tell me, do they?'

I stopped and thought for a moment and realised in all the time we'd been going out as a threesome it's always been me dipping into my pocket to cover the bill. Like today at the Bull, when Georgie insisted on a bottle of champagne to celebrate a new deal Jensen's company had just pulled off.

'No, I didn't think they did.' He answered the question for me, shaking his head as if somehow I'd disappointed him. 'You're probably not aware this situation has implications for me with Hawkeswood Estates.'

'How?' This was rubbish; he was simply trying to scare me. Well, it wasn't going to work. I knew Anna had cooked this up with him and there wasn't a shred of truth in it.

'Marcus is not happy,' he began to explain. 'If I can't curb your extravagances, he's threatened to take over responsibility for my finances. And that means he'll control the purse strings here.'

'It appears he already does if your beloved grandmother has got her hands on this statement first.' I said, shaking the papers at him angrily. 'Time you got a backbone, Talún, and stopped having an old woman push you around.'

After this outburst I didn't even wait for his reaction. I simply threw the papers into the air and left.

And now I'm in Exeter walking aimlessly. In a street full of busy shoppers I feel isolated and alone. I thought moving to Lynbrook would get us away from Anna's control but I know we'll never be free of her. She'll always be there, turning up to poison him against me, whispering in his ear, holding threats over his head to keep me in line. As I walk along I'm so wrapped up in my misery I miss my footing and accidentally slip off the edge of the pavement. I feel a stinging pain in my left ankle as I'm thrown forward and then suddenly strong hands are there breaking my fall.

'Are you okay?' a familiar voice says and then, 'good heavens…Lily,' and I find myself looking up into the concerned face of Max Warner.

JESS

For a moment I freeze. This is a bad omen. I thought coming here might lay the final ghost of my past to rest. I never thought I'd see him sitting here, leisurely skimming stones the way I remember him doing all those years ago.

Slowly, I take a step backwards and then another. If I can reach the edge of the trees and retrieve Caspar I'll be able to leave Talún to his solitude. After the embarrassing way we parted the other evening I would think I'm the last person he wants to see anyway.

I've almost reached the edge of the treeline when Caspar shakes his head, rattling his bridle. Talún turns at the sound and seeing me he's on his feet immediately, reaching the bank in seconds. Unable to move, I watch him walk towards me, his strides long and measured. He looks tense, which tells me he's not in a good place at the moment after his meeting with Anna.

'Jess, what brings you here?' he asks, his expression softening into the kind of smile which sends my pulse into overdrive.

'I thought I'd break my ride, give Caspar a drink.'

'I see.' His gaze drifts over my shoulder and he grins. I turn and realise how implausible my excuse is when my horse is tied up twenty yards from the water's edge.

'Oh well.' I give a guilty shrug.

'Actually, I'm glad you're here. About the other night. I've been meaning to see you to apologise, but it's been difficult, I—'

'You apologise? I think I should be doing that, don't you?' I interrupt. 'I didn't mean to push you away. It was just...well, we'd had too much wine I guess, and the last thing I wanted was for us to do something we might regret.'

'Oh, I doubt you could make the situation worse than it already is.' He sighs, rolling his eyes. 'I gather you had a visit from Anna this morning.'

'Yes, it was good to see her again. We had quite a chat.'

'Is this a place you regularly visit?' he asks suddenly, taking the conversation in a totally different direction.

'No. This is the first time I've been to the falls since I returned home. I've another place upstream where I normally stop. Why?'

'So what brought you here today?' he says, and I notice he's watching me closely. 'Are you spying on me?'

'Spying? Of course not. What is this? Are you suggesting I'm some sort of snoop for your grandmother?'

He blows out a deep breath. 'I don't know,' he says with a shake of his head. 'In fact at the moment...never mind. I'm sorry, forget it.' He waves a tired hand at me and turns to go, his long-legged strides taking him across the grass towards Achilles, tethered just inside the treeline on the opposite side of the clearing from Caspar.

As I watch him I realise I can't leave things like this. Although I told Anna I couldn't get involved something pulls at my conscience. We may no longer be lovers but we've sorted out our differences and are friends again. And at the moment he seems in genuine need of a sympathetic ear.

'Talún, wait,' I call after him, and run to catch him up.

LILY

'I've missed you. You promised to keep in touch,' Max scolds me playfully as we sit facing each other at a window table in All Bar One. Scooping me up from the pavement, he insisted I share a drink with him; for old times' sake, he said. As we walked he called his PA to say he'd be taking the rest of the afternoon off. Pocketing his phone, he then quizzed me about Josh and as I responded I could see he'd missed him too. Now we're seated comfortably he wants to know what I've been up to, and why my promise to keep in touch seems to have fallen by the wayside.

'I'm sorry, I've been busy,' I reply, which, of course, is a lie. I had consciously closed the door on my old life. I thought I'd be living too far away in Norfolk for people from the past to matter. Then when we came back to Lynbrook I got caught up with Georgie and Danni who never come to somewhere as provincial as Exeter – their words, not mine. Plymouth, it appears, just about qualifies as a place where they want to be seen shopping.

'What are you doing in this neck of the woods anyway?' he asks. 'Bit of a trek from Norfolk, isn't it?'

'Actually, Talún decided to come back and live in the

Hall. He's building his own stud there.'

'And what do you do while he's busy with horses?'

'Oh, well, I've made two very good friends in the village. We do all the usual girly things, you know, shopping, eating out. What about you? How's work? How's Davina?'

'Work is busy. We're doing very well. Davina,' he gives a thin smile, 'well, that's a different story.'

'Oh?' I lift my wineglass curiously.

'We're no longer together.' He answers quietly.

'You left her for someone else?' It's the only plausible explanation. Max is Exeter's version of George Clooney, a man dozens of women would kill to be with. Davina on the other hand is all sharp angles and geometric hair. I'm convinced no one would want such an uber thin unattractive woman, and yet...

'She's moved in with Tory Sharpe.'

'*The* Tory Sharpe?' I ask, referring to one of the doyennes of the fashion industry whose sexual preferences are well documented in the press. I've lost count of the times I've caught sight of her in one of her exotic creations in Hello or OK Magazine at some big fashion event. And now she's with Davina of all people! For a moment I'm stunned, and then I automatically reach for Max, slipping my hand over his. To be left for another man is one thing but this...

'Oh Max, I'm so sorry.' I say, totally shocked at his news. 'Are you still living up at *Bay Heights*?'

'No, it's on the market but I've moved out. I've got myself a luxury penthouse in a new development down by The Quay.'

'And is there anyone new in your life yet, or is it too early?'

He smiles as he hauls the bottle from the wine cooler and tops up both our glasses. 'There was only ever you, Lily. Surely you're aware of that.'

I laugh. Of course he's joking. Isn't he?

After another bottle of wine and a chat about old times I find myself opening up, telling him everything. He realises how sad I am, how confused and unsure about where I go from here.

'You need to go back and make your peace with Talún,' he says. 'I don't think for a moment he would lie about his situation. You need to meet him half way...it's all about compromise. Offer an olive branch. Suggest the monthly allowance you were telling me about. At least it shows you're prepared to put a cap on your spending and you're working with him, not against him. Make more time for Josh too, that's another way of showing you're on his side. And if things get tough, well, I'm always here. You can get hold of me any time, night or day on this number.' Reaching into the breast pocket of his jacket he pulls out a business card and hands it to me. Suddenly I find myself taken back all those years to the Golden Hind and Leo Hayden's similar promise after I'd seen off those pickpockets. But this is totally different. Max is nothing like Leo.

'Have you time to come back to the office and meet everyone?' he asks. 'I'm sure they'd all love to see you.'

'Of course,' I agree, feeling it would be good to see some of the old faces. I may have been gone only a few months but there are times when I do miss my nine-to-five and the interaction with work colleagues: the laughs, the gossip. I realise how living at the Hall has left me isolated, apart from Danni's and Georgie's company.

We make our way to the office and as Max opens the door and steps back, I walk into a familiar buzz of voices, phones ringing in the background. Nothing has changed; this place is always busy. Max introduces me to a young brunette called Jo who has taken my old job and loves it as much as I did. I stay for a while, chatting to Nick and the others, and as everyone begins to close down for the day I check my watch and make my farewells. Max walks me to the door.

'Keep in touch,' he reminds me, his hand on my shoulder as the automatic mechanism triggers and the glass parts behind me.

'I will,' I promise, giving his arm an affectionate squeeze and backing away. 'It's been lovely seeing you again.'

As I return to the car I know I may be about to lose Georgie and Danni as friends but now Max is back in my life, and that's worth a whole lot more.

JESS

I feel totally drained. My only intention was to listen, to give support to somebody who was clearly in need of a friend talk to. I still care about him, I realise, perhaps too much for my own good. All my noble intentions, however, have blown right back at me because it seemed once he began to talk he couldn't stop. It all came pouring out.

He had invested so much in this new beginning with Lily, but it's all gone wrong. He says he hoped she would settle down and they could make a life together. He thought running into her again and discovering Josh he had been given a second chance for happiness. New start. New family. But there have been problems. She dislikes Anna, although she did seem to have hit it off with Marcus. Not surprising I tell myself having seen how good she is at flirting with the opposite sex. However, as Talún continues, it appears Lily's behaviour – her extravagant spending and failure to take up her responsibilities at the Hall - have now pulled his grandfather into all of this. He has a month, he tells me, to sort things out, otherwise Amberleigh will take control of the Hall's finances.

During his revelations he stops occasionally, inclining his head silently as he looks at me, waiting for my response. I do what I can, calmly and impartially, aware of the anger I feel at the chaos Lily has caused.

When we eventually part, Talún pulls me against him, kissing my forehead as he thanks me for being there for him. Then he buries his face in my hair and hugs me, just like he did when we used to meet here all those years ago. As I breathe in those familiar scents of shaving soap and sandalwood, I quickly damp down on the memories and a feeling of wanting to be in his arms once more. That was yesterday and has no place in either of our lives now. All we can ever be is friends. As I watch him ride away I feel

I've done very little, but he assures me simply having someone there to listen has enabled him to get his thoughts into perspective. I feel I'm in the worst position anyone could be in: a helpless spectator in Lily's gradual destruction of yet another family.

I'm glad to see Bella in the bar as we set up for the evening. If anyone can lift me out of this gloom meeting Talún has triggered, it's her.

'How did your first day go?' I ask as I make a final check of the refrigerators.

'It was brilliant.' She grins, waving her hands in the air. 'Josh is amazing. He's not only cute, he's bright as well. He asks so many questions. We went to Buckfastleigh to see the butterflies and otters. He wanted to bring one home, said it could live in one of the ponds. You should have seen the disappointment in his little face when I told him it would eat all the fish.' She laughs. 'So we signed up to adopt one instead.'

By the time I'm unlocking the bar door, Bella has apprised me of her duties at the Hall. She gets on well with Jeanette, their house manager, and has the use of a white Range Rover and a horse. 'Talún feels Josh can go for short rides as long as his pony, Liquorice, is on a leading rein. That's tomorrow's project.'

Bella's enthusiasm is infectious. She's full of ideas about how to keep Josh entertained. Then as quickly as it's arrived, the upbeat mood changes. 'She doesn't love him, you know,' she says, referring to Lily. 'Today she wasn't even interested in what we'd been doing. He tried to tell her about Sparky – the otter we've adopted - and she just didn't want to hear any of it. You should have seen his face, poor little kid. She's an absolute cow.'

LILY

I took Max's advice and went to find Talún as soon as I returned home. After the way I had left him I braced myself for another round of verbal aggro. Josh's excited voice drew me towards the kitchen where I found him sitting with Talún, chattering away about his afternoon as he ate his tea. He was incredibly animated, full of excitement as he described his trip to see the otters and butterflies. I'd been subjected to his childish prattle earlier when I intercepted him and Bella on their return, so it was a relief when Jeanette came to take him off for his bath. As they left, Talún looked at me. He seemed sad and his voice was gentle as he said, 'Lily I don't want to fight. This is how I want our life to be: you, me and Josh sitting around the table like a proper family but before we can do that there are issues we need to sort out.'

We moved into the drawing room and after a long heart to heart we came to an agreement. Looking at it from my point of view I think I came away with the lion's share of the deal. I've got a monthly allowance, which I managed to bump up slightly from what was originally on offer. It won't be easy but I'm just going to have to learn to live within my limits. In exchange I've promised to spend more time with Josh, especially in the evenings when Jeanette usually takes care of him.

'All I'm asking for is honesty, Lily,' he said, as our conversation came to an end. 'We can't build a life on secrets and lies. And I'm sure, like me, you don't want to find yourself having to go cap in hand to Amberleigh for everything. Because be assured that's what will happen if we don't improve things here.'

'I understand,' I said, realising I was going to have to be very careful for a while, 'and I'm willing to work hard to change things for the better.'

'Good.' He pulled me into his arms, pressing his lips to my forehead, and then quite unexpectedly he said, 'It's your birthday soon. Is there anything you'd especially like?'

I interpreted this as an olive branch after his unreasonable behaviour towards me. I immediately thought of the health spa in Guernsey but I knew if he was aware that Georgie and Danni were going too, it would be a non-starter. As far as he is concerned they have played a big part in my financial crisis. The words *health spa* wouldn't go down too well either, as it's an indication of more idle extravagance. Think quickly, Lily, an inner voice nagged. Why would you want to go there?

'There is one thing...' I hesitated, 'but it's out of the question really.'

'Well you won't know until you ask, will you?' His smile was unexpected and gave me the courage to continue.

'True.' I drew a deep breath, 'Actually I'd like to spend a few days in Guernsey. I've an old friend living there ...Karin... she used to work with me at Warner Webb. I haven't seen her since she left. We used to keep in touch by phone and I always promised I'd visit one day. But bringing up Josh on my own there was never the opportunity...or the money. Since meeting you and having all these changes in my life, although we've not lost touch, it's something I'd completely forgotten about...until yesterday when I had a text from her. I realise it's short notice but she said she's hoping to get a few days off next week and asked now I'm settled here whether it would be possible for me to visit. Given how things were between us I wasn't going to ask but, as it's my birthday...' I took a breath, amazed and quite pleased at the speed with which I'd strung such a complex and believable collection of lies together.

'Why don't you ask her to come and stay here instead? Then she could celebrate your birthday with us.' he suggested, making my heart rate accelerate at the thought all this was about to go horribly wrong. I forgot; complex lying needs forward planning.

'Yes, that would be good idea,' I managed brightly, 'I know she'd love to see the Hall. But I'd want her to stay for a whole week... you know, make it a real break for her. Unfortunately, this time she's tied to two or three days. We could do it later in the year, though.'

'Fine,' he agreed, his smile returning. I breathed a huge sigh of relief and then offered him something I was sure would seal the deal.

'Right,' I said jumping to my feet, 'Let me give her a call

and sort the dates out and then,' I reached down and caught his hand in mine, 'for my actual birthday perhaps you me and Josh could do something together – a family day out maybe?'

'A family day out,' He repeated as he studied me quietly for a moment and then he smiled, 'Yes Lily, that's a great idea.'

'I think so too and I'll leave it to you to decide where we go. Make it a surprise.' I suggested as I leaned down to kiss his cheek. 'And I really am very sorry. I will change, I promise.'

Yes, yes, I know, I've lied again. But all I want is this one last trip, then I'll settle down and behave myself...I really will. I promise.

TALÚN

Lily flew out this morning. I dropped her off at Exeter Airport where she held onto me tightly and thanked me again for giving her the opportunity to meet up with Karin. Before she disappeared into the terminal building she promised to call me to let me know she'd arrived safely. Driving home, I felt we'd climbed a huge mountain. Of course I blame myself for not keeping a check on her spending. Her extravagant shopping habits were one of the reasons we left Amberleigh. I should have learned my lesson. Instead I took my eye off the ball and gave my total concentration to my horses. It won't happen again.

As I join the A30 I'm feeling more relaxed than I have for a long time. Things got off to a bumpy start between us but I think this last flare up has taught her a lesson. She's promised to keep within budget with the new allowance and I'm hopeful things will only get better from now on. Once I reach home I'll put in a call to Anna to tell her what's happened. She'll be pleased everything is under control and so will Marcus. I need to catch up with Jess too, to thank her. I know she feels she didn't do a lot but being able to offload all my thoughts onto someone else enabled me to clear my head and find a solution to my problem. I'm in her debt and although we have a shared past which didn't work out, I'm glad we're still friends.

LILY

I caught up with Georgie and Danni at the check in desk and we made our way to the VIP lounge. We were on our third champagne cocktail when our flight was called.

Now, after a very short spell in the air and a bit of a bumpy landing due to cross winds, a taxi has deposited us at this very plush hotel full of chrome and marble...and there are fabulous sea views! The manager, a rather tactile forty something Italian homes in on us as we are checking in. He says tomorrow a photographer is arriving to take photos of the hotel and the spa for a big group marketing campaign. Unfortunately there has been a mix up with the modelling agency and they can only send one girl which is no good. 'You lovely ladies, you would all be perfect for this,' he tells us in his effusive way, and wonders if we would be interested in helping him out. The shoot would only take a morning, no more, he assures us. Of course, Georgie, ever the sly negotiator, makes a big deal about it being a special break for and us and how helping him out would cut short our time for the things we've planned. I sense a deal brewing when she follows him into his office and closes the door. Ten minutes later she returns with a big smile on her face.

'Giovanni's phoned head office and they're offering to waive our bill if we do the photo shoot,' she says, punching the air. 'Girls, we are really going to have fun on this break.'

And fun we did have. The photography team arrived and took loads of shots of us – eating, drinking, in the pool, having spa treatments. Wow! I think if I could have my time over again I might have gone into modelling. I guess a lot of people think it must be boring having to strike different poses as some guy snaps you, but me? I loved it.

We spent our second evening in the bar with more of our favourite champagne cocktails both before and after dinner. God knows what kind of bar bill we ran up, but hey, we weren't paying, so why not? Halfway through the evening a small group of guys arrived. Drawn by our alcohol induced revelry they soon drifted over to our corner of the bar. James, Darius, Fletcher and Marc settled around us, expanding our high spirited group. It wasn't long, however, before I realised there was something going on. Even though I'd drunk quite a lot I was aware from the looks Georgie and Danni were giving a couple of the guys, they were looking for more than a friendly drink in the bar. Was I included in this? I hoped not. I started to feel panicky. Something like this could wreck my plans to marry Talún. Before everything spiralled out of control I decided to make it clear I wasn't going to be part of their plan and leave them to it. Pushing myself to my feet, I picked up my bag and said I would see them in the morning.

'Lily, you party pooper, where do you think you're going?' Danni protested, making a grab for me and missing.

'To my room. I'm tired and I've had far too much to drink,' I said, feeling my head spin. I needed to get to my suite but I wasn't sure in the state I was in I'd make it.

'I'll see her safely back,' Darius offered. I knew he'd been watching me all evening and was convinced he'd seen this as an opportunity to make his move. With his pale skin, thick dark hair and cold predatory black eyes, he made my flesh crawl.

'Thanks, but I'm fine,' I reassured him, and wishing them all goodnight turned and made my way a little unsteadily out of the bar. I was praying Giovanni was around and I could stop and tell him I felt unwell. I was sure he'd arrange for someone to take me up to my room, but he was nowhere to be seen. I reached the lift, swiping my fingers over the call button. I drew in a nervous breath as I turned to find Darius had followed me. He was obviously not about to take no for an answer.

'You shouldn't run off like that Lily darling,' he said as he closed in on me. 'Anything could happen to you.'

'Please,' I said, leaning against the wall, 'leave me alone. I'm fine.'

'You're far from fine,' he soothed. 'Let me take care of you.'

His hands crept to my shoulders and I felt his breath on my neck. Backed against the wall, there was nowhere to go. Gathering my wits as best I could, I was about to attempt a well-aimed knee to the groin when there was an angry growl and someone pulled him off me. The back of my head hit the wall and for a moment I saw stars. I leaned into the woodwork, shaking my head and trying to clear my vision. The first thing I was aware of was Darius making a hasty exit back to bar and next, the last person I expected to see. 'Max?' I peered at him, convinced after the knock to my head I was hallucinating. 'Is that really you? What are you doing here?'

'Saving your neck by the look of it.' He shook his great golden head of hair angrily. 'When you called the other day to tell me everything was back to normal with you and Talún you mentioned this trip and I knew there would be trouble. What is he thinking, letting you go off with those two again? Has he no sense? I've been at the bar all evening watching your so-called friends' antics. Two upper class tarts, Lily, game for anything. You're not like them.'

The irony of his words weren't lost on me. When all is said and done, despite what Max chooses to believe, the three of us are pretty similar. We're all with partners we don't love; men whose bank balances sustain our lifestyles. Yes, in the end sadly it's all about the money.

I hear the sound of the lift arriving and feel the warmth of Max's arm around my waist, keeping me upright. The doors part and he gently helps me inside. 'Come on,' he says, 'let's get you back to your room and sober you up.'

JESS

I love these perfect twilights. Ones where once the sun has gone, the far horizon goes through a whole spectrum of colour before melting into the deep, dark velvet of night.

Tonight, sitting here on my night off, I'm enjoying one of those moments. When Krister did the renovations one of the most important features was my new south facing conservatory. It gave me an uninterrupted view across open countryside and a magical evening vista, where the lights of Teignmouth dance along the horizon once darkness arrives. On this warm evening I throw the doors open and sit outside with a glass of red as I mull over the events of the day.

I can't believe how well the building is coming along. The daily increasing layers of brickwork are already transforming the site. Of course, I haven't a clue about the process, what happens where - Krister's the expert there. But being able to see physical change is exciting and I can't wait to see the first completed house, which should be ready by late autumn.

I top up my wine and sit back, listening to the sounds in the wood. There are those who are quite amazed I don't find it scary up here. I guess the majority of people wouldn't like to be this isolated but for me it's a perfect place to escape to.

Just out of my peripheral vision I notice the security light at the front of the cottage has been triggered. This usually means a fox or a badger is around, out on its night time hunt for food. As I draw a deep breath and close my eyes, savouring a fresh mouthful of wine, I'm aware of the soft nicker of a horse. It seems I have human company and wonder who could be riding in the woods this late in the evening. Leaving my glass on the table, I go to investigate.

TALÚN

After spending the evening at the stud sorting a few outstanding issues with Greg, I decide to take Achilles out. I used to do this when I worked for George years ago and needed to get my head around something. Riding in the wood at night gives you a totally different perspective. It's all about sounds rather than vision, although tonight there's a full moon which gives the landscape a ghostly feel as I direct my grey boy along the woodland pathway.

I wonder how Lily's reunion is going. She did text to say she'd arrived safely but since then I've heard nothing from her, but I guess she's got a lot of catching up to do with Karin. I'm pleased everything is settled. There's still a lot of work to do but I believe we're beginning to move in the right direction. With Fliss it was easy. Working as Marcus's PA, she loved the land and understood what her responsibilities as my wife would be. Lily is a town girl and I know it would be impossible – and unfair – to try to compare her to Fliss. We've still a way to go, but I'm certain we'll get there.

Up ahead I can see a light and I realise I'm near Jess's cottage. I pull Achilles to a halt. I realise it's late, but as I'm here, maybe I should drop in and thank her.

JESS

Approaching the front of the house, I hear the gate creak open followed by the sound of metal grating on metal as whoever is there secures it.

'Talún?' He stands there haloed in the beam of the security light and I wonder what has happened to bring him here this evening. 'Is everything all right?'

'Everything is fine.' He smiles, looking relaxed. 'I've been at the stud with Greg for most of the evening and...well, it was such a beautiful night I thought I'd take Achilles out for a moonlight ride. I saw your light through the trees and—'

'You wanted to chat?'

'A chat would be good.' The way he grins reminds me of how he was when I knew him first. But that was long ago, in another lifetime. Now he's twenty-eight and has a manor house, a stud, staff – and considerable responsibilities.

'I've wine around the back. Come and join me.'

He updates me on news at the stud: two newly pregnant mares and the anticipated birth of Achilles' foal at Amberleigh. As we sit drinking, he's amazed at the changes

Krister's made to this side of the cottage and comments on the comfortable rattan furniture.

'I wanted to make the most of this view,' I explain. 'Remember the evening we sat like this with those lights dancing out on the horizon? I thought it was such a magical sight.'

'And they're dancing for us again this evening. Nothing's changed, has it?' He remarks.

I remain silent, taking a mouthful of wine. He's wrong; everything has changed, for him and for me. 'So what really brought you here?' I quickly turn the conversation back to him.

He leans back into the softness of the cushions and twirls his wine glass between his finger and thumb thoughtfully before I'm gifted with his reflective green gaze. 'Well, first I wanted to thank you for the other day. You know, for listening; for being there.'

'It's what friends are for,' I tell him. 'And how are things at home now?'

'Much better.' He runs a hand through his thick dark hair and smiles. 'Lily and I had a long talk about all the problems we've been having. I think the row we had made her realise she'd not been very fair. Anyway, we've come to an agreement. We've made adjustments to her financial arrangements and she's promised to cut back on her spending and give the Witches a wide berth.' He flashes me an amused smile, 'Yes, I am aware of what the villagers call them.'

'So where is she this evening?' I ask, realising it's just past eleven and she'll probably be wondering where he's got to.

'In Guernsey for a few days catching up with an old friend.'

Alarm bells ring as I remember Bella telling me how the Witches were talking about their trip only days ago, when they were in the restaurant having dinner.

'Guernsey?' I echo, realising what she's done. 'I don't believe this. You've been played for a fool, Talún. She's with *them*.'

'Them? Danni and Georgie you mean?' His brows lift in surprise and then he shakes his head, 'No she isn't, she's spending a few days with a friend called Karin. They used to work together.'

'Are you sure?'

'Of course I am.'

He stops suddenly and shoots me a curious look. 'What made you think she was with them anyway?'

'Because they happen to be there at the moment on a four day spa break. Bella overheard them talking about it when they were in the restaurant at the weekend with Jensen and Felix.'

'Probably just a coincidence.' He shrugs and I can tell from his expression he believes her, the fool.

'Silly me, of course it is,' I snap, hearing the sarcasm in my tone, angered he can be so blinkered.

'Why do you dislike her so much?'

'What?'

'You hate her, don't you?'

My silence brings him closer. He cups my face gently in his right hand and turns it towards him. I'm so close I can see the amber flecks in those moss green irises. 'Jess?'

My fingers close around his wrist and I ease his hand away. 'It's private, Talún, and not up for discussion. Please...don't ruin our evening.'

TALÚN

I've never seen Jess like this. I came here this evening to thank her and let me know I've hopefully turned things around with Lily, and the word *Guernsey* became the trigger for a completely unexpected and hostile outburst from her. Now it appears she thinks Lily's away with those two dreadful women. There's always been this anger surrounding anything to do with Lily and suddenly I want to know the reason. Oh, I'm aware my wife to be is not the easiest of people to get on with. She has very few friends but I'm sure the tough upbringing she had made her wary of trusting people and forming relationships. So I

285

challenged Jess and straight away I could see the shutters coming down. The next moment she was warning me off the subject.

As the evening was cooling off we took ourselves indoors and settled in the kitchen where Jess extracted another chilled bottle of Pinot Grigio from the fridge and topped up our glasses. Pulling herself up onto one of the bar stools she sat silently, staring into her wine. It was clear something bad had happened between the two of them way back but exactly what had triggered it, I had no idea. And then all of a sudden it hit me.

'What caused your break up with Zac?' I asked, pushing myself away from the fridge freezer where I'd been leaning and slipping onto the seat next to her.

'Why the sudden interest?' She pinned me with an inquisitive stare.

'Curiosity I guess. When you arrived here you left a lot of unanswered questions behind in Milton Bay. Things probably too personal for you to share with anyone at the time. I think Zac was one of them.' I could see a flush creeping into her face and realised I'd hit a sensitive spot.

'I'm not sure why you're asking. People fall in and out of love. That's exactly what happened to Zac and me.' She shook her head, making her thick blonde hair fall across her face, probably to hide the discomfort I could see there. 'Sometimes your first love isn't destined to be your last.'

'No one helped it happen then?'

Pushing her hair from her eyes, she fixed me with a hard stare. 'And your point is?'

'Lily maybe? Did she take a shine to Zac? Come between you two? Is that why you appear to have this vendetta going on?'

I watched her fingers work their way around the base of her wine glass, not sure if I was about to get an answer or whether she planned to hijack the conversation and take it in another direction.

'Vendetta.' She rolled the word around her tongue, her expression thoughtful as she continued to play with the stem of her glass. 'I wouldn't go as far as calling it that. But

I can't forgive her for what she did to me.'

'Perhaps you need to get it out of your system then. Find some form of closure,' I coaxed.

There was a sadness in her eyes I've not seen before. 'I'm not sure what you're asking is possible,' she said with a slow shake of her head, 'but as far Zac's concerned, I'm willing to satisfy your curiosity.'

JESS

This wasn't how I'd planned my evening. When Talún arrived I was glad to have his company but the last thing I expected was this third degree over what happened between me, Zac and Lily. In the end I threw in the towel figuring as it was the lesser of her crimes it wouldn't hurt to tell him. As for Talún acting as my father confessor, or exorcist or whatever he figured he was, no matter how well meaning the gesture, I knew opening up to him wouldn't make any difference in my attitude towards his bride to be. And there would certainly be no forgiveness.

Taking a sip of my wine I begin, telling him it was Leo in his usual controlling way, who had mapped out my life for me. A life with well-heeled Zac Rayner, only son of a prominent local surgeon, was part of his plan. I speak about the downward spiral: dates he didn't turn up for, excuses he made. Everything was plausible, I say. I believed him. I trusted him.

'I was doing some temping over the summer and had an appointment at local stables.' I pause to take a sip of wine. 'There was an RTA and we were all diverted. The alternative route was through the western edge of Milton Bay.'

'The traffic backed up and I noticed this car which had stopped outside a row of terraced houses on the opposite side of the road. I had to do a double take but I was so sure it was Zac I pulled up a little way ahead and got out to watch. I saw him leave his car and go into one of the houses. The door opened and Lily was there. She threw her arms around him and kissed him. Then they went inside.'

'But why was Lily living with you when she had a house?'

'I have no idea. She told Leo her boyfriend had thrown her out and she was homeless. She was good at lying,' I say, shaking my head, and then tell him about the woman I talked to. 'There was a neighbour. She said Lily had been living there with a man but he'd left, and a girl - pregnant I think - was there now. I'm not sure why she lied to Leo.' I do really, of course - the money, but I want to stick to the facts, not give him opinions which might prompt more questions I don't want to answer. 'The neighbour also referred to Zac as the new boyfriend.' I add.

'I wanted to confront him but it took me a week to pin him down,' I continue. 'He wouldn't answer my calls and was never home. A group of us were meeting for a meal. He was supposed to pick me up but didn't show. Amber ran me into town where I met up with a few people for drinks, including Roo. When we arrived at the restaurant Zac was there. He'd been drinking and it was clear he wasn't in the best of moods. He hauled me out into the restaurant garden. Before I could say a word he laid into me, accusing me of sleeping with you while I was here on holiday.' I see his shocked expression as I reach for my glass again. 'However, it wasn't what I'd done as much as who I'd done it with that upset him so much.'

'The farm boy,' Talún says, remembering Zac's derogatory term for him. 'But where did he get such a crazy idea from?'

'Lily. She saw us together on the night of the restaurant opening.'

'But all we did was talk.' He pauses for a moment. 'Did she alert Leo? Is that the reason he arrived out of nowhere spitting pins?'

'Yes, it was all part of her plan to make sure Zac left me. She wanted him for herself. When I challenged him about what he had been up to with her he admitted it. Shrugged it off, said she was just a quick lay and she meant nothing to him. He also confessed to other incidents of unfaithfulness, justifying his actions by saying it was what guys did. Shortly after our row he dumped her.'

'Oh Jess.' Talún shakes his head, reaching out to give my hand a sympathetic squeeze. 'Still, I guess Lily did you a favour. I mean, at least you discovered what he was really like before it was too late.'

I pull my hand away. I'm not sure what I thought his reaction would be, but it wasn't this. It's as if he's saying Zac was the problem here and Lily's complicity in all of it didn't matter.

'A favour?' I snap, feeling the anger shimmer through me. 'You have no idea, do you? What I went through?'

He reaches for me again with an apology but I avoid his touch. I wasn't looking for anyone to take sides but the last thing I expected was for him to patronise me and sweep Lily's guilt under the carpet. But then what else did I expect? They may not be a love match but his willingness to marry her means he's bound to be biased.

Reminders of that summer have taken me back to a place I thought I had firmly closed the door on. I put my hands to my face and sob, wet tears trickling between my fingers as I give in to painful memories beyond those of Zac's infidelity.

I hear Talún's glass being placed on the worktop and then his strength and warmth as I find myself cradled in his arms.

'I'm sorry, Jess, I never dreamt this would cause you so much pain,' he says softly. 'I thought, well...'

'What?' I look up at him, wiping away my tears with my fingertips, 'that it was some girls' spat? She took everything from me, Talún: the little respect Leo grudgingly gave me, Zac, my life in Milton Bay. But worst of all she eventually took the most precious thing I had...you.'

I take a deep breath realising I've said more than I should have and must sound like a pathetic loser. 'I'm sorry,' I say, pulling back slightly, 'you must think I'm a complete—'

'Shh.' His voice is soothing, and I feel warm, strong fingers brush my cheek as they gently tuck a stray curl of hair behind my ear. It's a comforting gesture but when those same fingers slip under my chin to tilt my face towards his, it becomes something far more intimate. He considers me quietly for a moment, eyes dark with emotion, and I feel my pulse quicken as he slowly bends his head, his mouth claiming mine. The kiss is soft, almost hesitant at first, as if he's half expecting me to push him away or maybe even slap him. When I do neither, I feel him relax and continue, his tongue teasing its way into my mouth. As the kiss deepens I slip from the stool, my hands going to his shoulders to steady myself. Everything becomes sensation and the knowledge of what we are doing and where it will ultimately lead hits me. A warning voice tells me this shouldn't be happening, but suddenly I don't care. I want...need this so much. It's been too long. His arms wrap around my back to support me, and he pulls me gently between his thighs and against the hardness of his body. In this moment of contact I am aware of his arousal; that he needs me as much as I need him. As his hands slip under my t-shirt and I feel skin against skin I am past the point of no return. I no longer care what will happen tomorrow. All I want is this moment, and him loving me the way he did all those years ago.

LILY

The next morning Max arranges seats for both of us on the first available flight back to Exeter. We check out separately and I leave a hastily scribbled note for Georgie. I tell her a family emergency has meant I have to fly home straight away. I also explain the situation to Giovanni, hoping if they quiz him it makes my excuse a little more believable.

Thankfully the flight is a short one and after retrieving our luggage, he picks his Mercedes up from the airport car park. We drive home in silence. I'm still feeling hung over and I think he's obviously mad at me for putting myself in such a dangerous situation. As we reach Lynbrook I ask him to pull over.

'I'll make my own way to the house,' I tell him. 'The last thing I want is anyone seeing us together.'

'Don't be ridiculous.' He looks at me as if I'm mad. 'You? Wheeling a trolley case up the driveway? Someone is bound to notice and you don't want Talún asking questions, do you?'

'No, of course not.' I sit there quietly, suitably chastised.

Talún's Range Rover is parked at the front of the house when we arrive. Max sweeps the Merc around the fountain and parks up. He releases the boot catch and before I climb out to retrieve my case I reach for his hand.

'Thank you for being there.' I squeeze his fingers tightly. I really mean what I say. If not for him, goodness knows what would have happened to me.

He looks down at our linked hands and smiles. 'Just don't do this again Lily, please,' he warns gently. 'Keep away from those two women. They're bad news.'

'I will,' I promise, although I dread to think of what my life in this God forsaken backwater will be like without their company. I'm not cut out to be a country wife with the responsibility for running a home like the Hall. It's boring. All I want is freedom and fun. Surely that's not too much to ask? And although I hate myself for even thinking this, I don't want to be a mother any longer either.

'Can I buy you dinner some time?' I offer, needing to see him again as I suddenly realise he's become my principal means of escape from this dreary place. 'You rescued me from a bad situation, I'd like to say thank you properly.'

Max considers my offer for a moment and then nods. 'Why not?' He says, gifting me with one of his warm smiles.

'Great, I'll give you a call soon.' I promise as I vacate the passenger seat, 'And thank you again, you're a hero.'

I watch the Merc as it cruises back down the driveway and turn back to face the house, wondering if anyone saw us and not really caring if they did. If I have to face the music, so be it. Jeanette is there to greet me in her usual calm manner as I walk into the hall.

'Morning, Ms. Stevenson, you're back early.' She smiles. 'I was sure you said Friday.'

I'm not really sure where Jeanette's loyalties lie. She works for me but Talún pays her salary and I'm convinced the money wins every time. Because of this I'm always careful and it means right now I need to have a plausible explanation.

'Oh, an emergency came up. Someone called in sick which meant my friend had to go back to work. It was lovely to see her again, though,' I add.

She nods and I find myself, wondering whether Jeanette plans to ask any more about my time away. Thankfully she doesn't. Instead she arranges for one of the cleaning staff to take my suitcase to my room.

'What's happening this morning?' I ask, as the girl disappears up the stairs. 'Has Bella gone out with Josh?'

'Yes, she's taken him riding. I think Greg's gone with them too.'

'And Talún? I see the Range Rover is outside.'

'Not sure. At the stud I expect.'

'I'll catch up with him later.'

'Can I get you some coffee?'

I ask for a tray to be brought to the drawing room in thirty minutes which should give me time to shower and change. Jeanette nods and disappears. Later I'm about to head downstairs when I hear heavy footfalls coming along the landing. Opening my door, I come face to face with Talún. His eyes widen with surprise as he sees me. 'I thought you weren't coming back until tomorrow,' he says, as he pushes dark tousled hair out of his eyes.

'Caught you out, have I?' I respond, unable to resist a teasing smirk as I scan him from top to toe.

'What do you mean?'

'Take a look at yourself in the mirror. I hope she was worth it.'

TALÚN

Christ! What have I walked in to? I overslept at Jess's, which was to be expected I guess after the kind of night we spent together. Apart from sleeping with Lily a few weeks ago, which I still can't remember a thing about, I've not been with a woman since Fliss died. With Jess it was like stepping back in time; our coming together as natural and wonderful as it had been during that long ago summer. What happened there in the darkness wasn't simply sex; it was the reawakening of a powerful emotional connection. I knew then my feelings for her were still as strong and intense as they had been all those years ago. This morning she was very quiet as we said our goodbyes. I think we both knew there could be no future for us beyond our continued friendship. Despite what I've learned about Lily, in some ways I understand her behaviour. Brought into a comfortable middle class environment and indulged by Leo, it was only natural she coveted what Jess had. Of course I don't condone her actions, but I still stand by my view she did Jess a favour. Zac was an arrogant bastard. She deserved better.

I was still deep in thought as I reached home and headed for my room. What a shock to find Lily back early. 'I hope she was worth it,' she said. What did that mean? Had she guessed where I'd been? Surely not. For a moment I felt wrong footed, not sure how to respond, but I quickly recovered, saying I'd catch up with her once I'd showered and changed.

LILY

Where has he been? Messy hair, a swathe of stubble coating his chin, he looks as if he's just returned from an all-night party Has he been with someone else? No, of course not, he is far too moral. He looked absolutely horrified when I suggested it I wanted to laugh out loud. Well, it will be interesting to see what explanation he has when he decides to put in an appearance.

TALÚN

After a shower, shave and a change of clothes, I go to find Lily. She's in the drawing room flicking through a magazine when I enter. Coffee has been laid out and she looks up, her eyes fixed on me, as I close the door and join her.

'So,' I say, taking a seat opposite her. 'What happened to bring you back this early?'

'Oh, Karin had to go into work,' she says with a casual lift of her shoulders. 'Someone called in sick. What about you?'

'Me?' I draw in a breath as my brain does somersaults trying to come up with a believable response. I'm aware of pale blue eyes fixed on me as if looking for something in my behaviour that will give me away. Well maybe not; maybe I'm panicking like this because I'm so damned guilty.

'Yes, you look as if you've been out all night.'

'Not quite all night,' I tell her, having worked out my excuse. 'I couldn't sleep. Took Achilles out early.'

Lily nods and I realise I'm believed; off the hook. Abandoning her magazine, she leans towards the cafetiere. She pours the hot, black liquid into one of the cups, hands it to me and moves the milk and sugar nearer.

'So, did you get to do any sightseeing?' Now it's my turn for questions.

'A little,' she nods, 'she did take me into St. Peter Port for shopping, but there was nothing that caught my eye. A good start to my new spending regime, eh?' She jokes. 'To be honest I think maybe her call into work came at an opportune time.' She says as she splashes milk into her cup, 'Actually, I was beginning to feel rather bored.'

'Did you know Danni and Georgie were over there at some health spa?' I hit her with this information, keen to see how she responds.

She takes a sip and calmly returns the cup to its saucer. 'Really?' her eyes widen in surprise, revealing nothing.

'Yes, really. I'm surprised they didn't tell you. I mean,

you were always round there for drinks or lunching at the Bull weren't you?'

'Talún, what is all this about?' She frowns at me. 'Some sort of tit for tat because I suggested you'd spent the night with someone? I was only joking.'

I frown into my coffee, not sure what to say. I'm still trying to work out whether Lily is an incredible liar or Jess has made a huge mistake.

'You don't believe me, do you?' She gets to her feet and crosses over to where she's left her tote, pulling out her mobile. Returning to her seat, she scans through it. 'Here,' she offers it to me, 'this is Karin.'

I see a plump, dark haired twenty-something wearing beige trousers and a green patterned short sleeve blouse. I can just make out a gold name badge nestling below her left shoulder blade. I nod and hand the phone back to her. 'I'm sorry,' I tell her. 'I didn't mean to jump to conclusions.'

'Given what's happened recently it's to be expected.' She says quietly as she gets up and places the mobile back in her bag, before settling herself beside me. 'You know, I really do want to make this work,' she says, leaning her head against my shoulder. 'Guernsey gave me time to focus on the important things ...you and Josh. So,' she reaches up and kisses me on the cheek, 'have you had any thoughts about our family day out for my birthday?'

I close my eyes, hating to admit I was hoping she was lying. Had that been the case, I would have braved the consequences of taking legal action to secure Josh if it meant I could have Jess too. Instead nothing has changed, the arrangement stands and Lily and I are on still on course for our Christmas wedding.

JESS

It's been five days since I spent the night with Talún. The morning we parted there were no promises, no arrangements to meet again. Already I miss him: the strength of his arms around me, the familiar scent of his skin and the warmth of his body as he cradles me against him after making love. Would I see him again? Given the circumstances, probably not but secretly I hoped, oh how I hoped. However, last night in the bar Bella served me up a dose of cold, hard reality. I'd said how much I liked the new top she was wearing and she told me she'd bought it during a shopping trip to Exeter that afternoon. When I asked why she hadn't been looking after Josh she said it was because Talún had given her the day off. He had she said, taken him out with Lily for the day to celebrate her birthday.

As it was another warm evening, when I got home I sat outside for a while with a large glass of wine, trying to come to terms with my foolishness. Talún has chosen to marry Lily and despite what happened between us and the way I feel about him, fate has dictated our lives are destined to take separate paths.

This morning I got up determined to draw a line under the events of the past few days. I threw myself into the things that really mattered. I visited the site to meet Krister to see how work was progressing and arranged for more funds to be available to him. Afterwards I drove to the Bull and sat down with Rufus to help him begin planning next weekend's summer barbeque. Then, quite unexpectedly, I got a text from Talún asking me to meet him by the waterfall after my lunch shift had finished. Of course, if I'd had any sense I would have returned his text and told him I already knew they were back together so seeing him again was pointless. But fool that I am I wouldn't let go. Although I knew they were still together, I needed to know how it had happened - although it didn't take an Einstein to figure out Lily had somehow managed to blag her way out of trouble again.

I arrived at the waterfall twenty minutes ago and he's still not shown. Maybe he couldn't get away. Maybe some emergency came up at the stud...and then through the trees I hear the nicker of a horse. Talún greets me with a smile as he swings off Achilles' back and secures him to a nearby tree.

'Sorry I'm late,' he says as he reaches me, wrapping his hands around my shoulders, his lips brushing my cheek. I follow him over to the edge of the pool where we settle ourselves among the warm rocks. Bright sunlight dapples its surface, birds sing and in the background there is the musical rush of the falls. I watch him for a moment, his gaze fixed on the water. He shakes his head, clearing his thoughts no doubt and trying to decide how best to tell me what he doesn't realise I already know.

'I gather you're still together then.' Unable to bear it any longer it's me who breaks the silence, hearing the bitter edge in my voice.

He turns to look at me, his eyes widening with surprise, and then he frowns. 'Bella told you.'

'That you'd been playing happy families, yes.'

He winces at my sarcastic barb. 'She was already home when I got back to the Hall. Karin had to go into work to relieve a sick colleague so she flew back early. And before you say anything else, she does exist. Lily showed me a photo of her on her mobile. I'm afraid you were mistaken, she wasn't with Danni and Georgie.'

'There's nothing left to say then, is there?'

He stills for a moment, eases a hand through his thick dark hair then turns to look at me. 'Jess, please don't do this. I really want to be with you, but I can't,' he begins, reaching for my hand and wrapping his warm fingers around mine. 'You have to understand—'

'What? About being used?'

'I didn't use you Jess, I— '

'No?' I cut across him, 'well from where I'm standing that's exactly how it feels.'

He takes a deep breath but before he gets a chance to say another word I pull from his grasp as my eyes begin to fill. How brave I felt before he arrived, telling myself I knew the outcome of this meeting but it would be okay, I could cope. The fact of the matter is, I can't. Fool that I am, despite everything, I realise I still love him. It takes all my willpower to damp down the need to cry. I have to get out of here. Now.

Seconds later I'm running across the clearing towards Caspar. As I gather up his reins ready to haul myself into the saddle, I feel Talún's hands on my shoulders and he pulls me around to face him.

'You think this is easy for me?' he says, and I see the raw pain in his eyes. 'You think it doesn't kill me having to do this when I care about you so much?'

'You...care about me?' I respond, as my hardened gaze locks with his. 'Really?'

At that comment he releases me. He inhales deeply. He looks defeated; beaten. 'Do you want to know the real truth about Lily and me?' he asks, and I see the shimmer of moisture in his eyes. 'I've never had a proper relationship with her. She was the mystery woman in the pavilion with me on the night of your party. She'd tried to get in to see you. Good luck wishes for Exeter, she said. Rufus threw her out and when I suffered the same fate, I had a few sorrow drowning beers before I ended up sharing a bottle of red wine with her. One thing led to another and, well... Josh was the result.'

'How did you find out about him?'

'Warner Webb where she worked happened to be handling the sale of the Hall. I came down to see Max Warner in February and ran into her quite by chance. We had dinner on a couple of occasions and I accidentally caught sight of Josh when I dropped her home one evening. She was angry at first; denied he was mine. Then a couple of weeks later she asked me to meet her and admitted that he was my son. As you can imagine, after losing Fliss and Emily I felt I'd been given a second chance. But because of the circumstances I had to lie, creating a fictitious relationship with her to make things more acceptable to my grandfather. My relationship with Lily is really a business arrangement. I get Josh and in return, as my wife, she gets the lifestyle she's always wanted. I don't love her and she certainly doesn't love me,' he says with an angry shake of his head. 'Hell, I don't even sleep with her.'

I stand there, massaging my forehead, trying to fend off an approaching headache as I take in what he's just told me. That he's locked into little more than a business arrangement with Lily Stevenson. I suddenly understand how desperate he must have been to have Josh to agree to such a horrendous deal. But then the only other option would mean going through the courts and exposing himself and his family to the press. And, given his rather colourful past, it's something he would never risk. My heart breaks to see him go through with this arranged marriage to a woman I despise. I take a deep breath. With this dangerous hold Lily has over him it's impossible for me to walk away. I have to be there for him. I have no choice.

'If you'd experienced one day with Josh, you would know the sacrifice I'm making is worth it,' he says with a sad smile.

'I can well believe that.' I agree, remembering the morning I first saw him in the wood. 'He's a very special child.' I scratch around for how to say the next words I want him to hear. 'Look,' I begin quietly, 'I'm sorry I lost it for a moment just now but I had no idea this was what you were going through. If you need me, just call. If I can help in any way, I will.'

'Thank you.' He says and wraps his arms around me in a powerful hug. The sound of a dog barking in the distance alerts us both to the fact there is someone else in the wood. Talún quickly releases me and I walk Caspar into the trees, leaving him alone by the waterfall. Pulling myself into the saddle I head back to the cottage

LILY

Once Georgie and Danni were back I called them to apologise and offer an olive branch - lunch at The Swan in nearby Hendon. Although Talún doesn't approve of them, I'm reluctant to lose their friendship. They're good fun and they make a great job of stirring up these God-awful boring locals. With my soon to be husband back to his normal routine with his horses I'm confident I can easily continue to see them without him knowing. I'll simply have to find a suitable excuse to avoid the Bull.

They are already there when I arrive, sitting out on the covered decking which runs alongside the pub, heads together, chatting. Actually, it's not a pub any longer but a proper restaurant. I like it here. The place has an air of classiness that totally outshines Rufus Hayden's attempt at playing Pierre Marco White. Starched white table cloths and monogrammed plates are, for me, a true indication of up market dining.

'Lily.' Danni looks up with a smile.

'Hey girls, lovely to see you,' I say. They both stand and we go through our usual air kissing ritual. We take our seats and I notice they haven't yet ordered anything to drink. 'My shout,' I say, keen apologise for my hasty departure from Guernsey as I see the waiter approaching. 'Pimms as usual?'

'Actually, they do really good vintage champagne here,' Georgie says, fingering the wine list.

'Champagne?'

'Yes, champagne,' Georgie hands the list back to me with an expression indicating she doesn't expect an argument.

'Definitely.' Danni nods vigorously in agreement and moistens her lips. 'I'm absolutely parched.'

'Champagne it is then.' I try not to show my annoyance with their continued extravagance at my expense. This is my invite, my treat; I have no option but to indulge them.

The bubbly arrives and we relax. The talk centres around what car Danni should chose as a replacement for her Audi but it's not long before I find myself the subject of Georgie's curious stare again as she slowly rotates her champagne flute between her finger and thumb.

'So, Josh okay now?' She asks.

'Yes, he was running a high temperature but he's fine. A bit of a false alarm, you know what kids are like.'

'A temperature? I'm surprised you needed to leave in such a rush then,' she says, taking a sip of champagne and savouring the mouthful. 'After all, with Talún and Jeanette there...' she lets the rest of the sentence hang.

'Yes, but I am his mother.'

This statement produces a smirk from Danni.

'What's so funny?' I ask, annoyed I'm suddenly the cause of amusement.

'Nothing.' She gives an innocent shrug. 'Only you've never seemed the maternal sort. I mean, you have very little to do with him normally.'

'I know, but this was an emergency.'

'Are you sure the emergency was because of Josh?' Georgie is looking at me as if she's aware of to something I'm not. Did Giovanni tell them I was with a man? After all, he was there when Max settled his bill and actually ordered the taxi for us. Oh God! How the hell am I going to explain that?

'Of course it was because of Josh,' I respond indignantly, deciding to bluff it out. 'What other reason could there be?'

'Well you know what they say...when the cat's away—'

Before I can launch a *what the hell's that supposed to mean?* at her, the waiter arrives to take our lunch order. As he departs, Georgie requests another bottle of champagne, bumping up the bill even more.

'Here, finish this off before the next one arrives,' Danni says, topping up my glass before upending the bottle into the ice bucket.

I grab my glass, take a quick swallow and focus on Georgie sitting opposite me with her cat's eyes and halo of dark hair. She leans forward, elbows on the table, fingers linked. 'We know why you really came home,' she says, casting a quick glance at Danni who gives a supportive nod.

'Do you?' I stare at them blankly.

'Yes we do.' She leans forward. 'The thing is, Lily, you were very keen to warn us off Talún when we first met you. However, I really think you should have been paying more attention to another occupant of this village.'

While one part of me is relieved I've not been rumbled, the other is on high alert, remembering the morning Talún arrived home, looking as if....'

301

'And who exactly should I have been telling to back off?' I ask, after downing another mouthful of champagne.

Georgie and Danni look at each other with smug smiles. As Georgie is about to open her mouth and tell me, the waiter arrives with a new bottle of champagne and ice bucket. He opens and pours before taking the old one away and although it only takes a couple of minutes, by the time he leaves I'm almost at screaming pitch. I'm not only angry at the way they're enjoying this, I'm scared. I've deliberately kept Talún out of my bed and if he's found relief somewhere else I have a big problem.

'Well?' I fix them both with a hard stare. 'Go on then, tell me.

On my drive back from The Swan I was absolutely seething. I wasn't sure what made me angrier, the thought Talún had been unfaithful or the undisguised amusement in the faces of Georgie and Danni. Bitches! I'm determined not to have anything to do with them again. They even had the cheek to ask when I was going to invite them up to the Hall again to use the pool. The three of us work a rota, and yes, I guess it is my turn. But after the way they stitched me up with their gleeful news and a bloody big restaurant bill I was certainly not eager to play Miss Hospitality. I told them the pool had a leak and would be out of action for some time. I didn't fall out with them, in fact we parted quite amicably. It looks as if Max and Talún were right, they're so not my friends but I certainly don't want them as enemies.

And who was this threat I hadn't considered? Well, apparently they'd spotted him in the woods with Jess Hayden a week ago when they were walking their dogs. They were by the waterfall and he had his arms around her. Georgie and Danni seemed to know about their past connection, too. Thank God whoever told them wasn't aware of the part I played, otherwise they would have had another moment of triumph as they picked my carefully constructed personal history to pieces.

As I got nearer home my anger settled and I

concentrated on how exactly I was going to deal with the situation. The old Lily would have caused a hell of a fuss and thrown things. Then she would have gone round and confronted Jess Hayden. Now older and wiser, I know it would have done absolutely nothing to help this situation; in fact it would probably have made things worse. No, time has made me wiser and much more devious. I'm about to call up that insurance I set up a few months back. I didn't originally plan to use it in this way but needs must. It's the perfect solution to my problem and one which will guarantee Jess Hayden never bothers him again.

TALÚN

Lily is pregnant. At first I thought she was winding me up but then I remembered the night of the dinner party when I was drunk. The night when she put me to bed and climbed in beside me.

'I must be incredibly fertile,' she says with an amused laugh, as she runs her palms slowly up the front of my shirt after breaking the news. 'It was only the once with Josh, wasn't it? Shall we open a bottle? Celebrate?'

'Are you allowed to drink?' I ask, irritated by her cheerful attitude.

'One can't possibly hurt can it?' she says, rolling her eyes. 'Talún, what's the matter? Aren't you happy about this? It will be a brother or sister for Josh.'

I can't lie, this is not at all what I expected or wanted so instead I simply nod as my mind tries to get to grips with this latest disaster. 'When is it due?'

'Um, mid-March according to the online calculator.'

'So you'll be six months at Christmas? Have you seen a doctor yet?'

'Yes I will, and not yet, but I'm about to make an appointment...oh,' She pauses thoughtfully before continuing, 'that means we're going to have to bring the wedding forward doesn't it?'

'Yes,' I meet her gaze. Is it me or do I sense something lurking behind her happy pre-motherhood glow? She must be aware of my family's feelings about her. Did she do this on purpose? Surely not.

'I put a bottle in the fridge a while ago, should be cooled to perfection by now.' Her words interrupt my thoughts, her accompanying touch on my arm making me aware I've been staring at the carpet. My eyes meet hers once more and she smiles. This time it is soft and warm without any trace of guile. Confusion joins the anger I already feel, coupled with an urgent need to leave the room.

'Not now,' I reply irritably as I push past her heading for the door.

'Where are you going?' She calls after me.

'To phone Amberleigh. I need to break the news to my grandfather.' I reply as I close the door, leaving her alone.

My announcement is met with silence. I knew Marcus wouldn't be happy. He wants rid of Lily and I'm guessing he's already been working on a way to achieve this. Now any plan is in tatters. Lily isn't going anywhere and the Hawkeswoods have another great grandchild on the way. After a brief conversation he passes me over to Anna. She begins by telling me that Catkin has given birth to a foal. It's a filly with the same white blaze on its face as Achilles. Then I confirm the news about another soon-to-be birth and straight away I can hear the disappointment in her voice. She, too, wants Lily gone. I tell her about our new financial arrangement and how it seems to be working. I try to convince her a new baby might see Lily finally settling down but I can tell from her unenthusiastic response she's sceptical. The trouble is so am I and my words are trying to convince myself as well as Anna...and failing badly. I then make arrangements for us to travel up this coming weekend to discuss the wedding, which she agrees needs to be rescheduled.

'If we could move it to the first week in October...' I begin but Anna's already ahead of me.

'Tindersley Hall is out of the question now.' She says, her voice all business like. 'I'll ring and cancel.' She pauses for a moment and I hear a soft sigh before she continues,

'No use looking anywhere else. We'll simply have to move the reception here. We have space, we have staff, we have everything really...we can do it.' She sounds confident and upbeat and I know she's ready to take up the challenge. We'll have our wedding in October and despite her feelings about the whole thing, Anna will make sure it's a great success.

'I'll leave it in your capable hands then, we can firm up on the details at the weekend.' I tell her as I finish the call, realising I'll need to prepare myself for arguments. Lily is bound to take exception not only to Anna's involvement but also the change of venue. I replace the receiver and lean on my desk, my head cradled in my hands. As my thoughts clear, something else occurs to me, and I realise I desperately need to see Jess before news of Lily's pregnancy becomes public.

JESS

I look forward to Anna's early evening Skype call every week. Now her visits have become less and less regular since Talún's arrival at the Hall, I can keep in touch electronically and hear all the news from Norfolk. With my love of horses I'm always interested in what's happening at the stud and today there's great news. One of her best brood mares has delivered a foal. Her sire is Achilles and I'm sure Talún will be pleased to hear about this new arrival. As I'm about to mention this she tells me she's already told him and he's planning a trip to Norfolk within the next few days, bringing Josh with him.

'How is he getting on with Bella?' She asks.

'Wonderfully well.' I assure her, 'he adores her.'

'That's good to know.' I see her smile. 'Oh, and I forgot to mention, Lily is coming too. After their news we need to discuss bringing the wedding forward.'

'What news?'

'She's pregnant.'

'Pregnant?' I repeat, closing my eyes as I absorb the implications of what Anna has just said. I bite back my anger remembering the day at the waterfall when he revealed the desperate measures he'd taken to have Josh. Despite my feelings about Lily, his revelations had me promising to support him; to be there for him if he needed me. And now I realise there wasn't a shred of truth in anything he told me.

'Ah, I can see you're shocked.' I hear Anna's voice and take my concentration back to the screen once more. 'We were too. It's the last thing we expected...or wanted, and it strengthens her hold on him. Still,' she shakes her head as if she's resigned to it all, 'we can't do anything about it I'm afraid. Oh, and I don't think it's common knowledge in the village at the moment,' she adds, 'so I'd be grateful if—'

'I won't say a word,' I interrupt with my promise. Suddenly it's all too much, I can feel a tell-tale prick of tears behind my eyelids and I make an excuse that Rufus is calling me and I'm needed in the bar. Saying goodbye, I close down and sit there for a moment, my head in my hands. I'm determined not to cry, not to waste another moment on such a worthless liar. A soft tap on the door brings Bella into the room.

'Jess, are you ready to set up for...' She stops mid-sentence, 'Are you okay?'

'Yes, I'm fine.' I force a smile, tucking a wayward tendril of hair behind my ear as I get to my feet. 'Bit of a headache, that's all. Come on,' I ease her out of the door, 'let's get ready for our evening session.'

I haven't seen Roo for several weeks. He's been covering for one of the team who's on maternity leave but today he rings to say now he's on top of things he'd like us to meet in the bar of the Exeter Abode at one for lunch.

'Lovely to see you, Jess.' He arrives smartly suited and every inch the solicitor as he greets me with a kiss on the cheek. We settle ourselves on high stools at the bar. He orders wine and we chat, mostly about the building project. The one thing I love about Roo is his calmness. If he could bottle that and market it he'd make a fortune. I guess it's why I'm here today. Not to open up and tell him how Talún has bulldozed into my life and turned it upside down again, no. It's all about feeding off Roo's tranquillity and spending a little time escaping from the madness.

We're eventually shown to our table. He's been busy in court, a long drawn out case which he spares me the details of, only to say he's glad it's finally over. It's as he announces he's planning to take a well-earned break, an idea comes into my head.

'Actually, I was thinking of flying out to see Amber,' I tell him. 'And as you've been promising to visit for years, wouldn't this be an ideal opportunity for you to come too?'

To my surprise he's quite taken with the idea. Majorca is a popular tourist destination but there are still places like Cala Los Rosas which remain a haven for the Spanish and a few discerning tourists who want to get away from the mad rush. The more he thinks about it the more I can tell he's sold on a couple of weeks of sun and relaxation.

Over lunch we talk about the small resort and the beach restaurant, which Amber and her cousin Mads have run for the past five and a half years. During our fortnight we will be staying with my aunt at the restaurant which also has guest accommodation.

'I like the sound of this more and more,' he says, before we go our separate ways. He hugs me and thanks me for what he says is a brilliant idea, telling me how much he's looking forward to getting away on this, our very first holiday together since our uni days. 'Amber will be pleased to see you,' I tell him, 'You'll like Mads too. She has this incredible energy and is the total opposite of her laid back partner Juan. We are going to have the best time.' I assure him with a final hug.

I drive home with a new enthusiasm, something which seems to have gone a long way to banishing my blues. I convince myself I'm not running away, that would be too easy, and anyway my heart is here in Lynbrook. I simply need space; somewhere quiet to sort out my feelings before I have to return and live with this new situation. I make a quick call to Bella to check the dates we've chosen won't clash with anything she's planned. I think about phoning

Rufus but decide as I've already sorted everything out with Bella, it can wait till this evening. I call Amber to tell her we're planning a visit. She's really pleased Roo will be coming with me this time. With our flights booked I'm finishing a conversation with him, arranging a pick up time on Monday morning, when there's a knock at the door. I open it and suck in a ragged breath as I find myself face to face with Talún. Quickly ending my call with a promise to collect Roo just after ten, I slip my phone into the back pocket of my jeans.

'What do you want?' My voice is snappish and angry as I keep him on the threshold. I can see by his puzzled expression he's confused by my attitude but then he has no idea I'm already aware of what's happened.

'Jess,' He takes a deep breath and hesitates. 'Can I come in for a minute?'

'A minute? As long as that?' I can't prevent sarcasm creeping into my voice.

'Jess, what's the...' he begins, but I cut him off angrily.

'You lied to me,' I say, folding my arms tightly around myself, not sure whether it's a protective mechanism or simply to stop me lashing out at him. 'You bloody well lied to me. You told me you weren't sleeping with her so how is it she's now pregnant?'

'Oh God.' He runs his palm over his forehead, his fingers lacing deep into his thick black hair. 'How did you find out?' His dark brows pull together in a frown. 'The only people who know are...' He pauses. 'Anna...she told you?'

'Yes.'

Jess, you have to believe me,' he draws in a shallow breath, 'it was only once and I was drunk.'

'Just like last time then?' My response is scornful. I look at the man I thought I loved and feel nothing but contempt. What purpose does he think this visit serves? Is he looking for forgiveness? Well I'm done forgiving. All I want is for him to leave.

'Please, don't mock. I want you to know,' his voice cracks, 'that what we had—'

'Is gone, if it was ever there at all,' I say coldly. 'And I'd like you to go too.'

He doesn't argue. He simply turns and leaves. I close the door and lean against it. I hear his footfalls fading and the gate closing. The anger I feel suddenly implodes. Tears dampen my cheeks and I wipe them away, angry with myself for wasting any emotion on such a worthless man. I force myself to think of more important things. Like my imminent holiday. Quietly I make my way upstairs to begin packing.

LILY

I make my way to my room to begin sorting out clothes to take for our trip to Norfolk. I'm not looking forward to this at all. As soon as that bloody old witch has her claws into him again she'll be up to no good, filling his head with poison about me. Well, I'm not putting up with it. Anyway I'm entitled to tantrums. After all, I'm supposed to be pregnant so my hormones are all over the place at the moment, aren't they? Talún says she's handling the arrangements for rescheduling the wedding. And the venue has been switched to Amberleigh. Well we'll see about that.

TALÚN

It didn't cross my mind Anna would tell Jess about Lily's pregnancy. But then she has no idea of how entangled our lives are, or were...because from this moment I will cease to exist in Jess's life, just as she will in mine. I should have explained what happened that day at the river when I confided in her, but foolishly I didn't think it mattered. But it does and I've lost her. I could see it in her face, she loathes me. She thinks she's been used in some kind of cruel game and it breaks my heart. I still love her, I always will, but now I have to face facts, I'm well and truly tied into this marriage to Lily. And even if I could find a way out, I'm sure I'd be the last person Jess would ever want now.

LILY

I didn't know what to expect when we reached Norfolk. I knew, like Talún, they'd be convinced I'd done this deliberately. And I have, of course, but not quite in the way they all think. Surprisingly, they were both their usual charming selves acting as if everything was normal. But then I forgot the Hawkeswoods are old money so good manners come naturally, although no doubt under the surface they were both seething. The thought of that made me feel quite amused.

Since our arrival I've been constantly in Anna's company as Talún has been off on what he calls "estate business" with his grandfather, taking Josh with him. I suppose he felt it would make things easier leaving Anna and me alone to discuss the wedding arrangements. I thought she'd be difficult, with me being pregnant and everything having to be rearranged at short notice. But she wasn't. In fact she was very calm and business-like...those good manners surfacing again. She apologised for the fact we couldn't have Tindersley Hall any longer, then she took me over the house and explained what she had in mind for holding the wedding here at Amberleigh. Actually after hearing her plans I had to admit I didn't mind losing Tindersley. This is going to be bigger, better and much more me. Afterwards we sat down to run over the check list she'd made. Marcus is arranging the special licence for us and Anna has mobilised her 'corporate events team', which usually organises the Amberleigh New Year's Eve Ball, to begin work on everything needed to make my big day fabulous. I insisted on being responsible for the 'me' stuff though. I don't want either Anna or her team poking their noses in. This is personal and I'm doing it my way. Oh yes, with what I've got planned, all those well-heeled guests they've invited will be talking about me for months to come.

JESS

Rufus's annual barbeque went like a breeze. Dominic and his team delivered a fabulous spread and Bella and I ran the bar. My father, of course, was in his element playing host and was even persuaded to 'shake his stuff' – Bella's term not mine - out on the dance floor. I was glad I'd decided to stay and help before I escaped to the Med with Roo because there's nothing better than watching this village come together to enjoy themselves. Of course, there were the expected absences.

'All the jet setters are away,' Bella informed me, as she served someone with a glass of Pimms. 'Danni and Georgie are in Mexico test driving the condo their husbands have just bought and Talún and Lily have taken Josh up to Norfolk. Something's going on there,' she added, lowering her voice. 'I'm sure Jeanette knows but she's very loyal. You wouldn't get anything out of her. Josh just said he was going to see his great nanny and grandpa. Very excited, he was. I think they're very fond of him. Oh, and they're not back until Monday evening so I'm off nanny duties till Tuesday morning,' she tells me breezily, 'It means I'm available for the airport run if you want me.'

I gratefully accepted her offer. As far as I was concerned, Monday couldn't come quickly enough.

TALÚN

Our journey back to Harvington Cross has made me homesick for my old life. This weekend it has been great to see everyone again and catch up with news – engagements, weddings, new arrivals, promotions. Although I have a good team at the Hall, during my six years at Amberleigh I came to regard these guys as very much my extended family.

Lily and Anna seem to have negotiated some sort of truce. I don't think for one moment Lily's views about her have changed, but she was very impressed with Anna's rescue plan for the wedding and happy to leave all the arrangements to her.

We left Norfolk on Monday morning after breakfast with everything on course for our early October wedding. At one time I looked forward to this marriage and a new life with Lily and Josh. Now all I feel is trapped.

JESS

Our two glorious sun filled weeks in Cala Los Rosas have come to an end at last. We've had a wonderful stay and done so much in the time we've been here. There have been lazy days spent lying in the sun, and activity filled ones where we've explored the island by car and indulged in water sports such as scuba diving and paragliding. Roo has bonded with Amber and Mads, been shown around Juan's boatyard and was even allowed into Jorge's kitchen, which must be a first for any male visitor. The restaurant sits on the edge of the bay with a long, airy covered veranda overlooking the beach. Amber lives upstairs and there are two guest rooms with en suites in an attached annex. It's a welcoming place built of warm stone and wood, a haven for anyone who loves traditional Spanish food. On our last evening, Roo and I were given a table at the far end of the loggia where we could hear the gentle wash of the sea on the sand below and watch brightly lit cruise ships drift by on the horizon. After an amazing meal we sat chatting and finishing off the evening with a good quality bottle of red. As the last few diners vacated their tables, Roo topped up my glass and proposed a toast.

'To absent friends.'

'Had you anybody particular in mind?' I was curious to know who he might be missing.

'Actually, I have. I guess you could call her my guilty secret.'

'Her?' Immediately he had my full attention. 'A girlfriend? Are you serious?' I felt a smile forming on my face as my words came tumbling out in short, sharp bursts.

He nodded. 'Her name is Tegan Penrose. Detective

Sergeant Tegan Penrose.'

'A policewoman? Where? How?' I felt incredibly excited and pleased for him. As far as I'm concerned he's been on his own far too long.

He expelled a breath of laughter. 'Exeter nick, six weeks ago. We sort of collided in the corridor. My suit was treated to most of the coffee she was carrying. We both apologised at the same time. She offered to pay for the dry cleaning. I refused and invited her out to dinner instead. And,' he wriggled his eyebrows, 'well...so far so good.'

'I'm really pleased,' I said, overwhelmed by his news, 'and I have to say, about time too. What's she like?'

'Funny, smart...gorgeous in fact. You'd like her.'

'Let me guess...blonde?'

'Brunette...with the most amazing green eyes.' He rolled his and grinned. 'A brown belt too, which means I have to watch my step.' He paused thoughtfully for a moment. 'And what about your absent friend?' he asked, swallowing back a mouthful of wine.

'What absent friend?' I'm a little confused, wondering who he's referring to.

'Talún, of course.'

'Well, he's definitely absent but I wouldn't call him a friend,' I said a little too forcefully, which prompted a curious smile. 'Really he's not,' I insisted, gentling my tone. 'More of an acquaintance really.'

'Jess? What aren't you telling me?' Setting his glass back on the table, Roo gave me a one of his cool questioning looks.

'Nothing to tell.' I responded with a casual shrug and followed it with the kind of laugh even I wasn't convinced by.

'You can't hide from me.' He said picking up his glass again, 'What's he done? Is it anything to do with Lily Stevenson?

'Did I hear someone mention Lily Stevenson? What's she been up to now? ' I heard the curious tone in Amber's voice and swung around. She was standing only feet away, holding onto a tray of coffee. With Mads silently following behind, they were about to join us. 'Nothing,' I said with a shake of my head as they both seated themselves at our table, 'Her name came up in conversation, that's all.'

'Been hauled in for shoplifting again, has she?' She looked at us both curiously as she eased down the cafetière's plunger with the palm of her hand.

'Shoplifting?' Roo frowned. 'I wasn't aware she had form.'

'Oh there was a lot you didn't know about the lovely Ms Stevenson.' Amber said as she poured coffee into large cups while Mads handed them around. I could see by the expression on his face this had sparked Roo's curiosity.

'Exactly what don't we know about her Amber?' he asked, reaching for the milk.

Amber settled the cafetière back onto the tray and took a deep breath. 'Well, it's all water under the bridge now, Roo. I don't think it matters. Does it?'

'It matters a great deal,' he argued, spooning sugar into his cup, 'when she's marrying a client of mine.'

I took a deep breath, thankful Roo, ever the diplomat, had not revealed Talún's identity.

'But she's already married,' Amber said, shaking her head at what I could see she thought was the sheer preposterousness of Roo's comment.

'Married?' Roo and I echoed together.

'Yes, when she lived with us she had a husband, Pauli Stevenson.' She looked at me, pushing a stray curl away from her face. 'The house where she was seeing Zac…it was their home.'

'When did you discover this?' I was astounded. Why had no one said anything before?

'Around the time you left. I was curious and decided to check up on her. As a counsellor I had regular contact with Social Services. A friend gave me access to her file. I've never mentioned it because it wasn't relevant. She'd gone, you'd left for a new start with Rufus and I was planning to come here with Mads.'

'So where was Pauli when Lily lived with you?' Roo asked.

'On remand in Bristol. He was a petty thief, not a very good one either from the amount of times he came up before the magistrate.'

'More to the point, where is he now?' I queried realising this put a completely new complexion on their forthcoming wedding.

'Long gone, I expect,' Roo remarked, helping himself to the plate of small almond biscuits which had arrived with the coffee. 'I understand from my client that his family have already had her thoroughly investigated and everything appears to be fine.'

'This client of yours... rich then, is he?' Amber asked as she sipped her coffee.

'As Croesus,' Roo nodded, pushing the last fragment of biscuit into his mouth.

'I see.' Amber looked at me then at Roo. 'Well, personally given what I read, I find all this rather worrying. If I were you I'd make a few discreet enquiries yourself when you get home, just to make sure.'

SEPTEMBER 2013

TALÚN

I haven't caught sight of Jess since our return from Norfolk several weeks ago. I know Anna regularly Skypes her but she never mentions anything when we speak and, for obvious reasons, I would never ask after her. Although I told myself it was over, I can't seem to shake off this need to see her again. I tell myself I shouldn't care what she thinks of me. But I do and that's the problem.

I turn my thoughts to the wedding, which is just over a month away. I'm still angry with Lily but I need to push this aside and think about the baby. Whether I gain another son or am gifted with a daughter, this child will be as treasured as Josh is.

When I arrive at the Estates office Oliver is out and Sally, his PA, is in the middle of a call. I need to see him about roof repairs to one of the cottages. A few tiles are missing, something that must have happened during last winter's storms. The damage has only just been noticed and with autumn coming I need to get it sorted as soon as possible.

It looks as if Sally's about to abort the call but I indicate I can wait and pick up a magazine which is lying on Oliver's desk. I flick through the pages: a typical mix of upmarket properties, interviews and advertisements. As I'm half way through, Sally comes off the phone and joins me.

'Have you found it yet?' she asks, 'it's just after the Chanel ad. Here,' she reaches across and flips over a few pages. 'Oliver asked me to save it for you. Fabulous hotel isn't it? What I wouldn't give for a few days pampering like that.' she rolls her eyes and gives a dramatic sigh, 'and those other two women with Lily, they're from the barn conversions in Bennett's Orchard, aren't they?'

LILY

Time seems to be flying by. We're in the second week of September and Josh has started school. Talún has also managed to find someone to take care of him when he's home. She's the wife of one of the new grooms, a fully trained nursery nurse so she knows her way around kids. I occasionally see Georgie and Danni but our days of getting around together are gone. I realise because of them I nearly lost everything. Now Talún and I seem to have settled into a relatively calm phase in the run up to the wedding in a months' time. He was keen to have a fairly small affair with friends and neighbours followed by a big party on our return from honeymoon. I was happy with that, it seemed far more sensible than trying to host a huge one day event at short notice. Although I'm not a great fan of Anna's, I have to say she's worked a miracle turning everything around. She's even arranged for Greg to give me away. Oh yes, and Talún and I have been out to choose his wedding ring, a wide plain gold band. Mine is an heirloom. It's a patterned platinum band, nothing special really. Anna told me it's been worn by every Hawkeswood bride for several hundred years. Well, history doesn't mean a lot to me and once we're back from honeymoon I'm planning to get Talún to buy me something a bit more stylish, preferably set with diamonds. Oh yes, the honeymoon – Talún's booked us three weeks in Bali – I can't wait

This afternoon Naomi and her current boyfriend have disappeared to the cinema, keen to check out the latest Ryan Gosling movie. This leaves me alone in the kitchen making myself an expresso from the newly arrived built in coffee machine. It's the latest gadget to join the high tech wonderland that is the Hall's kitchen. Coffee made, I settle myself comfortably. Some long forgotten song is playing on the radio and I begin to hum along. I'm closing my eyes, savouring the taste of my latte and really getting into the music when something lands heavily on the kitchen table in front of me and I almost drop my cup.

I stifle a shriek, my eyes open and there's Talún standing right next to me, with an expression on his face the word anger doesn't even begin to describe.

'What is it?' I ask as I set the cup down. 'Why are you glaring at me?'

'Take a look,' his voice is low and icy as he points to the magazine in front of me.

It's one of those expensive glossies and I'm wondering why he would buy something like this when he's only usually interested in stuff to do with horses. As I reach out to open it up I can almost feel his rage. Why is he so fired up? I flip through pages of high end fashion, celebrity interviews and the latest food innovations and then...I stifle a groan. Shit! How the hell has this happened?

JESS

I had dinner with Roo and his new girlfriend yesterday at a recently opened fish restaurant back in our old stomping ground of Milton Bay. It seems another lifetime since our wine bar days in the run up to uni. Now here we are, with our respective careers, although back in those days becoming a property developer was definitely not one of my plans. I immediately took to Tegan and it's clear she's totally besotted with my tall, quiet best friend. She said she arrived six months ago. Having passed her exams she was looking for a transfer out of big city policing – Birmingham, to be precise – and said the move to Exeter had been the best thing she'd ever done. It was great to see them as a couple and note the way they interacted together. There was lots of laughter and affection between them and I have to confess to having an occasional twinge of jealousy. It had nothing to do with the fact Roo had this new person in his life; it was more about missing those same feelings I'd once shared with a special someone.

I returned home and opened a bottle of red before taking myself out onto the terrace to sit and watch the lights of Teignmouth dance on the horizon. I stayed there till late...very late. When I did decide to take myself back inside I realised I'd consumed almost the whole bottle. And this morning I'm paying for my over indulgence. I not only have the mother of all hangovers, I can't keep any solid food down. Although I connect the wine with my mega headache, the sickness is different and I'm putting the blame squarely on the moules mariniere.

By eleven the headache has gone and the nausea seems to have lessened but I'm not taking any chances so phone in sick. Rufus is understanding and says as Tuesday lunchtimes rarely see a stampede at the bar it's not a problem. He sounds concerned but when I mention my meal with Roo and the shellfish I ate I can almost hear his sigh of relief. He asks if I'd like him to drop round later but I tell him I'm fine. I'll take a couple of paracetamol and spend a few more hours in bed.

The next morning I feel fine and it's back to the Bull for my lunchtime shift. I was due to have a Wednesday evening off but Tanya, who covers for me from the restaurant, is on holiday so this evening I'm on with Bella. I can see from her face she's obviously bursting to tell me her latest gossip.

'Well, what is it?' I ask, as the bar eventually clears and I finish stacking glasses into the dishwasher.

'Lily's in big trouble,' she says. 'She lied to Talún about Guernsey.'

'How do you know all this?' I ask, knowing Jeanette would never divulge this sort of information.

'One of the stable girls came into the shop,' she tells me. 'There was this magazine which the Estates Manager had on his desk. Talún just happened to see it and there was a double page promotional spread for this five star spa hotel. Lily and the Witches were in the photos. She told him she'd gone to Guernsey to visit an old friend.' Bella says, 'Talún is furious because she'd promised to give the Witches a wide berth. The rumour is it's not the first time he's had trouble with her behaviour. The girls at the stud call her 'Lily Queen of Shops', you know after the Mary Portas programme, because she's always out buying clothes. Some up there even say he's had enough of her. If that's true, with the wedding only two weeks away, do you think he'll still go through with it?'

'Who knows?' I shrug, not really caring what happens to either of them. But, of course he has to marry her, otherwise he'll lose Josh. It's all coming back to bite him now and it serves him right. I have no sympathy whatsoever.

OCTOBER 2013

LILY

We're forty-eight hours away from the wedding now and preparing to leave for Norfolk. I didn't want to start married life this way but it looks as if I have no choice. Talún's anger on the day he discovered what had really happened in Guernsey was truly scary. Tears wouldn't move him. Nor would trying to explain the hotel had waived the bill and the only cost was the flight. In fact it made his eyes darken even more dangerously.

'What part of this don't you get Lily? You deliberately lied to me. There's even a photo of your so-called friend Karin here.' He shook the magazine at me. 'She's a hotel employee called Marcella Durand and you used her to cover up your deceit. Despite telling me were no longer seeing Danni and Georgie, you made arrangements behind my back to go with them on this...jolly.'

'I'm sorry, I'm so sorry,' I protested, wiping away the tears that didn't seem to want to stop. 'I won't do it again.'

'Damn right you won't. I've enough of your dishonesty.'

'What are you going to do?' I stopped crying, wondering what he was planning.

'I'm going to control your spending from now on. I'm stopping the allowance. You want anything, you come to me first.'

'You can't treat me that way,' I sniffed. 'I'm not a child.'

'Well you've behaved like one.'

'You're being unfair.' My upset gradually turned to anger as I looked for something to throw back at him.

'I don't think you can stop me.'

'Oh, I think I can.' I was dry eyed now, the pathway to getting the upper hand firmly in front of me. I pushed myself away from the table, feeling an adrenaline rush at the thought of having him just where I wanted him. 'What do you think Marcus and Anna would say if they knew you'd slept with Jess Hayden?' I asked, quite innocently, knowing I was taking a huge gamble. Georgie and Danni had told me they'd seen them together in the woods one afternoon. Of course, there could be a perfectly legitimate reason, in fact it might have been quite harmless. But their past relationship made me naturally suspicious and of course there was the morning I'd caught him returning from what he had said had been an early ride.

'Jess and I are friends,' his voice was calm as he locked his gaze with mine, defying me to argue.

'More than friends I'd say, wouldn't you, given the state you arrived back here on the morning I returned from Guernsey? You were with her that night weren't you?' Of course, it was all bluff, but the way he stood there, tight lipped and uncomfortable, I knew I'd accidentally uncovered the truth. 'The thing is,' I continued, 'I don't want to rock the boat. We've both been guilty, haven't we? My spending, your infidelity, they sort of balance out don't they? I'm not going to cause a fuss. In fact I'm quite happy to leave things as they are...' I gave him a thoughtful smile, '...for the time being.' I used those last words deliberately, making it quite clear I would hold onto his guilty secret and wouldn't hesitate to use it in future if he stepped out of line again.

'Jess was right, you are a complete bitch,' he said icily and then he left, slamming the kitchen door behind him.

JESS

Two days after my initial bout of sickness it came back with a vengeance. I couldn't keep anything down, even water. I guess I knew then it was something other than food poisoning. But I couldn't be pregnant – it was impossible. I was on the contraceptive pill. I hadn't worried when I'd missed my first period – it was something which had happened before on odd occasions. But then when the second failed to show, that, coupled with the sickness saw me dropping into a chemist in Exeter to buy a pregnancy testing kit. And this morning, on the day of Talún's wedding to Lily, I'm standing in my bathroom and staring at the small white testing stick which confirms I am going to have a baby. His baby.

LILY

My big day has arrived at last. I've had some very near misses with Talún on the run up to this wedding and I've come to a decision. It's impossible for me to stay in this marriage long term. However, I need to hold on long enough to make our eventual split believable to the outside world. I've got it all planned. A miscarriage by Christmas followed by depression should kick off the downward spiral nicely. Maybe I'll even name Jess as the other woman; spice the whole thing up a bit. And at the end of it all I'll be able to walk away with my *very* substantial pre-nup and begin a comfortable, independent life which if I'm truthful, is what I've always wanted.

I decided to relent and invite Georgie and Danni to my grand day. Well, I simply couldn't resist rubbing their noses in it. And boy, will I get some satisfaction when they arrive at Amberleigh for the reception and see the kind of money Talún's family have. They will be *so* envious.

The guest list, although small, reads like a local Who's Who. Everybody who's anybody will be attending, among them all those well-heeled, over-indulged young women who once thought they had a chance with Talún. Who would have thought it? Someone like me, with such a poor start in life, has beaten them to this amazing prize. Not that I'm feeling very enamoured with my prize at the moment. Since our confrontation in the kitchen three weeks ago he's been particularly obnoxious. He spends most of his time with his horses, working very late at the stud each evening. I mentally add neglect and unreasonable behaviour to my grounds for divorce.

This morning I woke up to brilliant sunshine. A good omen, I convince myself. I told Anna I didn't need her to help me get ready as I'd arranged for Jeanette to assist me. The photographer was in early, snapping photos of the house and of me drinking champagne as the transformation into beautiful bride took place. I have no bridesmaids. Normally they're siblings or friends and as I have neither I'm going to be star of the show...just the way I like it. Josh wanted to be a page boy but the last thing I wanted was him running about under my feet and getting in the way. He was disappointed but I told him this was Mummy's big day and that I needed him to be a grown up boy and stay with Anna.

It's been non-stop. Yesterday I took a trip into Norwich for my pre-wedding pamper – body scrub wax, facial, nails, the works. Early this morning two girls arrived from the salon I use in London to do my hair and makeup. The Swiss lace underwear I bought looks fabulous and now the very last piece of this ensemble...the exquisite silk Vera Wang wedding dress...has been slipped on and zipped up. I slide my feet into the ornate white Louboutins and Jeanette checks the small white flowers which have been arranged in my hair are in place, before guiding me towards the full length mirror to see the finished result. Wow! I look bloody amazing, even if I say so myself.

JESS

This morning I made a decision. I have to leave. Rufus will probably want to kill Talún if I tell him what's happened and Anna will never forgive me; she'll think I've let her down in the worst possible way.

After managing some dry toast I sit down and make a list of all the people who will be affected by my departure. My alibi will be a long term stay with Amber to cover for Mads absence. I know she has an elderly mother who's not too well so an excuse she's gone back to look after her following a bad fall is quite plausible. Only Roo and Rufus will know where I've gone. Everyone else will be told I'm abroad staying with an old uni friend. I lean on the table and cradle my head in my hands for a moment, realising this pregnancy, in its early months, has already created a whole chain of lies and deception. But I must protect my unborn child at all costs. Deciding what to do about the cottage, I immediately think of Adrian, still a lodger at the Bull. House sitting here will mean he has direct access to his allotment. Ben will see Caspar is regularly exercised and Bella can have use of the MX-5. Krister will be fine with the development and I can make arrangements for a regular transfer of funds as and when he needs them. When I have exhausted every possibility I can think of, I shower and leave to visit everyone on my list to break the news.

The next morning as the taxi driver loads my suitcase into the back of his vehicle, I take one last look at the cottage, wondering when I'll be able to call it home again.

TALÚN

The only thing that is keeping me holding everything together today is Josh and the new baby. I would lay down my life for this wonderful child and I shall love the new arrival just as much. As for Lily, I already detest the sight of her. How our marriage will work out is something I really don't want to contemplate at this moment. The honeymoon will take us to Dubai and then on to Bali. Three weeks of sheer hell to look forward to. At least once we're back I can lose myself in my work and take regular trips to Norfolk to stay out of her way as much as possible. But whatever kind of life I have to endure, Josh's welfare is my priority. I've already taken steps to employ someone who'll look after him when he's not at school. Tish Robinson, whose husband is a newly arrived groom at the stud, has been a great find.

As I dress, I'm suddenly remembering doing this all those years back for my wedding to Fliss. I remember it as a day of warmth and love; of two families coming together. I recall Fliss joking with me as we drove to the reception about how I was well and truly leg shackled. I'd never heard the term before and she explained it was Regency male slang, meaning married. I told her it made it sound like a long term prison sentence. Ironically, that is exactly what I feel I'm facing today.

325

When Marcus and I reach St. Swithin's, guests are already arriving: darkly suited men and colourfully dressed women looking like an array of exotic birds in their extravagant hats. I glimpse familiar faces and they smile and wish me well. I catch Marcus's serious expression. He never expected this day to arrive. In fact, I know he had already held talks with his solicitors about Josh. But now that's not an option he has some difficult decisions to make. Nothing has been said yet but I'm sure when I return from Bali he will want to talk to me about my future role within the organisation and the outlook isn't good.

We settle in the front pew and it's not long before Anna joins us. Tish follows behind with Josh. Insisting he needed his own outfit for the wedding - something Lily neglected to arrange - she's organised a dark suit, white shirt and a blue velvet bow tie for him. He looks amazing and gives me a mischievous grin as they slip into the pew behind us. Anna in shocking pink silk settles herself next to Marcus and whispers across to me, 'Lily's just arrived.'

As the strains of Mendelssohn fill the church, I wait. My thoughts turn to Fliss and then Jess, the only woman I've ever really loved. I feel my heartbeat accelerate as I'm aware of Lily arriving next to me on Greg's arm. Then the vicar steps forward to address the congregation, heralding the moment that is about to change my life forever.

LILY

I don't look at Talún as I arrive. Handing my bouquet to Jeanette, I keep my gaze firmly riveted to the floor. I'm deliberately playing the nervous bride because as soon as our eyes meet all I'll see is how much he still loathes me. I have him exactly where I want him now and he hates it. But it's his own fault. If only he'd left Jess Hayden alone.

I raise my eyes slightly as the vicar addresses the congregation, asking if anyone present knows any just cause or impediment etcetera, etcetera. I can think of one very big one. I hide my smile. I am confident. I am untouchable.

There's a sudden commotion at the back of the church. I turn to see what's going on. With brilliant sunshine spilling through the doors, I make out the silhouettes of two men and two women. I notice one of the women has a mass of curly hair and for a moment I'm thinking Jess has turned up to stop the wedding. As if that's likely to happen, I think, suppressing a giggle. The vicar halts the service and I see Marcus leave his seat and walk to the back of the church, where two of his security staff have intercepted the new arrivals. I can't believe he's actually talking to them when he should be getting them thrown out. I expel an angry breath and for the first time sneak a glance at Talún, who is also watching the conversation currently taking place.

Suddenly Marcus is returning, two of the four individuals following behind him. For a moment I wonder what they want, and then as they reach us and I recognise one of them, I know exactly why they're here.

JESS

I arrived in the middle of a downpour. Very un-Majorcan and a bit of a surprise. Thankfully, by the time I rescued my case from the carousel and had made it to the arrivals hall, the sun had come out and was scorching the pavement. Amber was waiting in her usual place and on the drive to the restaurant she quizzed me about my reason for returning only weeks after I had been here with Roo. I had to tell her the truth. An indefinite stay and a place of refuge warranted nothing less. She immediately pulled over and we sat for a while as I explained.

'So when Roo was here, the rich client he was referring to was Talún?' She looked totally shocked and then, of course, I had to tell her everything. By the time I had finished I felt quite drained and I'm sure she must have been too, after taking in all this new information. Wrapping her arms around me she told me not to worry, that we would get through this together. She also said her invitation was open ended, which meant I could stay on after the birth if I wanted to.

'About Lily,' she said, as we got underway again, 'she's not up to her old tricks again, is she?'

'I don't think so. I saw them together in the cricket pavilion. At the time I wasn't aware it was her but Talún confirmed it,' I told her. 'And he is Josh's father, they've had a DNA test done and that's something you can't fake. I'm afraid at the end of the day they have a child together, she is no longer married and by now,' I checked my watch, 'they should be man and wife.'

TALÚN

They arrested Lily in the vestry. I simply stood there too numb to do anything but watch as they handcuffed her and took her away. She didn't even look at me. While Marcus and the vicar went out to speak to the congregation, Roo and a dark haired woman in a navy trouser suit came over to talk to me.

'How did you find out about her?' I ask, still in shock from the speed in which I've gone from trapped bridegroom to liberated man.

'A conversation in Majorca a few weeks back when I was there with Jess.' He says, giving his companion a smile. 'One night after dinner, we were talking. Amber overheard us mention Lily. She knew all about her criminal record...and the fact she already had a husband, Pauli Stevenson. Didn't your family have her vetted?'

'I told them I'd arranged it myself.' I admitted, feeling all kinds of stupid, 'I lied because she told me if anyone went near her father he was the kind of freeloader we'd never get rid of. He was the last thing I wanted landing on my family. I was protecting them as much as her...and, of course, I desperately wanted Josh. Criminal record? Oh God... ' I rub a hand over my face. How much worse can this get?

'Just as well we followed it up then. Detective Sergeant Tegan Penrose,' Roo's companion, introduces herself before taking over the conversation. 'Because of Pauli's previous I decided we'd probably find him somewhere behind bars. And I struck lucky.' Her dark eyes spark with triumph. 'He's been in Wigan for the past two years. Getaway driver for an armed robbery that went wrong. He left Lily in 2008, just after their baby was born.'

'No, Josh is mine,' I argue. 'The DNA test proved positive and then there's his birth certificate –9th June 2008, nine months after the night I spent with Lily.'

'It's a forgery, I'm afraid.' She shakes her head sympathetically. 'His real birth date is 7th July. It means the DNA was falsified too.' She shakes her head and smiles. 'Lily's really up to her neck in it this time and so is the guy in the lab who tampered with the test results.'

'But the baby she's currently carrying is definitely mine,' I insist. The realisation this child will be born behind bars upsets me almost as much as knowing I no longer have any claim on Josh.

I walk away and stand looking out of the vestry window. Wedding guests are departing. I'm not sure how Marcus has dealt with them and at the moment with this dreadful news I care even less. 'I need to speak to my grandmother,' I say to Tegan. 'Could you find her and bring her here please?'

Roo's beside me again, his hand on my shoulder as Tegan leaves. 'You can rest assured Lily will be going to jail for a long time for this,' he says, as if subjecting her to the full force of the law is somehow enough.

I shake my head. I don't care what happens to Lily. I simply want this new nightmare to go away.

LILY

I thought I had everything sorted, that I was untouchable, but it seems my past has caught up with me. And what a time for it to happen, on my bloody wedding day! I was so glad I didn't have to be marched through the church. Instead, they took me out through a side door to the waiting police car. I think I would have died if Georgie or Danni had seen me. Obviously, none of this is new to me.

In my life with Pauli I had my brushes with the law but nothing as serious as this. There's no way I'll be able to blag my way out of trouble this time.

They took my beautiful wedding clothes and expensive heels away and I ended up in one of these crappy paper suits they normally give people when their clothes are needed for forensic examination. There was the usual booking in process at the front desk of the police station and then I got what I'd been waiting for, my one phone call.

I knew exactly who I was going to ring. The only person I could turn to, although I feared when he learned about the dreadful things I'd done he probably wouldn't want anything to do with me. My fingers were shaking as I punched in the number I'd committed to memory. He answered straight away and as soon as I heard the sound of his voice everything fell apart and I couldn't stop crying. Between my sobs I explained where I was, what had happened and that I didn't know what to do.

'Don't worry Lily, I'm on my way,' was all Max said and then the line went dead.

JESS

Roo phoned this morning with the shock news about Talún and Lily's wedding although it wasn't that much of a surprise, the press having already beaten him to it. When Mateo, Jorge's kitchen assistant, returned to the restaurant with the morning papers there was Talún plastered over the front of the tabloids. Someone had managed to get a sneaky shot of him leaving the church with Amber and Marcus. His head was down and he looked tense. Settling herself out on the loggia with an early morning coffee Amber read out the details to Mads and me stopping frequently to shake her head and murmur, 'Good Heavens' or 'Oh my.' Finishing, she closed the paper and looked across the table at me.

'Well,' she said rolling her eyes, 'Looks as if Lily has done it again. What a catastrophe.'

I nod in agreement; my first thoughts are for Anna and Marcus who were uneasy about Lily right from the start. How they must hate the embarrassment and this unwanted media intrusion into their lives. I always knew Lily would cause this havoc and I feel a sudden niggle of guilt wondering whether if I had been brave enough to tell both Anna and Talún what she had really done to our family all this could have been avoided. But even if I had, would they have believed me? Lily was such a convincing liar. No doubt she would have turned things around, accusing me of being Talún's spiteful ex-girlfriend stirring up trouble. Oh yes it would have definitely been viewed as a case of sour grapes and me? Well I'd have ended up looking spectacularly stupid.

I'm still angry Talún lied to me about sleeping with her and part of me says he deserves everything that's happened. On the other hand, I do know how devious Lily can be. She must have realised Anna and Marcus had begun to have doubts about her, therefore getting pregnant was a way to secure her future. I'm glad she's looking at a long spell behind bars, but my heart goes out to poor little Josh, what will happen to him now? Amber is right, it is a catastrophe.

TALÚN

I feel I've been sleepwalking through the last forty eight hours. After the blow of discovering Josh is not mine I've had the added stress of wondering what will happen to our unborn baby. Will Lily be able to keep it or will the courts grant me custody? I can't bear the thought of a child being born in a prison hospital wing. Lily didn't love Josh and no doubt she'll see this new arrival as yet another millstone around her neck.

Anna has been my rock. I don't know what I would have done without her. Marcus, too, has ridden out the storm. It can't have been easy to have had such an embarrassing public incident happen on home territory. However, he tells me everyone is fine, his PR department has done a great job with the press, and he has been inundated with messages of support for all of us. Of course the first thing I did was apologise to both of them. I was so keen to have Josh as my son I deliberately bypassed one of the most fundamentally important things – having a proper check done on Lily. And I realise if I had done, I wouldn't be in the position I find myself in today and neither would they.

I guess by now the news of this awful day has arrived in Lynbrook. Georgie and Danni will have seen to that. I don't know how Jess will take it or even if she will care. She probably thinks after the way I brushed off her concerns over Guernsey and lied about sleeping with Lily, I deserve everything that's happened to me. And the way I'm feeling at the moment, she's probably right.

Josh has been taken into care and is currently with foster parents in Norwich. I've been visiting every day as I can't bear to think of him alone with strangers. His whole world is upside down at the moment and he keeps asking when he can come home. The couple he is with are very supportive and assure me he will get all the love and attention they can give him while he's living with them. So it's all very much a waiting game to see what happens next.

Lily, I gather is back in Exeter living with Max while she awaits trial. I can't see her lawyer has a case, but if it does end up in court it means the inconvenience of an appearance for all of us and more unwanted publicity. An unexpected message from Pauli Stevenson, asking to see me, has me travelling to Wigan today. Apparently he wants to talk to me about Josh and that means much as I would love to ignore his request, I have to see him.

LILY

I must have a charmed life. Max, my knight in shining armour, has ridden to my rescue I'm out on bail and living in his luxury apartment until the trial date. During my interview I kept my response to "no comment". I wanted to give the smug, brunette sergeant a hard time, snotty cow. Max brought in one of his slick lawyer friends, whose very persuasive arguments eventually resulted in me being released on bail. When Max and I walked out of the police station, the look on that cocky copper's face was priceless. It really made my day.

I've been here for a few days now. I can come and go within daylight hours as long as I stay within the city and report to the police station once a week. Max has bought me a new mobile and given me money to buy clothes. While I've been here I've not been wasting my time. Already I've touched base with Pauli's old friend and forger, Gav. Not just to replace the passport the police currently hold, but all the documentation I need for a completely new identity.

I never liked my name anyway, so getting to choose a new one has been quite exciting. I've only one very slight niggle of regret, and it's about Max. He's been incredibly good to me, says he's going to sort things out, and he's putting money by to fight my case. He talks about looking after me, of being together once I'm free – me him and Talún's baby which he's determined to make sure I keep. I haven't had the heart to tell him there is no baby and he's dreaming because if I stay I'm going to be locked up for a long time. Attempted bigamy and deception is bad enough, but when it involves a powerful family like the Hawkeswoods I know they'll throw the book at me. No, my lawyer has simply bought me valuable time which I'm using to organise my escape.

Max has begun hoarding money here at the apartment. I'm guessing this is his fighting fund for me, although it could be cash he's hiding away from Davina as he told me he's already set the wheels in motion for the divorce. It's become a ritual when he returns home each evening, depositing bundles of notes in a large floor safe in his fitness room. And now I've sussed out the combination. I checked this morning and I couldn't believe how much was there – more than enough to give me a very comfortable start far away from here.

TALÚN

How life changes in the blink of an eye. Yesterday everything looked bleak. Today there is a glimmer of hope. I had no idea what to expect when I got to the prison. Roo drove up to be with me. Although I was seeing Pauli alone, he thought it best I have some moral support. Josh's father is an unknown quantity. The fact he made his life with Lily made me wonder whether, like her, he was an unpleasant piece of work.

When I walked into the small room they had allocated for our meeting, I could immediately see the likeness between father and son. It hit me then that the resemblance to Marcus I'd been convinced I'd seen in Josh had simply been wishful thinking. I didn't think Pauli looked like a criminal, just a short, stocky guy with cropped hair and a sad face. I settled myself in the chair opposite, under the watchful eye of an attending prison officer, and sat back to listen while he explained why he'd asked me here today.

'I left home when Josh was a few months old,' he said. 'I don't know him at all but I gather he's currently in foster care.'

'Yes, he is.' I confirmed.

'I read in the papers about his life with you, what a lovely happy boy he was.'

'He was...is,' I agreed, amazed at how the attention of the tabloids had shifted away from Lily and me, choosing instead to focus on this small boy who had been taken into care.

'The thing is,' he leaned forward, 'Lily and me, we're the only proper family he's got. My folks are dead and hers, well, they're not the sort I'd want taking him on. They will though, if they think there's a chance of money coming their way. Anyway, I'm not going to be out any time soon and she won't be either. This may seem strange coming from a man who walked away from his responsibilities but, I want to make sure he's going to be okay. I know how much you care for him and, well, I was thinking, if you are interested in adopting him then I'll give you my full support. I want him to have the best chance in life.'

I was stunned. Keeping Josh was the answer to my prayers, but I was puzzled. I'd expected Pauli to be looking for some sort of financial payoff in exchange. But when I asked him he simply shook his head and said no. It appeared despite his life of petty crime, beneath the surface Pauli Stevenson was a decent human being after all.

'There is a slight problem,' I warned him. 'I do believe in order for a child to be adopted, both parents have to agree.'

'She'll be glad to be rid of him,' he said, shaking his head. 'You know that woman hasn't got one maternal bone in her body. There were complications when she had him; means she can't have any more. Thank God for that I say.'

'What?' I gaped at him, unable to believe what he'd just said.

'Didn't she tell you?' He barked out a hollow laugh. 'No, I expect she strung you along, didn't she? Promising you a wagon load of kids to fill that big house of yours.' He gave a slow shake of his head. 'Well, sorry mate, it never would have happened.'

I left Pauli, walking out into the autumn sunshine to where Roo waited in the car. As we drove back to Amberleigh I told him of the conversation I'd had about adopting Josh and also the phantom pregnancy. He didn't make any comment, but promise he'd get things underway regarding the adoption as soon as he got back to his office. I smiled as the countryside sped by. I felt my luck was changing; everything was beginning to come good. But the biggest challenge of all still lay ahead – fixing things with Jess.

Two days later I arrived back in Lynbrook. I knew there would be questions at the Hall so I got everyone together and explained what had happened. I needed to give them the true version and not what the papers had been feeding the general public.

That afternoon I rode out to see Jess. On the last occasion I had seen her she had slammed the door in my face. I was hopeful this time she would at least allow me to say what I had to...even if she did decide to slam the door afterwards. I was under no illusions about the huge task I had ahead of me to win her back. But I knew I still loved her and I was fully prepared to go the distance.

When I reached the cottage I noticed Adrian's van was parked up in the trees. I was also aware I hadn't seen him since he'd left his job at the Hall. That meant there was more bridge building to do.

I couldn't see any sign of him in the cottage garden so I knocked on the door. When it opened there he was, sandwich in hand, looking very much at home. Which I discovered, to my surprise, was because he now lived there, Jess having left on a long break abroad. He said he was sorry to hear what had happened at Amberleigh and hoped Anna and Marcus were okay. I said they were fine and asked him to come back to the Hall; that his old job was there if he still wanted it. He grinned, slapped me on the back and made one of his usual dry observations before accepting. It felt like old times.

That evening I settled in front of my desk to catch up with paperwork. Calling it a day around ten, I poured myself a glass of twelve-year-old malt and sat for a while, trying to work out what would make Jess leave so suddenly. And where exactly had she gone? Adrian said she'd never been specific about location or length of absence. I phoned Anna and discovered they had recently talked on Skype. She confirmed what everyone else seemed to be saying; that Jess was staying with old uni friends somewhere outside the UK but again, everything was vague. I remembered my own departure all those years ago when I felt life here without Jess held nothing for me. Had history repeated itself? Did she leave because she couldn't bear to stay here seeing me married to Lily? Well if that was true maybe it meant she did care and there was still a chance for us. But first I needed to find her.

LILY

This is it. Goodbye UK, hello Grand Cayman. Well, it had to be somewhere hot and exotic didn't it? No doubt the police will think I'm still hiding somewhere in the UK or maybe somewhere on the Costas. Hopefully it should keep them busy looking in the wrong direction for months.

I decided not to have any conscience over the money I've taken from Max. I need it; end of. Much as I'm aware I owe him so much and at one time I had a certain fondness for him, at the end of the day, honourable men are fools, born to be used by women like me. With my new identity – Nicole Carter – and the small fortune waiting for me in my new bank account, I'm looking forward to enjoying a new affluent life somewhere much hotter.

On my way here in the taxi I did briefly think about Josh and what will happen to him. It's good to be free and single again without the ties of motherhood. It's what I always wanted. I content myself with the thought that whoever he ends up with, they've got to be a vast improvement on someone like me.

So here I am at the boarding gate, following behind all the other passengers bound for New York. The first step on my journey to sunshine, white sand and blue sea...oh, and hopefully a liberal sprinkling of hot millionaire playboys.

JESS

I've not been in touch with Roo recently but I gather from Anna, who called yesterday, he's working with Talún on some legal matters at the moment. I was really anxious for news about Josh but as Anna sounded a little down, I thought it best not to ask. My thoughts then move on to Lily's pregnancy. As she'll be going to jail I know once the baby is born it will be kept in a special unit within the prison for the first eighteen months of its life. I take a deep breath and run my fingers across my stomach. I feel for her poor unborn child. At least my baby will have a mother who loves it and more than that...freedom

I've been to the market with Mateo this morning. He's an elderly cousin of one of the waiters and helps out in the restaurant. Although most of the produce is delivered from the wholesalers in Palma, there are a few things Jorge likes sourced locally.

We're back by ten-thirty with our supplies, and leaving Mateo to unpack I go to look for Amber. She's sitting on the secluded side terrace drinking wine and surfing on her laptop.

'Got something to show you,' she says with a grin, as she sets her glass down and searches for the item. 'It's Marcus's investiture at the Palace.' She swivels the laptop around for me to see. I'd forgotten all about the knighthood. There's a photograph taken outside the Palace with a couple of paragraphs about him underneath. Anna's looking very elegant as usual and Talún is there with Josh...and a young dark haired woman. I take a deep breath, wondering how only weeks away from the fiasco with Lily he's begun another relationship.

'Are you all right?' I hear Amber's concerned voice. 'You've gone quite pale.'

'I'm fine.' I take another breath and pull out a chair.

Amber calls out to Mads to bring me a glass of water.

'You still love him, don't you?' She gives me a wistful smile.

'Yes,' I admit, knowing it's pointless to lie to Amber. 'But it's a wasted emotion isn't it? You can see for yourself what he's like. The wedding was six weeks ago and he's got someone else already.'

NOVEMBER 2013

TALÚN

In only weeks things have settled down. I guess I should be thanking Lily for skipping bail and disappearing without trace. Pauli's agreement coupled with the fact Josh had already been living with us quite happily for several months, means he's back. We're fostering him at the moment and Roo is investigating whether, due to the circumstances, there's a possibility we can go ahead with adoption. We're not there yet...but at least everything seems to be going in the right direction.

Josh has settled back at the village school and has been reunited with Bella. This afternoon I've taken time off to pick him up. As I approach the school gates I see her helping him button up his jacket before slipping on his small back pack. As she takes his hand and they begin to walk towards me, she sees me and waves out.

'Good day?' I ask as they reach me and Bella hands him over into my care.

Josh looks up at me and nods vigorously. As she runs an affectionate hand over his head I decide to pitch the question no one has so far been able to answer.

'You don't happen to know where Jess is, do you?'

'Abroad, that's all I know.' She raises her dark eyes to mine and shakes her head. 'Adrian said you came out to see her at the cottage when you got back.'

'I did. He didn't know either. Abroad could be anywhere.' I brush a frustrated hand through my hair.

'Rufus would definitely know. I can ask him if you like.' she offers helpfully.

'Not a good idea. We have history. Jess obviously didn't tell you?' I try to make a joke of it but the fact he probably holds the key to the one thing I need makes me feel even more frustrated.

'Well what about Roo?' she suggests, 'He's her best friend. He's bound to know.'

'Roo? I reply, and then feel like a total dummy. I've been so immersed in the fall out from this wedding fiasco, Josh's future and Marcus's investiture, the obvious hasn't hit me.

Bella rolls her eyes and grins. 'You men, what are you like?'

I manage to get a quick ten minutes with Roo between his final client and lunch. As I'm shown into his office I see he's signing the last of a batch of letters. Handing them to his PA, he motions for me to sit, caps his pen and settles back in his chair. I get straight to the point, asking him about Jess's disappearance and whether he knows where she is.

He watches me silently for a moment before he answers. 'Why do you want to know?'

'Because I need to talk to her. The last time I saw her we argued. I want...need to put things right between us.'

Roo continues his silent hazel-eyed survey of me, and then sits back, his eyebrows drawn together in a puzzled frown. 'Can I ask why?' he asks.

I'm not sure whether I should open up my innermost thoughts to this man. He's so cool, so detached; I can't read him at all. I'm aware they're very close and although we've formed a bond through the work he has done for me, there's a possibility this request might be a step too far. I wait a few more moments then deciding it is I slowly get out of my chair. I turn to leave, apologising and telling him I was wrong to come here.

'Talún do sit down.' There's a slight impatience in his voice as he waves me back to my seat. 'I'll answer the question for you, shall I? You're here because you love her and you want her back. It's as simple as that, isn't it?'

I nod silently.

'Jess told me about your conversation, that Lily was the mystery woman with you on the night of the party. She caused so much trouble.' He looks across at me. 'She changed the course of history for both you and Jess.'

'I know,' I agree quietly. 'Now all I want is to have her

back in my life.'

'Have you considered it's not what Jess wants now? That it might be too late?'

'Of course,' I realise I sound more confident than I feel. 'She's strong, determined...even cussed at times. But I can't let her go without a fight.'

Roo nods, a slight smile lifting the corners of his mouth, probably at the word *cussed*, which no doubt he totally understands. Levering himself out of his chair, he reaches for his jacket. 'I could do with a drink,' he says as he slips it on. 'Fancy some lunch?'

Unsure of whether or not it means I'm going to get the answer to my question, I follow him out of the building and into the street.

JESS

The weather at this time of year takes a little getting used to. Back home there would be rain and autumn leaves tumbling from the trees and carpeting the wood. Here it's pleasantly warm, very warm in fact, although Amber tells me this kind of weather during November is exceptional and has a lot to do with the wind coming across from North Africa. I've fallen into a pattern living here and although I miss home like crazy, I've come to terms with the fact I have to stay here at least until the baby is born.

The sickness returned soon after I arrived. I couldn't keep anything down. Deciding to make my condition public brought a wave of excitement in the restaurant. The Spanish love children and even though I only have a small bump at the moment, I am fussed over like an invalid. Although technically Amber is my step aunt, she has quickly taken on the role of new grandmother-to-be, organising my journey into motherhood. I now have regular doctor's appointments set up and have been booked into a private clinic for the birth. I've also been introduced to retired midwife Lydia, an ex-pat who lives locally and along with her husband Frank, are regulars in the restaurant. Amber has rounded her up to take care of the ante-natal classes later on in the pregnancy. So it seems I have the whole package sorted...or rather Amber has. And now it's all about day to day living in this idyllic spot and enjoying moments of peace like the one I'm currently having, sitting on a sheltered cluster of rocks at the edge of the bay which I've earmarked for sunbathing.

Across the beach the town surrounds the small harbour in a protective arc of whitewashed and stone houses. There is a generous stretch of golden sand, a promenade and a small car park and here from my eyrie I have a view of the town, the harbour, Juan's boatyard and El Barco Rojo.

It's great to wander to the town square, where the weekly market is held. In its winding streets the small independent shops sit side by side and there is colour everywhere, both in their multi-coloured canopies and the many flower tubs and window boxes. On occasions when I have accompanied Mateo on early morning visits to the local bakery, the aroma of freshly baked bread is out of this world. And although I really miss Lynbrook, this place is a great substitute.

This morning, the local boats are out as usual in pursuit of langoustine while some of the older Spanish men have arrived, carrying fishing rods and heading for the breakwater, in search of a suitable place to cast their lines. I see Mateo and Mads leave in the van, probably en route to the wine merchants. I watch as the vehicle slowly climbs the hill out of Cala Los Rosas and heads west on the Palma road before my attention is taken by a huge motor yacht slipping past the bay. Finding my sun cream, I give my arms and legs a liberal coating, put on my sun hat and settle back with my Kindle. Moments later, my mobile intrudes. I'm expecting a call from Rufus but instead find myself looking at a text from Roo. He's organised a surprise visit, arriving on a mid-morning flight tomorrow. I smile knowing he won't be alone, that as he promised me a few weeks ago, he'll be bringing Tegan with him. Although it will be great to see them both, I realise it means I'm going to have some explaining to do about my current condition.

TALÚN

I knew once I discovered Jess's location, getting to see her would be the next big hurdle. Over lunch Roo told me where I could find Jess but what I didn't expect was that in his usual calm way he'd take control of everything. And at last here we are, in the arrivals hall at Palma airport, being ushered out to a waiting limo.

Josh is with us and has had the time of his life. His first flight ever and I don't think he's stopped asking questions since we checked in at Exeter Airport. Now we're in a new country with all sorts of strange sights and smells...and even more questions needing to be answered.

As the limo eats up the miles to Cala Los Rosas, where Jess is staying, Roo tells me about El Barco Rojo, Mads and Amber's restaurant. Soon I'm able to see for myself as we reach the outskirts of the town and follow the road which winds down the hill towards the small harbour and its adjacent crescent of golden sand.

Amber comes out to greet us and her lack of surprise at seeing me means Roo has already been in touch with her about my trip here. She embraces us both and makes a fuss over Josh, whose eyes are like saucers at the sight of the beach.

'Jess isn't here at the moment,' she says. 'She's gone into town with Mateo to pick up some spices. She'll be back within the hour. I've not told her you're coming. She thinks you've brought Tegan with you,' she says, shooting a glance at Roo.

She takes us through to a covered veranda which runs along the front of the restaurant and faces the beach. Settling us at one of the tables she disappears to organise drinks. On her return Amber's younger blonder cousin Mads joins us with her partner's son Santiago, who she tells me is a year older than Josh. At first these two small boys watch each other quietly across the table. Curious brown eyes meet inquisitive blue ones as they take their measure of each other silently and then gradually small smiles begin to emerge. Once our drinks are finished Mads asks Josh if he would like to accompany them to the harbour to watch the fishing boats come in. He turns to me to ask if it's okay for him to go and my nod of approval sees him slipping down from his seat and taking Mad's hand, eager to be off.

The hour seems to drag and as we sit drinking and chatting I try to distract myself. I push away the concern I may have come all this way for nothing. That she won't want me back. I'm not sure how I'll cope if that happens. Amber brings me out of my musing as she asks me all about my new family. It seems she already knows about Josh.

'He's a lovely child,' she says, as we watch an animated Santiago explaining something to Josh as they stand side by side watching an incoming fishing boat. 'I can't believe Lily gave birth to him.'

'Neither can I,' I agree. 'Are you aware she skipped bail?'

'Yes, your aborted wedding and the subsequent fallout attracted a lot of media coverage. And talking about publicity, I found Marcus's investiture online...a lovely photo of you all. Who was the dark haired woman?'

'Tish. She's Josh's childminder.'

'Jess seemed to think you were together.'

'I think her husband might have something to say about that,' I smile, amused. 'He works for me at the stud.' Then a sudden thought crosses my mind. 'Why? Did it bother her?'

Amber gives me a slow smile which says far more than any words could. It occurs to me if Jess was affected by the thought of me with someone else, then maybe...

The sound of approaching feet along the boarded veranda brings me out of my deliberations. Roo gets to his feet, deliberately blocking me from Jess's view, and I hear her voice and her laugh as she embraces him.

'And where's Tegan?' I hear her say. Then as she slips past him, eager to find his partner, she comes to an abrupt halt. Her hand goes to her throat, eyes wide with shock, as she comes face to face with me.

'What the hell is he doing here?' I spin around to look at Roo, whose innocent, light brown eyes meet mine.

'You'd better ask him that yourself,' Roo replies, turning to look at my unwanted guest and then at Amber, who quickly clears away glasses and leaves. Talún gets to his feet and even after all that's happened I still can't stop the way his nearness affects me. My breath catches in my throat as I watch him, wishing things were different; that we were together again. But that can never happen. He has someone else in his life now, someone important enough to be invited to the Palace for Marcus's investiture.

'You had no right to bring him here,' I continue to direct my anger at Roo. 'I trusted you to keep my secret.'

Roo takes a deep breath. 'Believe me, I didn't take this decision lightly but I know I've done the right thing. Talún has been trying to find you since he returned to the Hall.'

'And that was excuse enough for you to not only tell him where I was but to bring him here as well?' I expel an impatient lungful of air and try to calm myself. 'For what reason?'

'As I said before, I think you'd better ask Talún that.' Roo steps back and I find myself face to face with the cause of all this upset.

'Well?' I stand there impatiently, wondering what excuse he's about to give.

He looks uncomfortable but his eyes never leave mine. 'I've been trying to find you Jess. No one knew where you were. I desperately needed to see you.'

'I can't imagine why.'

I watch as Roo walks away, leaving us alone on the veranda.

'To tell you I love you,' he says, stepping forward and reaching for my hand, 'and I want you to come home with me, we—'

'Are you mad?' I interrupt, moving out of his reach before giving vent to my feelings. 'Firstly, I'm not going anywhere with you so I'm afraid you've had a wasted journey. Secondly, I'm not at all happy with you dragging Roo into all of this. He had no business telling you where I was. And thirdly,' I take a deep breath, 'it's obviously slipped your memory but you're already in a relationship.'

'Am I?' He looks confused. 'Who with?'

'The woman who was with you at the Palace for Marcus's investiture.'

'Tish?' he says. 'You mean Tish?'

'If that's her name, yes. Slim, dark haired?'

'Yes, she's Josh's childminder, Jess. She's also married to one of my grooms. Josh is fostering with us at the moment. I'm planning to adopt him.'

His explanation ushers in relief that Josh is going to be okay but hot on its heels I'm hit with a barrage of confused thoughts.

'Jess, I've made so many mistakes but this isn't one of them,' I hear him say, 'and I know it may be difficult for you to take in, 'but the truth is I love you so much and I can't bear the thought of living my life without you.'

I feel confused. Part of me has longed to hear those words. I really do want to believe him, but...

'I'm sorry.' I push past him. 'I really can't cope with this at the moment.'

'I haven't finished.' He catches my arm and swings me around to face him just as Mateo emerges from the interior of the restaurant. Taking one look at Talún's grip on my upper arm, the small Spaniard moves forward to confront him.

'No upset Señorita Jess!' he says, waving an angry finger at him. 'Bad for baby.'

'Baby?' Talún releases me. 'You're having a baby?' I can see the shock in his face as he takes a step away from me. 'My baby?'

'Yes,' I confirm with a nod, 'And because of that I had no choice, I had to leave. You were about to marry Lily, and it was the only thing I could do to avoid the gossip that was bound to arise. By the time I returned I figured people would probably believe the father was someone I'd met here.'

'You mean you would have passed my child off as someone else's? That I would never have known? How could you?' Now it's his turn to be angry. Not simply angry but from the way his eyes darken, absolutely furious. 'Bloody hell!' he snaps, and leaves me, taking the steps down to the beach two at a time. I inhale deeply and rest my hands on the veranda rail as I watch him stride across the sand, taking his outrage with him.

I see Mads approaching from the direction of the harbour with Santiago and, to my surprise, Josh is with them. I had no idea they'd brought him along. He's wearing blue shorts and a Bob the Builder T-shirt. I'm so pleased to see him, relieved to have this immediate distraction from the turmoil surrounding me. He's delighted to see me too and as I crouch down he throws his arms around my neck and plants a kiss on my cheek. He then treats me to an excited, wide eyed description of his journey here, leaving me under no illusions that planes have joined tractors as his favourite thing. Roo emerges from inside the restaurant and suggests they take a walk into town. There's a promise of ice cream and I know he's doing this to get him away from all the anger here. 'Is it true what Mateo has just told me? You're having a baby?' he says, with a mixture of surprise and disbelief, 'And you didn't think to tell me?'

'I'm sorry, I did what I thought was best.' I give a tired shrug. 'Please don't be mad at me.'

'I'm not angry, Jess, but I think you need to make peace with Talún,' he says, nodding in the direction of the beach where he's currently wandering along the shoreline, the wind teasing his untidy dark hair.

'Any idea why he's so mad at me?'

'I could hazard a guess.' Roo says, as he continues to watch Talún, 'Pauli Stevenson asked to see him. He wanted to know if he'd be willing to adopt Josh. During their conversation he mentioned Lily had had a tough time giving birth and couldn't have any more children. She faked her pregnancy to make sure she held onto him. Of course a few months after the wedding there would have been a convenient miscarriage. But by then the wedding band would have been safely on her finger.'

The news comes as both a shock and a relief. I felt sure Lily was out there somewhere carrying Talún's child, a weapon she could still use against him. 'Okay, Lily lied,' I protest indignantly, 'but I didn't.'

'You decided to keep the truth from him. In his eyes it's the same thing. Something I've learnt in my dealings with Talún is he's very honest. And he expects that same honesty from those he cares for... and,' he fixes me with his light brown gaze, 'he does care for you, Jess, deeply. I apologise for springing this surprise but I'm not sorry I did it. He needs you and I honestly believe you need him...and your baby,' he gestures towards my stomach, 'needs both of you.'

Roo turns to go. Josh slips his small hand in his and gives me a final wave before they head off up the road towards town. I hear his chatter, bombarding Roo with questions as they walk.

Digesting Roo's words, I turn back to look at the beach and find Amber beside me.

'Go to him,' she says, giving me a hug. 'Roo's right. Your baby needs both of you. Talún didn't come all this way to find you on a whim. He loves you and he wants to take you home. Please don't throw away your chance for happiness.'

'I think I might be too late,' I say as I turn my attention back to the beach. I notice the tension in Talún's shoulders, hands thrust deep into his trouser pockets as he stares out to sea, no doubt trying to decide whether there's time to catch the next available flight back to the UK.

'Well, there's only one way to find out. Go on, shoo!' she says, before stepping back.

Slowly, I take the steps down to the beach. I kick off my sandals before beginning my walk across the sand to join him at the edge of the sea. As I reach him he turns, and I'm relieved to see the anger has left his eyes. Instead, all I see is a deep sadness. I feel relieved because it means he hasn't closed the door on me; on us.

'Forgive me,' I say, reaching up to gently touch his

cheek. 'I never meant to hurt you. Lily was pregnant, the wedding imminent. All I wanted to do was to protect myself and our baby.'

He nods quietly and pulls me into his arms. 'I'm sorry too. I came with great intentions and all my words sorted. Sadly, nothing went to plan.'

His lips gently brush the corner of my mouth and I look up at him and smile. 'Oh I don't know, it wasn't all bad,' I reassure him, 'at least you got to say the most important ones. *I love you*?' I explain to his frown.

'And I meant it, Jess. I do love you, so very, very much.' He wraps his arms around me, pulling me into the warmth of his body and kissing me once more. 'I want us to be together: you, me, Josh and our baby. I want a new start for all of us at the Hall, one that comes with the promise I made you all those years ago – Always and Forever.'

I remember those three words which accompanied the gift of his grandmother's ring that long ago summer when we were together. I look up into the face of a man who, despite everything we've been through, I've always loved. A good, caring man. One who is prepared to raise another man's child as if it was his own. A man I want to spend the rest of my life with.

Reaching up to brush my lips against his, I whisper, 'Let's go home then.'

He smiles and slips his hand in mine. I feel his warmth, his strength and his love, and as we make our way back across the sand towards the restaurant, I know *Always and Forever* really does begin today.

THE END

About The Author

Jo Lambert was born and brought up in rural Wiltshire.

Her first novel, *When Tomorrow Comes* was published in 2009 and four other books - *Love, Lies and Promises, The Ghost of You and Me, Between Today and Yesterday* and *The Other Side of Morning* followed. They formed a series charting the loves and lives of four Somerset families over several decades.

Summer Moved On, her sixth novel, is the first part of a two book love story set in South Devon.

Jo now lives on the eastern side of the Georgian city of Bath with her husband and a green MGB (the other love of his life). She loves travel, red wine and rock music and is known to take a photo or two.

A Message from Jo

Dear Reader,

Thank you for reading Watercolours in the Rain. I hope you enjoyed the conclusion to Talún and Jess's journey. Feedback is always important to authors so if you have a few moments I would appreciate a review. And if you'd like to get in touch with me I have Facebook and Twitter accounts and would love to hear from you.

Printed in Great Britain
by Amazon